MY DARK DESIRE

L.J. Shen &
Parker S. Huntington

scan me for playlists, triggers, & more!

Before you begin, thank you for taking a chance on Zach and Farrow. We like to joke that these two are just like us both—a clash of cultures that somehow work. Neither of us has ever written a book like this. It's a privilege to even have the opportunity to do so.

I (Parker) never thought I'd be able to share my culture with the world, especially through a love story. I'm part-Viet and part-Chinese, raised in both Orange County and the DMV by my zany, amazing, tightknit family. A lot of what's in My Dark Desire is based on my personal experiences. They're wild, almost unbelievable, and addictive. I can't wait to pass along tiny doses of my life to you. And Leigh, you're a saint for agreeing to write this book with me and listening to me drone on about my childhood.

Speaking of...I (Leigh) enjoyed every second of writing this book with my best friend. It's decadent, full of delicious banter, and a reflection of my friendship with Parker. (One percent of our conversations are about work. The other ninety-nine percent is split between food and family.) Parker is my work wife, and considering the divorce rate among Asian Americans is 12.4%, chances are we're in it for life.

So much of what I love about Zach and Fae comes from the day-to-day convos we share. I'll wrap this up, so you can dive into the story. Enjoy!

xoxo,

Parker and Leigh

(P.S. Y'all, the aunt is real. So is the stolen car incident. I couldn't believe it, then Parker showed me the receipts. I NEED CELESTE IN MY LIFE. – Leigh)

"EVEN MIRACLES TAKE A LITTLE TIME."

— *Fairy Godmother,*
CINDERELLA

PROLOGUE

Zach

My father always said that people are paper and memories are ink. Little did I know, my book would be dipped in tar, then ripped to shreds.

I grew up with a generous father. Money. Identity. Love. A nice set of morals—and an even nicer set of teeth. He gave me them all.

But the most precious thing he ever gave me? *His life.*

Age Twelve

Like all calamities, the worst day of my life started innocently enough. Dad and I rode in the backseat of his Flying Spur Bentley, our driver veering in and out of lanes in a desperate bid to beat the heavy traffic. A never-ending chain of honks filled my ears. The sky poured above us, a storm that had followed us from the auction house. The radio played "Bookends" by Simon and Garfunkel too loud to hear my own thoughts.

I could feel Dad's eyes glued to the back of my head as I blew hot air onto the car window and drew a sword over the frost.

He sighed. "You could really use a hobby."

"Hobbies aren't useful. That's why they're hobbies." I drew fingers curled around my sword and blood dripping from the tip. "Besides, I have hobbies."

From the front, our driver snorted, flicking on the left signal.

"You have talents," Dad corrected. "Just because you're good at things doesn't mean you enjoy them. And sitting idly all summer as you wait for your best friend's return does not constitute a hobby."

Stupid Romeo Costa. He just upped and left one day. Didn't even say goodbye. First to Italy in elementary school. And now, some boring summer camp his dad forced him into. He came back from Europe a total bummer. I half-expected him to return this time with a chunk of his brain carved out.

I blinked up at Dad. "Why do I need to enjoy the things I do?"

A soft smile curled his lips at the edges. He was huge. Or maybe he just looked huge because I hadn't shot up all the way yet. But he filled up the entire backseat with his body. With his *presence*. With his onyx hair and laugh wrinkles on the sides of his eyes. And the wicked scar on his forehead he got while chaperoning Cub Scouts. An eagle had tried to snatch me, and he'd lineman-tackled me at the last minute, bumping against a sun lounger and splitting his forehead.

Dad rapped my temple with a curved knuckle. "Because if you don't appreciate the journey, how would you enjoy the destination?"

"Isn't life's destination *death*?" I pinned him with a glare, so I wouldn't have to witness my art evaporating from the condensation on the window.

He laughed. "You're too smart for your own good."

"That's not a no," I murmured, itching to cover my ears to avoid the sound of cars honking and the pelting of the rain.

"The destination is family. Love. A place in the world to call your own."

I flicked a small twig from the side of my sneakers. "You have lots of places."

"Yes, but only one of them is my home. And that's where you and your mother are."

I studied him with a crunch of my forehead. "What did we ever do to make you so happy?"

"You exist, silly. That's enough."

I sprawled in my seat, tap-tap-tapping my knee, bored to the max. "If we make you so happy, why do you always buy stuff to feel good?"

"Art is not *stuff*." He put his hand over mine to stop me from tapping my knee. "It's a person's soul poured into material. Souls are priceless, Zach. Try to protect yours any way you can."

I inched closer to him, peering at the velvet satchel between us. "Can I look at this one?"

"Not until your birthday."

"It's mine?"

"Not to carry around. It's dangerous."

"Even better." I rubbed my hands together, turning my attention to the hand-carved canton box cradled between his palms. "How about this one?"

We'd just picked up the spoils of Dad's bidding war at an antique auction. Well, Dad did. I sat in the car, solving a Rubik's cube without bothering to actually look at it as he trudged through the identification verification process. Art had never interested me. Dad spent the past twelve years drilling his wisdom into me, hoping some of his obsession would penetrate my skull. No such luck. I could debate the merits of gongbi versus ink and wash painting, but I couldn't force myself to actually give a crap about a bunch of lines on paper.

Sometimes I secretly wished I had a dad like Romeo's. He let him handle guns and hand grenades. Rom even knew how to operate a *tank*. Now *that* was a flex.

Dad slid the heavy lid off and slanted the box my way. "Your mother's anniversary present."

Clasped between satin walls sat a round jade pendant chiseled into the shape of a lion. A red cord looped around the curved edge, leading to stacked beads, an oversized pan chang knot, and double tassels. A cool two million dollars, and for what? Mom wasn't even gonna wear this thing. Adults sometimes made the dumbest decisions. Dad called them impulses and said they were human. Maybe I wasn't much of a human, because nothing made me too excited. I always thought things through and craved nothing. Not even sweets.

I slumped back into my seat. "It looks like the slab of cheese mold growing in the Tupperware in Oliver's locker."

My other best friend had the hygiene of a wild boar. Though that wouldn't really be fair to the boar, because the latter didn't have the option to shower daily.

"Sha haizi." *Silly kid.* Dad flicked the back of my head, chuckling. "One day, you'll learn to appreciate beautiful things."

The rain intensified, knocking on the windows like it was begging to enter. Red and yellow lights gleamed through the distorted glass. The honking grew louder.

Almost there.

"Are you sure Mom will like it?" I rubbed my nose with the sleeve of my shirt. "It looks like the one Celeste Ayi got her years ago." Pretty sure my aunt bought it at an airport souvenir shop on her way out of Shanghai.

"She'll love it." Dad's finger hovered over the pendant, moving along the edges without actually touching it. "It's a shame I had to fly to Xi'an in January. By the time I heard they added the other pendant to the D.C. auction, someone had already bought it."

"There's another?" I drew an octopus on the glass this time, only half paying attention as a stormy Potomac crawled by. Another few miles and we'd turn onto Dark Prince Road. "Doesn't that lower the value?"

"Sometimes. But in this case, the pendants were crafted as a his-and-hers set. They belonged to star-crossed lovers during the Song Dynasty."

I perked up. Finally, we got to the good part. "What happened to them? Were they beheaded?"

"*Zach.*"

"Oh, that's right." I snapped, then sliced my finger across my throat. "They did death by a thousand cuts back then. Their arms must have been *ripped*."

Dad massaged his temples, staring at me with a slight smile. "Are you done?"

"No. When they cut people's noses off without anesthetics, do you think they died instantly or bled out?" The traffic jam loosened, and the car gained speed. *Finally.*

"Zachary Sun, it's a wonder that you're my chil—"

A blaring horn sounded, drowning his voice. The rain. The entire world. Dad cut off, eyes wide. The car swerved violently to the side, as if trying to escape a collision. Dad tossed the box away and launched himself at me, wrapping his arms around my torso, clutching me painfully. He pinned me flat against my seat. The blinding flash of headlights blazed across his face.

The Bentley tipped over, on its side, flipping onto its roof. We landed upside down. He was still on top of me. Still shielding me. It happened fast. Loud, piercing ringing. Then, pain. Complete, utter pain. Everywhere and nowhere all at once. I was both numb and in agony. I blinked fast as if it could help me hear or even see.

"You're okay, Zachary. You're fine." His lips shaped the words, his face less than an inch from mine. His whole body shook. His eyes swung down, between us, and he closed them, taking a ragged breath. "Wo cao."

My eyes flared. He cursed. Dad *never* cursed.

Something sticky and dark dropped onto my right leg, coming from Dad. I shook it off.

Blood.

It was blood.

Dad's blood.

And then I saw it. A landscape rake pierced through his gut. Spearing him into the door. The jagged edge poked my stomach, grazing it. I sucked my belly in, struggling to breathe at the same time.

I blinked fast, hoping this nightmare would wash away. Dad came into focus, his entire face bloodied, shards of glass sticking to his skin like hedgehog spikes. Blood everywhere. Sliding down his temple from the forehead scar to his chin. His blood—warm, metallic, stinky, *sticky*—soaked into my clothes, my skin, my hair. I wanted him off. I wanted to scream. His lips moved again, but this time I couldn't make anything out past the ringing in my ears.

I can't hear you, I mouthed. *Say it again.*

I tried to move, to touch his forehead, stop the bleeding, but he was too heavy, and I had to keep sucking my stomach in to make sure the rake didn't cut me open.

The red pouch.

I reached for it, stretching my hand as far as it would go. The rake sliced a tiny hole into my skin, but I managed to grab the satchel, dumping it upside down. A knife. I wrapped my hand around its handle and tried to cut off my seatbelt. It tore at the side, making no difference. I still couldn't move.

Henry, I tried to scream our driver's name.

No response.

I glanced over my right shoulder, finding Henry's forehead pressed against a deflated air bag, creating a constant, piercing ring with the horn. I knew he was dead, even without seeing any blood. He looked like a lifeless puppet, his pupils black and flat.

Dad's lips moved again. His eyes begged me to listen. I wanted to, I really did, but all I could hear was the horn.

A tear fell from dad's cheek to mine. A hiss slipped out of my throat, like the drop burned me where it landed. Dad *never* cried. His lips moved slower, his body still covering mine. Protecting me from whatever was happening or had already happened. A cage of bent steel boxed us in. I couldn't move out from under him if I tried.

I managed to form a fist, clutching onto his shirt before he collapsed on me. My hands tremored with his weight, the other still wrapped around the knife handle. Dad's eyes remained open, but I knew he wasn't alive anymore. His soul had already drifted away. And I finally understood what he meant when he'd said souls were priceless.

My senses returned one by one, trickling like rain.

First, my hearing.

"Is there anyone else in there?"

"A child."

"Alive?"

"Damn... I doubt it. That truck went straight into them at full speed. They stood no chance."

Then, my skin receptors.

Dad was cold. So cold. Too cold. I knew what it meant. A piece of his flesh melted from his face, dropping onto my chest. If it was hot, I couldn't feel it. I trembled all over, screwing my eyes shut, fighting down the bile rising up my throat, my stomach still clenched tight.

Get off me. I don't want to feel your death. I don't want to feel, period.

Finally, my ability to talk.

"Alive," I croaked out, hearing people groaning, grunting, shouting, trying to flip the car upright. "I'm alive."

But I didn't feel like I was.

"You hang in there, buddy," a voice called out. "We're coming to get you. It's just gonna take some time, okay?"

"Okay."

Not okay. Nothing was okay.

I squeezed my mouth shut, listening to them talk.

"Wait. Isn't this...?"

"Yeah. Bo Sun. *The* Bo Sun." Silence. "Jesus fucking Christ."

"Is he...?"

"They're going to have to cut him off before they can get to the kid. He's speared onto the rake through the melted metal."

"Goddammit. Poor kid."

CHAPTER ONE

Farrow

"I heard her hair stylist has less Instagram followers than she does." Tabby snapped her gum from the backseat of the Mercedes GLE. "And she has, like, four thousand? I mean, just let the butcher at Balducci's do your hair and be done with it."

"She's flaunting those bangs like it's 1999. No one has the guts to tell her they look awful on curly hair." Reggie snickered. "And her balayage is downright orange." Tabitha and Regina Ballantine, ladies and gentlemen. My stepsisters. Between them, they produced enough venom to kill a well-populated island.

My stepmother Vera tutted from her spot behind the steering wheel. "Now, now, girls. That's not very charitable." The words didn't match her vicious giggles. "Sylvia is a nice girl. A little plain, but that's not her fault. Have you seen her mother?"

Tabby scoffed. "Unfortunately."

I bit my lip as hard as I could, stifling the urge to point out that Sylvia Hall had just passed the bar after graduating magna cum laude from Georgetown. Her head had more to offer the world than an overpriced haircut.

But I wasn't in a position to say anything. One, because the Ballantine women hated my guts, and everything I said would be used against me. And two, because I was quite literally not in a position to speak—nestled in the trunk, balled into a fetal position, breathing as shallowly as possible to keep my presence unknown.

The SUV rolled past Potomac's manicured lawns. Outside, the air had thickened with blooming flowers. All I smelled was Tabby's riding boots. A mixture of manure, hay, and whatever stable boy she'd wrapped her legs around this week.

"Are we almost there?" Reggie smacked her lips, snapping something shut. "I'm low-key excited, you know? I've never been to Zach Sun's house."

"Take a picture, because this'll be your first and last time." Tabby snorted. "I don't even know why you're making us go, Mom. Everyone knows Constance Sun would carve out a kidney if it meant her son will marry whomever she chooses."

"Zachary Sun has a mind of his own. If he decides he wants one of you ladies for a bride, no one will stop him."

If nothing else, I admired Vera Ballantine's eternal optimism. Tabby and Reggie were about as desirable as chronic wasting disease. A lethal combination of high maintenance and low IQ.

"Besides…" Vera switched the station to classical, even though she didn't know Yo-Yo Ma from *Yo Gabba Gabba*. "There'll be other rich, influential men there, ready to be bagged. There's that duke… Oliver something?"

"Von Bismarck." Tabby gagged. "The man is a certified skirt chaser. He'll probably give me an STD if he breathes in my direction."

Reggie snorted. "It's cute how you pretend you're not interested."

"Pulling out my Uno reverse card, sissy."

"For your information, he once invited me to his mansion on the Amalfi Coast."

"Only you and every other woman with a pulse." Tabby clucked her tongue. "Wow. If I were you, I'd start designing those wedding invitations right away."

I tightened my arms around my knees, mentally sifting through months of research. My plan was bulletproof. Go in. Take back what's mine. Slip out unnoticed, cloaked by the night and a designer gown I'd commandeered from Reggie. It wasn't my first hustle, and it wouldn't be my last. I'd been a survivor since birth. From the moment my no-show egg donor placed me in a Costco cardboard box outside Dad's door with the note:

All yours. Should've answered my calls, asshole.
An abortion doesn't cost as much as a kid.
Tammy

By that time, Dad had already married Vera after a whirlwind romance. According to Tabby, Vera urged Dad to "get rid of the thing."

How can you even know she's truly yours? She huffed throughout my childhood, knowing full well I heard her.

But I didn't need a DNA test. Mother Nature vouched for me. I shared Dad's arctic-blue eyes. The golden hair that curled in thick waves, framing our faces and ears. The same delicate bone structure, long-limbed body, and even the same beauty spot just under our right eyes.

Vera sighed. "It's a shame Romeo Costa is off the market."

"As if we ever had a chance."

Reggie yawned. "As if we *wanted* a chance. I heard he's a sociopath."

"Really?" Tabby's hair swung over the headrest. "I heard he donated a new maternity ward to Johns Hopkins as soon as his wife got pregnant."

"Probably because they'll need to bulldoze the entrance to wheel her in on delivery day. My facial girl told me Dallas Costa ate her way through half the bottom layer of a three-tiered cake at the White House dinner yesterday, and the entire thing collapsed on some oil baron."

Things 1 and 2 disintegrated into a fit of giggles.

"Does anyone else smell bleach?" Reggie sniffed. "I swear, the scent of Farrow clings to my nostrils these days. You have to kick her out, Mom. She stinks up the whole place."

"And where would I put her, exactly?" Vera cranked the A/C up to max. "We need the rent money for all the shitholes your father left behind. People are already starting to talk. When I signed the lease on this car, I didn't even opt for the AMG." She paused. "I suppose we could stuff her in the pool house…"

"Not the pool house." Tabby jerked forward, by the way the entire vehicle bounced. "I'm converting it into a second closet."

I couldn't believe I intended to plow through hundreds of people as self-obsessed and superficial as my stepsisters for the next hour. But I had no choice. Zachary Sun possessed something of mine.

The jade pendant should've never ended up inside the sprawling Sun château. Naturally, this had the telltale fingerprints of Vera's greed all over it. When Dad passed, she'd auctioned off his belongings, biding her time until the insurance money kicked in. Apparently, Zach Sun bid three times higher than the closest offer. Now this spoiled billionaire possessed the only memory I had left of Dad.

Not for long.

Vera flicked on the turn signal, jouncing the vehicle over a gravel path. "Here we are. Goodness gracious, look at the line." *Finally.* She shushed an argument between my stepsisters, tsking as we waited. "Christ alive, look at the security at the gate. A bit much if you ask me."

I scooted deeper into the backseats and swathed myself in black fabric. The handmade material I'd sewn blended so well with the rest of the empty trunk, I knew they wouldn't rummage around.

"Open." A security guard rapped the trunk window. It popped out, creeping up at an excruciating pace. The flashlight's intense ray impaled the fabric that cocooned me before the door slammed shut. "All clear. *Next.*"

Vera threw the vehicle into park with a screech. My step-monsters evacuated the car, swapping places with a valet. Just as I'd predicted, he parked it on a driveway furthest from the two-acre property's entrance on Dark Prince Road. He joined a golf cart packed with other valets, hitching a ride back to the main road.

As soon as the headlights faded, I crawled from the trunk to the driver's seat and cracked the door open. The Sun terrarium glared down at me, lit up from end to end with blinding floodlights, daring me to trespass. Even a few hundred feet away, it cast a menacing shadow across the trimmed lawn. I tiptoed on a bollard-lit path to the main house, crouching between rows of luxury vehicles when a valet cruised by in a Lotus Evija. Reggie would kill me once she saw the state of her dress. Cool sweat made the satin cling to my flesh. I'd torn the slit several inches higher while squatting in the trunk.

Another thing I'd discovered during my research: this party marked the official inauguration of Zachary Sun's bride hunt. Quite literally. I had no doubt the prospective brides in attendance intended to go *Hunger Games* on each other's asses until one victor remained standing. If the DMV rumor mill was to be believed, Zachary Sun—to appease his fed-up, desperate-for-grandchildren mother—would begrudgingly select a single candidate to date by midnight.

They were all lovely in different ways. Tall and short. Curvy and slim. With their silky gowns and silkier manners. Daughters of Singaporean billionaires and former Salvadoran oligarchs. Of Korean chaebols and Hollywood producers. But they all shared one thing in common—they wanted to be the next Mrs. Sun.

I ducked my head, hoping to blend with the crowd as I shouldered past ballgowns and tuxes. I excelled at being invisible, a skill I'd honed by preschool. Mainly to save myself the abuse Vera and Things 1 and 2 hurled at me whenever they had a bad day.

The château towered over me in commanding splendor—stretches of pale French limestone, imperial columns, and polished gardens that rivaled Versailles. I swallowed the lump clawing my throat and flowed inside, carried by the volume of eager bodies. Curved grand staircases flanked the foyer. My eyes crawled up the one leading to my target. Zachary Sun's office. Suited guards blocked the bottom, hands clasped at their fronts, Bluetooths tucked in their ears.

In the corner, my stepfamily laughed too loudly at something men in designer suits said. Vera clutched an hors d'oeuvre to her chest, attempting a frown past a barricade of Botox. She'd aged like milk in a sauna and flaunted a sour personality to match it. I needed to avoid being seen, but I wasn't overly worried. No one else here knew me.

Dad had been too mortal to brush shoulders with this crowd. As for me, I always avoided any event that involved sucking up to Potomac's deepest pockets. Marrying seemed like a total waste of time. You should only ever have one love of your life. Yourself. And, perhaps, a dog.

I waited until a staff member rushed up the steps to shadow him. The symphony of voices below chased us upstairs. I moved my lips without sound, feigning a conversation to thwart the guards' suspicion. Once we rounded the corner, I redirected to the library that housed the office. I'd memorized the mansion's floor plan by heart. *Thank you, Zillow.*

When Zach had purchased the manor from the Swiss royals who had occupied it before, he'd barely made any changes, other than converting the subterranean garage into a high-tech art gallery. Initially, I thought I'd have to somehow break into it. Alas, I'd stumbled upon last month's *Wired* cover. A feature on Zach's latest hostile takeover. There it was. Immortalized on the magazine's shiny double-spread, almost unnoticeable under the power of his soulless glare. The pendant. Perched on a shelf. Secured by glass.

Lo siento, sucker. You're about to be one piece of art short.

I sauntered down the hall, passing paintings that probably cost more than the entire Ballantine estate. Especially now, with Vera and her daughters sinking Dad's company to depths even the Titanic hadn't reached. I had no idea what he was thinking, splitting the ownership of the cleaning company four ways. Three of us had never worked a day in their lives.

The library door loomed before me. I white-knuckled the handle, expecting it not to budge. I'd spent two months learning to pick endless locks with the kit tucked into my bra. But the door slid open effortlessly without a sound. A burst of crisp air lapped my skin, raising goosebumps across my flesh. I edged inside, closed the door, and plastered my back against the wood, allowing myself one quick moment to regulate my heartbeat. This wouldn't be the first time I did something that could land me in jail. But it marked my first time stealing from one of the most powerful men in the world.

I didn't take the time to appreciate Zach Sun's office, even though I'd never stepped foot anywhere this extravagant before. Not with the pendant beaconing me like a lighthouse. In the same glass box from the *Wired* spread, right beside an identical copy. A his-and-hers set.

Well, this seems fitting. One of them is his, the other is mine.

There would be no confusion. Dad's pendant bore one imperfection that made it uniquely ours. As a kid, I'd given the tassels a "haircut." The strands dangled about an inch shorter than they should.

I whizzed past the desk, ignoring paperwork as it somersaulted to the rug with the gust of wind. Finally—*finally*—my fingertips kissed the thick glass. Right above Dad's pendant.

"Sorry it took me so long." Tears pricked the backs of my eyes. "He locked you in a golden cage. Don't worry. I'll get you out of here."

Since Dad died, I'd kept his favorite pendant in my nightstand to hug close whenever I woke up in the middle of the night, missing him. Before Vera sold it, a waft of his scent still clung to the intricate knots. I bet the scent was sullied by now by Zach's clinical existence.

I'm getting this back, Pops. I promise.

Hiking up the tattered hem of my pale-blue dress, I unhooked a portable glass cutter from the waistband of my underwear. The blade clicked as I swung it out, spearing the corner of the glass. Violent thumps hammered between my ears as I began whittling a circle around the small lock.

Then I heard it. Loud enough to pierce my heartbeats.

"What do you think you're doing?"

Fuck.

CHAPTER TWO

Farrow

The chilly voice didn't hold a candle to its owner. I swiveled, pasting on a vacant smile of the Reggie variety. The type that screamed: *I have nothing but dust and the latest Chanel collection between my ears.* "*Ohmigod*, it's you. Zach Sun. I've been wanting to meet you forever."

I was not above stroking men's egos if it meant they left me alone. They were normally simple creatures, easily distracted by compliments. Unfortunately, Mr. Sun appeared about as thawed as Iceberg B-15.

"I asked you a question." He stepped forward, his eyes a dark vortex, so empty I feared I'd fall into their pits. "Now would be a good time to answer."

It didn't help that his presence distracted me. That he was tall, his angled jaw so defined I could sharpen knives on it. His hair and eyes blacker than the tip of a raven's wing. He wore a tux with a tailcoat, hair parted on the side and slicked back. He was power, elegance, and beauty. Dripping charisma like it was molten gold. And yet, too clinical. Too cold. Like a lifeless, deserted planet. I'd seen him countless times—unbeknownst to him—and I could never get used to his magnificence.

His right brow popped up. "Cat got your tongue?"

More like I'm pussying out after getting caught.

"I got lost trying to find the art gallery." I bowed, peering up at him behind a curtain of heavy lashes. "I'm *so* sorry. I couldn't help myself. The rumors precede it."

"The art gallery is in the garage." Zach reached for the switch, edging the dimmer up to its highest setting. White light poured from the ceiling. "And if you know it exists, you're also aware that it is strictly off-limits. Besides, you don't like art." He said it with such confidence that, for one jarring moment, my breath stuck in my throat. Like he could see right through me. He closed the door behind him, leaning against it to block my escape route, arms folded over his chest. "Let's try again—why are you here?"

With a parting glance, I dragged myself away from the jade pendant and sauntered across the room, eating up the distance between us with swayed hips. In lieu of a sword, sex was a great weapon. "I don't like parties."

Or you. Or the fact that you waltzed into my life and snatched what's mine so easily, as if I'm nothing of consequence.

I buried the words beside my pride and dove in for the kill, adjusting the neckline of my gown. His eyes didn't even budge. Ouch. Onto Plan B.

I fanned my face, tossing my hair over one shoulder. "I needed to catch my breath, and my legs led me here."

"Well, I respectfully ask that they lead you off the premises, unless you wish to spend your night in a jail cell."

That he wasn't a nice guy didn't surprise me, but he was being a downright prick. Then again, I *had* come here to steal from him. I floated around the room, ignoring the way his words hung in the air like a blade. My knuckles fluttered over business books, paintings, and upholstered couches.

Zach discarded his whiskey tumbler on an end table, his eyes tracking my every movement like a hawk. "Are you dumb?"

Dumb? No. Determined? You bet. And I had a feeling Zach wasn't accustomed to women who didn't fawn all over his every request.

The Go board nestled between two tufted sofas caught my eye. Kaya wood. Yunzi stones. Mulberry bowls. He must've dropped an entire mortgage payment on this baby. Stones littered the board as if someone had abandoned a lengthy game. Or more likely—run away. On instinct, I plucked a black stone from the bowl and set it beside a star point.

From across the room, Zach's brows snapped together, his eyes dropping to the board. "It's not chess." His low voice reeked of ridicule. But something else had laced into it. A pang of panic. He didn't like it when others touched his things. Classic only-child syndrome.

"Obviously." I gauged Black's thickness, fingertips tingling with the urge to snatch another stone. A lifetime had passed since I'd last played. "Chess dolls are cute and pointy. These circle thingies are for checkers."

His eyelid twitched. All that money, and he couldn't afford a sense of humor. *Tsk. Tsk.*

Before me, the stones broadcasted all I needed to know about the players. Black—cautious, generous, and gentle. White—ruthless, aggressive, and decisive. *Zach is White,* I decided.

I arched a brow, burying my curiosity about Black's identity. "I assumed it was Black's turn."

"And why would you assume that?"

Because I can count.

I opted for something slightly more offensive. "Because White was dumb enough to respond to Black's ko threat, so I imagine after destroying his own group, he begged Black for a timeout in order to lick his wounds and regroup." I shook my head. "Didn't have the balls to resign, did he?"

Silence. I flicked an errant blade of grass from my dress, deciding I liked Zachary Sun best with his mouth shut. His expression remained an impenetrable fortress, blank and unreadable. He didn't look at me. Instead, his entire attention clung to the board. There was something so detached about this man that I seriously doubted he was capable of functioning humanly. It made him unpredictable. And *that* made him a very dangerous opponent.

"Yikes." I rolled my lower lip into a pout, tilting my head sideways. "You're White, aren't you? Don't worry. Your secret's safe with me."

The slight flare of his nostrils was the only telltale he was breathing. "I didn't avoid resigning."

I eyed the door, wondering whether he'd notice if I wormed my way out. "Glad to hear it. That would be *terrible* sportsmanship."

The French windows tempted me. Not like I needed my ankles intact these days.

"No." Zach stalked toward me, one deliberate step at a time. His scent, of citrus and dark woods, burned through my nostrils, warning me that danger lurked nearby. "I did not back out," he insisted, so close to me now that our shoulders almost touched. We both glowered at the board. He gestured to the high point. "Look."

I did. At his hands. Hands that had never seen a day of hard labor. Perfect, clean, and cut cuticles. Long tan fingers. Smooth, even skin. Thick wrist with a De Bethune strapped to it. So perfect. So glamorous.

So *soulless.*

"I smell a bet," I challenged, realizing this so-called genius hadn't caught on to my intentions. Holy hell. I was actually going to get away with trying to steal from him. My feelings ricocheted between relief and disappointment for not capturing the pendant. *Yet.*

"All I smell is bullshit." He claimed the seat across from Black, dropping his elbows to his knees and lacing his fingers together with a frown. "Sit." Sit. Go. It wasn't lost on me that every command he'd given me could be mistaken for a dog's.

"Why?"

"Because I'm about to wipe the floor with you. Your journey will be shorter from the settee."

I studied him, half-scandalized, half-frightened. "You really think you're smarter than the rest of the world, don't you?"

"The theory is backed by facts." He meant it. Poor whomever-he-decided-to-marry. I hoped for her sake his dick was as big as his ego.

"I think—"

"You *believe*," he amended. "Most people lack the capacity to truly conjure real, original thoughts. Even dissertations are recycled theories of greater minds. I couldn't care less what you believe. Now sit down, or I call security."

I blinked. "Are you forcing me to *play* with you?"

"Yes."

"Let me guess—you weren't the most popular kid in the playground."

"Never been to a playground." He pushed his sleeves up, lifting the mulberry lid covering the white stones. "Though my parents did rent out Disneyland for a weekend for my fifth birthday. Flew my entire grade there. Didn't hear any complaints. *Sit.*"

I did so obediently, figuring the game would be a welcome distraction while I calculated my next move. "Ah, rich people. They're just like us."

He didn't even ask who I was. For my name. The sheer intrigue and outrage of the prospect of being outsmarted at a dated mind game made him throw all caution to the wind.

Zachary Sun wasn't used to losing. *What a terrible existence.* If you couldn't mourn your losses, how could you celebrate your wins?

I eyed his relaxed shoulders. "Don't you have a party to go back to?"

He hadn't once glanced at the door.

Zach ignored me, collecting a stone between his index nail and middle fingertip. Without pausing to think, he blocked my attack. It happened in less than a second. All with flawless stone etiquette. He reclined against the plush upholstery, propping one leg over the other, finally gifting me a sliver of his attention. His slacks rode up until the hem revealed his sock—black. Just like his heart.

"Where'd you learn to play Go?"

I knew an accusation when I heard one. Used to it, unfortunately.

"Korea." I didn't offer more, leaning forward to assess my next move.

Outside, music, laughter, and champagne glasses clinking together seeped past the door. My hectic thoughts drowned them out. I needed to escape. I'd come for the pendant another day. Another time.

His left brow arched a millimeter. I was sure he wanted to ask what a white American girl was doing in Korea, but he held himself back. I had a feeling he prided himself in not caring about others. Or perhaps he simply didn't care, and pride was his default setting.

I stole a quick glance his way, checking to see if his face still made my pulse accelerate. It did. "If it makes you feel any better, I participated in some Go competitions when I was there."

His lip curved up in a snarl. "Why would it make me feel better?"

"When I annihilate you."

"Now who's being cocksure?"

"Please, Zach. There's only one dick in this room, and I think we both know that it's you."

Yup. That just left my mouth. Vera was right. Maybe I was impossible to civilize.

Zach moved another stone. He'd cornered me, both literally and figuratively. He was a fantastic player. Calm, pragmatic, steadfast. It didn't surprise me. Just annoyed me. I'd grown used to having an edge analytically. Dad always warned that the price of stupidity is always paid. Maybe that was how Zachary Sun had built his wealth from Forbes-worthy inheritance to the nominal GDP of Luxembourg. He possessed no weakness to exploit. Had no stupidity to pay for.

I twirled a stone in my palm as I waited for his move, ignoring stone etiquette, knowing it would bother him. "Shouldn't you go back to your guests?"

"No," he said decisively. "They'll have more fun without me."

He maneuvered a stone, leaning closer to me to do so. I did not interest him in the slightest. One could argue that I was practically half-naked, on a platter before him, completely at his mercy. He didn't care. Those poor girls downstairs didn't stand a chance. Zachary Sun didn't do love, nor passion. Humans did not thrill him. Numbers and mind games did.

I cleared my throat. "You have a nice house." I needed to fill in the silence somehow. To keep him from asking questions about me. At the same time, I worried he'd recognize my voice. All the other times we'd met, we both wore masks.

A few moments passed before he looked up in my direction. It didn't even last a second. "That's not a question."

Christ.

"Is it true that your mother is forcing you to marry by the end of the yea—"

"I wish to play in silence."

I buried my knuckle into my temple, hoping to relieve the building pressure. "And then you'll let me leave in peace?"

"And then I might let you leave in *one* piece. That's my best and final offer."

"That's not much of a bargain for me."

"I think it is. Unless you're fond of prison food."

"I'm not picky." At the very least, I'd no longer have to fork over rent to live in my own childhood home.

"Neither are the people who will corner you in the showers."

"Are you imply—"

"I do not imply things. I outwardly say them. And right now, I am outwardly saying, 'Make your move. Without a word.'"

I obeyed him. For the next two hours, we lost ourselves in the game. Every twenty minutes or so, someone would knock on the door and attempt to lure him back to the party. They were all met with lazy waves, a wordless instruction for them to leave. Zach's full attention remained on our game, which was why I tried hard to prolong it as much as possible. I didn't want him to start interrogating me again. But dammit, he had skill. If he told me he competed at the Majors, I'd believe it.

Sweat beaded at my temple. We entered our third hour with flourish. Me—with burning feet, ready to sprint out the door as soon as he'd let me. And him—with a perpetual frown etched onto his lips. His frown morphed into a full-blown scowl when our stalemate became evident. We'd reached a dead end. The music and chatter subsided downstairs, indicating most guests had left. The host had spent the entire party here. With me.

Sure enough, we hadn't talked. Not a single word.

I broke the silence first. "I'm going to have to think about my next move." I rubbed my cheek, jutting out my lower lip. I hated losing. Plus, I wasn't even sure what getting out of the lion's den would look like. This afternoon, before I'd arrived, I'd parked my car two blocks away from his mansion with the intention of strolling to it, prized pendant safe in hand. Obviously, I'd gotten too cocky.

Zach's eyes didn't budge from the board. "You're about to lose."

"Keep telling yourself that." I stood, stretching my arms and feigning a yawn. He rose to his feet, too, that scowl still wilting his lips. I snapped the stone bowl shut. "Well, thank you for th—"

"When will we finish the game?" He removed his phone from his pocket and thumbed through it. His calendar app flashed before me. Goodness, it didn't even occur to him that I'd say no. His thumb shot up with each scroll, probably sorting through dates convenient for *him*. "Tomorrow is no good for me, and I have a meeting in London the next day, though I will not be staying overnight."

My jaw clamped shut with an audible snap. It shouldn't have surprised me. Zach wanted to be challenged. No, he *needed* to be challenged. Everyone around him bored him. Unfortunately for him, I would rather drive home blindfolded and handcuffed than spend another second in his presence.

I scratched my cheek. "I, uh, have a busy schedule."

"More parties to crash?"

I smoothed a hand over my dress, my palm sweaty. "That's rude."

"But not wrong. Who are you?" His eyes were like two barrels of a gun, digging into the soft flesh of my temple, threatening to pull the trigger. Death lurked behind those eyes. I wondered what they'd witnessed to suck the soul out of them.

"I'm a guest."

"I'd remember if I invited you."

"I'm someone's plus one."

"Name that someone."

Would it kill him to budge?

I conjured the name of a man I guessed would be here. "Pierre Toureau." A client of mine. A very wealthy one. He owned restaurants, malls, and a fleet of Mid-Atlantic conservatories. I bet Zach had invited him and his pretty grad student daughter Anamika.

A vein bulged in his neck. "Really?"

"Really."

"Interesting. Does his wife know?"

Shit. "I'm his niece."

"The one from France?"

"Y-yes."

"Where are you from in France?"

Jesus. He wasn't supposed to be hot *and* smart. Again—not a surprise. Just alarming to be on the receiving end of a lethal dose.

"Uh... Yes?"

He shook his head, like I was a lost cause. "You're not one of us," Zach concluded, hands resting in the pockets of his slacks, jaw harder than the granite surrounding us. *Shit.* Also—*screw you.*

"How do you know?"

"For one thing, you're wearing a nightgown."

Double shit. It was the only dress of Reggie's that didn't have feathers, leather, or other dead animal parts. Should've known it was too good to be true.

"I don't know what you're talking about." I kept my chin up, retreating a step, my fingers patting my surroundings, searching for a weapon. How much jail time would I get if I clubbed him with one of these sleep-inducing finance textbooks he couldn't possibly have finished? "It's okay not to like my dress, but don't offend it. I don't tell you that you look like a penguin in that tux."

He stalked toward me, stoic and unrelenting. "Give it up, little octopus. You're wearing holed sneakers."

Little octopus? What?

"They're comfy. You never know when you need to make a run for it." Another step back.

"Now would be a good time." He stopped about ten inches from me. Close enough to be intimidating, but far enough not to touch me. "I'll even give you a head start, seeing as you're such easy prey."

He underestimated me. Normally, I loved proving people wrong. But with Zach Sun, I doubted my own abilities. Both physically and intellectually.

I extended my neck to look him in the eyes. At 5'8", I wasn't often dominated by men, but Zach made me feel miniature. Smashable as a tender teenage heart. He was lean, tall, and muscular. Proportioned like a Roman sculpture. Everything about his face was divine. The arches of his thick brows. His bottomless eyes—so dark I couldn't see where the pupils ended and the irises started. And the pillowy, hand-drawn lips any woman would die to call her own. They were all bracketed inside a jaw so square, between cheekbones so high, he looked half-human, half-demon. An art collector that was a work of art himself.

"Look…" My back hit the door. I grabbed the knob digging into my lower back on instinct. The pendant behind him all but winked at me. *Fuck.* I needed to return for it somehow. By inviting me back, he'd offered me a gift, packaged with sharpened spikes and wrapped in poison ivy. But a gift, nonetheless. Too bad I didn't trust either of us to open it. I raised one palm. "I can explain."

One final step, and he cornered me completely. His body pinned me to the door, not quite touching mine but close enough that the invisible hairs on my arms stood at attention. "I wholeheartedly doubt it."

"You can't do anything wholeheartedly. You don't have a heart." I didn't know what made me provoke him, but I couldn't stop even if I wanted to. Not with the surge of momentum behind me. With the zap of electricity bleeding into my veins. And beyond logic, not with every fiber of my pride wishing to chisel a scar onto Zachary Sun.

His face remained unmoved. "I may have no heart, but my brain compensates for its absence, and it is telling me to punish you for your—"

I didn't stick around to hear what he had in store for me. I whipped around, jerked the double doors open, and bolted outside. Zach was at my heels in seconds. His smart shoes clanked against the marble in long strokes. I sprinted to the edge of the stairway and hopped onto the banister, zipping down the handrail as fast as I could.

Zach snapped his fingers. "Chase her."

In an instant, two people materialized, scrambling up the stairs after me. Zach was still the closest, but even he wasn't as fast and nimble as I was. *Olympic material, baby,* I wanted to taunt. In another life, Zach and I would be friends. Maybe. We'd play Go. Do mental math. Exchange ideas. I'd win. Sometimes, anyway. Keep him on those even-heeled toes of his.

At the bottom of the stairs, I sprang off the handrail and did a little twirl and wink before charging for the exit. The place had emptied out. No one but cleaners and an event manager milled about. They shrieked at my sudden intrusion. A mop went flying out of a hand, jetting soapy water across what was probably an original Baselitz. *Oops.*

Without missing a step, I burst out the front doors, startling a valet on a cigarette break. The crisp air did nothing to cool my flesh. I picked up speed, thighs burning with the strain. Andras would perform a human sacrifice if it meant I trained this hard every practice.

My heavy pants drowned out the choir of crickets. Sweet summer sweat crawled down my spine. The gown's slit tore higher with every stride. I was scared as hell. *But also more alive than you've been in a while.*

I snatched a discarded water hose from the grass and pointed it at his employees, spraying them down and knocking them over like dominos. Breathless laughter hiked up my throat. *What are you doing, Fae?* Having fun. Something I'd almost forgotten how to do.

I tossed the hose aside and picked up pace. By now, I'd lost the employees. Only Zach could keep up.

"Wouldn't do that if I were you." Somehow, he sounded composed. Neither out of breath nor dumbfounded by my sudden bravery. "You can run, but you cannot hide. What I want, I get. And right now, I want answers."

My sneakers sank into the soft ground, ruining his carefully trimmed grass. The sprinklers turned on, no doubt on purpose. Water sprayed me from every angle, weighing down the nightgown until the satin plastered to my body. But I refused to slow.

A dark chuckle curled around my wet skin like ivy. "You're top entertainment, Octi."

"Why are you calling me Octi?" I screamed into the air. I didn't want to show how much he riled me up, but I couldn't help it. Of all the nicknames in the world, I couldn't conjure a single one less flattering. Not even if I workshopped it for a decade.

"Because you're an octopus." He said it conversationally. Like I wasn't running, and he wasn't chasing me. "Exceptionally smart. Hands everywhere. And venomous. Plus, female octopuses hurl shells at males that harass them."

"If you know you're harassing me, *stop.*"

"How's Friday for you?" He managed to scroll through his phone while picking up speed. What a weird, weird man. "I can fit in a game between eleven p.m. and one in the morning."

One in the morning? For Go?

There was only one thing I wanted more than turning around and flipping him off—surviving this bizarre encounter. I swallowed my pride, legs pumping so fast, I was seconds from igniting a friction fire out of Reggie's nightgown.

"Octi."

I wasn't going to answer this stupid nickname. I wasn't.

"Octi, you need to stop. I'd hate to put a hole in your skull—yours actually contains something inside it—but we both know I will."

"It's the only hole you're interested in tonight," I hissed, hiking up the gown's slit when I almost tripped. "Too bad the female population of Potomac hasn't caught on yet."

He ignored me. "Friday, eleven p.m.?"

"The next time I'll voluntarily be in the same room with you is to attend your funeral to make sure you're dead."

A sudden whoosh pierced the air. The scent of metal burned my nostrils. A fancy gold knife landed in the grass mere inches away. Shit. He'd thrown that at me. Actually tossed a *knife* at me. That escalated quickly. Vera always said my smart mouth won me stupid prizes. But I never thought I'd anger someone to the point of assassination. I shifted to zig-zags, knowing it would slow my pace but also not wanting to leave here with a souvenir the shape of a second asshole. Zach's dark and broody laughter rang behind me. *He's enjoying this.* Sociopath.

According to legend, Zach Sun never laughed. Barely ever cracked a smile. That he was a morose man, tough as nails, his heart full of rust.

This was what cracked his façade?

I'd get revenge on this prick if it was the last thing I did on Earth. In my haste, one of my sneakers loosened from my foot, spearing into a pocket of mud. I had no time to look back. To stop. I continued galloping forward with only one shoe on. Water doused my bare foot in an instant. When I reached his iron-wrought gate, I knew he thought he had me cornered. I also knew once I made it past the bars, Zach wouldn't be dumb enough to stab me. Self-defense was hard to prove when your victim sported a hole in their back, even if you were the fifth richest man on Planet Earth and everyone treated you like you wielded a gold-plated dick.

Watch and learn, sucker.

With flourish, I planted my foot on the metal bar and scaled the monstrous twelve-footer. The rails were absent of nooks, but I had enough momentum and core to hoist myself over it. Once I leapt to the other side, I bowed theatrically, this time clutching the muddy hem of the gown for emphasis. When I tipped an invisible hat his way, his jaw squared. The tiny reaction felt like a victory. Octopus: 1. Lobster: 0.

I was drenched like a stray cat, my hair a mess and my heart a wreck, but I would never give Zachary Sun the pleasure of seeing me break. "So long, Lobster. And thanks for the fish."

"Lobster?"

"Octopuses' favorite snack."

I disappeared into the night before the heavy gates crawled open. His men hunted me like hounds, flashlights piercing through the night, golf carts humming in my ears. But I evaded them, cutting through the wooded acres surrounding the property.

The thing about octopuses? We camouflaged very well.

When I returned home, I mustered just enough energy to crawl into bed. Mud dried in thick cakes around my calves and ankles. Tomorrow, I'd wake up with a cold from the drenched dress. Tonight, all I could do was spend every minute until morning weeping into my pillow. For the pendant I couldn't retrieve. For the dreams that had fallen out of reach. For Dad.

Next time, Pops. Promise.

CHAPTER THREE

Zach Sun: Grand Regent. Ninety minutes.

Ollie vB: Pass. Wicked party last night, Sun. But I'm still recovering from the previous week's sexcapades.

Romeo Costa: You mean the legacy gala your hotel held?

Ollie vB: Yep.

Zach Sun: The one where 90% of attendees were on Social Security?

Ollie vB: No one gives a hummer like a gummer.

Romeo Costa left the chat.

Zach Sun left the chat.

Ollie vB renamed the chat Social Security Administration.

CHAPTER FOUR

Zach

I tilted the grimy shoe in my hand, studying it. It was so worn out, I couldn't make out the brand. I'd done some online research and narrowed it to either Vans or Converse. By the power of deduction—and fucking logic—I guessed it was the cheapest out of the two. The girl looked too poor to afford air.

"And then she climbed over your gate, hopped to the other side, and *bowed?*" Romeo punched buttons on the panel to the cryochamber. "Are you sure you experienced it and not, well… dreamed it?"

Sweat drenched my shirt from our morning workout—notably not as taxing as my little run with Octi last night. I tugged the back, slid it over my head in one swoop, and balled the performance fabric in my fist, dumping it into a hamper. "I'm positive my mind did not conjure a con woman who knows how to play Go and walks around in see-through lingerie."

Romeo flicked the lights to the ice room on. "Why not? Sounds like your fantasy."

I have no fantasies, you fool. Let alone about women. Human flesh disgusted me.

He stretched his arms. "Maybe it was the alcohol? That Jamaican rum was potent as fuck."

"I wasn't drunk."

"But I was." Ollie moseyed in from the bathroom, stark naked, swinging his dick in the air. That thing was longer than a lemur's tail. I hoped he taped it to the side of his thigh on dates. His entire existence was one big sexual harassment. "I was *smashed.*"

He stopped by the panel, shouldering Rom out of the way and choosing the advanced option. Below -266F. Four minutes. The screen monitored the temperature inside as it plummeted, right along with my patience. He'd spent the entire morning bitching about his hangover.

Since the three of us lived on the same street, it took all of two seconds to break into his home, pull him out by the ear, and drag him to the decked-out, three-story penthouse suite in his family-owned luxury hotel. He'd moaned about a headache before we even lifted a single weight.

"Oliver, put that thing away." My lips curled into a sneer. "It's dragging all over the floor."

"By the way, Zachy, I hope you're not dead set on a virgin for a bride, because I popped a few cherries last night." Oliver ignored me, scratching the side of his ass. "Okay, fine. A whole bag of cherries. Those industrial ones you get at Costco."

Romeo barked out a laugh. "When have you ever set foot inside a Costco?"

"Never, but I've heard stories. Who'd you end up choosing, and why do you have Oliver Twist's shoe in your hand?" Ollie whipped his curly blond head, frowning at me. "Please tell me it's kink-related. The only way anything about you would ever make sense to me is if you tell me right now that you have some kind of filthy feet kink."

"*Christ.*" I scoffed, shaking my head.

"What? I'm not judging. We all know my relationship with dog leashes."

"One cannot have a relationship with inanimate objects." I said it slowly, hoping it'd seep into his skull but knowing it wouldn't.

Ollie jerked a finger toward Rom. "Tell that to his wife and her fridge."

Contrary to general belief, Ollie wasn't an idiot. He just pretended to be one so he'd be spared all the expectations and obligations a man in his position usually had to endure. It was actually a clever setup. One I hadn't thought of myself. He would be the last bachelor standing out of us three, because he'd engineered his image so that nobody, alive or dead, wanted their daughter to date him, wealth and status be damned. He was so thoroughly corrupted, so depraved, that most families would sooner accept a pet fish for a husband than Oliver von Bismarck. He'd also quietly doubled his natural wealth through investments no one ever asked him about because they all assumed he shared a single brain cell with a discarded sperm. In the thirty years I'd known him, he'd never broken a heart, never had to stammer his way out of ending a relationship, and never made a single business mistake while careful to appear as though he had no idea what he was doing and managed his achievements through sheer luck.

He cruised through life without being interrupted by pretending to be an idiot. Which was the most genius thing one could do.

I pushed my running pants down and dumped Octi's shoe on a wooden bench. "It belongs to someone who trespassed here yesterday."

Rom chuckled. "A hot nerd who came wearing lingerie and fed him a nice dose of his own bullshit. There's only one problem—he doesn't know her name."

This was the least of my problems, actually. Even if I could, indeed, consider someone as an actual wife, the little octopus definitely wasn't prime material. She was a liar, clearly below my station, and a blonde. My mother would never consider her for the position. Even if she did, I wouldn't. She possessed none of the qualities that had made it to my list. And yes, there was a list: filthy rich, open to a clinical arrangement, and above all—obedient. I did not tolerate love. Couldn't stand romance. Actively loathed homo sapiens. And she was very human indeed. All messy flesh and blood. Hot temperament and even hotter body.

The cryochamber screen beeped three times, signaling it was ready.

"What's the problem?" Ollie stuffed his giant feet into slippers, yanking the door to the walk-in cryotherapy room. White-blue smoke rolled out in thick waves, tumbling along the floor. "Just go through your guestlist."

I followed him, teeth clenched. "If she were a part of the guestlist, we wouldn't be having this conversation."

I was not in a great mood. I did not like to be outsmarted. No, let me rephrase—I was not *used* to being outsmarted. The child bride of Satan blew into my life like a tornado. Slipping into my castle, going through my shit, very nearly winning a Go game against me. And then, to top all of that off, she'd run away cartoon character-style, climbing over my towering gate like a lizard. Whoever she was, she wasn't a cushioned heiress with extravagant dreams in her head and a black Amex in her vintage Birkin.

Rom entered the chamber last, closing the door behind him. "I can't believe I'm saying this, but Ollie is right." The digital clock above our heads began counting down from four minutes, white clouds of ice obscuring it for the most part. Both men shivered. I, as always, felt nothing. Rom rolled his neck, flexing his abs. "Even if she wasn't on your guestlist, she came in with a guest. In their car. There is literally no other way to get past security. It's too heavily guarded. And you have that shoe to go by."

"It's a common shoe," I growled. But it was not a common shoe size for a woman. Size ten, narrowed trim. She was tall. Sprightly. Almost androgynous in frame. An amorphous creature. I couldn't even tell if her face was traditionally attractive or not. I just remembered wanting to look away every time our eyes met, because she stared at me like a Rubik's cube she wanted to figure out, not like a meal ticket.

"You're a resourceful man." Ollie flicked a chip of ice from his shoulder. "And it worked for the prince from Cinderella."

"That was a fairytale." Those appalled me. I detested the idea of happily-ever-afters. Downer-tragic-ending was more my brand. "Plus, in the Brothers Grimm version, Cinderella's stepsisters amputate their feet to fit the shoe."

Romeo jogged in place to shake off some of the cold. We worked out six times a week, together when our schedules allowed it, then went through the ritual of the ice chamber, ultra-red lights, the dry sauna, and IV drips, usually at my place but occasionally at The Grand Regent when I craved a space Mom couldn't find me.

"Fairytales exist." Romeo gestured to himself. "Look at me."

My upper lip curled into a sneer. "What you have with your wife isn't a fairytale."

"What would you call it, then?"

"The worst financial investment in the history of humanity."

"He's not wrong." Oliver barked out a laugh. "You know I'm a fan of Dal, but I've met private jets more cost efficient than her."

Rom blew out a cloud of air. "You don't believe in fate?" As if he'd believed in it before he'd become wildly obsessed with his other half. Or should I say—his other quarter. His wife was a tiny thing, but she made a lot of noise.

"I'm more of the chaos theory kind of guy. And she seems like anarchy, personified."

Romeo had forced Dallas into marriage, which resulted in a

whirlwind relationship with ups, downs, and enough angst for three historical C-dramas. Over one year and four-point-three million dollars in the red later, he seemed happy with his wife. But I'd met some people who felt happy while infected with Lyme disease. Humans largely had no standards.

"Anarchy or not, she caught your attention, and no one else has in the thirty odd years I've known you." Romeo glanced at the timer. Probably counting down the seconds until he reunited with Dallas. The two of them sickened me. "That must mean something."

"It means she's deranged," I supplied. "Completely unhinged and stupid enough to enter my lair uninvited."

"She got in and stayed there for a few hours." Ollie graduated to cupping his balls to protect them from the cold. "That means you enjoyed her company."

"I'm not looking for her." I watched my skin as it turned a nice shade of blue, wondering why it still felt the same, before and after. The clock showed two minutes. Ollie and Rom had started chattering, shivering, jumping around. They were so soft. So alive and in tune with their stupid bodies. I couldn't decide if I was jealous or annoyed by it.

Rom migrated toward the exit. "Why not?"

"Because I have no use for her."

"You haven't finished that Go game." Ollie snapped his fingers. "You know you won't be able to live with the knowledge she could've beat you at it."

"She couldn't have. She barely survived the duration of our game." I was certain I'd forget her soon. Her measly existence hadn't exactly left an imprint on my life.

"He's going to look for her." Romeo ran a hand over his dark mane, staring at the clock above our heads. "Fuck, it feels like I've been here since Thursday. Time crawls when you're freezing to death."

"I will not be looking for her," I countered, not moving an inch, the icy smoke not penetrating my flesh even remotely. I was numb. So numb. Always fucking numb.

Ollie elbowed Rom, leaning in to whisper. "What do you think they'll call their children?"

Rom shoved him away. Ollie's dick swung with movement. It hadn't shrunk a centimeter smaller in the subzero cold. It was probably a medical condition. One of many, if I had to guess.

"*Get the Fuck Out* and *Stupid Egg*," I hissed out through clenched teeth.

Ollie quirked his head sideways. "Is that in Chinese?"

Romeo trembled. "It's in Zach."

Twenty seconds left. They'd progressed to pacing around aimlessly, trying to gather some heat. I stayed put.

Oliver fingered his chin. "She's the first woman he's ever talked about."

"And the last person he should be with." Romeo elbowed Ollie away when he tried to huddle for body heat. "She's a con woman. Remember?"

Ten seconds. I refused to partake in this conversation. I had no reason to encourage these two morons to explore this topic further.

"Zach's life is neat as shit." Oliver began strolling toward the door, making a show of rubbing the ear we'd grabbed him by this morning. "He needs a little mess. She'd be good for him."

Five seconds.

Romeo shook icicles off his hair, following Oliver. "I'd pay good money to get a front-row ticket to his downfall."

The buzzer from the clock above our heads erupted. We strolled out, single-file. Ollie grabbed the digital thermostat and pressed it to the back of his leg. Then Romeo's. Then mine.

"Shit, Zach. You're still at sixty-five." Oliver cackled. "Are you fucking kidding me? Are you even human?"

I was not, in fact, very human at all. And I wished to stay that way. Humanity was messy, mediocre, and prone to mistakes.

I'd made up my mind. I wasn't going to find her.

I was better off forgetting she'd ever existed.

CHAPTER FIVE

Zach

"Zachary, pay attention. What about this one?" Across the office, Mom dangled a Polaroid of a long-haired, scarlet-lipped beauty. "I do adore her family. Her mother is in our country club. She's a tax lawyer. Works at Clarke & Young. Not a partner just yet…" Her delicate brows slammed together as she skimmed her file. "No, no. She won't do. Too lazy. She only volunteered twice in college."

Mom boomeranged the photo into the trash pile on the rug. Dozens of pictures scattered across the coffee table, coating the entire surface. All potential brides for yours truly. All eligible. All as boring as a freshly painted white wall. This particular batch had missed the soirée, during which I'd failed my task—choosing a bride by midnight. Yesterday, Mom had barged into her friend's dating agency and confiscated these dossiers. This marked the birth of Plan X. She'd labored through A to W over the last five years when it became clear that I'd need divine intervention to drag me down the aisle.

I yawned, keeping my feet propped over my desk, ankles crossed, as I tossed a tennis ball up to the ceiling. Back and forth. Back and forth. "So what if she isn't a partner?"

"She's already twenty-five. She should be well on her way to owning her own firm by now." Mom's head snapped up. "You surprise me sometimes."

Perhaps because you're the one who's changed, Mother.

Sun Yu Wen—American name Constance—had a one-track mind. To find me a bride. She was running out of time, and I was running out of options. Especially after she'd chalked up the ball as a terrible failure. She'd thrown it for me to pick a future wife. In reality, I didn't even leave my office.

At this point, my best bet was a mail-order bride. A mail-order bride would not huff when I lodged her in the guesthouse. Would not flinch when I made her go through IVF to avoid touching her. Would not sulk when I retreated into one of my dark moods, where I didn't want to see or hear from anyone. Would not protest when she realized all I had to offer her was money and premium sperm.

I tossed the ball. "Why does it matter that she's not an overachiever?"

I knew I'd poked the bear, but I had trouble accepting my fate— and a whole entire wife I did not desire. Mom wanted to live vicariously through me. She knew she'd never remarry. Never open up to someone else. So, she'd decided, unilaterally, that I needed to stuff her void with a picture-perfect daughter-in-law, grandchildren galore, and more people for her to take care of. And it *was* a void. After Dad's death, Mom even changed her last name from Zhao to Sun, a huge deal because one) Chinese women did not change their surnames, and two) "Zhao Yu Wen sounds lightyears better." Her words, not mine.

Mom smoothed her tweed Chanel jacket, her lips twitching downward. "Are you saying you'd like to marry a bum?"

"I'm saying you remind me of Grandma."

The same grandma who never approved of her marriage to Dad. A sore spot for Mom. One I prodded only when necessary.

Mom shook her head, pinching the corner of a Polaroid so tight, her fingers reddened. "I didn't raise you to behave like this."

"Must've been one of the nannies."

We'd had three on rotation. I still sent them postcards, mooncakes, and fruit baskets every New Year, much to my mother's chagrin. Mom did not approve of me treating them as humans. When it came to the nannies, her jealousy reared its ugly head fast. She still hadn't realized I didn't actually have a relationship with them. I just didn't have one with her, either. After Dad died, she'd spent the remainder of my teens zoned out, lost in grief, until my aunt snapped her back into shape.

Speak of the devil. Zhao Yu Ting—American name Celeste (but Celeste Ayi to me)—burst into my office, clad in a gauche Juicy Couture tracksuit and a Gucci fanny pack, looking like a caricature of a rich tourist. "I've arrived." She held three designer bags on each forearm and boba tea clasped between manicured fingers.

I dug my fingers into my eye sockets. "You were never invited."

She rushed to me, awarding me with air kisses a solid foot away from each cheek. She knew better than to touch me. "My apologies for missing your little soirée, Zachary. You know I fly to Seoul for my facial every fifteenth of the month."

"It's fine."

I did not invite her to the party, either. Mainly because Celeste Ayi could not be trusted with a credit card, let alone other people. She'd probably cause a diplomatic crisis.

"Aren't I glowing?" She did a little twirl, smacking my temple with her Birkin. "Rejuran Healer, Chanel injections, Aquashine, and Baby Face Cell Therapy. It's the only way for me to maintain my 22-year-old skin." She did not have a 22-year-old's skin. In fact, she barely had skin anymore. She was 99% fillers.

I dodged her Birkin when she darted to the couches to hug Mom and came face-to-face with the Go board I'd managed to avoid since the party. I'd set up a perfect KO to finish off the little octopus. What a coward she was, running away from her inevitable failure. Celeste Ayi squeezed Mom's head to her chest, forcing her into a half-crouch.

"We were just going through our options." Mom swatted Ayi away, gesturing to the impromptu dating agency, formerly known as my coffee table. They spoke in Mandarin. "Because Zachary *failed* to choose a wife at the soirée. Care to tell us your thoughts?"

"Why, yes, of course." Ayi discarded the shopping bags on the floor, darting into the seat beside her older sister. She slammed her boba on the table, rubbing her hands together. "Finally, you two are smart enough to beg me for my opinion."

Technically, it was Mom who'd asked for it. I had no idea as to why. Celeste Ayi was a total nutcase, and I said that with as much sympathy and admiration a man like me could possibly muster. She'd moved into my childhood mansion a few homes down the road to help raise me when Dad passed away and never bothered moving out after I left for college. Seventeen years ago. The sisters still lived together but could not be more different.

Mom was a straitlaced, PhD-holding former professor, who dedicated her life to raising me to be everything society expected me to become. Successful. Put-together. An impeccably mannered overachiever.

Celeste, however, was a thrice-divorced, childless singer-songwriter who made infrequent visits to China to perform, cash in, and fuck off with a new boy toy in the country of the day. She inhaled more conspiracies than she did books, considered malls to be an extension of her closet, and cared a little less about what others thought of her than she did about color coordination.

Ayi tore up a picture, tossing the remnants behind her. "Too much like Tao's mistress."

Tao—one name only—and Celeste were the Sonny and Cher of China, only uber-sexualized. Once upon a time, newspapers hailed Celeste Ayi as the nation's most provocative, controversial female singer. She'd framed the articles, as if they were something to be proud of. Then, she caught Tao in a hot tub with three women. Two months later, he went from second husband to second ex-husband. Now they merely tolerated one another in public long enough for the occasional concert or photoshoot.

Ayi tapped a picture with a painted nail. "What about this one?"

Mom shuddered inside her fashionable suit. "Absolutely not. Her dad went to jail for tax fraud. Now her family lives in a tiny, rundown home in McLean that barely Zillows at 1.3 mil. The entire neighborhood petitioned the city to condemn the thing."

The poverty didn't bother her. The problems that came with it did.

Sure enough, Mom snatched up the picture and tossed it onto the trash pile. "I don't even know what it's doing here. Remember, Zachary—you inherit the problems of your in-laws, so choose wisely."

I yawned, ignoring the dozen or so texts Ollie bombarded the group chat with. "Sounds like the solution is to not have any in-laws."

"And this one?" Ayi pointed at another photo, squinting. "She's pretty enough. Round eyes. Milky glass skin."

"Are you describing a goat?" I missed the tennis ball. It bounced off the desk, onto the hardwood, and then to the coffee table, where it rolled until it covered a Polaroid. "On second thought, a goat would require less maintenance than a wife. Carry on."

They ignored me. Mom's lips twisted down. "She's beautiful, yes, but she's an *influencer*." She punctuated the word with bunny ears. "That is not a proper job."

"That's not a job at all," I interjected. "It's a hobby you get paid for until the algorithm changes and you lose your clout." I absolutely despised social media. The only upside to it was that it seemed to bring us one step closer to the end of civilization.

"Oh, this one is a great option." Mom plucked another Polaroid from the table, holding it to the natural light sifting through the curtains. "She's a doctor. A neurologist."

"At twenty-two?" I watched from the corner of my eye as Mom scurried toward me with a folder. "A perfect age for a brain doctor— before hers has fully formed."

"She's your age." Mom ignored the quip, setting down a background check in front of me. "Not ideal if you'd like four children, which is frankly the bare minimum."

This is not a daycare. I don't need a full roster of babies to keep myself afloat.

I opened my mouth, then clamped my lips shut, thinking better of the words. Anything to do with death triggered her. Whereas I'd gone numb, she'd gone shrill. Both were a nuisance to deal with, but only the latter elicited a headache.

Mom tapped her finger over her lips. "However, she comes from a good family and is actively seeking a husband. I approve of her."

"I approve of her, too." Celeste Ayi sashayed to the drink cart, helping herself to a double scotch on the rocks. "She must know a good plastic surgeon. I've been meaning to get a mini-lift for a while now. Everyone has one."

A bitter laugh stuck in my throat. How cruel was life that the only things my father had wanted for me—a wife, children, and happiness— were the things I reviled the most?

And yet. *And yet.* I couldn't let my mother down. When Dad passed away, he'd done so protecting me from sure death. If he'd never shielded me with his body, he'd be alive. Mom would have a husband to dote on. Celeste Ayi would be free to find a fourth husband. The world would operate exactly as it should've. But he'd left us behind. And discounting my unhinged Ayi, I was Sun Yu Wen's sole living relative.

I'd felt precisely one human feeling my entire life. *Guilt.* Guilt over killing my father. Guilt over destroying my mother. Guilt over ruining my family. Letting go of it would separate me completely from my species. I clung to it as proof I wasn't a complete psychopath. Its burden felt delicious against my bones, its suffocating pain reminding me I wasn't completely numb.

"There she is." Mom thrust the Polaroid in my face. I kept my feet

MY DARK DESIRE | 37

on the desk and angled the picture with a lopsided tilt of my head. "Her name is Eileen."

Eileen was objectively attractive. Warm smile. Nice figure. All the right credentials. And still—she bored me to death before we'd even exchanged one word.

I handed my mother the picture back, shaking my head. "Too wholesome."

My phone buzzed with another text from Oliver. I sighed, deciding to answer it before he found a way to escalate. God forbid he, too, barged in here.

Ollie vB: You sure? I know a PI who can track down your little con woman in no time.

Zach Sun: The last time I hired someone upon your recommendation, I ended up with a stranger's dildo clogging my pool skimmer. Hard pass.

Zach Sun: I'd trust Frankie Townsend before I trust whomever you recommend.

Ollie vB: Ouch. Short temper. Maybe it's time to get laid.

Romeo Costa: By something other than his hand.

Ollie vB: His poor dick. Probably goes to bed screaming, "Help! My owner beats me every night."

Romeo Costa: Impeccable grammar. A+.

Zach Sun has notifications silenced.

Meanwhile, Mom hadn't stopped rambling. She tucked the photo onto the glass edge of the custom frame that held an original Twombly sketch. "Wholesome is bad?"

"For someone with an IQ in the 200s, wholesome can be boring."

"She's actually into archery." Mom cleared her throat. "And can cook."

"Surgeons work unfathomable hours. She wouldn't be a good fit as a mother."

"I said neurologist, not neurosurgeon. If she were the latter, I wouldn't even ask before booking you a wedding venue." When she didn't draw the smile she'd aimed for, she sighed. "Besides, she's planning a sabbatical before transitioning to part-time."

I stood, pacing across my office. An office that smelled less and less like my kingdom since Octi had paid it a visit. Her scent clung to the air—oranges, artificial fruit, cheap soap, and a hint of some cleaning product. "She's no good," I growled, fixing my gaze on that unfinished

Go game that mocked me more than that nameless woman's smile.

"She's brilliant." Mom shadowed me while Ayi stacked the remaining photos and used them as a coaster. "Your father and her father were good friends in college. They met at Tsinghua before Dad left for Oxford for his master's. They were xué zhang and xué di." *Senior* and *Junior*. They must've been close. That stopped me in my tracks.

I pivoted to face Mom, startling her into a stop. "Dad knew her?"

Mom's pinched lips curved into an innocent smile that did nothing to hide her real motive. "He met her many times prior to her family moving to Berlin for business. He was her godfather, actually. I'm sure she has some stories of him to share."

I grabbed Eileen's picture again. For a moment, the idea of meeting her semi-charmed me. Doctors were analytical people, were they not? Perhaps I could explain my situation. My terms and conditions. All the fine print. We'd walk into this pragmatically, eyes wide open, each with something to gain. I could give her the wealth, the status, the perks. Just not the love, the devotion, and everything else that came with a real partnership. She'd get the kids, too, and wouldn't even have to pretend to enjoy getting impaled by my supersized cock. We could have a comfortable arrangement. A business deal of sorts.

But there was another part of me, a greater part of me, that knew no sane woman would ever subject herself to this kind of existence. Not in a free world, anyway. They all wanted the romantic dinners, the Instagram-worthy vacations, the conversations into the night, the candlelit sex. The touching. The touching. *The touching.*

I couldn't touch humans. That was my worst-kept secret. I loathed the feeling of foreign, sticky hot skin against my own. I did not shake people's hands. Didn't slap people's backs, nor kiss people's cheeks. I did not hug, cuddle, or make out. And sex? Entirely out of the question. The mere thought of someone laying on top of me made me violently sick. Flashbacks of the time I'd spent trapped under my father's lifeless figure lashed against my skin like a spiky leather belt each time I went as far as contemplating kissing someone.

I decided to spare my father's goddaughter.

"No." I tore the woman's Polaroid between my fingers, letting pieces of her sprinkle to the floor like confetti. "Not interested."

"I'm never going to wear the dress I bought for his wedding." Celeste

Ayi shook her head and knocked back the whiskey in one sip, slapping the tumbler against the drink cart. "I should just wear it for a date."

Mom straightened her blazer, calculating her next move.

I bared my teeth. "What?"

She stood tall, chin up, suit impeccable, not a hair out of place. But inside, I knew she was falling apart. That every day, I broke her heart, woke up, and did it again.

"Are you gay?" It came out in one whooshed breath. Not laced with judgment but rather desperation. A plea to explain the past decade. Anything that made even a little sense, so she could decode my inability to find a wife. She must've been holding the question in for years.

"No." *If I were, I wouldn't be alone.*

"You know you can tell me—"

"I'm not gay. It's not about that."

"Then what is it about?"

My inability to tolerate whomever I cannot use or exploit, let alone be affectionate with them.

"I have standards."

"No one meets them."

"Well, they're not very social. Just like their owner."

"I did hear a rumor." Mom knotted her arms behind her back and strolled to the opposite wall. My Damien Hirsts and Warhols bracketed each side of her. "That you were here with some young woman at the party?"

My jaw locked at the mention of the little fugitive. "She was a nobody."

"A nobody you spent three hours with." She appraised me, returning to the coffee table and retrieving the Polaroids from beneath Ayi's boba. She swatted off the condensation. We were alike, Mother and I, in the sense that we did not tolerate imperfections in anything we did.

"We played Go."

She stopped. Sneered. "Is that code for something?"

"Yes." I resumed my aimless journey, searching for a shred of evidence my unwelcome guest had indeed intruded a couple nights ago. "It is code for playing Go."

I touched ornaments, documents, and furniture. Made sure everything was where it should be. So far, it did not seem as if the little octopus had helped herself to a souvenir. Everything was here, not an inch out of place.

"I heard that she's…" Mom's shoulders rattled with a slight shudder. "A *blonde*?"

Funnily enough, I didn't even remember her hair color. I remembered that it was pale. And that she wasn't horrible to look at. That I didn't feel bile rising up my throat when we stood too close for comfort. That I did not immediately step back when her scent invaded my system.

"Is she now?" I stopped in front of the shelves behind my desk screens, inspecting them. "That may well be. I didn't pay attention to her. Only to the fact that she had two brain cells to rub together and might be considered a decent player by a mediocre player."

Behind me, Mom's breaths came out in tremors. *Not the news you hoped for, is it?* Then again, I hadn't given her the kind of news she wanted for years now.

"Is she smart, then?" She sniffled, trying to muster some enthusiasm. "What does she do in life?"

"Don't know."

"Well, what are her degrees in?"

"Not sure she has any kind of formal higher education." I adjusted a carved wooden figurine of Shou Xing on my shelf. The God of Longevity. A lot of that missing in the Sun household. I moved on to the next shelf. "Frankly, I doubt it." Octi appeared too feral to sit through four years of tertiary education. Something peculiar caught my eye.

Mother gasped. "How much do you know about her?" She raked her fingers through her hair, ruining her new blowout. She snapped her fingers at Celeste Ayi. "We need a credit check, criminal record, and extensive psychological profile before you can publicly be seen with her."

My thoughts drowned out her voice. The little *shit*. Octi had tried to steal my jade pendants. The his-and-hers. Dad's final acquisition. A deep, crescent hole hugged the lock. She hadn't lied. She *had* come here for the art. Only she'd failed to mention she came to fucking steal it.

I did not get along well with humans.

I got along even worse with thieves.

"Zach? Zachary?" Behind me, Mom started pacing, her steps thumping on the hardwood despite her negligible weight. "Are you listening? What of the fact that people said her dress was completely inappropriate? Would you at least consider sending her to my personal shopper? I'll pick up the bill."

But why would my mystery guest be fascinated with this particular art piece when I had hundreds more pricey and less secure lying around the house? She could've picked the figurine right next to it. Unlocked. Unguarded. In plain sight. It would go for double the price, too.

The pendants must've meant something to her.

Or, at the very least, one of them did.

"...come to terms with the fact that she is blonde, but I won't accept an unschooled harlot for a daughter-in-law." Mother droned on in the background. "In fact, I won't make promises to accept her at all. Oh, this is horrible. Why couldn't you have taste?"

"Because then he'd be fun." Celeste Ayi, who'd long advanced to her third drink, slammed a bottle down at the whiskey cart, guzzling another glass like it was water. She squinted out the window with the tumbler burrowed into her chest. "It's just my luck to have the most boring nephew possible. A fortune-teller told me so when I went to Hawaii for that bachelorette party. You know the one. She said he'd be nothing but a headache. And you know what? I do blame him for my Advil addiction."

Neither Mom nor I paid attention to her. I sifted through mental images of all the art I'd purchased this year until I reached the pendant. Sotheby's. Newly widowed housewife. I'd contacted the seller privately and offered far more than the evaluation before the auction even began, refusing to entertain a bidding war. Not when Dad had wanted to complete the his-and-hers collection.

I remembered the seller. 50s. Stocky. Bleached hair. Too much plastic in her face for anything that wasn't a cheap garden chair. She talked a mile a minute and kept offering to introduce me to her daughters. Daughters that could include the little octopus. They didn't appear genetically related, but perhaps the father compensated for the cotton candy the mother had between her ears. There was only one way to find out.

"Are you listening? Zach? Zachary?" Mom snapped her fingers in front of my face. "I'm taking you to Shanghai next month to find a match. I will not be—" Her voice sunk in the turbulent ocean of my thoughts.

I knew I'd promised myself not to seek her out, but that was before I found out she'd tried to steal from me. Now, the peculiar encounter transformed into something else completely.

Little Octi needed to be taught a lesson.

And I was an excellent teacher.

CHAPTER SIX

Ari: So? Got the pendant?

Farrow: Nope.

Farrow: He caught me.

Ari: HE CAUGHT YOU? ZACHARY SUN CAUGHT YOU?

Ari: HOW ARE YOU SO CALM? Do I need to get there and post bail?

Ari: I've always wanted to do that. It looks so cool in the movies.

Farrow: He let me go.

Ari: That's… charitable of him?

Farrow: This man wouldn't perform a single act of charity if the future of the continent depended on it. He caught me snooping, not stealing. It was bizarre. We somehow ended up playing Go.

Ari: I'm confused and slightly turned on by this chain of events.

Ari: Did you at least win?

Farrow: We never finished the game.

Ari: You left without giving him your number?

Farrow: He chased me down his front yard and tried to stab me.

Ari: I see. Good thing you didn't give him your number, then.

Ari: Did he actually try to stab you, though?

Farrow: He tossed a knife at me. I can still smell the steel, three days after.

Ari: Clearly you left an impression. Do you think he knows who you are?

Farrow: Hard no. My own family barely knows who I am, and I live under their roof.

Ari: So, what are you going to do now?

Farrow: Find my way back in there and get the pendant when he's out of the house. It's going to take some leg work, but I can do it.

Ari: You're crazy.

Farrow: Crazy, but lucky. I might not have won at Go, but I won at Catch.

CHAPTER SEVEN

Farrow

Like all calamities, mine came to me at a low point. I scrubbed leftover lasagna, the brain-like texture soaking into my sweatpants when the doorbell rang. Tomato paste brushed across my face like war paint. Tabby had decided the family's cleaning business, Maid in Maryland, was not for her. She'd started pursuing a career as a food blogger. The fact that she was a terrible cook did not deter her one bit.

From the second floor, Reggie's voice pierced the veil of an Olivia Rodrigo song. "Someone get the door." Sometimes I wondered if she was twenty-two, like me, or twelve.

"Too busy." Something collapsed in the dining room, followed by Tabby's loud groan. "*Ugh*, stupid superlong selfie stick."

"Farrow." Vera cranked up the living room TV. *The Real Housewives of Potomac*. She once cornered the producer at a bar and begged for a cameo. "Do something useful with yourself and get the door."

I gritted my teeth, doing my best not to yell past them. "Cleaning." *Your grown ass child's mess.*

One of Tabby's Le Creuset dishes hadn't made the journey from the oven to the island counter. The beginnings of candy-red bruises coated my knees from 20 minutes of scooping Bolognese from the tiles into a bucket with a spatula. The flesh on my hands and arms tingled and burned, courtesy of the empty bleach bottle beside me. My mind failed to conjure a single valuable thought past the cloud of fumes I'd inhaled all day. I'd cleaned two twelve-thousand-foot mansions all by myself because Vera had decided to fire most of our staff to "trim the fat." God forbid she or her daughters make up for the lack of manpower themselves. These days, I started my work days at four in the morning.

The doorbell rang again. The Ballantine household made the collective decision to ignore it. A sharp, angry knock rattled the door

"Jesus." Reggie groaned from upstairs, pausing her music long enough to assure we could all experience the full force of her irritation. "Can't be Amazon because they have more tact than to keep bugging us." She blasted the song back up.

Vera shut off her show. "Why do I have to do everything in this house?" Heavy, vulgar thumps followed her feet past the kitchen and into the foyer.

I pinched my inner wrist to distract myself from the aches snaking up my thighs. The owner of that knock had better leave soon or come bearing wine. The last thing I needed was company. Not that we had much, anyway. The step-Ballantines loved pretending to be pillars of the local community. In reality, our neighbors didn't even know their names, and we'd lived here for almost twenty-three years.

Vera flung the door open and gasped. Then, there was silence. Lots and lots of silence. Not even getting man-handled by security for harassing the producer had made her speechless, so I took this as a sign of the apocalypse. Which I was down for. I could use some time off.

"M-Mr. Sun." The spatula fell from my hand with a clank. I stopped breathing for a moment. Vera continued fumbling over words. "Why… I… This is unexpected."

Dammit. How did he figure it out?

Reggie and Tabby materialized from whatever holes they'd hid themselves in, zipping to the entryway. I shoved the bucket into the nearest cabinet, dumped a rag over the stain, and dashed into the pantry. Not the finest hiding spot. But I couldn't make it past the island without being seen.

Ours was the oldest home on the street. Tiny, dated, and hanging on by a thread. But moving out wasn't in the cards. The memories Dad and I shared here remained engraved in every scratch, dent, and tear. No way in hell would I give that up. Plus, every lawyer I'd spoken to warned me against moving, should I contest the will. I fully intended to. I'd bet my fencing hand that whatever will Vera had summoned at the reading was fake. Too bad I didn't have the money to hire representation to fight her. Until then, I planned on playing nice and lowering her guard.

"Mrs. Ballantine." I recognized Zach's husky, concise tenor. He dripped authority. The kind of person you'd trust, even if he told you to dip your head in lava. "I hope I'm not intruding."

"Intruding?" I pictured Vera literally waving the idea away. "Absolutely not. Come on in, please. My daughter was just making dinner. How do you like lasagna?"

However he felt toward the dish as a concept, he sure wasn't going to enjoy licking scraps off the floor. Tabitha had been shocked to discover the dish's handles were hot and dropped the entire thing.

A horde of footsteps stampeded down the hall.

"I'm not here for long." Zach's voice—confident, bored, and formidable—grew closer. "In fact, I have an unconventional ask of you."

I squeezed my eyes shut as if it'd make a difference. *Please, don't stop in the kitchen. Please, don't stop in the kitchen. Please, don't—*

Bright white light crept past the shutters on the pantry door. I held my breath, inching my entire spine as tight against the shelves of canned goods as possible. Chairs scraped the tiles, not even a dozen feet from me. *Shit, shit, shit.*

If the bastard wanted sugar for his coffee, they'd open this pantry and I'd be busted. My fingers itched to stab his beautiful face with the spatula in my hand. Why'd he come here? It wasn't like I'd actually managed to steal the pendant. Yet.

From the horizontal slats, I saw Vera lean toward Zach. "Anything." She edged nearer when he sloped back. "These are my daughters, by the way. I don't think you had the chance to properly meet them at the party—thank you so much for the invite, by the way." No answer. "This is Tabitha, and this one is Regina. Tabitha is an acclaimed food vlogger, and Regina is the marketing director of our housekeeping company."

Tell me your children are jobless without telling me they're jobless.

Tabby and Reggie stopped fighting for the seat beside Zach to wave.

"Heeey," Reggie screeched in a fake voice. "*Ohmigod*, thanks so much for inviting us to your party. Like, grateful doesn't begin to cover it."

Ha. If Grateful met Reggie in a dark alley, it would run screaming. I wasn't sure she could spell the word, let alone feel it.

"No need to thank me. Your mother included it as a clause in the pendant sale." *Ouch.* He was extra arctic today. I already felt the frostbite.

Tabby hip-checked Reggie out of the way. "I'm so happy we finally get to meet one-on-one." She offered a hand. "You and I have hung out in the same circles forever. Seems like we always miss one another."

Zach ignored her outstretched limb. "What a travesty."

From the tiny cracks in the shutters, I couldn't get a good view of him. I itched to crack the door open and peer at them, but I knew better than to yield to temptation.

Judging by Vera's gasp, she'd finally caught a glimpse of the remnants of her daughter's mess on the floor. "Is that... blood?"

Tabby crept behind Reggie. "It's Bolognese."

One could argue that two pounds of ground beef in a burnt jumbo loaf topped with a can of San Marzano tomatoes couldn't be considered Bolognese, but what did I know? I wasn't the acclaimed food vlogger.

Vera swiveled back to Zach. "I am so sorry, Mr. Sun. Believe me when I say I'm utterly horrified. The home isn't usually so messy, but our maid slacks off without strict supervision. I'm afraid it's difficult to find good help these days. You know how it is." By maid, she meant me. And by screw you, I meant her. Vera gestured to the mess behind her. "Oh, I hope this doesn't ruin your impression of me."

Zach began rolling his sleeves up to his forearm. "About my ask—"

"Would you like anything to drink?" Vera drew a palm to her chest. "My goodness, where are my manners? Not anywhere within reach, it seems. I blame the long work hours. I've taken over my husband's business, you know."

What you've taken over is the living room couch.

I was the cleaner, the bookkeeper, and the administration executive. All she did was bark orders and call me useless. Even that, she only did once in a full moon. She spent her days shopping with money she'd gotten from pawning Dad's things, gobbling up daytime soaps, and ordering takeout on the corporate card.

Irritation rolled off Zach's body like a thick fume. "I don't want anything." He finished his sleeves and set his forearms on the counter. "Other than to ask my question, if I may."

"Oh, sure." Vera sobered. "What is it?"

He fished something from a white gift bag he'd brought with him, holding it to the light. Was that...? No way. It couldn't be.

But it was.

"Does this shoe happen to belong to anyone in your household?"

Chapter Eight

Farrow

M^{*otherfucker.*}

otherfucker.

The billionaire asshole was out to get me. He'd actually taken time off his schedule to parade my busted-ass shoe all over Maryland like it was a deer's head. Men in power were such sadists. He simply couldn't let it go.

Fear nipped its way up my spine. Goosebumps replaced the bleach tingles on my arms. The center of Zachary Sun's attention was a very bad place to be. He had the means to destroy anyone with a simple phone call. What was I thinking, slipping into his residence to retrieve the pendant?

Silence blanketed the kitchen. Without a doubt, Vera, Reggie, and Tabby knew the shoe belonged to me. Not a single day passed without them teasing me for my attire. They couldn't understand why I didn't let the price of my clothes determine my value as a person.

A briny drop of sweat trekked down my forehead to my eye.

Breathe. Just breathe, Farrow.

But I couldn't. My chest caved. I smothered my mouth with a palm, hoping it stifled the sound of my breaths. Another second of silence, and they'd hear me. Surely.

For once, Reggie's shrill voice saved me. "Oh, that's awkward. I believe this one's mine, actually."

"No, no. I think it's mine." Tabby elbowed her out of the way. "I always bring a flat pair when I go to parties. I don't know if you know this, but I'm quite the dancer—"

"But don't you remember, Tabby…" Reggie clamped a hand on Tabby's shoulder, probably digging her acrylics into the bone. Her tone carried an eerie threat. "…that I borrowed those… *shoes* from you that night because mine got lost when I saved an injured bunny in Mr. Sun's garden?"

I dug my teeth into my inner cheek, wrangling back a frantic laugh. As low as I'd gotten, I hoped I never became this pathetic. This Cinderella bull crap was right up their alley. I bet if Zach had come in with a used menstrual cup, asking if it belonged to one of them, they'd give him a demonstration to prove they were the rightful owners.

Vera put an end to the debate before Reggie made a valley out of Tabby's shoulder. "It's Tabitha's shoe." Tabby was the costliest of her two daughters, so I supposed Vera wanted her off her hands sooner rather than later. She nodded, reassuring herself she'd made the right decision. "Definitely hers."

More silence. Unfortunately for my so-called family members, Zach Sun was too smart to buy into their bullshit. Good news for him. Devastating news for me.

His fingers tightened around the shoe. "Do you have any other daughters, Mrs. Ballantine?"

My shoulders tensed.

"What? No. These two are more than enough. They keep me busy. Trust me." Her hands curled into fists. "Ha. Ha."

More silence. Zach didn't feel the need to fill the void with meaningless words. It was probably the only good thing about him.

Finally, he set the knockoff Vans down on the island. "Are you certain, Mrs. Ballantine?"

"Well, I would know if I had an extra daughter tucked away in the house, would I not?"

Oh, the irony.

Reggie and Tabby began to squirm. I could tell, even from this angle. Tabby cleared her throat.

Tabitha Ballantine, don't you dare choose this moment to be honest for the first time in your life.

"Lovely." Zach's chair scraped across the floor as he stood. "In that case, both the Ballantine sisters should accompany me to the police station. In fact, the D.A. happens to be a good friend of mine. We'll go straight to his house. I've been meaning to check out his new renovations, anyway."

Vera stood taller, finally dropping the sweet aunt charade. "W-what are you talking about?" She couldn't even land a direct-to-streaming role with that acting.

I often wondered what my father saw in her. Part of me kind of knew the answer. He wanted someone—*anyone*—to be his. He'd grown up an orphan in Scotland. Moved here with no ties. No friends. Nothing. And Vera? She had the entire package. Sisters, aunts, and a daughter with another on the way. Too bad that, in gaining one family, he'd betrayed another. *Me.*

Zach plucked the shoe off the counter, dangling it from his index finger. "I'm talking about the fact that whomever this shoe belongs to tried to steal my pendant the night of the soirée. Since it came from your household when I bought it, I am going to go out on a limb here and guess that someone got too attached and thought they could get away with stealing it back. Well, theft is illegal in all fifty states. Your daughters should be taught a lesson."

"Oh, this is all a misunderstanding. They don't want that useless piece of cra—" Vera stopped herself at the very last second, drawing in a deep breath and replacing it with a superficial giggle. "I can assure you that the girls could not care one bit about the pendant, Mr. Sun."

"And still, this shoe proves to me that one of them did," Zachary insisted, milking the truth out of her without her even realizing it.

"It's probably Farrow's," Tabby rushed out.

And I'd thought Vera would be the one to rat me out. My cheeks flamed. Freaking Tabby.

Zach lowered the shoe. "Farrow?"

"Our stepsister." Tabby's cheeks flushed, no doubt excitement at the sudden opportunity to please Zach. "She dresses like a homeless person and our dad—her biological dad—used to own the pendant. She kept it in her room before we sold it. She always gets into trouble."

Up until now, I might've saved Tabitha if we were ever in a Mufasa-and-Scar situation. I made a mental note not to. The woman was as likeable as a deadly virus.

"So, there *is* a third sister." Zach sounded like he was trying to fleece nuclear codes from a toddler.

"Sh-she's not really a sister." Reggie fussed with the collar of her Oxford dress. "Though I wouldn't say no to sharing her metabolism…"

"My stepdaughter is estranged from us." Vera tried to sound dignified. "I've tried my best with her, I have, but—"

Zach cut her off. "Where is Farrow?"

"Somewhere in the house." Tabby's shoulders sagged, now that she was no longer at risk of jailtime. She gestured to the rags on the tiles. "She needs to finish cleaning up here."

The sting of her words pinched my cheeks. Heat exploded from my sternum, buzzing up and down my entire body. My lousy excuse for a family had no idea how they sounded. Or maybe they did, and this was their goal all along.

Working as a cleaner didn't embarrass me. I prided myself in my stellar service. But being paraded as the lowly maid of my own family? I found myself surprisingly embarrassed. Surprising because I didn't usually give half a crap what people thought about me. But somehow, I did when it came to Zachary Sun. Once upon a time, and for three hours only, I'd managed to capture his attention. Something no other woman had ever done. Yes, I liked the idea that he thought of me as mysterious and alluring. Not as someone who scrubbed her step-monsters' toilets.

"Find her for me." He snapped his fingers once as if he were delivering a decree to his devoted subjects. I could practically hear the prick sitting back like the brusque king that he was. "Or you'll find yourself in one hell of a lawsuit."

The commotion that followed made my head spin.

Vera pointed to her daughters. "Reggie, you look upstairs. Tabby, do the pool house and the basement. She can't be far. Her car's parked out front. I'll check here."

A flurry of feet charged in several directions. The door to the backyard whined open. The lighting fixtures rattled with the heavy footsteps above. Cabinet doors creaked open in rapid succession.

Zach yawned, possibly... *amused* by my life circumstances. "She wouldn't hide in a cabinet."

Vera swung another open. "Why not?"

"Because she is not a complete idiot."

"Trust me, she is—"

"I don't."

"W-what?"

"I don't trust you. Keep looking." He checked his wristwatch. "I want her head on a platter, and I want it before my six o'clock appointment across town."

I saw the words for what they were. A declaration of war. If he thought I'd sit down and take it, he had another thing coming. Just because I accepted abuse at home to ensure the protection of my assets didn't give him free reign to make me his new favorite game. Before Dad passed, I'd spent my entire life giving my step-monsters hell. To the point where Vera had all but begged for me to move to Seoul, Reggie handed me brochures of every reputable plastic surgeon, and Tabby marked a map with all the foodie hotspots. (I didn't even know she could read a map.)

I know how to fight, Zachary Sun. Gloves off. No mercy. Until I draw blood.

"I wouldn't put anything past her." Venom seeped through Vera's tone. "I've tried with her, Mr. Sun. I really have. But Farrow is beyond repair. It's those genes her mother gave her, I think. She's…" She exhaled but didn't finish the sentence.

"She's what?"

"So unladylike."

"Expand."

"Unruly, feisty, mannerless. A *tomboy.*" The word burst past her bared teeth. Vera slammed a cabinet shut, pausing to shake her head. "She got into so much trouble growing up. Can you believe they kicked her out of private school at sixteen? She gave away the morning-after pill to students who needed them. For *free.*"

And I'd do it all over again. Fuck the patriarchy. While we're at it—screw Vera, too.

"Did she ever finish high school?"

At this point, did it matter?

Ironically, the closest I've ever come to using my GED is via the research skills required to break into your home.

"Barely." She tossed her hands in the air. "Her father had the mind to ship her off to a fencing academy in Seoul. It's what she wanted all along, anyway. She always looked down at me and my poor daughters. Wouldn't let me choose her clothes, get her nails done, or cut that god-awful hair."

"College?"

Vera snickered, waving a hand. "Not even community college.

Tabitha, however, has a B.A. from Columbia and my sweet Reggie went to the prestigious—"

"No need to finish the sentence. I assure you, no part of me cares."

Even if every part of him cared, Tabby did not, indeed, have a degree from *that* Columbia. But Columbia College of Maryland didn't exactly have the same ring to it.

Vera opened the fridge. What did she think? That I'd stuffed myself between her gallon of probiotic yogurt and double-XL pickled onion jar? Somebody call Sherlock and tell him he might be out of a job.

Mr. Sun was obviously not as thoroughly appalled as Vera wanted him to be because she proceeded to the fake-crying portion of the program, except she couldn't quite siphon out a tear, so her nose just scrunched up and down. Vera swiped her cheek. Dry as a Chilean desert. "She fought me over that pendant. Gave me hell. But we needed the money. Her late father worked on very slim margins, and my girls need to be provided for until the insurance money kicks in." She spoke as if Reggie and Tabby were children, not capable women in their mid-twenties. "I am beyond embarrassed at Farrow's behavior."

I was embarrassed, too. To be affiliated with this hot mess. Thankfully, not through DNA.

Zach cut through her moaning. "Mrs. Ballantine?"

"Yes?"

"Try the pantry and put us both out of the misery that is this conversation."

"Oh. Right. Good idea."

Her footsteps neared.

My elbows dug deep into my hips. The spatula almost fell from my clammy grip. Tiny hairs leapt up from the nape of my neck. I rocked back on my heels and drew in a breath, preparing myself for the worst.

Vera's fingers stretched out. I chanced one final glance at Zach through the slats and regretted it. He wore a ghost of a smile, his back against the island, one ankle crossed over the other. With eerie precision, his eyes found mine through the shuttered door.

I jerked back, slamming my head into a can.

He'd figured it out.

He knew.

The bastard knew.

CHAPTER NINE

Farrow

The bright chandeliers blinded me for a moment. I blinked to adjust my eyes. I felt bare. Naked and exposed. I knew what I looked like. With my tattered clothes and my hair pulled back. Tomato stains up and down my arms. A freaking spatula nestled in my fist. Normally, I wouldn't care. But I wanted Zach to see me as his equal.

Vera pointed at me, turning her gaze to her guest. "There she is." Everything—from her voice to her fingertips—shook.

Zach folded his arms across his chest, the epitome of casual. His presence filled up the room like he'd been carved into it, sculpted in marble. An immaculate haircut highlighted that thick, glossy tar hair, not a single strand out of place. With his navy cashmere sweater pulled over a smart dress shirt and pale gray slacks, he would auction for a billion dollars and some change.

A tiny smirk pulled at the right side of his mouth. Almost too slight to see. He peered down his nose at me, so tall and larger than life. "Mrs. Ballantine?" Even as he spoke to Vera, his eyes never budged from me. As if I'd somehow escape if he gave me an inch.

The gravity of the situation crashed on me. Back pressed against the shelves. A cornered animal. Utterly humiliated. Didn't mean I had to accept it. I deposited the spatula on a random shelf, jerked my chin up, and met his gaze head-on.

Vera scuttled to his side. "Yes?"

"Privacy, please."

"Farrow, get you—"

"No, Vera." Zach straightened to his full height, stepping away from the island. "*You* are leaving."

"But…"

"I did not ask for your opinion. I asked you to kindly fuck off."

Holy shit. He really was pissed. *Well, you* did *try to steal something of his.* Scratch that. Something of *mine.* I needed to remember that. It made all the difference.

"You and I aren't done." Vera pivoted back to me and wagged her French-manicured finger in my face. "Not by a long shot."

"Don't worry, *Mommy.*" I winked at her. "I'm not going anywhere, whether you like it or not." Sure, I had to play by her rules, but that didn't mean I had to be a good sport.

Nothing about Dad's death made sense. One moment, he'd stood before a restaurant entrance, waiting for the valet to pull up. And the other, the valet crashed into him at the speed of light. The tests came back clean. No alcohol. No drugs. The valet claimed his foot got stuck on the accelerator and received a five-year sentence. The judge felt sorry for him. For his sick wife. For their innocent baby. I felt bad for him, too. But I felt even worse for myself. That was two years ago, and I was still licking the wounds, which showed no signs of healing.

With a displeased grunt, Vera tromped her way into the living room. Still close enough to eavesdrop, of course. The minute she evacuated my personal space, I ventured out of the pantry.

"No." Zach strolled to me, raising one palm. "Stay where you are. Rats fit right into dark holes."

I slipped out, anyway. "Speaking of dark holes, anyone ever told you you're an asshole?"

"Not aloud, but I'm sure many share the sentiment."

On instinct, I drifted to a utensil drawer, yanking it open to arm myself with the sharpest thing I could find. He slammed it shut with his hip before I could reach for a steak knife. *Killer instincts.* Noted.

He *tsked.* "If I were you, I wouldn't try anything funny." His colossal frame blocked any path I could take out of here. Not that it mattered now that he knew my identity. There'd be no escaping him. "Not only can I outsmart you, I can also out-kill you. And I am currently very tempted to do so, little thief."

A burst of pure energy flooded my veins. "Fuck you, big bucks. You and your stupid friends don't scare me."

No way had I grown that paranoid the past couple days. I'd felt someone following me, the little hairs on the back of my neck saluting the stranger each time I entered and exited a new home to clean. A private investigator, perhaps, since I doubted these trust-fund babies would ever perform manual labor personally. And if it wasn't Zach, it must've been one of his fancy friends. I'd heard the rumors. All three of them were thick as thieves and prone to throwing their weight around the DMV to get whatever and whoever they wanted. Well, not me.

I swiveled past Zach, headed for the door. "Go pester another kid on the playground."

He unleashed a dramatic sigh. That was when I felt it. A metallic thing kissing my lower back. Cold, sharp, and unmistakable. A *knife*. What kind of psychopath walked around with a freaking *knife*? In broad daylight, too? Then, I remembered he'd sent a fancy one soaring in my direction when I'd escaped him at the party. Zachary Sun loved his weapon. He was a far cry from the unimpeachable and elegant version of himself, who popped onto Bloomberg panels to discuss rising start-ups. A savage in designer suits. And he was officially, unapologetically my problem.

"I strongly advise you don't run away from this particular conversation."

I shuddered, more from the baritone rumble of his voice than the knife digging into my lower back. He wouldn't stab me. I just didn't know how far he'd take this. I stopped but didn't turn to face him.

Zach pressed the flat edge deeper into my flesh. "Unless, of course, you aren't very fond of your ability to walk."

He should be worried about my ability to castrate him with an épée. Because that just officially became my new goal in life.

Though he couldn't see it, I plastered on a smile, ignoring my skyrocketing pulse. "I'm flattered, Mr. Sun, that you think my measly life is worthy of a life in prison for you."

"I'm surprised, Miss Ballantine, that you think I'd ever be subjected to such a fate. I am far too rich, powerful, and smart to serve even a minute in any six-by-eight room that isn't a sauna. Plus, if you turn around, you'll notice something very interesting about my knife."

I twisted on my heel, taking my sweet time, building anticipation, not showing an ounce of the panic I felt. If Zachary Sun wanted my complete submission, he'd have to rip it from my bloody hands.

When my body faced his, I noticed our distance. At least two giant steps separated us. My eyes crawled down to the knife stabbing my hip bone. Thick black velvet hugged everything but the blade.

My breath caught inside my throat. "Velvet doesn't catch fingerprints."

Of course, he knew that. What the heck didn't this man know? His eyes held mine. "No weapon, no crime."

"This can't be legal."

"Everything is legal when you know the right people." Something deliciously dark gleamed in his eyes. "Laws are for people like you. Lawyers are for people like me."

"You're a fraud. Nothing like how they portray you in the media." The words burst past clenched teeth. If I lessened the pressure of my bite, even a smidge, my teeth would clatter from angry, vicious tremors. "How many people know that you're a monster?"

"Not many. Only those who bother to look past my exterior. It's too convenient not to, though. I'm a highly useful creature to most."

The tip of his knife drifted from my hip bone toward the space between my navel and the waistband of my jeans. A pool of heat gathered between my legs. *What the hell is wrong with you, Fae?* But I couldn't help it. Something about the power he oozed got me. I'd lived in one of the richest zip codes my entire life, yet I'd never experienced anyone quite like Zachary Sun.

His knife stopped just shy of my sex. He licked his lips, subconsciously. "You could be one of them, you know."

My whole body came alive, my pulse stuttering beneath every inch of my skin. I wanted more. And yet, I wanted nothing to do with him at all. Logic dictated that someone like him would be shit in bed. He had all the wrong traits of a talented lover. Too selfish. Too beautiful. Too narcissistic. But I still would. My eyes jerked up, crashing into his. He had no trouble meeting my eye contact. He wasn't a psychopath. No. He was something else completely. The only monster of his kind.

"A deal with the devil?"

He stared down his nose at me, every inch of him a frozen tundra. "The only thing you lose out of striking such a deal is your soul, and that isn't worth too much."

An impregnable lump blocked any words from escaping my throat. I cleared it, curling my nails into my palm. "How do you know?"

He shrugged, his knife still digging into my core, to the space where warmth swirled. "Most people do not possess them in the first place."

"Maybe I don't have a soul, either."

Are you really talking to Zachary Sun about souls right now? What is wrong with you? The answer, of course, was a lot. A whole bunch, in fact. But every minute we spoke was a minute he didn't stab me.

Yeah. That's why, Fae. Keep telling yourself that.

He drew slight circles with the flat edge of his knife, sending fireworks from my core to my toes. "You do."

"How do you know?"

"You reek of it." His jaw clenched under smooth golden skin. "And I'm a soul collector."

Are you drunk? He didn't look it, but he sure sounded it.

I meant to ask, but all I could manage was, "You collect souls?"

"The most underrated currency in the world. Everybody wants one, and they're hard to come by. That's why people purchase art. Art makes you feel alive."

"Only if you're already living."

"Even if you're a breath away from death," he countered, drawing an indecipherable pattern against me. Just when I'd thought nothing affected him, he spared a single glance downward. The blade grazed the tiny sliver of bare skin above my waistband. "Once I have someone's soul, they're a pawn in my hand."

This man's brand of fucked up made Michael Myers resemble a Teletubby. A thesis could be written on how well he managed to hide it with ethereal looks and flawless manners. I wondered if Vera and the girls were eavesdropping on us. From this angle, we couldn't see beyond the vacant doorframe, but I wouldn't put it past them. They loved good gossip almost as much as they enjoyed seeing me punished.

I tapped my lips. "Know what I think?"

"No. You can keep your two cents. You look broke."

I ignored his quip. "You're hiding something. You don't seem like the type to carry weapons around." I realized, after I said it, that I wasn't really scared. Enthralled, angry, and ready for battle? Of course. But scared? As crazy as it sounded, even with his knife aimed directly at me, I didn't truly feel unsafe.

He shook his head. "You have no idea what kind of man I am."

His dusky, gleaming eyes scraped down my frame. I seized the opportunity to grip the knife. I aimed for the handle, but my fingers accidentally brushed against his. Zach hissed, pulling away like my touch had branded him. His expression turned feral. He stumbled back, eyes glazed over with something I'd never seen before. Not on him. Not on *anyone*. His back bumped into the sink with a loud thump. I was so surprised by his visceral reaction, I staggered in the opposite direction, too.

"Do *not* touch me." The words came out harsher than he'd ever spoken to me. For once, he didn't whisper, hiss, or husk. That simple statement lacked any control.

Against all logic, I straightened, forcing my shoulders back. The idea that I'd somehow turned the tables thrilled me. *Whatever your weak point is, I'm going to find it. And then I'm going to press it until you bleed out.*

I white-knuckled the edge of the counter behind me, forcing my bloodlust to retreat. My heart beat so hard, I feared it would break my ribcage and rip out of my flesh. I couldn't afford *that* hospital bill.

Zach clasped the knife with shaking fingers. I replayed the last few seconds. He'd ordered me not to touch *him*, rather than his knife. It could be nothing, but my gut said otherwise.

I conjured all the confidence I could muster, certain I was onto something. "So, what? You're going to kill me now?"

The muscles in my stomach burned. I felt charged. A live wire. Buzzing with anger and ire and *life*. I wanted to pounce on this man and strangle him. To finish that Go game. To show him what I was made of. I couldn't remember the last time anyone had made me feel much of anything other than Dad. Friends, boys, acquaintances—they all came and went.

Zach held his jaw, working it back and forth. His knife still pointed at me, just in case. He seemed thoughtful all of a sudden. I needed to pry him away from his own thoughts.

"You had a deal to offer me," I reminded him. "I'm listening."
Reluctantly.

His lips curved up in a snarl. "You think you deserve a deal?"
Pretty boy, ugly soul.

"I think you're still here, and you've put some thought into my identity, so obviously, you found something you've been seeking in me. Don't let your pride get in the way of your objective. I'm sure there's enough people out there to stroke that giant ego of yours. I don't need to be one of them." I could tell by his expression that he thought I spoke too much, fought too hard, and was a general headache.

He never wavered in his stance. "You're the hired help."

Summing up my entire existence through my job description. Nice.

"I'm a housekeeper," I corrected, straightening my spine, not ashamed in the slightest. "Well, if you want to get to the real nitty-gritty of things, I own Maid in Maryland with my fa—" I started to say family, but they didn't deserve the title. Not by a long shot. "With my stepmother, mostly."

Zach treaded closer, collecting himself after that weird moment between us. "Your stepmother is useless."

I could smell him again. His inimitable, outdoorsy scent that made me think of Scandinavian woods and merciless winters. I might be smart, but my body was obviously a dumbass. Even if Zach Sun were the devil, I'd willingly let him drag me into darkness. I was Persephone, eagerly following him into the underworld.

"That's not true. She has many uses. If you ever struggle to fall asleep, ask her to talk to you about her wardrobe woes."

"What I don't get is..." He tightened his grip on the knife, placing the blunt edge on my collarbone and gliding it up my throat, ever so slowly. My breath hitched. "...why the only person in this family with an actual functioning brain became everyone's designated bitch, *Octi*."

Ah. A question for the ages. I contemplated lying to him for a moment. The truth was, by far, the most vulnerable thing one could share about themselves. But I decided against it. Zachary Sun would call me out on my bullshit before I even finished my sentence. There was no point hiding things from him, even if I knew *he* was full of secrets.

Distinctly aware they could very well be eavesdropping, I lowered my voice, swatting the knife away from my chin. "I have some issues to sort out before I can part ways with them. Legal stuff." I scowled. "Anyway, didn't you come here to yell at me for the pendant?" Yes. I was so desperate to change the topic that I didn't mind being shouted at.

"Yelling is hysterical and pointless. You deserve punishment, not a slap on the wrist." With the tip of his knife, Zach tilted my chin up to meet his eyes. "Which brings me back to our deal."

I swallowed hard, somewhere between pissed off and intrigued. I really ought to be scared of this man. I didn't know why I couldn't bring myself to conjure that particular emotion. Maybe because he seemed too controlled to kill someone offhandedly. Or maybe it was something else. The way he held his knife almost reminded me of how my elderly neighbor clutched onto his walking cane. Or how the toddler across the street held onto her blankie. As if he used it often. Casually. Like an accessory to help him with his daily tasks.

I pinched my lips together. "Aw, what will you do? Force me into marriage like that psychopath friend of yours?"

Everyone knew Romeo Costa had dragged his Southern belle wife down the aisle by the ear, kicking and screaming. That they were now the most praised and admired couple in this zip code didn't matter in the slightest. Their origin story had forever seared into my brain. How he'd locked her in that golden cage of his. How she rattled the bars, bent them into the shape of his heart, and wore him down, chipping his exterior bit by bit until he was completely and undeniably hers.

A legend of a dark Romeo and a stubborn Juliet, the rumor mill whispered. *A rewritten classic where everyone got their happy ending.*

I wasn't Dallas Costa, though. If, by some wild stroke of disaster, Zach Sun forced me into marriage, I wouldn't play the long game. I'd probably stab him in his sleep with my épée.

Zach reared his head back, staring at me as if I'd hallucinated him. "No offense, Miss Ballantine, but I would sooner marry a wild coyote than you. At least the coyote would be exceptionally more pleasant to spend time with. Plus, if I feed it, I might have a chance at domesticating it."

I smiled, making sure to flash my canines. "Careful. It might also kick your ass at Go."

"Easy there, Little Octopus. I do recall you ran away from the game because you'd backed yourself into a trap."

I could finish that game fine. I'd replayed it in my head every night since the soirée. The side effect of a stellar memory and an unhealthy obsession with victory. I knew where each stone rested. Anticipated every move he could make. And most importantly, how I'd use them against him. I narrowed my eyes, glancing at the clock on the wall behind him. "What do you want, then?"

I had lots of work to get to. The leftover lasagna on the floor wasn't going to clean itself, and at this rate, the Ahmadi family had every right to dock my pay for showing up late.

Zach took his time answering, standing before me in all his unapologetic, unreasonably attractive glory. Hard, cold, and unrelenting. A flawless sculpture abandoned before the varnish.

"You."

CHAPTER TEN

Farrow

My spine slammed against the wall. A bad time to realize he'd walked me back, step by step. Cornered me. Invaded my space without actually touching me. That was the thing. Zach never truly pierced my personal bubble. Not with his body, anyway.

Using the flat edge of his knife, he tilted my head to the side, toward the family room. I had a clear line of sight to my step-monsters. The level of precision with which Zachary Sun operated stunned me. He'd started steering me here ten minutes ago, aware of his goal while I'd rambled about souls.

Vera, Reggie, and Tabby stood in a tight circle, bickering with one another like three frenetic hens. So, they hadn't eavesdropped. Too busy tossing the blame for what had happened between themselves.

"…looked at me like he was going to ask me out." Tabby threw her hands in the air. Her Dior skirt rode up, revealing a generous stretch of her thighs. "What was I supposed to do?"

"…could swear he smiled at me when I told him the shoe is mine." Reggie sniffed into a handkerchief, blowing her nose in decibels more suitable for a distressed elephant. "Also, is that my skirt? *What* made you think you could pull it off, Tabs?"

"Look at them," Zach instructed, every ounce of him stone-cold. "These are the clowns holding you hostage. You live in an upside-down world, where the dog has the human on a leash."

"Is your punishment to make me feel like shit?" I slapped the knife away from my face. "Because mission accomplished. Now, can you leave?"

"Not before I hire you to be my help, *Help*."

The shock lasted only for one second. Followed by an urge to strangle him with my bare hands. But he didn't deserve my emotions.

So, instead, I offered him my defiance. I tilted my head back against the wall and pulled my lips in an empty smile. "Leave. Before I kill you. I won't even need a weapon for that. Trust me."

"You'll be working for me—*under* me—at my whim," he continued, undeterred and unimpressed by my rejection. "You'll serve, obey, and cater to me. Paying off your debt for trying and utterly failing to steal from me—"

"Listen here, Sir Jerk-a-lot. I didn't *actually* steal from you. No proof, no crime. All you have to show for your accusation is a small dent on a glass case. I'm not my stepsisters. You cannot stress me into being your bitch."

"I never mentioned a dent on a glass case."

Oops. I never made stupid mistakes like this. Never got so heated I abandoned my wits. Zachary Sun had managed to upend years of strict self-control. Of the practiced calm expected of a world-class fencer. Well, *former* world-class fencer.

The telltale pulse of regret crept up my neck. "You did five seconds ago." I doubled down on my lie and lifted a hand to stop his retort, refusing to fall into the hole I'd dug for myself. "Before you say anything, remember—no proof, no crime. I simply got lost in your library. That dent in the glass was already there."

"The surveillance cameras tell a different story." He raised his phone with his free hand, wagging it. A clear shot of my face flashed at me.

Shit.

Shit, shit, shit.

I'd checked for cameras on the ceilings, but it hadn't occurred to me to check for hidden ones. *Fine.* It had. But my desperation got the best of me.

I pulled my shoulders back, feigning confidence. "The surveillance cameras don't have a mouth. My lawyer, however, will, and I bet she can get pretty creative about what happened there. A powerful man. A cornered woman in a nightgown." I cocked my head to the side. "You do the math."

In fact, said lawyer wouldn't have to make up a single thing. Zachary Sun had trapped me in his office and forced me to stay, dressed only in lingerie. A pesky little thing called false imprisonment. A felony punishable by up to thirty years in prison. I'd looked it up first thing in the morning.

Zach arched a single brow. "You can't afford a pair of shoes that stay on your feet, and you expect me to be concerned about your legal representation? Last I checked, Google can't represent you in a court of law." He stared me down. "Who's letting their pride stand in their way now, Little Octi?"

And still, I refused to back down. I opened my mouth, a saucy retort ready to launch at him. He stopped me with his knife to the mouth. He used just enough pressure to part my lips. Whatever he saw had his pupils dilating. It lasted half a second before his eyes tapered.

He shook his head, washing away whatever the heck that was. "The deal isn't an offer. It's your only choice to survive."

"You want me to dust your shelves and suck your toes to remind you that you're better than me? Hard pass. I'm not fulfilling whatever sick fantasies live in that twisted head of yours."

"I can assure you that the absolute last thing I fantasize about is your touch."

"Fine." I backed away from his knife and pushed up my sleeves, feeling uncharacteristically hot all of a sudden. "I'll fess up."

"I doubt you'd even recognize honesty if it hit you in the head with a nametag."

His dig bounced right off my shoulder.

"Say, hypothetically, that I wanted to steal from you. So, what?" I shrugged. "It's not like I succeeded. Nor is there ample proof. The room remains perfectly intact. At worst, I'll get some probation time and community service for trespassing. Bring it on."

With that, I whipped around, ready to bolt, but he snatched my wrist. *So much for not fantasizing about touching me, jackass.* A sneer hiked across my lips. I pivoted, eager to point that out. But by the time I turned, Zach had already released my hand and stumbled back. Sheer confusion laced with revulsion marred his flawless features. He stared at the hand that had touched me, then at my face, then down at his open palm again. He looked like he was waiting to see if it would burst into flames.

Ouch. How horrid was I to him that he'd almost yelped? Another foreign emotion snuck into my gut. *Hurt.*

I crossed my arms, digging my short nails into my elbows as much as I could with their abysmal length. "If you find me so disgusting, don't touch me."

He straightened his back, loosening his jaw into the same terrifyingly neutral expression. "You will work for me." The words came out slow as he stitched together his composure, thread by thread.

"I will *not*." I shook my head, looking around us. "Why the hell would you want me to, anyway? You think I tried to steal from you. Are you begging for a repeat or something?"

"You need to be put in your place."

"My place is nowhere near you."

"Your place is to serve anywhere and anyone who can afford you. I can."

"I'm not some object you can own."

"You are a subject I *will* own," he countered, eyes dead. "Until I feel I've had enough of you. Which, worry not, should be very soon. I'm offering you an extremely short and economical deal. You'd be a fool not to take advantage of it."

Finally—*freaking finally*—the thousands of alarm bells that should've gone off an hour ago blared in my head. Why, of all people, did he want to hire *me*? Sure, I challenged him in Go. But so could some 9-dan prodigy at the Ing Cup. Why me?

Why does it matter? You promised Dad you'd get his pendant back. You can lie to everyone but him.

"Fine." I flicked a tomato chunk off my shirt, aiming for his shoe. Only fair. "If you give me the pendant back, I'll give you a three-month contract."

"The pendant is off the table. You'll never have it." He checked his watch, shaking his head at the time. "Six-month contract, and I'm your only client. Hours are eight-thirty to six-thirty. Five times a week. Weekend rates are triple the wage."

Did he want a maid or a roommate? In what universe would I agree to such outrageous hours?

I fought an eye roll. "I have a company to run. I do three to four mansions a day."

"You'll do one, and it will be mine."

"We'll lose clientele. No, thank you."

"Why would you lose clientele? You're not the only cleaner in the company."

My blank stare said it all.

His face morphed from boredom to revulsion. "You're a one-woman operation, and you split the profit with your stepmother? Are you a crosswalk? Is your purpose in life to be stepped on?"

Actually, she got a sixty-forty split out of the deal. But I was too embarrassed to tell him.

I tilted my chin up. "That's rich coming from you."

"I'm offering a reasonable exchange. She's offering you forced labor."

"The fact remains that I can't work solely for you."

"You can, and you will, once your stepmother hires more help, which is what she'll do by the time I'm done with her."

Why are you doing this? Why are you helping me?

Obviously, he had an ulterior motive, but I didn't know what I could offer that no one else could. Other than Go, we shared nothing in common.

"I'm not doing this out of the goodness of my heart." Zach read my mind, pulling his phone out of his pocket and checking his emails.

"Then, why are you doing this?"

"Because you deserve to be taught a lesson."

"And that is?" I regretted the question as soon as it left my lips.

"In this world, there are masters, and there are servants. I'm a master. You're a servant. Act accordingly, and I will let you go."

I didn't buy what he was selling. No one would go through these lengths to prove something to someone they didn't care about. At the same time, I knew better than to think he wanted to woo me. Zachary Sun gave off strong asexual vibes. I'd seen him several times, eyes clinging to his every move both up close and afar. He'd never so much as glanced at another human appreciatively. His eyes never halted on blush-stained cheeks or generous chests. Men did not interest him, either. He treated humans as stones in his Go game. *Speaking of...*

"You want to finish the game." A tiny smirk interrupted my scowl. "That's why you want me close."

"You've caught me." Sarcasm dripped from his lips. "Your intelligence knows no bounds."

I slid past him, waltzed over to the counter, and opened an overhead cabinet. "You think you'll win."

He watched as I fished out a cup, filled it to the brim with tap water, and downed the whole thing. "I think the words you are looking for are *thank you*."

"I still didn't say yes to the deal."

His thick brow tilted up. "Aren't you going to offer me any water?"

I gave him a slow once-over, allowing myself the liberty to appreciate all the good parts. "Your legs and hands seem to be in perfect health. I trust you can handle the task."

"I haven't poured my own water in..." He scowled, trying to recall. "*Ever*, I believe."

I set the cup down in the sink, wiped my mouth with the back of my hand, and clucked my tongue. "There is nothing quite as wasteful as lovely, useless hands."

His jaw locked, and I knew I'd hit a nerve. It was a rare occasion, so I took that as a win.

"So." He drew the word out, his free hand flexing, perhaps with the effort not to strangle me. *These next six months will be hell for you, buddy.* "Do we have a deal?"

I took my sweet time rinsing the cup. The Ahmadi home needed to be cleaned, but somehow, I trusted that Zach would follow through on his promise and wipe away my extraneous responsibilities. The raw pink skin of my hard-labored hands winked at me beneath a steady stream of water. Water I couldn't afford. Under lights that still needed to be paid for. A mere six months, and my troubles might wash away. Could I do it? Could I sign away my soul to a monster in Armani?

A foot away, Zach's untarnished hands taunted me. Smooth, long fingers. Absent of calluses, save for a single one beneath his right middle finger. *From Go*, I deduced. We were moonless nights and perihelion days. Arctic cold and equatorial heat. Old money and no money.

I tore one-fourth of a single paper towel sheet from a holder, wiped my hands as dry as I could with the tiny scrap, and tucked it in half over the crest of the faucet to dry. The only reason we hadn't switched to a washable tower roll stood in the living room, arguing with her sister over who would make a more suitable bride for the devil before me. We couldn't afford another clogged sink from Tabby.

A quick glance at Zach told me he'd never been poor enough to reuse paper towels.

Well, if you want me in your life, you better get used to my penny-pinching habits.

I marched to him, determination fortifying each step. But the minute I reached his six-foot personal bubble, he got out of my way. *On instinct,* it seemed. Like the mere idea of my filthiness rubbing into his goldenness made him want to vomit. He really didn't like the idea of us touching. I was beginning to take offense.

"You're asking for some serious overtime and unconventional concessions." I folded my arms over my chest. "Come back to the negotiation table, and we might just have a deal."

"You're in no position to negotiate."

I shook my head, sighing. "You think too logically. There's one thing you're not considering."

"What is that?"

"*Emotions.* I have them. And right now, most of them are dedicated to hating your guts. So, you'll have to meet me halfway."

He tucked his phone back into his pocket, sliding the knife into its concealed holster. "What is it that you want?"

I wondered if he realized that the picture-perfect veneer he'd worked so hard to erect had begun to crumble before me. Sure, a lot of moving parts made up Zachary Sun, and I didn't understand 99.99% of them. But I'd figured out one important thing. Something dark and unusual lurked beneath the most eligible bachelor in the Northern Hemisphere. Something terrifying he didn't want the outside world to see.

"You can keep your crappy traditional wage structure. I want no part of it." I inched closer, just to push his boundaries, reveling at the way his jaw set at my proximity. "You'll pay me in the form of legal fees. Cover the six-figure retainer and hourly fee, then pay me minimum wage over the table and fifty bucks per hour under it." The last thing I wanted was to line Vera's pockets while enriching my own.

Zach didn't even flinch at the number. "You don't want the money to reach your stepmother."

"Correct. And money is no issue for you."

"I'll do you one better. I'll hire you the best fucking lawyers in the DMV."

I swallowed, trying hard to keep the emotions at bay. I knew it sounded too good to be true, and yet, I couldn't stop myself from hoping. Hope was the cruelest form of punishment. Normally, I knew better than to let it trickle into my system. But I was tired and foolish and, for the first time in my life, a little sorry for myself.

I held his gaze. "You understand that, whatever goes toward that lawyer, I can never pay back, right?"

"I can afford a whole continent of you, Farrow." *Of* you, not *for* you. Just one letter shy of romantic. "And you'll have representation so ruthless that Mrs. Ballantine will run to the settlement table before you even file the first motion."

I shook my head, frantic eyes darting in her direction, cursing myself for forgetting our proximity. "She can't know I lawyered up."

He frowned. "Why not?"

I pressed my lips together, staring hard at his throat. At the long, elegant column. Masculine and thick. I'd never uttered these next words to anyone before. But I needed to. He was my only shot at this. What a cruel twist of fate. My salvation had come from the devil.

"There's a second clause to our agreement." I tucked my upper lip in my mouth, biting down, toying with the words I feared would sound crazy. "I need you to hire a private investigator to look into the will. Dad would never keep me out of it. He just wouldn't."

"Consider it done."

He didn't question why I'd fight for a cleaning business, like the lawyers had during the free consults. Didn't advise me to abandon Dad's legacy. Didn't judge me for mourning the future I'd lost. The one where I retired from fencing with an Olympic gold, and Dad and I ran Maid in Maryland together. Just the two of us.

In fact, his face never wavered from its default blank canvas. No judgment, no disbelief, no condescension. Just boredom and a dash of impatience for whatever meeting had him glancing at his watch every now and then. I appreciated the simplicity of his selfishness. Zachary Sun cared about himself and only himself. Anything outside of that purview didn't deserve his concern.

Zach casted a warning look. "No more asks." He produced his phone, did a few swipes, and handed it to me. "You should not be rewarded for your appalling behavior."

I peered down at the screen, noting the name of an AI app he'd just acquired by force. It transcribed conversations and converted them into contracts in real time, discarding all the useless back and forth in between. We operated on different levels, him and I. The sooner I accepted that, the less miserable the next six months would be.

I scribbled my chicken-scratch signature on the screen and licked my lips, half exhilarated, half shocked at what just happened. I'd thought he'd intended to pull me into his lap and give me a good spanking. Instead, I escaped with a new job far cushier than my current one and the opportunity to finally run away from a horrible fate.

He retrieved his phone from me, careful not to make physical contact.

I squinted. "You can't possibly be doing this as a slap on the wrist or to beat me at Go." But I wasn't so sure. Rich people spent their money in crazy ways. That's why the rest of us wanted to eat them. "What else do you have to gain from this?"

"I wouldn't want to ruin the surprise." His frosty tone warned me to toss his phone down the garbage disposal and escape while I could. "Now, if you'll excuse me, I have some words to exchange with your... *mother.*"

He stalked toward the living room, not sparing me a glance on his way out of the kitchen.

"Hey, Zach?"

He stopped but didn't turn around. "Yes, Little Octopus?"

Was the stupid, absurd nickname actually growing on me? It wasn't sexy at all, but I kind of liked the meaning.

I grinned. "I figured it out."

"Figured what out?"

"How to get out of the pickle I got into during our game."

My words were met with silence. I thought I saw his broad shoulders shaking, just a bit, in—dare I say—*laughter.*

"Monday. Eight-thirty." He rapped his knuckles on the doorframe. "Don't be late."

"Sure. Try not to stab anyone when you lose your pants this time."

CHAPTER ELEVEN

Zach Sun: @OllievB, call your hound off my little intruder.

Ollie vB: My PI?

Ollie vB: How'd you find out? Whatever he discovered was supposed to be my sorry-for-dicking-my-way-through-your-prospective-bride-list surprise gift to you.

Ollie vB: [SpongeBob One Eternity Later GIF]

Ollie vB: That's it? No details?

Ollie vB: Maybe they're fucking as we speak.

Romeo Costa: …

Ollie vB: Right. It's Zach. He's allergic to cooties.

Ollie vB: You never know… This girl might be the one to cure him.

Ollie vB: They could be fated. Like me and Frankie.

Romeo Costa: For the millionth time, my sister-in-law is practically a child. Stay five feet away from her for the law.

Zach Sun: And an extra ten feet for Jesus.

Ollie vB: It's a good thing my dick expands.

Romeo Costa left the chat.

Ollie vB: Was it something I said?

Ollie vB: Wait… @ZachSun, you back?

Ollie vB: Hello?

CHAPTER TWELVE

Farrow

"Lazíts, Fae. Accuracy requires a clear mind and a cleansed soul." A fencing mask blanketed Andras' face. "You are inside your own head, and that is not a good place to be. Focus. Mérd fel a távolságot."

Check your distance. My Hungarian skills hovered somewhere above fetus and below toddler, but Andras repeated the same commands often enough that I'd memorized them all.

He swatted my calf with his sabre. "You are standing too far. You are showing me your weakness. I can smell it all the way from here." Each admonition sounded harsher in his formal, contraction-less way of speaking.

I only half-tracked his quick leg work as he completed a balestra, replaying yesterday's showdown with Zach in my head. His taunt bounced between my temples.

I wouldn't want to ruin the surprise.

With my luck, the surprise would be worse than the punishment I'd barely escaped.

I backed away from Andras, nearly tripping on the piste as he launched himself at me.

"Retreat." He trained the point of his sabre at my masked face. "How do you expect me to prepare you for the Olympics if you lose focus in such a simple training?"

I didn't expect him to get me to the Olympics. Not after I'd already tried once and blown it in the most spectacular fashion. It would hurt less if I'd lost out on a roster spot due to my shortcomings as a fencer. Nope. My demise was my own doing. A part of me—a big part of me—knew I didn't deserve a second chance after what I'd done.

I yielded my sabre, refocusing my attention on my fifty-four-year-old coach. "Shit, my bad."

"Nyasgem." He punctuated his curse with a disgusted grunt. "Next time your eyes wander from my sabre, I will stab you with it."

Focus, Farrow. Before he makes a sieve out of you. We'd switched it up today, using sabres to work on my leg speed. I'd gone for a long stretch of time without any training, courtesy of my new sixty-hour work weeks. But thanks to my devil in shining armor, this would soon change. Working for Zach freed up more time for fencing.

I grinned behind my mask. "Don't blink."

Without mercy, I advanced, taking advantage of our size difference. *My turn.* I aimed for Andras' head when he parried, directing a thrust at my shoulder. But I was faster than a bullet. I shifted, catching his masked face with the point of my sword. The buzzer rang across the room, adding a tally to my half of the scoreboard. I didn't need the electric wires to tell me I'd earned the point. Behind the sword, you just *knew*.

Andras tore the mask from his face and dumped it at his feet, shaking his gloved fist at me. "Where were you the entire match? You came to life twenty seconds before we finished."

I pulled my mask off and shrugged. "20 seconds is all I need to win."

I'd lost any right to be arrogant after The Incident, but with Andras, I could. He never judged anything outside of technique and effort. Never made me feel like a lesser person for making *that* mistake.

I set my mask on a bench outside the piste lines, listening to his bitching. I deserved every single insult thrown my way. Luckily, most of them were in Hungarian, so I couldn't understand. Andras had graciously agreed to rework his schedule to fit mine. He trained me at six in the morning, three times a week. He deserved one-hundred percent of me.

Andras followed me as I padded to the orange cooler. "You look like a novice who watched *The Parent Trap* and decided to take on fencing. An embarrassing amateur."

I hovered my lips an inch shy of the tap, gulping ice water. "Won't happen again."

He tailed me as I headed toward the locker room. "Of course, it will not. If you show up in this condition on Thursday, I am suspending you as an instructor."

That stopped me in my tracks. I whirled around in the middle of the hallway. Two amateur fencers bumped into me but apologized quick, even though it was my fault. "You can't do that."

Andras planted his fists on his waist. It used to creep me out when his light-blue, almost translucent eyes bored into mine. Now, I found comfort in them. With Dad gone, no one else cared enough to stare at me like this.

Wrinkles stacked on Andras' wide-set forehead like Jenga blocks. Short and wide, he didn't have the perfect stats for a fencer. And yet, the world considered him the best instructor to ever grace the sport. *The Fourth Mouseketeer.* A living legend.

People shouldered past us, rushing to sessions with their instructors. Potomac Hills Country Club offered Olympic-grade, professional fencing facilities. If you could afford them. *Or* if your coach was *The* Andras Horvath.

The supersized digital clock fixed on the far wall reminded me my student would arrive soon. I needed to prepare. He didn't appreciate tardiness.

I dropped my voice to a whisper, sweeping my eyes across the club. "I need the money."

Not really. I needed the client. But God forbid some asshole overhear our conversation and pass it along to Vera. For someone as lazy and allergic to math as my stepmother, she sure kept a militant eye on my finances.

"My academy, my rules." Andras charged forward until our noses almost touched. A whoosh of apprehension somersaulted in my belly. "I am not here to help you maintain your hobby. I am here for the gold medal, and you are my best shot. You are the most talented student under this roof. If we do not share the same goal, the same discipline, you know your way out."

Oh, Fae. So delusional of you to have called that straight-out-of-The-Shining Kubrick Stare affectionate.

Something so silly as human emotions couldn't possibly penetrate the thick cloud of Andras' one-track mind. He lived and breathed fencing. Nothing else mattered to him but an Olympic gold.

I swallowed down the bitter comeback lodged in my throat. There was a lot I wanted to say. That I didn't have time. That sometimes I saw two of him when we dueled and the sleep deprivation played tricks on my mind. That the calluses from cleaning had overridden the fencing calluses, and now the sword handle felt strange in my hand. And mostly, that I wasn't even sure I could qualify for the Olympics with my record and the fine I was still paying off.

In the end, all I said was, "Duly noted. Now... may I please get changed before my student arrives?"

Without a word, he swiveled, storming in the opposite direction toward the reception area. Andras always walked like that. Like an Axis general from the '40s.

I chewed on my inner cheek, finally making it to the locker room. There, I pulled out my fencing gear and raked my fingers along my upper arm. Andras had left a mild cut there, just like he'd promised he would. Only he had ever managed to pierce my fencing lamé and padded plastron. They must've torn beforehand, and he knew it. A gross violation of the sport's ethics. And exactly something Andras would do.

Asshole. A thin trickle of blood ran down my arm, snaking all the way to the elbow. I turned on the tap and rinsed it with warm water, before pulling a first aid kit out of my locker and bandaging myself up. Sweaty, uneven locks of yellow-white hair fell into my eyes. Haircuts were for people with money. Pretty soon, it would reach my butt, and Andras would curse me for my frugality, then hack at it with a rusted pair of kitchen shears. Rinse and repeat.

I checked the time on my phone. Eight minutes until the lesson. Andras paid me under the table (to save himself employment taxes), but that wasn't why I'd chosen to teach. I only had one student, and I'd taken him on because I needed intel. In fact, this very same student once said in an interview that data is the new gold. I couldn't agree more.

Seven minutes left. Enough time to reply to the string of messages my best friend from the fencing academy in Seoul had left me.

Ari: I cannot believe you aren't here when I'm planning a WEDDING.
Ari: The betrayal cuts so deep.
Ari: [Christian Bale Covered in Blood, Lighting a Cigar GIF]
Ari: When do you start work for American Psycho again?
Ari: (They should totally reboot this as a new movie, starring the Suns.)

I grinned, my thumbs flying over the screen as I answered her.

Farrow: Not until Monday. Why?
Ari: I want you to have hot, angry sex with him.

Farrow: I really don't think he's interested in me in that way.

Ari: Then, I wish you'd just let me lend you the money you need to pay for the penalty and fight your stepmom. Seriously, you can pay me back little by little. You know my family can afford it.

Farrow: I know. But it's my journey. I really appreciate it. I just wouldn't be able to live with myself if I did that.

Ari: Ugh. I hate you.

Farrow: I love you.

Ari: Fine. Love you, too.

Farrow: Say hi to Hae-in for me.

I glanced at the overhead clock suspended above the old blue tiles. *7:02 a.m.* Fuck. With a huff, I collected my hair into a tight ponytail, gathering it all the way inside my fencing mask. I double-checked the mirror for flyaways, tucked them each beneath the tongue, and shimmied my gloves on, collecting my gear from the floor.

The hallway had emptied in the past ten minutes. I forced myself to take leisured steps. To decelerate my heart rate. A uniformed teen pushed open the door for me. I flexed my fingers beneath my gloves, soaking in the scene. A dozen fencers in full gear danced on pistes planted all over the massive room. Swords clinked in a unique symphony that never failed to send goosebumps down my spine.

A week had passed since our last lesson. Six days since the soirée. One final Friday before my official starting date at the king's lair.

My student stood alone on a piste, the only fencer still waiting. Back to me. Hands clasped behind him. His face staring out the window in silence as if the lowly pupils around him didn't deserve his attention. The épée—his discipline and weapon of choice—complemented him. It made for the slowest, most deliberate combat. With the entire body as a target. More importantly, the right of way did not apply to this fencing style. Therefore, of the three disciplines, this was the most savage. Which was precisely why it suited Zachary Sun.

The man wasn't a knight in shining armor. A hero of high morals here to save the day. No, he was a sleek predator. A monster who struck whomever and however he wished, so long as it got him closer to his goal.

Somehow, this ruthless predator had convinced Vera to hire three cleaners for our company before he'd left the other day. I couldn't believe my own ears when she sat me and my stepsisters down to break the news. She couldn't stop gushing about him. How he admired her business plan and how he'd offer her more ideas to expand it in due time. *"This is a new era, girls. I opened the door to the greatest business opportunity. Your mother has achieved something your father never could."*

"Jane Doe." Zach still stared out the window, roping me back into the present. "You're late."

For weeks, I'd hardly spoken to him while we trained. With his shrewdness, it wouldn't take much for him to recognize my voice. I couldn't risk it. Not with so much intel about his party to collect. Now, there was no need to preserve my cover.

I sauntered to the piste, taking position in front of him. "Sword. Mask. Posture."

He spun on his heel and narrowed the distance, draping his mask over his godlike face and picking up his épée in the process.

I inclined my chin. "En garde."

His stance melted into position as if he'd been born into the art of fencing, the movement so effortlessly, I wanted to scream. His right foot out front, angled toward my position, knees over toes. Back straight. Always. Arms nice and loose. Nothing to critique.

I paced on the strip, slamming heavy breaths against my metal mask. "I'm going to be ruthless today," I warned.

"Give me your worst."

The fencing apparatus' timer began to tick down. I sank into a deep lunge. For an épée fencer, Zach favored aggressive play. He skipped the probes and advanced mere seconds into our first three minutes. His lithe body spliced through the air, the point of his sword aimed straight for my heart. I dodged, retreated, then stepped forward. He disregarded the move as a threat. *Arrogant bastard.*

I made sure he regretted it, springing forward and rocketing into a dive, all the way to the floor, cutting him at the knees. He growled at the contact but managed to bite his tongue. The apparatus beep punctuated his retreat. *1-0.*

He settled on his en-garde line. "Again."

"Your instincts…" I snapped my fingers, turning away from him and returning to starting position. "…they're not as good as you think."

"I'm not paying you to talk, Jane." He rearranged himself back into proper stance. "I'm paying you to fence."

Be this way, and I will shred you into ribbons.

The next match, I bullied him by circling my sword the entire time it was in the air, hiking up his guard until his parries became fidgety. He returned the favor with long, impressive strokes that kept me on my toes, plunging into my personal space when I least expected and coming at me with such hostility, you'd think I'd beheaded the Terracotta sculpture inside his home library. He wielded a lethal combination of strength, speed, and combat joy. A true fan of the art of war.

The point of his sword kissed my shoulder. I grunted as if the contact hurt, pulling back with a yelp. "Ugh." *1-1.*

Zach retreated, strolling away as he admired his sword. "Be graceful in defeat." *Famous last words.*

We returned to our en-garde position and began again. *2-1. 3-1. 3-2.* As the bout progressed, I had to admit Zach could probably cinch a spot on the Olympic team. He possessed all the coveted traits. Speed, agility, inhuman precognition, and superior observation skills. He moved like a dancer with elegance and unparalleled discipline.

Midway through the second period, I'd stopped keeping track of the score. All I knew was that I would beat him. I never lost.

I hurled the sword at him. "Why fencing?"

He dodged artfully. If my question surprised him, he didn't show it. This was more than I'd spoken to him in all four months we'd practiced together. Without a cover to keep, I indulged my curiosity. Correction: I intended to blow my cover on purpose. I wanted him to know it was me who had taught him how to use a sword. That I knew how to impale one's heart, and his was no different.

He executed a perfect passe arriere. "The touch of a blade is preferable to the touch of a human."

"What's wrong with humans?"

"Everything." He attempted to hit my shoulder, but I ducked, twirling in place. "You, for instance, talk too much for my liking."

"Find another trainer."

A frosty chuckle chilled the air. "We both know you're too talented to replace, something that cannot be said about the majority of workers."

"Andras is a better instructor than me."

"Andras is a dead horse. Bitter and mad at the world. A victim cannot become a victor. And I do not employ losers."

Our swords zinged, meeting, pulling, then turning away from one another. "You think so highly of yourself," I growled.

"Only because most creatures are so lowly. Don't you agree, Jane Doe?"

I advanced, lunging so fast, I left a gust of wind in my wake. Through sheer athleticism rather than technique, he dodged my two jump flicks and tried but failed to aim at my heart. I attacked him faster, relentlessly, refusing to give him a break between parries. He stumbled, falling to the floor, his back plastered against the piste.

Get used to this position. After all, it's how cooked lobsters are served.

Zach tried to recover. To spring to his feet. No matter how stellar his reflexes, he couldn't match my practiced speed. By the time his neck lifted off the alloy, his mask met the tip of my sword, making up for the two times he had his knife aimed at me.

The scoreboard beeped. *9-7.* A knot untightened in my stomach as I pressed my foot against his knee, stopping him from standing. With a flick of my sword, I tossed the épée from his hand.

Zach remained on the piste, calm and collected under his mask, his chest barely rising with his breaths. "That's one very red card, Jane Doe."

"Red happens to be my favorite color." I used the point of my épée to remove his mask, neck to scalp, careful not to graze his beautiful face with my blade. As much as I hated to admit it, ruining such art would be a waste.

Zach was revealed to me inch by inch like the slow draw of a theater curtain, his stoic face unwavering and utterly breathtaking. Somehow, his eyes tangled with mine through my mask. A shiver ran down my spine. We weren't touching. Not really. Layers of heavy fabric and pads separated my foot from his knee. But I considered my sword an extension of my arm, and its point caressed the tip of his forehead, right where his widow's peak led to a perfect lock of coal hair draping over his right eye.

He stayed perfectly still as I brushed it aside with my épée. "Interesting."

"How so?"

"You're an octopus, not a bull."

My heart stopped in my chest. I'd done it now. I'd revealed myself to him. With my stupid mouth and smartass attitude. *You wanted this,* I reminded myself. Somehow, it felt more like an accident than a goal. I said nothing, fortunate enough to remember to breathe.

"Did you know..." His husky tenor pierced all the protective layers of my uniform, gliding down my skin like black velvet. "...Aristotle thought octopuses were dumb? Do you take it as a personal offense?"

Silence. I'd frozen in place, replaying the past two periods, wondering what had given my identity away. Zachary Sun being Zachary Sun, he didn't let me bask in the unknown for long.

"Even behind a mask, your poker face is as mediocre as your Go skills." His gaze tangled with mine so easily, I almost forgot that I still wore a mask. "You looked like you were sitting on a carpet of needles. Out of place and out of sorts. Quite different from my usual teacher."

I peeled my mask back, staring down at him with a sneer. Unruly blonde locks cascaded past my waist, bracketing my entire body. Sweat glistened on my skin. Our eyes locked. I couldn't stare this man down without my body humming the angry beat of a heavy metal song. Being in constant forced proximity to him would be a problem. My body ran too hot near this man.

"So, this is how you found out about the soirée." He tipped his head back, allowing my blade to run over the curve of his forehead and nose with the faintest touch. Adrenaline stormed through my veins. He was playing with fire. "I mentioned it in passing to you during one of our sessions."

I didn't respond. Per usual, he already had it all figured out.

He assessed me with critical eyes. "You really aren't one of them, are you?"

"One of whom?"

"*Them.* People. Average. Simple. Dumb." I said nothing. "My, my. I'm going to have so much fun with you." A slow smile spread across his lips. So faint. He was incredibly stingy with his happiness. "My own shiny toy. To enjoy. To abuse. To break."

The gravity of my mistake rolled through me. I'd miscalculated. Made a wrong turn somewhere. I shouldn't have agreed to work for him. To put myself in his vicinity on purpose. To my horror, I did the very thing I'd once accused him of doing. I abandoned a game. Retreated to the lockers to lick my wounds and regroup. His dark chuckle followed me as I vanished, slinking into the shadows of the hallway, leaving him on the piste to soak in his victory.

Zachary Sun didn't bother to get up.

He knew he was already at the top.

Chapter Thirteen

Ollie vB: Saw Zach's parents bride shopping for him after brunch today.

Zach Sun: For the last time, my aunt is not my parent.

Ollie vB: She raised you, you are eternally embarrassed of her, and she says the cringiest shit. For all intents and purposes, this woman is your parent.

Romeo Costa: I cannot believe I'm saying this, but I agree with Oliver.

Romeo Costa: Anyone who fucks you up to this extent is a parent.

Romeo Costa: Now define bride shopping.

Ollie vB: Glad you asked. They literally approached innocent women, asking them for their birthdates and list of hereditary illnesses. Your Ayi even pointed to one and said aloud, "This one's too small to carry Sun-sized babies."

Zach Sun: [Retreating into a Bush GIF]

Romeo Costa: ON THE STREET?

Ollie vB: No, you uncultured swine. In Hermès.

Romeo Costa: And they say love doesn't have a price.

Ollie vB: Whatever the price may be, Zach would say it's inflated and refuse to pay.

Zach Sun: This is embarrassing.

Romeo Costa: Not as embarrassing as having your dick pic enlarged in a court of law as part of a bitter custody trial between your former lover and the vice president.

Ollie vB: I wouldn't go as far as calling that an embarrassment. Perhaps a mild inconvenience?

Romeo Costa: Jesus, Ollie. People made shirts with the imprint of your cock on them and the slogan HE HAS MY VOTE.

Ollie vB: I found it rather flattering. And I'll have you know my dick pic was the least offensive thing to cum out of politics in the last decade.

Ollie vB: The only downside about it is—now people want to take a picture with it because it's famous.

Romeo Costa: How is that a downside? You've made enough sex tapes to open your own Pornhub.

Ollie vB: It's not hookups asking for pictures. Just randos on the street. And apparently, graciously obliging them is considered 'indecent exposure.'

Zach Sun: That explains it.

Ollie vB: Explains what?

Zach Sun: "No one gives a hummer like a gummer."

Ollie vB: Ah. Boomers. The last great generation. Horny, experienced, and incapable of working an iPhone camera.

Ollie vB: Anyway, back to Zach's misery.

Ollie vB: Feel that fur-lined collar tightening around your neck, sonny boy?

Romeo Costa: Marriage is not a punishment.

Ollie vB: I'd literally pick the electric chair.

Romeo Costa: [Eye roll Emoji]

Ollie vB: Every. Single. Time.

Chapter Fourteen

Zach

I made it a point not to leave my office the first day of Farrow's employment.

Firstly, and most importantly, I had work to do. Work provided comfort and joy. Trading stocks. Taking companies by force. Digesting them into my own.

All those traits that made me unapproachable and odd as a human—my lack of consideration, desire, and empathy—were pros in the business world. It didn't matter that I'd already amassed an offensive fortune. Making money was my blood sport of choice. The stock exchanges—my arena. And every being with a pulse—my opponent. I sat on my gilded throne on Dark Prince Road. The undefeated champion.

Secondly, and less importantly (but notable, nonetheless), Farrow needed time to adjust to the estate. To familiarize herself with the property I called home. To roam the grounds, explore every nook and cranny, and make herself comfortable. I read her like an open book and decided to accommodate her. Not because I actually cared whether she acclimated to being here, but because the woman was a walking, talking headache without a cure.

Only after she simmered down could I execute my plan in peace.

The little octopus was living proof that luck hadn't abandoned me. Initially, I'd paid her a visit in her pint-sized kitchen to taunt her. Maybe even execute her punishment. Then, something happened. Something wonderful and horrible, all at once.

I touched her and didn't cower. Didn't shiver. Didn't vomit.

For two entire decades, not a single human could lay a finger on me without physically sickening me. Not a doctor. Not a woman. Not even my mother. It never occurred to me that an antidote for my problem existed. That Farrow Ballantine could drive a Disney princess to suicide could only be considered the universe's idea of balance. I'd heard the saying. *God wraps every gift with a problem.*

I didn't know what it was about the fierce, unruly maid that prevented my body from revolting at her touch. Certainly not her misplaced fashion sense. Or the bite with which she delivered every word. Or even the choppy blonde mop on her head. I'd seen supermarket sashimi cut with greater precision.

All I knew was that I never let an opportunity go to waste.

My Little Octopus would fix me. The *how* didn't matter. So long as I could endure another woman's touch—and thereby fulfill the promise I'd made to Dad after he'd shielded me from certain death.

And so, for today, I buried myself in numbers and trade markets sprawled across the split screens.

No one would miss my presence, anyway.

Chapter Fifteen

Zach

The first semblance of normalcy since discovering that my "elite" fencing instructor moonlit as an unpaid maid came from six uninterrupted hours of work. By the time I raised my head from the computer screens, my watch read half past noon. On the dot. My internal clock functioned properly again.

Natalie cracked the door open, poking her head past its cavity. "*Yoo-hoo.* May I interrupt?"

You already fucking are.

I reclined in my leather chair, ripping the black thick-rimmed reading glasses from my face and placing them on their stand. "Yes?"

"Your lunch is ready, Mr. Sun."

I ate the same lunch every day since seventeen. Eight strips of sashimi, one toro inari, cold shishito peppers, and a cucumber salad. Variety didn't interest me. I found no pleasure in food, and type 2 diabetes seemed like a less appealing prospect than Chapter 9 bankruptcy.

"Send it in."

Natalie invaded my domain, jostling a cart past the double doors. She followed me to the coffee table, set down a cavernous porcelain bowl of water, and handed me a fresh towel after I washed my hands in it. As far as assistants went, she was tolerable enough. Former Phi Beta Kappa at Johns Hopkins. No scented beauty products to nauseate me. Capable of taking orders with above-average executive function. A little heavy on the dialogue, but I supposed I'd yet to encounter anyone who could keep their questions, answers, and reactions to my preferred two-syllable limit.

She transferred the tray of dishes from the cart to the table, then collected her iPad, clutching it to her chest. If possible, the powder-

MY DARK DESIRE | 85

blue blouse wrapped around her torso like Saran Wrap tightened with the movement. She'd coupled the shirt with a gray pencil skirt and a pair of Louboutins so high, she probably had an eagle-eyed view of the Washington Monument.

I cocked a brow, curious what had given her the idea that she was welcome to stay. "Yes?"

An audible gulp traveled down her neck. "Mr. Sun…" She painted a circle with the tip of her ridiculous shoe, white-knuckling the edges of the tablet screen.

I stared at her. She knew better than to expect me to fill the silence. Natalie fidgeted under my scrutiny. "There's something else."

After studying her for ten straight seconds, I gathered that she had no intention of completing the thought. "Well, I'm on pins and needles here, Natalie. Whenever you're ready. Preferably in this century."

Another gulp. A shaky breath. I should've finished my lunch by now, which I preferred at the forty-seven degrees Fahrenheit I expected it served at.

The Go board caught Natalie's attention. She drew a palm to her chest. "Aw. You haven't touched your checkers game in forever."

"It's Go." *And so should you.* "You were saying?"

"Right." She cleared her throat. "Forgive me for overstepping, but I couldn't help but overhear your mother's conversation with Celeste the other day when they visited for lunch." She forced herself to maintain eye contact with me. No easy feat. My default expression was set to hostile. She flattened her free hand over her skirt. "I know you're auditioning women as potential… umm, you know, life partners."

Poor Natalie. She didn't think she stood a chance, did she? I had nothing against my assistant. In the same way I had nothing against people who wore Crocs. Just because I found them fundamentally tasteless did not mean they did not deserve to breathe.

Or so society insisted.

Natalie was excruciatingly average. Pretty—but not beautiful. Hardworking—but not genius. She'd attended an Ivy League college for her master's, but those had steadily produced idiots since their inception. She lacked any real personality or talent. In fact, I'd only chosen her as an assistant because she didn't possess the usual aversion to long hours and basic math.

"And I was thinking…" She licked her lips, dropping her gaze from my face to the floor, brushing her mousy brown hair back. "I think you should definitely consider me. I'm hard working and quiet." *Not right now you aren't.* "I take directions really well. I'm dutiful and a team player." Team player? How many people did she think I planned on inviting into my sack? "I will not give you trouble. I… I…" Her cheeks turned scarlet. She pinched her lips together before forcing nonsensical words to tumble out. "I will do whatever you want—however you want it—in bed. I'm not even asking for exclusivity. I'm a survivor. I want a good life. And I have a feeling you're a survivor, too, Mr. Sun. I don't know how or why, but I see it in you."

I didn't ask her what she saw. I did not care. But Natalie was in the zone, already too far gone to notice her reluctant audience was unimpressed by her lackluster performance.

She closed her eyes and heaved in a breath. "You have this air about you, like you're ready for war at the drop of the hat. I know that look. I wear it, too, sometimes."

"I appreciate a good hustler, Natalie, but I am in the market for something rather specific."

Her eyes clung to mine. "What is it?"

"Whoever gets Constance Sun's stamp of approval."

She shoved out an awkward, stilted laugh. "Is Constance your cult leader?"

"In a way. She *is* my mother."

"Why would you let her dictate who you marry?" She hiked the iPad up her chest like it would shield her from my answer.

Because her husband died protecting me, and there hasn't been a single day since that I didn't wish it were me instead of him.

"I took away her partner. The least I can do is let her choose mine."

Natalie's shoulders caved downward, her entire being liquifying into a slump. I disliked people with bad posture. She was disqualified before she even opened her mouth.

"But it's not fair—"

I held up a hand. "As is life. You're over the age of three. I thought you'd already gotten the memo." I fanned the cloth napkin over my lap and picked up the set of steel chopsticks. "Anything more you'd like to discuss before I have my lunch? I wish to do so in silence."

Natalie opened her mouth then clamped it shut, showing off her best trout impression. "If nothing else, you're about to get your wish." She tucked her iPad under her armpit, voice cracking.

I lifted a brow. "They're canceling federal taxes?"

Surely, I did not have this good of luck. I was born on the fourth day of the fourth month. The unluckiest number in Chinese culture. In Mandarin, four shared similar pronunciation with the word *death*. Already, the cure to my physical aversion to humans landing headfirst in my lap seemed like an uncharacteristic stroke of fortune.

"Well, not *that* wish." Natalie set her iPad on the cart, busying her hands by collecting the porcelain washing bowl and depositing it on top. "Your mother called earlier to inform you she is letting some girl borrow her Astteria necklace. The custom jade and gold one you keep in a safe for her."

The state of modern dating must've hit an all-time low since I'd last checked, because she sniffed, failing to keep an errant tear at bay. It was a particularly gruesome punishment for my sins that I had to endure the tears of women without even getting the pussy.

Natalie progressed to clenching her fists around the cart handles, challenging their load-bearing capacity. "Constance said the girl is going to drop by today and asked that you *show her around*." She used her fingers as quotation marks, her lower lip curled in a barely contained pout.

This again. Hadn't Mom realized blind dates didn't work after Plan N?

I burrowed my fingertips into my eyelids, massaging the area with a heavy sigh. "What's the woman's name?"

Natalie scrunched her nose. "Electra? Exotica, maybe?"

"Eileen."

My mother would dine on a bowl of eyeballs before trying to match me with a woman named Exotica.

"Yeah. Something like that. Very bland name if you ask me."

Good thing I didn't.

"When am I expecting her?"

"Three o'clock."

Might as well make an effort with Eileen to please my mother. Even if I felt like dying before doing it.

"That's fine. Let her in when she arrives. I'll take care of it."

"Really? You never accept anyone unannounced."

I did not answer Natalie.

She shook her head, huffing. "Every woman in this zip code would die to have your attention, and you only have eyes for your mother. What a travesty."

"Watch your mouth, Miss Mikaylov, unless you're eager to lose your job."

Natalie remained standing in the middle of the room like an out-of-place piece of furniture you had to keep because a close relative had gifted it to you. There seemed to be more she wanted to say, but the idea that I was paying her an hourly rate to try to convince me to marry her instead of spending the money on something more useful—like dry cleaning or getting Oliver's Cane Corso's anal glands expressed—rubbed me the wrong way.

I plucked a translucent sliver of budo ebi from the sashimi plate, bringing it to my lips. *Too warm.* "Will that be all, Miss Mikaylov?"

For a reason unfathomable to me, I nursed the foolish hope that she'd tell me Farrow had tried to set the house on fire, auction my entire art collection, or otherwise commit a heinous crime on my property. Something to give me an excuse to seek Miss Ballantine out and breathe fire at her blizzard existence.

But Natalie merely exhaled again, head bowed. "No, sir, that will be all."

She retreated with the cart, leaving me with a surprise date I did not want and a low-security dating agency server to hack into.

CHAPTER SIXTEEN

Ollie vB: Dinner tonight?

Zach Sun: Busy. Pass.

Zach Sun: Especially if you plan on showing up in the same shirt as last time…

Ollie vB: What? Ashamed to walk beside me as I rock my wife pleaser?

Romeo Costa: Wife pleaser?

Ollie vB: It's a wife beater but rebranded with better PR.

Zach Sun: It should be burned. No man this side of the Jersey Shore wears a tank top outside of the gym.

Chapter Seventeen

Zach

The news of my surprise blind date ruined the cadence of my schedule. On a normal day, I'd be midway into the selection process for a hostile takeover. Eileen Yang had just saved a company at the expense of my mood.

The doorbell chimed at exactly three o'clock. At the very least, she'd arrived on time. I valued punctuality. It showed character. Well, the bare minimum, anyway. I strode to my window, passing my uneaten lunch. A white Bentley parked beside my fountain, sparkling from a recent wash. A fine choice. Nothing too offensive or gaudy. No bright-pink Range Rovers or neon-green Lamborghinis.

Stuffing my hands into my front pockets, I strolled out the office and down the staircase to greet my blind date. To be fair, this could hardly be considered a *blind* date. Not when I'd cruised by a measly layer of security to get to Eileen's file from the dating agency.

Eileen Yang. 33. Indeed, a neurologist based in Manhattan. Three degrees from two Ivy Leagues. Multiple Doctors Without Borders stints. The author of a popular A.P. Bio study guide. Last year, she'd drained her royalties to pay off the 12-million-dollar mortgage for a condo on the Upper East side. It seemed Mom had found the perfect girl for her. Which, of course, meant she'd found the perfect girl for me.

Now all I had to do was not fuck this up. Easier said than done. When it came to humans, I had more expertise in fucking up than succeeding. Women, specifically, found my entire existence a personal slight. I never paid any real attention to them. But when I did, it usually came in the form of brutal honesty, informing them that I found their conversation to be as mind-numbing as sorting grains of sand by size.

You literally know how to split atoms, Zach. Surely, you can make this girl not hate you.

I moseyed down the hallway, descending the stairs, noting that the house looked particularly pristine today. I was a little disappointed Farrow had yet to try anything fishy. I'd been under the impression we'd battle it out as soon as she arrived. Perhaps she had something up her sleeve for me for later. No part of me believed she would lay down and take it. Accept me as her boss and behave herself.

When I opened the front door, I found my mother's ideal woman. Tall and slender with glossy dark tresses that reached her shoulders and a sage-green Burberry suit. She wore her hair parted down the middle, tucked behind her ears, in a cut that could only be achieved with a ruler. A neutral expression decorated her face, her posture proud and linear.

"Good afternoon." She sounded almost robotic. Not necessarily a bad thing for someone who wasn't a fan of homo sapiens. "Zachary?"

Regrettably. I did a slight bow, stepping aside and gesturing for her to come in. "Eileen."

Every fiber in my body shriveled at the idea that she might try to hug or kiss me. Thankfully, she marched inside with practiced ease, not bothering to glance my way as she placed her black Ferragamo studio bag on the credenza. She removed her sensible heels, neatly arranged the Malone Souliers together, and tucked them beside the door. An Hermès scarf wrapped around her throat, designed to shelter the delicate skin from the sun. She unknotted it, retying the silk into a fashionable bracelet around her wrist.

I pressed my lips together, stifling a grimace. It was as if my mother had personally raised her.

"I won't take too much of your time." The words came out with practiced eased, as if they'd been spoken dozens of times. How many blind dates had Eileen suffered through to reach this level of robotic? "If you could lend me the necklace, I'll be on my way. I'll inform our mothers we conversed and reached the conclusion that our future plans do not align. I would, however, appreciate the necklace. There's a St. Jude's charity event this evening, and your mother will ask questions if I don't wear it."

I wanted nothing more than to send her on her merry way, out of my life with that necklace. But I'd made a promise to marry Mom's chosen bride, and Eileen was the entire package. A piñata of good manners and superior upbringing.

"Would you like a tour of the house first?" I asked through gritted teeth. "You've made it all the way here, after all."

We stood about eight feet from each other, neither of us eager to bridge the distance.

"Oh, really. I don't wish to impose."

Translation: please, don't make me suffer through another second of this.

"Impose away." My lips barely moved as I spoke. "The stock market closes in fifty minutes, and I've already put in the hours today."

She stared at me like I'd just announced I bathed in cat urine every evening to unwind. "You finish your work day at four?"

"I work all hours of the day," I clarified. "*And* nights." *In case you ever plan to ask for any of my time as a wife.*

"Are you always so lax?" She frowned before smoothing out her expression. I was not worth the wrinkle.

"Only today." I forced myself to smile, sourness exploding in my mouth. "So? Care to join me?"

Eileen stiffened ever-so-slightly, an exhale sailing past her lips, a touch too rushed. Obviously, she'd hoped I wouldn't ask. "I'll take a tour, thank you." She didn't want to be here just as much as I didn't want her to be here. The fact that I wouldn't have to pry her off me was oddly comforting.

With a swift nod, I cocked my head sideways toward the east wing. We strolled a good distance away from each other, with me spewing boring anecdotes and facts about each room and the art that decorated it. Eileen nodded at all the right moments, pretending to care, but I'd caught her checking her thin leather Cartier often. I could do worse than to marry someone who didn't want to be in the same room as me. In fact, I preferred it to the alternative. Fending off a needy wife seemed like a new circle of hell.

On our way to the dining room, I caught sight of Farrow. So much for giving her space on her first day. She kneeled in the corridor, scrubbing away a persistent mud stain from the porcelain tiles. I'd gotten used to witnessing her in this state—sweaty, sporting a bird's nest on her scalp, her clothes peppered with bleached pigments.

She looked pitiful. The product of poverty and exhaustion. So opposite of me and my genteel guest. And, I realized, for the very first time, so fucking beautiful I couldn't breathe. With her sharp features, golden hair, and sparkling blues. And those overgrown bangs—a little wavy and out of control—that made her look like a cool grunge girl on a double spread of *Vogue*.

The line of thought startled me. I never admired humans. I certainly never admired them for something as temporary as their beauty.

This is good. This is fine. As long as you remember she's a means to an end and not an actual three-dimensional person, you can admire her looks.

To prove my own point, I sidestepped her like she was a puddle of puke, sneering down at her as I guided Eileen along the hallway. "You missed a spot."

Farrow glared up at me, no doubt stabbing me in her mind. "Sorry, Boss, but you're a permanent feature."

There she is. At my maid's smart mouth, Eileen released a tiny gasp, turning to glance between us.

I stopped at the junction between the dining room and the guest wing, my eyes still pinned on my new housekeeper. "It's Mr. Sun to you."

Farrow slumped against the wall and blew a lock of hair from her eye, appraising me and Eileen. No part of her seemed ashamed or distressed at being seen like this. At our feet. Scrubbing my floor to high shine. She inclined her chin and offered a toothy grin directed at Eileen. "Did he tell you he sucks at Go?" From her lips, it sounded just as Mom had suspected—like *Go* was code for something else, and she'd just accused me of being bad in bed.

Eileen's brows shot to her hairline, her slender fingers kissing her collarbone. "Are you going to let her talk to you like this?"

"Hope not." Farrow picked up her rag and resumed scrubbing. "My wet dream is to have him fire me."

Astonishingly, I found myself wanting to be part of her wet dreams. In fact, I was hard-pressed to conjure something I wanted more than to watch her with her legs spread open, buck naked, showing me how wet she was. I'd officially lost it. Sailed deep into murky, unchartered waters with these foreign thoughts and unchecked desires. A speck of dirty water splashed from the rag onto my bare toe with her thorough scrub. My eyelid twitched.

She batted her lashes, awarding us an angelic smile. "Not to be confused with him firing *at* me. Because he did that, too. Did he tell you he likes throwing knives?"

I was going to kill her.

But first, I was going to fuck her.

Because—and this was important—for whatever unknown reason, she seemed to be the only woman I could even contemplate being intimate with. In fact, I discovered, I hadn't stopped thinking about her face. Her body. Her derisive smile. The way she moved on the piste. Like Tinker Bell if she were an assassin. So lethal and so soft at the same time.

Eileen jerked a step back, spinning her head to me. "You own a throwing knife?"

"Some antique blades." I shot Farrow a withering look. "As part of my art collection."

"He owns a tank, too." Farrow grinned, obviously enjoying herself. "It's the only thing he drives. G.I. Jerk."

"It's not a tank. It's a Conquest Knight XV."

"It's made from aluminum." Farrow cackled, clutching her stomach, not caring that she'd just added another dirt stain to her shirt. "I took it for a spin, by the way. He really shouldn't leave his keys where everyone can see them."

I bet she did. And I didn't know why, but it uplifted my mood to know she'd misbehaved.

"Anyway, I see you two have a lot to catch up on." Farrow put two fingers to her forehead, saluting us. "Have fun, kids. I'll leave you to it."

Eileen frowned, palm tightening around the nape of her neck, clearly unimpressed with the verbal battle I'd gotten myself into with the help.

"Sorry about that." I gestured for Eileen to continue up the stairs. "A pair of hikers found her in the woods just five years ago. She was raised by wild coyotes and grew up thinking she was one of them. I agreed to hire her as part of a rehabilitation program that focuses on integrating low-IQ individuals into society."

"Interesting. Only five years ago." Eileen shadowed my steps, swiping at her suit as if she could brush away the encounter with my feral octopus. "Her command of the English language is immaculate."

We climbed the curved staircase to the soundtrack of Farrow's bell-chime giggles. They echoed down the cavernous foyer, amplified by the sheer size of the mansion. Up until now, I'd never considered my home to be too big.

"Her English is fine." I led her to the opposite hall from my office. "It's the content spilling from her mouth I take issue with."

"You seem to share good chemistry."

"Hardly."

The only chemistry we shared was radioactive. Farrow and I were two corrosive elements, bound to blow up in spectacular fashion, but I always did like science.

Eileen followed me into my bedroom closet, stopping just shy of the safe. True to her mannered upbringing, she turned to grant me privacy while I punched in the twenty-two-digit combination and withdrew the imperial-jade necklace my mother lent her. It wasn't lost on me that Farrow would not only watch me enter the code but also memorize it to use at a later date. The two women couldn't be any more different. And for some wild, incomprehensible reason, I preferred the one with the manners of a starving bear.

I deposited the engraved case on the closet island between us. The recessed lights casted cold, blue shadows over Eileen. When I looked at her beneath them, not a hair out of place, tidy, stylish, and deliberate, I knew there was no way I'd ever be able to touch her—with or without Farrow's help. This could never work.

I sucked in a breath, loathing myself for breaking my promise to Dad, yet again. Just as I'd started to send her on her way, Eileen surprised me by blurting out, "I brought mooncakes."

I crossed my arms. "What?" Not only was this not the time for them, it was literally not the time for them according to the calendar.

A small smile tipped up her lips. The first human thing she'd done since stepping into my domain. *Rich, coming from me—I know.*

She rested a hand on the island, surveying the closet, as though the idea of getting caught sharing the space with me was as disagreeable to her as it was to me. "Mooncakes. From Chinatown. The real deal. Made by this ancient lady, who felt bad for running out of them last Moon Festival and cooked up a special batch for me. They're triple yolked."

Sounds like a recipe for clogged arteries.

It occurred to me that she'd abandoned the stilted formal speech, though I didn't have a clue as to why.

"Grandma sent me all the way to this third-floor apartment in the middle of the night to pick them up." When she noticed she'd left a fingerprint on the glass counter, she wiped it with the Hermès scarf swaddled around her wrist. "She said they'd win you over. I… I'm not even sure I want to do that." Her lower lip twitched as if she'd suppressed a wince. "Win you over, I mean. This has nothing to do with you. You're overqualified, like I knew you would be. But I don't like…" She paused.

"You don't like what?"

Mingling? Being set up by your family? Humans?

"Men," she finished in a whisper, peering down at her toes.

This explained a lot about her single status. And, to be frank, her lack of interest in my dick.

A knot in my shoulder began to loosen. "You're gay?" I could work with this. A marriage on paper. No expectations of emotions, interaction, *sex*.

"No." She tucked her lip into her mouth, deliberating her next words. "I don't like women, either. I don't feel any desire toward anyone."

Oh. Mom truly had found the female version of me. Well, up until Farrow Ballantine barreled into my life. Now, I one hundred percent *did* want to touch someone. In fact, I wanted to do a hell of a lot more than that.

Eileen's gaze traveled up to my ceiling. Tears rimmed the lower ledge of her eyes. She blew out a raspberry, the sound almost jarring coming from her.

I blinked. "You don't want to fuck me?"

"I wouldn't even want to hug you if we ever got married. Which, by the way, I've only contemplated because I really don't want to die alone. I want children. I want a family. I want to experience what other people enjoy."

I stroked my chin. This could work. Eileen Yang wasn't likeable, but she wasn't horrible, either. Sufficiently quiet. Sufficiently independent. And we both appeared to share the same problem.

"This is dreadful." She shook her head. "I'm so sorry I came here. I knew the necklace was just an excuse. I'm wasting both our tim—"

"Miss Yang?"

"Yes, Mr. Sun?"

"Let's have those mooncakes. We have a lot to discuss."

CHAPTER EIGHTEEN

Zach

"So, which was it?" Eileen perched on the seat across from me in the conservatory breakfast room, pouring us another cup of tea. The mooncakes sat between us, untouched. She placed the teapot back on the golden tray, angling its handle symmetrically between our cups. "I'm referring to the assortment of household items that magically materialized whenever we misbehaved, growing up. Flip-flop?"

I reclined, sipping the loose-leaf tea, inspecting her behind the rim. "Believe it or not, my parents never threatened me." Perhaps this thing had legs after all. That she stirred nothing in me was a feature, not a bug. She could never crawl under my skin, never sway me one way or the other.

"Ah." She nodded, almost to herself. "The wall."

I set the teacup on its saucer and thumbed away a drop that spilled over the edge. "My quads have been rock hard since I could talk."

She cupped her mouth, giggling into her palm. For the first time in years, I felt at ease. Confident I'd fulfill the promise to my father. I knew Eileen wouldn't bust my chops if I taunted her. She was safe. A smart, logical choice. The coup de grâce was that she reminded me of my mother in personality and experience, which meant I could never develop feelings for her in the long run, no matter how much time I spent with her.

"I always thought Mr. Sun would be formidable." Eileen tilted her head, a distant glaze coating her eyes. "Growing up, I remember him so stern."

"He was strict," I confirmed. "But he had a soft side, too. He only showed it to me and Mom. What else do you remember about him?"

"I remember he adored you. He always spoke about you to my dad." Eileen met my eyes, turning serious. Her manicured fingers sank into the red velvet of the upholstered seat she occupied. We were both trying to share a tender moment. And failing miserably. "I always listened, because I knew they both wanted us to marry each other one day."

Silence crackled between us. Filled with tension and trepidation. My meeting with Eileen Yang was always destined to happen. Now that it did, we had a decision to make. In our circles, people frowned upon lengthy dating periods. Loyalty, commitment, and preservation of bloodlines mattered most.

"I will never love you." I rested my ankle on the opposite knee, lounging back in my seat. "And I will never touch you, either. Not to kiss you at the altar. And certainly not to impregnate you. In fact, it's unlikely that I'll ever feel comfortable enough to hug my own spawn."

Not true, I reminded myself. *Not if Farrow cures you.*

Maybe one day—far, far, *far* down the line—I'd feel comfortable enough to hold my future spawn's hand when we crossed the street.

"Affection does not…" I cleared my throat. "…come naturally to me."

As I said the words, violent flashes of memories attacked me.

Burnt flesh. Blood everywhere. Screaming. The scent of seared skin assaulting my nose. Dad, Dad, Dad.

This was why I needed to put up with Octi. To fix the damage Dad had left behind.

Eileen nodded, staring at her hands. Her fingers tangled with one another. Long and narrow, like the rest of her bone structure. We'd make fine-looking children, no doubt. And they wouldn't be dumb. Always a nice bonus.

"I want to try sex." She peered around as if someone could pick up her whisper without piercing her personal bubble. "See if perhaps it could grow on me with time."

"You still can." I pushed the saucer in. "As long as you're discreet, I don't mind if you take on a *cinq-a-sept* lover. Provided he or she is willing to sign all the necessary paperwork." I refused to be a laughingstock, but I didn't expect my future wife to sit around cross-legged, just to appease my phobias, either.

Eileen tapped a beat on her knee. I found that little quirk annoying. I wondered if Farrow had quirks, too. If so—what were they? Nothing would surprise me. Including killing puppies.

"I'm okay with that. Does that mean...?"

I nodded. "Insemination. *If* we decide to sign this deal."

She sighed, nodding to herself. "This is actually very comforting. Sex was the one thing that always stood in my way of starting a family. Every time I tried to date, I'd end up tumbling into bed and stopping before we actually did it. Regardless of how intellectually attracted I was to him, it never felt like what my sister described. It felt... almost nonconsensual."

"Well, this won't be an issue for us, because I don't want your body."

She divided a mooncake in perfect quarters with the tine of her fork. "Then, what do you want?"

"Your cooperation. For you to co-parent my children. Wear my ring. Stand by my side during social functions. We can be cordial. Friendly, even. After all, we'll have much to share—children, goals, wealth, power."

Eileen smoothed her dress. "Just not love."

I nodded.

She drew in a breath. Did she have to breathe so loudly? How did she expect me to tolerate her existence when everything she did got on my nerves?

"Are we actually considering this?" Eileen asked, re-tucking her hair behind her ears. "I mean... forgive my directness, but should two people this fucked up reproduce, anyway? I know we look good on paper..."

"But paper is just a paper," I finished for her. "Easily destroyed." I'd contemplated this before and came to the same conclusion every time. "My children won't be miserable. I'm like this because my circumstances made me like this. Take away those circumstances, and I'd be as horny as every other sleazeball in this country."

Eileen winced at the crass words. "And we take this secret to the grave?"

"Does it matter? Most marriages in this tax bracket are a contract between two acquaintances who once upon a time enjoyed screwing one another. If anything, since the only exchange of bodily fluids will happen in a medical setting, we'll be the least filthy couple in this town."

She nodded, pushing back her shoulders. "I want to continue

working." It felt too soon to lay down her terms and conditions. At the same time, it was exactly what I'd craved. Someone who saw marriage as a business opportunity. Eileen pushed away her plate, getting down to business. "I love my work. I know my mom told yours that I want a sabbatical—"

"Work as much as you want." I raised one palm up, stopping her from launching into a speech. "With the exception of the last trimester of your pregnancies. My heirs must be taken care of and arrive in Like New condition."

This was the only part of reproducing that actually made sense to me. Creating a genetically superior workforce from scratch to continue my business after I croaked. After all, I couldn't drag the money into Hell with me in a Louis Vuitton carry-on.

I added, as an afterthought, "The less I see of you, the better. No offense."

"None taken." She regarded me. "I have money, but…" she trailed off.

"But not my level of money. I dug into your finances during the background check." I produced my phone and pulled up my contract app, setting the device on the table. "You come from a family of six with most of the inheritance passing down to your brothers. I'll give you assets in the neighborhood of twenty million, but you'll sign an iron-clad prenup."

"Of course. And it will include some of my own conditions regarding my lifestyle budget and charities of choice."

"Agreed on principle, subject to changes and fine print. My wife must be appointed to the boards of some companies I own."

"The time commitment?"

"Three hours per week."

"I want compensation for my time in the form of an apartment of my choosing in Shanghai."

"Done."

Another pause. If this was everything Dad wanted for me, why did it feel fundamentally wrong?

"I want no more than two children. Three is too many and might interfere with my career." She cocked her head to the side, studying the ceiling as if trying to fleece every demand she could think of from her brain. "And a wet nurse for each child. Up to twenty-four months. I refuse to raise IQ-deficient idiots."

"Not a problem, so long as we split custody if you plan to continue practicing in New York."

Mom would want to see her grandchildren on a regular basis. And *that* would tear her attention away from me. Two birds. One stone. Plus, I still held onto stupid hope that Dad wanted me to have a family for a reason that didn't include saddling me with unnecessary bills, headaches, and sleep deprivation.

"This sounds acceptable enough." Eileen inspected my face, possibly for signs that I'd run out the door. The only person I wanted out the door was her. "And... you're sure you'll be okay with this arrangement?" She tapped her knee again. *Tap, tap, tap.* "That you won't suddenly decide you want love and teddy bears and all that nonsense. My sister says every man ends up only wanting one thing. Se—"

"Money," I finished for her. "The rest of life's vices bore me. I won't change my mind."

"That reminds me—separate beds?"

"Separate *wings*."

"Am I really that unattractive to you?"

"It's not you, Eileen. It's me."

Actually, it's you, too. For being my mental clone. I already have sex with myself. It's called masturbation.

Silence engulfed us. With nothing more to discuss, I stood, brushing away wrinkles on my trousers. Eileen mirrored me, rising to her full height. I imagined I'd one day resent the way she wore her lips—pursed in the shape of an asshole—because her expression was eternally sour.

I saved the contract draft on my app, eager to escort her off the premises. "I'll have my people contact yours for further negotiations and instructions."

"I don't have any *people*." She air-quoted the word with her fingers. "But yours can reach me on my cell. How about we shake on it?"

And then, without an ounce of consideration for how nauseating her touch was, she forced her hand into mine and gave it a firm, wet, *hot* squeeze.

Immediately, acid churned in my stomach. I stood frozen for

a moment, stunned and appalled, my gaze pinned hard on the spot where our flesh connected. My arm had gone slack, my hand limp in hers. I hated how pathetic I looked. How pathetic I *felt*. My mouth hooked into the shape of a scream, but nothing came out.

Let go of me.

Stop touching me.

Just fucking leave.

Bile traveled up my throat. I swallowed it down, everything rigid except the arm she'd taken. The contract. The marriage. The promise. I wanted to forget them all. To wash away my entire encounter with this inconsiderate imbecile. But Dad. *Dad, Dad, Dad.*

All my effort concentrated on waiting for Eileen to withdraw her hand first instead of jerking it away. When she finally did, I nearly keeled over with nausea. The whole thing lasted less than two seconds but felt like an entire day.

Eileen pressed her thumb onto a cluster of mooncake crumbs she'd spilled on her dress, sprinkling them into her unfinished teacup without a care in the world. Then, she reached into her wallet and fished out a business card from its depths, pressing it into my hand again.

More touching. Great.

"Call me."

"*Argh.*" My throat clogged up with a scream. I could not produce actual words. "Leave." Not exactly polite but the most I could manage.

"Sure. I'll show myself out." Eileen' eyes ping-ponged between me and the conservatory door, as attuned to my misery as a prostate exam. "I'll send you some Shanghai apartments via email. Please be sure to star me as a primary contact."

My fingers curled into a fist, the unmistakable burn of human flesh spreading across my skin where she'd touched. It felt like I'd been sullied. Marked, stained, and contaminated. An allergic reaction if I'd ever felt one. My windpipe narrowed. I couldn't breathe. It still felt like she was touching me. I needed to get her off, get her off, *get her off.*

And finally—goddamn fucking *finally*—Eileen vanished out the open double doors. Just in time to miss her future husband collapsing onto the hardwood planks.

CHAPTER NINETEEN

Zach

Weak, useless, and pathetic.

I didn't have time to dwell on how unsuited for civilization the broken shell of my body was. The minute Eileen disappeared, I raced to the teapot and showered my hand with its hot liquid. When it ran out, I hustled in the direction of the nearest bathroom.

Natalie caught me halfway through my journey, a batch of documents in her hands. "Oh, hey. Mr. Costa and Mr. von Bismarck were wondering if—"

I sidestepped her, barking out behind me, "The answer is no."

The bathroom door burst open in my rush, flinging against the wall. The crystal handle attached to the interior shattered all over the tiles. I kicked the door shut and stepped on spiky glass shards with my bare feet, barreling to the sink. Blood pooled at my heels. The pain didn't even register. I just needed to get her the hell off me.

I flipped the faucet to extra hot, thrust my hand into the pouring stream, and tipped my head back, groaning. The water came out fire-hot, lashing my flesh, stinging every inch like electric wires. I closed my eyes, practicing deep breaths. The "good" thumb—the one that hadn't been contaminated by Eileen's touch—rubbed soothing circles over my infected skin. Images of dead, rotting flesh plastered against me assaulted my brain.

Blood. Skin burned down to the muscle.

"Just wait, Zachary, we're coming to get you."

"Shit, Stan, that kid's gonna be fucked up. No way is he coming back normal from this."

"If that were me, I'd want to die, too."

I slapped the faucet handle with my quivering free hand, trying to get it hotter, but it had already maxed out. The water hissed as it scorched my skin beneath it clean to the bone. I didn't withdraw. *Couldn't.* Not when I needed to rid myself of her touch. No matter the price.

The door behind me jiggled, shaking on its hinges.

"G.I. Jerk, are you okay? I saw you running."

Of course, it was her. I couldn't catch a break.

Another rattle. "Hey, is this thing jammed?"

"Go away," I growled.

But she didn't. She wouldn't. She never followed instructions.

"What the…?" Her voice came from behind me, but I was too deep inside my trance to figure out how she'd managed to get inside despite the broken doorknob. "Jesus. *Zach.*"

The water shut off. I still had my eyes screwed shut, my jaw rock-hard to prevent the bile lodged in my throat from projecting all over the marble. It scorched my larynx with its sourness.

"Holy shit, dude. Your skin is pink."

Farrow. She was here. Inside. Right beside me.

My eyes shot open. She came into focus like a restored painting, familiar yet new. Blue eyes flared. Full mouth opened. Why did her stained maid uniform look more delectable than a Burberry dress suit? Seriously. When did Farrow Ballantine start to look so breathtakingly beautiful to me? Even now, with her hair tied up in a messy bun and her crooked wavy bangs glued to her forehead with sweat.

"How did you get here?" I snarled, shaking away these useless thoughts. "The doorknob shattered."

"The outer lock is still intact." She raised a bobby pin between us before tossing it into the sink. I recognized the moment she processed my current state of duress. She slapped a hand over her mouth, pupils running wild in their sockets. "What the fuck, Zach? Look at you."

Farrow surveyed our surroundings, grabbed a decorative vase, and used it to guide me away from the sink, herding me like a shepherd.

She knows I don't do touching. She figured it out.

The idea that she knew my darkest, most depraved secret—*and respected it*—made my stomach twist into thick knots. It was so typical of life to thrust me into such a cruel situation—just to teach me an even crueler lesson. Salvation came from the most unexpected places. Sometimes it came from religion. Sometimes it came from forgiveness.

And sometimes it came from the girl you finally realized you didn't actually hate.

Farrow backed me all the way into the opposite wall of the bathroom. "Your skin is raw. It's gonna blister. You have, like, third-degree burns. It's all gonna come off if we don't treat you."

She returned to the faucet and flicked it on, setting the water temperature to cool but not cold. While she waited for the temperature to change, she started tossing open cabinets, searching for something.

"Upper cabinet to your left." I slid my back down the wall, sitting on the floor and clutching my wrist. "What kind of idiot keeps their first aid kit on the lower level?"

"Maybe the same one who voluntarily gave himself a third-degree burn because he doesn't like being touched but doesn't have the balls to own up to it," she snapped, popping a red-and-white box open and rummaging through it.

I tried to swallow and failed. She was more perceptive than my childhood friends. They'd taken far longer to discover my secret. For the first time, I wasn't amused by Farrow Ballantine. I was worried. There was nothing more dangerous in this world than a smart woman.

"Petroleum jelly." She withdrew a tab of Vaseline. "Bingo. Hey, why is most of it gone?"

Fucking Ollie.

I mustered the courage to examine the skin slowly melting from my hand. Bright red. Purplish at the edges. Swollen and blistered fingers. I'd seen worse, but she probably hadn't.

Farrow deposited the Vaseline on the counter, continued sifting through the kit, and swore. She dumped the contents onto the marble and snapped her fingers. "Up on your feet."

I stood without question. Not sure when I'd started taking orders from my own maid, but here we were.

Her finger darted beneath the faucet, double-checking the temperature. "Put your hand under the running water. I'll be right back. Don't go anywhere." She wagged a finger in my face. "I swear to god, Zach—if you move an inch from this place, I'm going to find you and smother you with a bear hug."

With that, she left.

The cool water felt good against my skin, which surprised me, since I rarely felt anything at all. I heard Farrow moving in the nearby kitchen, slamming drawers, cursing in... Hungarian? It wasn't lost on me that I should've been more disturbed that she knew my secret. Maybe because *I* knew all of *her* secrets and could dangle her own weaknesses in her face. No.

The truth was, I kind of trusted the little shit.

Farrow smacked the door to the bathroom open, holding a roll of Saran Wrap in her hand and a jumbo bottle of Advil in the other. She discarded the painkillers on the counter and turned off the tap. Then, she plucked out a cotton swab, smeared it with Vaseline, and applied a thin layer to the scalded area in long, gentle strokes.

She pulled out a strip of the film and tore it with her teeth. "You better throw in a bonus for all the stuff I do for you."

I ignored her. Farrow opened a hydrogel pad and clamped it to my hand, careful not to make physical contact with me. The burn intensified, licking at my flesh like fire. I groaned.

"Stay still," she instructed. "Don't worry. I'll wrap you up without touching you."

It was on the tip of my tongue to tell her that a woman like her couldn't possibly worry me, but now wasn't the right time to be prideful. I shut my trap and extended my arm her way. She maneuvered the roll of film with surgical precision, managing to wrap the affected area and hydrogel pad without touching my skin with hers. A foreign sensation exploded from my hand, shotgunning to my gut. *Pain?* Something I hadn't felt in so long that I almost didn't recognize it. I didn't know whether I liked or hated that I felt pain when she was around.

Her deft fingers worked another layer of film over my skin. "Was this a hot date?"

I scowled, leaning against the sink. "Are you trying to be punny?"

"*Succeeding,*" she corrected. "A hot date. Get it? Because you got yourself *burned.*"

"Funny people don't have to explain their jokes, and it wasn't a date."

"Thank God. You were really cold and unapproachable. I would've bailed at hello. And that house tour? Dude, you are not the President. No one cares about the decorative driftwood in your master bedroom."

I pinned her with a warning glare.

She ignored me. "If it wasn't a date, what was it?"

"A possible business arrangement."

For absolutely no logical reason, it felt deeply wrong to talk to her about Eileen.

"Does Natalie know?" The corner of Farrow's mouth coiled into a smart-ass smirk. "She kind of has a thing for you."

"I have a thing for her, too."

"You do?"

"Yeah. Boredom."

"Poor Natalie." She shook her head, applying a third layer of the film around my skin. She nodded to the wrap. "Can I pin it with my finger? I'll have to touch you."

She would have to touch me through three layers of polyethylene. I'd survive.

Despite all efforts to fight it, a hint of heat crept up to my cheeks. "It's fine."

Her thumb dug into the wrap at my pulse. I watched in awe as her nimble fingers worked the clear sheet. It still felt uncomfortable to be touched, but I didn't mind it so much through a barrier.

She collected the Advil bottle from the counter, gathered two pills, and discarded them into my healthy hand. "Swallow those while I secure the film."

I popped them in my mouth and gulped them dry, glaring at her. Why did Farrow tending to my burn wounds excite me more than eating triple-yolked mooncakes with my immaculate bride-to-be? This made no sense at all. And sense was the one thing I could always count on.

I slanted my head, watching the film ripple as her breath fanned across it. "What I don't understand is, how can you be so poor when you don't have to pay rent and utilities, co-own a relatively successful small business, and have a side hustle as a fencing coach?" The answer had landed in my lap during a deep dive into her life, but I figured I should establish some sort of discourse between us before I broached the subject of fucking her.

Farrow's throat rolled with a swallow, her eyes trained on my injured hand as she worked. "The house is paid for, and the deed is under my and my stepmother's name, but I do pay rent in the form of property

taxes and half of the utilities. Regardless, I'd gotten myself into a…
situation. I have to pay a large fee. I'm still working on it."

"What did you do?"

But I already knew. What I really wanted to ask was—*why did you
do it?* She didn't seem like the type.

"It's none of your concern."

"You're in my house. Your character is my concern."

"Should've thought about that before you hired someone who tried
to steal from you. Allegedly."

The knots up and down my back began to loosen, even though she
still touched me through the film. "Do you have a boyfriend?" I didn't
actually care. It didn't factor in my decision-making, though it might
become a headache to use another man's woman.

She squinted. "I'll repeat myself—it's none of your concern."

"Can we make one thing clear?" I rested a hip against the vanity.
"Everything you do, everyone you communicate with, and every single
fucking breath you take is my business. I made you my business the day
I hired you, and I am a *very* good businessman. Now that that's out of
the way, you can either volunteer the information, or I can extract it in
other ways. The choice is yours."

"What choice? You're leaving me no leeway." She stepped back and
picked up the phone she'd discarded on the tiles when she'd busted into
the bathroom, pocketing it. "You'll get the information either way."

I shrugged. "Might as well fess up."

"I don't have a boyfriend." Her nostrils flared. "And I'm not
interested in one, either."

"The male population of the world is surely devastated," I drawled.
But she seemed completely unbothered by my quip. Maybe even
relieved.

"That's a pity." She flashed a grin. "You know how the saying
goes… *If you can't handle me at my worst, then I've got news for you. My
personality will only deteriorate from here on out.*"

"That is *not* the correct saying."

"It's the correct saying for *my* personality." She dusted off her hands
on the apron of her uniform. "Anyway, do you like her?"

Why? Do you care?

I played dumb. "Who?"

"Audrey Huffborn."

"It's Hepburn," I corrected.

"Not your bride. She is put together and elegant like the real thing, but she's obviously miserable." Farrow slanted her head. "So? You into her?"

"Yes," I lied. I had to. She kept staring through me, deep into a soul I didn't think existed, searching my face for something she'd never find. *Emotions.*

"She's very pretty." Farrow's frown smoothed out. "Glossy hair, red lips, almond eyes—"

"You're better than that," I interjected, wondering internally if she truly was.

"Better than what?"

"Describing minorities through food."

She seemed surprised, but not defensive. "I never thought of it that way."

I arched a brow. "How would you feel if I said you have pancake eyes?"

She tipped her head back, snorting. "Duly noted. Although…"

"Yes?"

"For the record, I love almonds. *And* pancakes." She groaned. "God, I love pancakes. Ooey, gooey chocolate-chip pancakes topped with extra almonds."

She was ridiculous. Completely unhinged. Yet, my lips twitched, fighting a smile.

"You may leave now."

She squinted. "Aren't you going to thank me?"

"For what?"

"Your hand!"

"Thank you for my hand?" I blinked, deliberately not getting it. "You didn't stitch it back together, Octi. You merely wrapped it in film."

"Wow, you're a jerk."

She pivoted, stalking out of the bathroom.

And you're mine. I'd make sure of it.

"Don't forget to clean the breakfast conservatory," I called after her. "My date left some crumbs."

CHAPTER TWENTY

Farrow

The Sun manor sparkled by the time I finished. Sure, I'd commandeered Zach's obnoxious war vehicle for a joy ride and flipped the stone penis on the Roman statue in the garden maze upside down. (Not like I was the one who broke it in the first place.) But overall, I'd left the place in better shape than I'd found it, granted it'd already come in tip-top condition. Nothing out of place. Not even a toothpick.

When I yanked the double doors open and slugged toward my ancient Prius, my lock screen read half past seven. Way too late to trek down a quarter-mile driveway in the pitch dark in any other town but Potomac. All the other homes on Dark Prince Road lit up with lights. Not Zach's. Nope. He preferred to broadcast what a hellish existence he lived.

I trudged down the driveway, cursing my new boss.

This morning, when I'd pulled up to the iron gates, a guard had instructed me to park outside the property. He'd shrugged. "Boss' order."

I didn't doubt it. It sounded right up Satan's alley to torture me, just for the fun of it. Cheap entertainment to see me running all the way to his mansion in the rain. What a total asshat. And yet, something fragile lurked beneath his surface that I couldn't explain. The way he almost shriveled into himself when faced with human touch broke my heart.

I couldn't hate him all the way, even when I knew I probably should.

Autumn leaves crunched under my boots. The gurgling water fountain washed over my ears as I lumbered past it. I made it to the security gate, walking through it rather than climbing over it this time. Across from me, the sprawling Costa mansion glowed with creamy lights, even from this distance. I stopped and stared from afar, too exhausted to be concerned with how pathetic I looked.

A food truck rumbled past their private gate and sailed up the long driveway, leaving the scent of ginger, lemongrass, and cinnamon in its wake. Catering. For a normal weekday dinner. A current of drool fought its way past my teeth. I hadn't eaten all day.

I spotted the blurred figure of a very pregnant woman. Dallas Costa, perhaps? She burst through the entryway, racing to the truck in a glamorous off-the-shoulder canary-yellow dress. Behind her, her husband tugged her back, sweeping her into his arms, so she didn't have to walk. They cooed into each other's ears as an army of servers carried trays out of the trunk and into the house.

My heart wept with jealousy. I wondered, for the millionth time, how different people could lead such different lives in the same zip code.

To my left, Oliver von Bismarck's gates remained permanently open as a queue of luxury cars filed through. Music blared into the street. He was probably throwing another salacious party. And by party, I meant orgy. Rumors traveled fast in this town.

"*Oliver is a self-proclaimed vaginivore,*" Reggie once told Tabby. "*He finds pleasure with anyone he deems pretty enough to become his next meal.*"

I bet he didn't have a care in the world. I bet he never had to wonder how he'd pay a debt or preserve his father's legacy. *Stop the pity party, Fae. Struggles aren't bad. You enjoy the view more if you climb there.*

A honk pulled my attention away from the mansion. Thick mud splashed my sneakers as a Maybach rumbled to a stop beside me. The rear window rolled down, revealing a woman whose age I couldn't quite pin down. She wore a Lululemon jacket over an Ernest Leoty bodysuit that showed off her Pilates build. A tartan Burberry gym bag consumed the rest of the leather bench. It shocked me that this stunning woman had given birth to a son whose feral smile resembled a health crisis.

"Farrow." She removed her AirPods. "Do you have a minute?"

Zach's mother knew my name? The Sun family sure did their homework. Then again, I recognized her from my own research.

I nodded, but it didn't matter. Her chauffeur had already shifted the car into Park. He exited, swung open Mrs. Sun's door, and offered a hand. She accepted it, stepping out with grace. Judging by the flat line of her lips, I suspected I'd enjoy conversing with her as little as I did her spawn. Still, I gave her the benefit of the doubt, pasting a polite smile on my lips.

She arched a brow. "You're Zachary's new housekeeper, correct?" I shrugged but didn't say anything. "I'm Constance. His mother."

"I know."

She didn't offer me her hand, but I knew it had nothing to do with a phobia. Didn't matter. Dad always said—*No one can devalue you without your consent.* Well, permission not granted.

Constance tightened her perfect ponytail. "You were at Zach's party, weren't you?"

Another nod. And a… *bark?* Three fluffy Corgis peeked their heads from the gaping window. They wore matching outfits, better dressed than I'd ever be.

Constance petted one of their heads through the window, her eyes still holding me hostage. "Zach seems to have taken a liking to you." Truly, there was no need for the disgusted tone. Her words made as much sense as the annual turkey pardoning.

Behind her, the Maybach blocked my Prius. Still, I fished a key from my backpack, jabbing the unlock button. The car beeped twice. I considered it my reply.

"Not a big talker, I see. Just as well, I suppose." She dusted fur off her hands, nodding. "Let's cut straight to the chase. My son is an excellent predator. As such, he decided to bring home his prey. But you're wrong for him."

"Am I, now?" I knotted a cheap scarf over my neck. The heater in the car was one of many luxuries I couldn't afford.

"No offense."

"None taken. It's a compliment. Your son is very… *peculiar.*"

The dig bounced off her, probably cushioned by the truth laced into it. "I have nothing against you."

"Great to hear."

"It's just…Zach is at an important juncture in his life. I fear you might interfere with his decisions. That he's confused and blinded by your…your…" Her eyes scraped a path from my choppy hair to my muddy shoes, searching for one positive thing to say about me. "…Cunningness, perhaps." I wondered how long this conversation would take. I needed to do my stretches and run a few miles before dinner. She toyed with the simple Chanel necklace resting between her collarbones. "Look, I'm sure you're a lovely girl, who will make someone very happy. But that someone isn't my son."

The cold bit into my flesh like a ravenous animal. I arched a brow, hoping to end this before I succumbed to frostbite. "You do know I spent the entire day cleaning his toilets, right? Not pole dancing on his Greek columns."

"French, not Greek. Nevertheless, you need to quit."

"Maybe." I walked around the Maybach to my Prius, tossed my backpack into the passenger seat, and opened the driver's side. "But I need the money more."

And all the help Zach promised would come along with it.

"I'll write you a check."

She slammed my door before I could slip in, plastering herself against the rusted metal. Her toned figure barely covered a fraction of it. A ridiculous thought entered my head—how could something so small birth someone so big?

Constance stretched her arms wide, blocking me. "Name your price."

"That's the thing." I folded my arms over my chest. "My integrity doesn't come with a price tag." Rich, considering what I'd done to get kicked out of competitive fencing, but she didn't need to know that.

"Your integrity *will* come with a price tag if it ensures my son's happiness." She tipped her chin up, refusing to move. "And there is nothing more important to me than his joy."

Wow. Okay. I'd tried to be polite, but she'd shattered my patience. The knots in my back taunted me. I didn't need to deal with her son's demands *and* hers, too. For once, I wanted to be the sword, not the fencer.

"Oh, I don't know about that." I brought a hand to my chest, brows furrowed in mock sorrow. "I caught him in his closet after his date, crying into a bottle of champagne. Poor guy. Seems to have truly lost it. Vomited all over a brand-new Armani suit."

The astonishment on her face practically pried her jaw off its hinges. I glanced around, wondering how Zach planned on destroying my life if his mother died of a heart attack right here.

She snapped her jaw shut. "I want you out of his house and away. Do not be ridiculous. Take the money and go." On cue, her driver lowered the window on our side, handing her a checkbook.

I reached into the Maybach to pet her dogs. One rested its paws on my hand, licking my wrist. "Two million dollars." I didn't know where the number came from. It seemed obscene. But it wasn't like she didn't have that kind of money. I bet her freaking sneakers cost more.

"You cannot be serious." She waved at the pup, shooing it away from me. Apparently, it wasn't just Zach I wasn't good enough for.

"I accept cash and Bitcoin only. Wouldn't want the feds to take their forty percent." I straightened, gesturing to my Prius. "Now, if you'll excuse me."

Constance Sun glanced at her Apple watch, shook her head, and stared up at the sky, which had decided to sprinkle rain onto this already miserable encounter. "One-point-five." *Oh my God.* She was serious.

"Two million, or you'll have to suffer through sharing a dinner table with me every Thanksgiving." I grinned. "I'll buy you the ugliest sweaters for Jesus' b-day."

"We're atheists."

"I'm not. Zach will respect my religion." I cocked my head to the side. "Are you a small or extra-small? And do you prefer space pizzas or Christmas lights?"

Panic skated over her face. She'd actually taken me seriously. "Fine. Fine. Bitcoin."

I was momentarily speechless. She wanted to give me two million dollars to quit? A part of me—a big part—wanted to take it. But another part told me Zach had offered something far more precious than cash. The most talented, connected lawyers and private investigators and unlimited resources to get to the bottom of what happened to Dad.

"Actually." I scrunched my nose. "I think I'll stick around, after all. Nothing like a job that gives you a bit of gossip."

Her hand flew to her chest. It took everything not to burst into laughter. Rich people weren't used to being rejected, especially after flaunting their money. If she'd approached me politely, without condescension and cruel assumptions, I might have said yes. But we'd never know now.

"This isn't over."

"I'm not afraid of you, Mrs. Sun." I drew out the words, maintaining eye contact. "You won't bully me into submission."

She pinned me with a look before disappearing as fast as she'd come. Sensing something—*someone*—I twisted my head, looking up to the grand bay windows of Zach's manor. He stood there, staring out the glass. At me. Our gazes tangled. His didn't waver.

I'm not going to back down, my eyes said.

He smiled, and I could almost hear the word on his lips—*good.*

CHAPTER TWENTY-ONE

Ari: How was your first day?

Farrow: A delight. I started out by busting my ass for ten hours.

Ari: It's a great ass, though, so glass half full.

Farrow: Then, he and his date watched me clean the tiles together, which was also a treat.

Ari: Clean the tiles? Is that code for something?

Ari: I swear, the weirdest kinks come out of America.

Ari: Wait. He brought a date home? What a fuckboy.

Farrow: They had mooncakes and tea in the conservatory overlooking the Potomac River.

Ari: Okay. I take that back. That sounds pretty picturesque.

Farrow: Oh. And then his mom chased me around, offering to pay me not to work for him.

Farrow: I turned down TWO MILLION DOLLARS. Now's a good time to tell me I'm stupid.

Ari: You're not stupid. You have morals. But WHY?

Farrow: She thinks he likes me too much. I bet she's worried I'll steal his sperm while I tidy up his bedroom.

Ari: I mean... is that completely off the table? He IS hot. LOL.

Farrow: Bitch, I would birth the next grim reaper or something. The man is lethal.

Farrow: But enough about my glamorous life. What are you doing with your life?

Ari: Choosing catering for my wedding next summer.

Farrow: Wish I could be there. I miss Seoul.

Ari: Seoul misses you.

Farrow: Come visit soon.

Ari: Promise. <3

Chapter Twenty-Two

Farrow

I took the egg hurled at my temple as a sign from God that I'd made the right decision signing my soul over to Zachary Sun. If anything, kicking my step-monsters out of Dad's home would give me some much-needed peace and quiet.

Reggie's wails boomed from the kitchen into the entryway. "I think I'm having a panic attack." I would, too, if I'd missed my calling in baseball. With that arm, she could've been the next Spencer Strider.

I shut the front door behind me and ignored the splattered yolk, feeling like a semitrailer had run me over several times before someone scraped me off the road, hurled me into a dumpster fire, then shot my remainders. Every inch of me felt bruised, malnourished, and bone-tired.

When I hauled myself into the kitchen, the contents of the freezer greeted me. Frozen veggies, chicken nuggets, and ancient half-pints of ice cream—checkered across the floor.

"I can't find my macaroons." Reggie tromped out of the pantry with a face full of makeup and a dress straight out of *Stepford Wives*. "Please tell me you didn't eat them, Tab. How can I complete my vlog?"

"That shit gets three hundred views on a good day." Perched on an island stool, Tabby ran her tongue over her teeth in front of a compact mirror. She scooped the car keys from an ugly fruit bowl. "Admit it, Reggie, it's not a career. It's a money pit. Be an Elsa, not an Anna."

"An Elsa?"

"*Let it go.*"

With a sigh, I jerked the fridge open, grabbed a yogurt cup, and commandeered someone's half-eaten tray of raspberries. Neither Thing 1 nor Thing 2 noticed me, even after I slammed the door shut with my hip and started trudging my way to my room. I'd clean everything tomorrow. I was dog tired.

Reggie stomped around behind my back. "You're just jealous I actually have a career."

I tossed a few raspberries into my mouth and wondered what kind of mouthwatering dinner Zach's chef made for him tonight. Grabbing the banister, I took the stairs two at a time, shaking my head. It got warmer the further I traveled down the long, narrow corridor. Mine was the last room and by far the smallest. It suited me fine. Easier to heat up in the winter.

I kicked the door open, thinking nothing of the fact that it was already slightly ajar, when I found Vera sitting criss-cross applesauce on my bed, surrounded by a halo of scattered documents.

I set my dinner on my study desk and rushed to the bed, collecting all the papers. "What the hell are you doing?"

My birth certificate. An engagement letter with a lawyer that had already dropped me six months ago when I couldn't afford her retainer. Some legal documents regarding my fencing federation penalty. All there. *Check, check, check.*

Vera stood, rearranging her Gucci belt over her waist. A secondhand treasure she'd snagged at a thrift store. "Don't look so scandalized, child. I knew you were up to something, so I decided to sniff around."

"You went through my stuff?" I spat out, collecting everything into my arms and opening the blue folder I'd organized them in. "Who gave you the right?"

She flung her bleached hair to one shoulder. "This is my house, you know."

"*Ours,*" I corrected, shoving the documents inside and clutching the folder to my chest. "It belongs to me, too."

Vera peered around the room with distaste, already calculating what she could do with the space. "I'll buy it off you eventually."

"With what money? I'm the only one here who *works.*"

She waltzed into my closet. The hinges creaked and groaned. "Don't give me this attitude. You deserve everything that's coming your way."

Every muscle in my body clenched as she began sifting through my clothes, searching for... What? Secrets? More documents? Things to help her figure out what I was up to? She already knew I planned to contest the will as soon as I had the means. Anyone with a functioning brain could guess that.

"Why?" I rushed after her, rearranging everything she tossed, pulled, and tugged. "Why do you hate me so much?" A genuine question. I didn't believe in fairytales with one-dimensional villains and angelic heroes. I believed in the gray area between bad and good. Where good people could make bad choices and still try to be better the next day.

Vera balled a shirt of mine and chucked it on the floor, pivoting to me. "You really want to know? Even when the answer is so obvious?" Heavy pants rattled her shoulders. "You were his biological daughter, Farrow. Who looked just like him. You had the DNA advantage. And he was obsessed with you. Loved you far more than you deserved. He only pretended with Reggie and Tabby." She drew a hand to her chest, the globe-sized engagement ring Dad had given her twinkling under the light. Tears sprung to her eyes. "Oh, my sweet girls. They tried so hard to please him."

My jaw clamped. I struggled not to cry. I missed him so much, not because he was the best father, but because he was the only person in my corner. It sucked. The aloneness I'd felt since he died clung to me like a latex dress. Sometimes, I'd close my eyes and fight the constant tide of loneliness by recounting the earliest memories Dad and I shared. Lately, it had gotten harder. Memories were a lousy ex. When you wanted them gone, they stayed. When you wanted them here, they left.

Vera jerked away from the clothing rack and hugged herself. "And he put all of his resources and time into your fencing. We always came second to you. He cheered you on at every single competition you've ever had, yet he never made it to Tabby's ballet recitals or Reggie's pickleball matches."

Now wasn't the time to point out that they'd both sucked at their crafts and lasted point-three seconds. Tabby's entire ballet career could be summed up in one three-minute home video of her starring as a tree in *The Nutcracker*. The part didn't require her to move. In fact, it *encouraged* stillness.

"You wanted him to give me away when my mother left me at his door." I clutched one of Dad's sweatshirts she'd discarded to my chest. "Your cruelty cannot be excused."

"Yes, I did." Vera's eyes met mine. She stood tall, proud and unapologetic. "You were a healthy cherub of a baby. Not even a month old. You would've found a wonderful family to adopt you, somewhere you didn't have to compete for attention. I tried to do you a favor. You weren't foster care material."

"Oh. Wow." I shook my head, a bitter chuckle escaping me. "You did *not* just say that."

But of course, she did. Vera Ballantine had no limits.

I flung the door open, waving a hand at the cavity it left. "Get out of my room."

Vera advanced to me, shoving her face in mine. "Don't contest the will, Farrow."

"It's not the real will."

Her face was so close to mine, I could see the rage swimming in her bloodshot eyes. "How do you know?"

"Because he would've left me the business."

And the pendant, too. The one I'd get from Zach, no matter what. Dad wanted me to have everything he cherished, because he knew I'd keep it close to my heart. Keep his memory safe.

"You little idiot." She raised her hand. I flinched, anticipating her strike. Instead, her grin widened as she pretended to wipe something off my shoulder. "You will never take me and my girls down."

With that, she stalked off.

CHAPTER TWENTY-THREE

Zach

Brett Conner was one of the least palatable people I'd ever encountered. A truly grotesque testament of his character, considering I found the gross majority of my peers unworthy of oxygen. Unfortunately, Brett Junior was the COO of a company I intended to acquire. Dot Cum. An up-and-coming NSFW social media platform with a search growth above 4900% and eighteen million active users per month, a figure growing by the minute. You could say Brett Senior's love for pussy was both his blessing and his curse. It had earned him a company worth over three billion dollars... but also a son whose sole contribution to society was keeping niche designer boutiques afloat.

"Hey." Brett Junior plowed into my house, wearing neon Prada sunglasses and a gold Gucci tracksuit. "Yo, O.C., my man." *O.C.* As in: Orange Chicken. Truly, that he managed to survive his twenties without being stabbed in the face by a steak knife could only be considered a miracle. He raised his fist for a bump, his signature idiotic grin the only indication of cognitive function. "Brought some champagne made in Italy. The real stuff."

I didn't have the heart to tell him he was wrong. Frankly, I did not have a heart at all. Had I possessed such an organ, I surely wouldn't spend one beat of it on this man. Tragically, it also seemed like my pulse would not be affected by Miss Eileen Yang, who had spent the last couple dates sending me real estate links in Shanghai. She'd already proved to be a headache.

Brett Senior trailed behind the disappointing byproduct of his sperm, followed by Dot Cum's head of accounting, some suit named Jasper. When I ignored his fist bump, Junior swaggered past the Guan Yu statue in my foyer, arms spread for a bro-hug. I sidestepped him as he launched himself at me, causing him to collapse onto my floor.

"Ew." He cupped his balls, still face-down. "Why'd you do that?"

"Not big on hugs." I used the tip of my shoe to turn him over so he laid on his back. "Do not drool on my floor. My cleaner doesn't need any extra work. And for future reference, do not call me Orange Chicken, unless you are prepared for me to call you Unpurposed Flour."

Junior rubbed his knee, frowning. "Flour? But I'm not even Floyd."

I closed my eyes, drawing a breath. Senior winced, bowing his head and reaching out for a shake before remembering I didn't do those. He slipped his hand back into his pocket. "My apologies, Mr. Sun. My son is quite... overwhelmed with his corporate role." He took off his hat, smoothing back white tufts of hair. "I suspect you'll be making a few changes in management if this deal goes through?"

I turned my back on all three of them, heading toward the dining area. "I'll be appointing my own team."

I'd opted for a quiet dinner rather than an official meeting. The data I needed already sat in a vault inside my head. This morning, I'd determined the price I was willing to pay for the company. It hovered somewhere under half of *Forbes'* projected valuation. Now it was just a matter of bending the Bretts to my will and fucking them over. The only kind of fucking I did.

"Thank you for your hospitality, Mr. Sun." Jasper matched my pace with Senior trailing not far behind us. "We could've hammered down the finer details in an office, so I appreciate the extra touch—"

"Kindly withdraw your tongue from my ass. It is not a kink I indulge in." My feet carried me through the grand brass-and-ivory gallery. "Oh, and let me save you the awkward question—I will not be keeping you on payroll, either."

He clamped his mouth shut.

Junior scraped himself off the hardwood, jogging to catch up with us. "I get the whole hardball routine. I do, man. But I'm not gonna let you eat our lunch or anything. Lay out a welcome mat beneath my ass, and I'll let you pound a deal outta me." He circled his finger next to his temple, whistling. "Don't be delulu, yeah?"

Nothing—and I was certain of it—could make me loathe this guy more. That we spoke the same language yet couldn't understand one word from the other's lips was a testament to how far our lingua franca had fallen.

"The fact that you wanna buy Dot Cum says it all." Junior pounded his chest. "We did a good job. We deserve to stay."

"Don't confuse luck with talent. You stumbled into a hole in the market, no pun intended. You have three reputable developers chasing your tail and a litany of incompetent staff running your marathon. Your adversaries *will* catch up with you, and when they do, you can kiss Daddy's black card goodbye."

He scratched his temple. "Adversaries?"

"Competitors. Opponents. Rivals. People far smarter than you. You have no idea how to monetize your own brand. I'm the Jesus to your Lazarus, kid." I waltzed past two servers, who held each double door open, revealing a columned dining room with floor-to-ceiling French windows. "You're not here to bargain. You're here to make carpet sounds and let the grown-ups talk."

"They said you're a cold bastard, but I thought they were exaggerating."

"They didn't." I stopped at the chair at the head of the long oval table. "In fact, they probably lowballed it."

People forgave me for my cutthroat attitude because I was too rich and too powerful to cross. Also because I'd collected a long list of favors over my thirty-three years, and the prospect that I'd demand their souls in exchange made them tremble in their sleep.

Four servers rushed to pull out our chairs. The catering staff hovered around the table, popping wine bottles and angling them into our glasses. Junior gestured for a waitress to continue pouring. That idiot needed alcohol in his system like I needed a second dick.

Jasper and Senior fretted with their napkins, glancing at me, unsure what to do. "Sit," I ordered. They did.

I shook my head, producing my phone from my inner pocket.

Zach Sun: SOS.

Ollie vB: FUCKING FINALLY. Told you those formative Pilates classes were gonna pay off. And not just because of the bored trophy-wife pussy.

Romeo Costa: WTF do you think SOS stands for, Ollie?

Ollie vB: Sucked One's Sausage. What else?

Zach Sun: Rom.

Ollie vB: Huh? His name doesn't even have an S in it.

Romeo Costa: @ZachSun, yeah?

Zach Sun: I need you to crash my business dinner.

Romeo Costa: Do I want to know why?

Zach Sun: Don't trust myself not to kill the guest.

Romeo Costa: The Asters?

Zach Sun: Worse. The Conners. Junior is a pain.

Ollie vB: Had a fivesome with him once. Might be overcompensating.

Romeo Costa: That explains it. I'm bringing Shortbread.

Zach Sun: If you must.

Ollie vB: Wow. You really are desperate. I'm bringing a date, too.

Zach Sun: You're not bringing anyone.

Ollie vB: Why?

Zach Sun: Because you're not invited.

Ollie vB: Why not?

Romeo Costa: Because then I'll have two people I need to stop Zach from killing.

Ollie vB: [Kim K Crying GIF]

Ollie vB: But where else will I have the opportunity to wear my wife pleaser?

Zach Sun: @RomeoCosta, how fast can you get here?

Romeo Costa: Already on my way.

Zach Sun: @OllievB, you can come, but leave the wife pleaser and the date in the car.

Ollie vB: Aww, but Daddy, why?

Zach Sun: Because they're probably a fugitive.

Ollie vB: First of all, thanks for the vote of confidence.

Ollie vB: Second of all, her lawyers are in talks for her surrender, and it was only a DUI.

Zach Sun: Respectfully, Oliver, fuck off.

Ollie vB: Fine. I'll bring pink coke.

Zach Sun: Don't you dare.

Ollie vB: It's rude to come to a dinner empty-handed.

Zach Sun: Then don't come at all.

Ollie vB: I love it when you play hard to get. You know I have a weakness for unattainable holes.

Zach Sun: You're about to acquire a brand new one between your eyes if you don't shut up, courtesy of my knife.

Romeo Costa: We'll be there in ten minutes, Zach.

Ollie vB: And I'm bringing the pink coke. <3

As we texted, the caterers piled more dishes onto the table. Piri piri chicken. Jollof rice and egusi soup. Kanpachi crudo and miso carbonara.

"More food. My goodness." Senior patted his ample stomach, snapping my attention back to him. "You really do spoil us, Mr. Sun."

I cut my gaze to the entrance, following his line of sight. Farrow swept in through the double doors, dressed in her tight-fitted black maid's dress with the white Peter Pan collar. She carried a silver tray, not sparing me a glance as she glided past. But I knew that with a single word, I could wipe off that stoic expression from her face. Conjure sweat at her temple, ruining the French braid she'd twisted her pale hair into.

In the few days she'd worked for me, Farrow had befriended all of my staff. The cook, the gardeners, the house manager. She was a breath of fresh air in this lifeless mansion. Problem was, I didn't like air. Suffocating suited me fine.

I slid my phone back into my pocket, my fingers twitching in my lap. Each time she moved, the A/C vent forced a current of her scent my way. I held my breath to prevent it from trickling into my system. Wordlessly, she set down caviar pots, her lithe, athletic body leaning over my plate. She tested my limits, constantly inching nearer. Stretches of empty space unfurled on either side of me. Farrow could've occupied any piece of it, but she'd decided not to. I had no choice but to conclude that this was her dipping her toe into the water to check the temperature. Had she figured out her purpose here? It was entirely possible she'd put everything together.

The fact that I could picture myself touching her did not provide me any comfort. On the contrary. It made me feel like an inferno seared beneath my skin.

Junior whistled low and rubbed his hands together, his eyes running up and down Farrow's body. "Nice staff, man."

My blood—normally a frozen, useless liquid in my veins—sizzled into lava within seconds.

"I see what you've done here." Junior winked, licking his lips. "Very smart. No need to settle down, saddle yourself to one chick. A rotating staff is the way to go. Where's she from, anyway? Norway? Holland?"

"Your worst nightmares," Farrow muttered under her breath.

"Aw, she talks, too." Junior slapped his thigh, cackling. "Baby, you're no nightmare. A wet dream, maybe."

"How about we test the theory with a sharp object?" She smiled, batting her lashes as she set down the last caviar pot. "I'm pretty good with handling those." Understatement of the century.

I knew she could hold her own. But I wanted to kill him for her.

When she tucked the empty tray under her arm, pivoting to leave,

I stopped her with the tip of my butter knife. It kissed her elbow each time she exhaled. I leaned in for privacy, hissing out, "You should not be serving food."

My fingers rebelled against my brain, twitching, eager to latch onto her wrist and drag her out of here in front of everyone. I didn't recognize myself these days. I needed to do something about it. Perhaps a lobotomy, since narrowing my masturbation window from every 48 hours to every 24 hadn't worked. Normally, I jerked off for the sole purpose of healthy sperm circulation. Not to fantasize over Farrow's lips rolling down my shaft.

The little octopus pried away my butter knife. "They're short on staff." She rearranged my utensils on the wrong side, her elbow nearly touching my chest. I could hardly breathe. "The manager of the catering company said you scared someone off. You caught her on a break in the garden and kicked her out?"

"She was smoking."

"So is this chick." Junior threw a thumb Farrow's way. "Smoking *hot*."

Farrow tossed a smile back. "Burn in hell." She had no idea how close he was to this fate.

"Might take you up on that offer." Junior rubbed his hands together. "You coming with me?"

Latching onto the steak knife, I leaned forward, leveling my eyes with Brett's as I slammed the blade an inch from his pinky finger. He jumped back in his seat, gasping.

"I will say this once, and I will say it nicely—never, *ever*, under any circumstances, look, touch, talk, or breathe in this woman's direction. Am I understood?"

But I obviously wasn't. Because Brainless Brett responded by tossing his empty head back and laughing wildly, nearly coughing out a lung. "Damn, bro, chill. She's just the help. I have a dozen like her waiting in my house if you wanna do a little switch-a-roo."

"*Junior*," Brett Senior barked from my left.

My chair scraped the floor as it shot back. I started to stand, ready to put a knife between Junior's eyes, when two things happened at once.

One, Dallas Costa's annoying, high-pitched voice ripped through the air as she singsonged from the foyer, "Oh, *Zacharyyy*."

And two, Farrow Ballantine brushed her fingertips on my wrist.

CHAPTER TWENTY-FOUR

Zach

Putting Dallas aside—all the way on another continent, if possible—I focused on Farrow's touch. It scorched a path through my flesh and bones. I suppressed a hiss, jerking my hand away and fixing her with a glare. "What are you doing?"

"I don't know." She toyed with a small smile. "Pushing you out of your comfort zone, maybe?"

"Well, don't. I fucking like it there."

But the bite in my voice wasn't there. Nor was my knee-jerk reaction to rush into the bathroom and scrub my skin clean until I peeled off the infected layer. A flash of Dad, dead and stiff above me, still zapped through my head, except it didn't linger. And I didn't have the same horrible reaction I normally had to people touching me. All I felt was… buzzed. And a little seasick. Farrow backed away, blowing a loose strand of hair out of her eye as she made her exit.

Dallas leaned in for air kisses. "Look at all this food." Her pregnant belly poked into my personal space. A dire reminder of the thing my mother expected of me. An heir. Someone to continue the Sun bloodline.

Romeo endured Brett Junior's bro-hug, steering him away with a finger to his forehead. "Check that your wallet is still in your back pocket," I hissed to Rom, shooing away a busser when he tried to collect the knife speared in front of Junior's plate. Let it serve as a warning for the—hopefully brief—remainder of the night.

"Everything looks so good." Dallas clapped, bouncing on her feet as much as she could with that thing cooking in her stomach. "Other than the company, I hear."

She was a lovely creature, Dallas Costa. With lush chestnut curls tumbling past her shoulders. Emerald doe eyes, wide smile, and a figure most men would go to World War III for. And yet, she stirred nothing in me. Too loud, happy, and simple for my taste.

"White truffles." She plucked a cavatappi noodle from a shared plate with her bare hand, catapulting it past her lips. "You got this for me, didn't you?"

"All yours, now." I gestured for a server to fetch me another steak knife, though my appetite had already shriveled into nothing.

Dallas slapped her Birkin to Romeo's chest and hauled the entire oblong plate off the table, rushing to dump it on her placemat. Within the chaos, Senior and Jasper remained silent. Too starstruck by the man in front of them to worry about our meeting being interrupted. I supposed my guests required an explanation.

With Farrow gone, I relaxed, snapping my napkin open over my lap. "Rom and Oliver consult me off the books."

A lie, of course. I wouldn't take Oliver to a brothel without worrying about his conduct, let alone a business meeting. But Ollie and Rom kept me in check. For the most part.

"Oliver von Bismarck, I assume?" Senior—who did not come from money and never ceased to be enthralled by anyone born into it— leaned forward on his elbows and ogled me. "The duke?"

"Prussian nobility." Oliver swept into the room, clad in a pale gray three-piece suit, swiping a hand over his golden curls. Considering he did not have a job, I had no idea where he'd come from looking like this. "Quite a useless title, once you've gone through most willing women in the world, if I'm honest." He stole Jasper's untouched wine glass on his journey to his seat, placing a kiss on the crown of Dallas' head along the way. "Looking fabulous, Mrs. Costa. How's my goddaughter doing in there?"

"Coming along nicely," Dallas replied, chewing on a Boudin Blanc sausage at the same time. The girl had less class than a cum stain.

"You're high if you think I'll put my trust in you with any female, let alone my own daughter." Romeo claimed the seat next to his wife, while Oliver slopped beside Junior on the other end of the table. "Zach's the godfather."

"Get your head out of the gutter." Oliver feigned disgust, glowering at Rom. "I would never try anything with the daughter of my own best friend."

Romeo raised a brow. "Really?"

"Yes, really. That would be bad manners, seeing as I fully intend on seducing his sister-in-law." Ollie tipped his glass, snapping his fingers in a server's direction. "Grey Goose martini. Three olives. Actually, make it two. I'm drinking for Daytona Beach, as well."

"It's Dallas." She pried a grape off the centerpiece and popped it into her mouth before discovering the hard way that it was decorative. "And please don't make me your enabler."

I steered the conversation to familiar territory. Sex—and everything that came with it—was not my area of expertise. My attention settled on Senior, the least infuriating of my guests. "I trust you received my official proposal."

"We did." He sliced into the buttery wagyu, scooping a dash of potato espuma and shiso chimichurri. "While it's an interesting offer and we're flattered, we do believe you undervalued our company by a billion dollars." Actually, I'd undervalued it by *two* billion, but he wanted to meet me in the middle.

"I did no such thing, Mr. Conner." I reclined against the upholstery, ignoring my food. I didn't do fine dining. I ate to survive. "In fact, all I've done was deduct my liability fee, which is sure to come."

Junior frowned, angling his body forward. "Liability fee?" His sunglasses perched on top of his nose. *Indoors.* Had Oliver arrived in his wife pleaser, he still wouldn't be the worst dressed in the room.

"Yes, liability. I'm sure you're familiar with the word, seeing as your existence sums it up." Reluctantly, I turned to look at Junior. "Your company serves people who let others watch them suck toes and grind against public subway seats. This whole operation is a lawsuit waiting to happen. Therefore, I reserved the money I calculated I'll need to hose the legal fecal matter off Dot Cum when shit hits the fan."

Jasper tilted his head, reaching for his wine before remembering Ollie had stolen it. "You deducted one billion dollars because of an imaginary lawsuit?"

"It's not imaginary." Oliver cut into his steak. "People sue companies every day. If they can find a reason to sue a diaper company, what makes you think they can't find a good reason to piss on a site where anyone can say they're over eighteen and create pornographic content?"

"Not to mention, ad revenue for social media companies runs in the high nineties." I fixed the utensils arrangement Farrow had screwed with until they aligned parallel to one another. "And about eighty percent of family-friendly corporations would never consider advertising on your platform."

"It'll be a bitch to bring the boys to your milkshake yard." Romeo, who'd lost his mind almost two years ago, finished cutting his wife's entire steak. "You can't treat your estimated market value as a true and tested number."

"Exactly." Ollie snapped his fingers, receiving his martini and tipping my server a hundred bucks like he was at a restaurant. The man was as in touch with reality as a space cowboy. "Nobody wants to advertise their product next to a dick pic."

Dallas grinned at Ollie. "Speaking of, wasn't *yours* splayed on the cover of the *New Yorker*?" The little troll.

"Well, yeah, but that is one photogenic penis." Ollie popped a tiger prawn into his mouth. "It deserves an *Esquire* cover, leaning over a horse in cowboy gear."

"I see you've given it some thought."

He nodded. "Even hired an art director to give me pointers in case my beautiful penis is ever invited for a photoshoot."

Dallas tipped a shoulder up. "Seen better."

"You're biased." Ollie yawned, taking a swig of his martini like it was beer. "Another penis impregnated you. You have skin in the game."

She patted her husband's lap. "Rom actually has the most beautiful circumcision."

Why were these people my friends? Why had I not opted to live in a cave in the Alps? I had zero desire to discuss other people's genitalia.

"*Dad.*" Junior finally ripped the sunglasses off his face, stomping his gold Versace sneakers. "You can't sell it at a bill under the market value. That's crazy."

Senior glanced Jasper's way. The latter rolled his tongue along his teeth, rearranging his new glass of wine by its stem without a word. His gaze shifted back to me. "Is one billion your best and final offer?"

"While I'm still in the race." I laced my fingers together. "I have a terrible attention span when it comes to acquiring new companies. The industry is ever-changing. So is my mind."

"Dad, *no.*" Junior's eyes clung to his father's face. "They're pressuring you, so they can rip you off. Let's not sell. I'll pull some more hours. This time, I'll even come to the office every day. I swear—"

"Shut up and let me think," Senior barked, smacking the table. Utensils and plates clattered. Some food rolled off the edge.

Dallas groaned. "Not the stuffed cherries."

The staff burst into the room, collecting the plates from our second entrée and replacing them with fresh ones for the next round. A hand grabbed my untouched food. I eased in my seat a little, knowing it was Farrow near me. That, even if our elbows brushed, I wouldn't keel over.

She bent over the table next to my right arm, trying to reach a side dish. Her short dress rode up her thighs, revealing the curve of her round ass. Miraculously, my fingers itched to claw onto the back of her knee. To ride up north along her inner thigh. To cup her pussy through her underwear from behind and slide a pinky into her panties, rubbing the seam of her tight, little pussy. Desire singed my neck, coiling in tight ribbons down my body, sliding past my chest and stomach to my dick.

I was hard. For the first time in my life, I was hard because of a woman. A woman with flesh and blood. In theory, I'd always appreciated women sexually, but never up-close. The realization that I actively wanted to touch Farrow Ballantine floored me.

I wasn't merely not-disgusted anymore. I was actively yearning.

"Excuse me, Mrs. Costa, gentlemen." Senior stood. "I'm going to need a minute with Jasper." Junior jerked to his feet, running his tongue along his teeth. His father shook his head. "*Alone.*"

Junior blinked in disbelief. "Are you kidding me?"

I gestured toward the door, voice thick with the pain of untapped desire. "There's a drawing room to your left."

After Jasper and Senior strolled out, Junior dragged his fingers through his hair, tugging hard as he glanced around. He squinted at Oliver. "Hey, didn't I have a threesome with you at some point?"

"*Fivesome.*" Oliver shook his head, checking his phone with a frown. "Though two backed out at the sight of your sword. Or should I say, your pocket knife."

Dallas giggled. Romeo sighed.

"Why, this is shocking." Farrow's breath fanned my ear. She collected more dirty dishes from the table. "I'd have never assumed."

I didn't know why, but there was something fundamentally wrong about seeing her serving us. Dallas, especially. Farrow deserved to sit shoulder-to-shoulder with the Southern belle. To gossip and flaunt a designer frock. To have everyone's attention and adoration. She deserved the fucking world. I hoped one day someone gave it to her. Even if the thought that it wouldn't be from me made it hard to breathe.

Dallas head bobbed, erecting a hang-loose sign. "Right on, sister."

Junior sneered at Farrow. "Nobody asked your opinion, Cinderella."

"Watch your mouth when you talk to her." Yet again, I speared the table with a steak knife, eliciting intense reactions from everyone seated. "Or I'll make sure you don't have enough teeth to speak."

"Oh." Oliver plastered a hand over his forehead, slithering it down with a shake of his head. "Not the help, Zachary. Who would've thought you, of all people, would turn out just like Chris?"

Rom paused mid-slice. "Chris?"

"Christopher Marshall."

"Never heard of him. Is he someone whose life we've ruined?"

"The Senatorial candidate," Farrow provided, unfazed by it all. "In that J-Lo movie."

"Finally." Oliver stood, showering her with golf claps. "A woman of depth and culture. *Maid in Manhattan*. I tear up every time." He scooped up an invisible tear with the back of his finger. "Though I'm sure Zachary over here is more about the Maid in Maryland life."

It didn't surprise me that Ollie knew all about Farrow and her cleaning company. Mom probably vented to him over almond cookies and freshly imported da hong pao before whining to Romeo.

"Shut up." I pointed a fork at my best friends—a reformed psychopath and a fuckboy with more mileage than a used car. "Both of you."

Farrow turned to Dallas, ignoring me. "Hey, you should totally try the stuffed bone marrow elote we're bringing in a sec. They're to die for." She jerked a thumb toward me. "I scarfed down all of this buzzkill's portion in two seconds flat."

Dallas drew a palm to her chest. "Did we just become best friends?"

"I believe so."

Dal whipped her phone out. "I'll get us T. Swift tickets."

Farrow wiggled her brows. "I'll make friendship bracelets. Fave colors?"

"Purple and green."

Junior pinned Fae with his dilated pupils, ready to launch into another tirade. "Speaking of being stuffed…" He fought a bout of sniffles, coked out of his mind, nose snowed in more than a Syracuse Christmas.

But she didn't pay attention to him. She was already on her way out, balancing 7 dirty plates in one palm. Junior swiped his nose and stood, following Farrow. "I'm going to make a quick dash to the bathroom."

Oliver pulled his chair back and sighed. "I'll make sure he behaves."

"No." I got up, raising my palm. "He's past a little spanking. Stay here." I paused. "And maybe call my lawyer."

Junior flattened out his tracksuit, muttering incomprehensible things. "Gotta teach this girl a lesson…"

My jaw locked. "*Definitely* call my lawyer."

I stalked Brett as he traced Fae's steps, cracking his neck and knuckles. She entered the main kitchen, oblivious to the men following her. Brett and I filed inside, watching as she unloaded the plates into an already filled sink.

"*Oof.*" She planted a hand on the counter and wiped her brow. "What a piece of work."

"What a piece of *ass.*" Junior advanced, stopping short of the counter, mere inches from her.

She didn't look up from the dishes, flipping the faucet on to rinse the plates. "I wouldn't try anything stupid if I were you."

"Yeah?" He scooted closer, boiling the blood in my veins to a temperature more suitable for the sun. His sniffing was out of control. "Why's that?"

"Because I can hit harder."

"Oh, so you like it rough, do you?"

I watched with painstaking stillness as Junior raised his hands, wiggled those sticky fingers, and stretched them out, aiming for her ass. He neared his destination, almost rounding the curve between the cheek and those toned legs that moved with graceful skill on the piste.

"*Farrow.*"

The strain in my own voice surprised me.

Junior's hand froze midair.

Octi whipped her head around, blinking at me, surprised. "What?"

"Are you squeamish?"

"No."

"Good."

I slid my knife out and tossed it right into Brett Junior's outstretched hand.

CHAPTER TWENTY-FIVE

Zach

"What the fuck?" Brett gawked at his missing fingertip. "What the fuck, what the fuck, what the fuck?"

Good question. What the fuck, indeed.

No worries. Nothing to see here. Just protecting my antidote. Surely, protection of private property laws will hold up in a court of law.

"Nooo." He shed fat tears onto his injured hand, holding it up to the light. "Not Palmela Handerson."

What a shame that my aim never failed me. I'd hit bullseye. The tip of his middle and index finger. Not enough to cause real damage other than some missing tissue and nerves. *Pity.* A little to the right, and I wouldn't have to hear him screech.

"What the fuck, bro?" He clutched his wrist, keeling over and firing out an anguished cry. "You fucking sliced me, man. Sliced me!"

I did, and I wish I can do it again.

Junior patted the floor, trying to find his discarded fingertips. They'd splattered onto the tiles like confetti. Even now, blood gushed from the jagged cavity they'd left behind.

This marked the first time I'd tossed a knife at a target outside the practice range. The first time that I'd hit anything with this particular knife—Dad's gift to me—*ever*. Even though I knew the paperwork was going to be a hassle, I did not regret it.

"What the fuck." Brett Junior progressed to screaming, stomping in place, staring at the fountain of blood spurting from his fingers. Guess he decided not to look for his missing organs, after all.

"The fuck is—you fucked with the wrong person. I told you not to get anywhere near her. She's mine."

"It was just a friendly squeeze."

"What a coincidence." I strolled forward, collected the knife, and waved it before him, pinching the handle. "Just a friendly squeeze. Now your right hand won't be of much use, even to jerk off to the thought of her."

"I'm calling the police."

"And telling them what?" I wiped the blade off on the edge of his shirt and tucked it into its holder. "That you came into my house high off your ass and sexually harassed my staff?"

"I'm losing blood," he whimpered, stomping out of the kitchen as loud as humanly possible, hugging his wrist to the Gucci emblem on his chest. "Dad! Daddy!"

Finally, I spared a glance at Farrow. She'd kept quiet the entire time, assessing me in that way of hers that made me worry that she could untangle all my secrets from my façades.

I yawned. "What?"

"You've lost control."

"I'm in perfect control," I countered. "It's Brett Junior over here who can't keep his hands to himself."

"I'm not yours." Her baby blues blazed with fury. "Why would you say that to Brett?"

"You will be." The truth slipped out without warning or consent from my brain.

"I won't."

"You will."

"What makes you so sure?"

"I always get what I want." I darted my tongue out, swiping it over my lower lip. "And I want you like I've never wanted anything in my life."

If I thought she'd be done for at my unusual confession, I had another thing coming. She wasn't one of the fangirls. In fact, my answer seemed to piss her off even more.

She snatched a washcloth that hung over the faucet, cleaning Brett's blood from the floor. "Was it really worth it?"

I didn't want her touching anything that came from him, but I stopped myself from yanking the rag out of her fist. I needed to rein in this obsession before it spiraled out of control.

"Now you'll get into trouble, and for what?" She sprayed an organic cleaning solution on the tile. "My ass has been pinched before. It always ends the same. With a shiner for the guy who did it and swollen knuckles for me."

The mere thought of men thinking they could touch this woman without consent made me want to do heinous things. I needed names, addresses, and schedules. And knives. Plenty of fucking knives.

"I won't get in trouble."

From the drawing room, Senior lost his shit at volcanic decibels. "How could you be so stupid?"

I jerked a thumb back in their direction as Jasper and Senior reprimanded Junior, proving my point. "I'll add a few million to sweeten the deal when I buy the company." A grim, lopsided smile slashed my face. "That's always been the plan. I lowballed them hard."

"You treated me as an object. As a possession." She paused to stab me with her glare. "I may work for you, but that's where it ends."

"Au contraire. It's only the beginning. I have so many other plans for you."

Her eyes tightened at the corners. "*Zachary.*"

"*Farrow.*"

She hurled the heavy, drenched rag into the sink. Blood splattered over the plates and mugs. "You got something to say to me?"

"Sure." I stalked to her, stopping just a foot shy. *Progress.* The column of her throat bobbed at the proximity. I palmed my knife, fingered the bloodstained collar of her maid outfit with the tip of the blade, and flashed her a smirk. "You look good in red."

With that, I left, making my way to the master bedroom. Her crumpled Chuck Taylors squeaked against the marble floor. They stomped the steps behind me, loud and unapologetic. Outside of parties and formal dinners, I didn't even allow shoes in the manor. She'd ignored the rule from Day One.

We passed Junior without a word. He slumped against the post on the first step, getting stitched up by Ollie's family doctor while his father and Jasper fussed over him. Across the hall, Ollie, Rom, and Delhi laughed, glasses clinking, utensils hitting porcelain plates.

I jerked the golden handle to my bedroom open and slipped inside. It clicked shut behind Fae, who twisted the lock. She followed me into the bathroom, where I flipped my faucet to its coldest setting and stuck my hands under. The water turned pink beneath the blood. Our gazes tangled through the mirror. If she was freaked out about me slicing a man for almost cupping her ass, she certainly didn't show it.

After I finished cleaning up, I waltzed into my closet and began unbuttoning my shirt. Farrow rested a hip on the doorframe, her uniform and bare legs still caked with blood. Slowly, I rolled my shoulders down, aware of her eyes pinned on the fabric. It fell to the rug without a sound. I stood shirtless before her like a statue in a private viewing, allowing her a few more moments to soak in my six-pack, the contours of my sculpted arms, and the deep V that ran into my slacks. Her eyes widened like saucers. Heat pooled beneath my navel, all my blood rushing to my cock. I knew that look. Wore it myself whenever I hunted for a deal. She was hungry. For *me*.

You have no idea, Little Octopus. I'll give you seconds and thirds. Desserts and snacks in between. You are going to be so full of me, your pussy will be the shape of my dick.

The thought was as startling as the idea. I couldn't even bring myself to touch her right now.

I broke the ice, snapping my fingers in the direction of her face. "My eyes are up here, by the way."

We stood about ten feet away from each other. But unlike any other time, with anyone else, each foot felt like an entire continent.

"There's nothing behind them." She folded her arms. "Your torso is a much better view."

I picked a crisp white button-down, slid the empty velvet hanger back on the rack, and padded to her, still shirtless. "You shouldn't let anyone talk to you like Brett did. Or Oliver, for that matter."

Her smile dropped. "They get away with it because they know they can. I'm not Dallas Townsend. I have no one to protect me."

I slipped the fabric over my arms and took another step toward her. "Yes, you do."

Then another, fastening a button with each stride.

"And who would that be?"

"*Me.*"

Silence clawed the air. Then, I heard it. Tinkling laughter bubbled from her throat like wedding bells carried by the wind. It trickled straight into my stomach and burst in every direction from there. Only, it didn't feel like butterflies. It felt like bats from hell.

"What was that?" I demanded.

Her smile vanished—and so did the strange murmur inside my chest when she'd made that sound. It was not unpleasant. And did not feel like cardiac arrest. I might have wanted it back.

She blinked. "What was what?"

"That sound."

Her brows shot up to the edge of her hairline. "I... laughed?"

I noticed that her brows were a shade darker than her icy blonde locks. That they made her beauty wilder. More dramatic. Her eyes, too, weren't the traditional blue. They were pastel—the palest shade on the palette—rimmed by a navy circle.

It occurred to me that I could look at her face for hours on end without getting bored. Which was a preposterous thing, really. Women usually bored me. Their faces, like their bodies, were interchangeable and entirely unexciting.

"Laugh again," I ordered.

Her delicate brows crashed together. "Make me, then."

"Impossible. I have no sense of humor."

"Develop one."

"It's not a fucking film roll, Farrow. It's going to take more than a couple hours."

"Why do you need me to laugh, anyway?"

Because I felt something inside my chest, and I am desperate to feel it again.

It marked the first time since Dad had passed. And possibly the last. But I wanted to try.

"Just do it."

"Can't fake it." She shrugged, leaning back. "Though I bet you're used to women faking things for you."

No, I am not. I never let them get close enough.

"I'm not funny. And neither are you, judging by your last joke."

"Make an effort." She tipped her chin up, maintaining eye contact. "You vowed to protect me. Said I was yours. Well, the path to a woman's heart goes through her mouth. You have to make me laugh."

It's not your heart I'm after, I wanted to remind her.

Too bad she wasn't Dallas Costa. *That* mouth didn't need any laughter. Just beignets.

We stood chest to chest now. Not touching, but close enough to do so if she tried. Which I wanted her to. Desperately.

My heart was beating out of my chest, *thump thump thump*, trying to rip away from my arteries. I delved into my brain, struggling to conjure amusing things. I didn't laugh much. Or at all, to be honest. Very few things pleased me. When I truly thought about it, Farrow topped the short list. Though I supposed making fun of her wouldn't make *her* laugh.

"This is ridiculous."

She tilted one shoulder up. "Not my fault you've never had to impress a girl in your life. Thirty-three is a good age to start."

She'd Googled me. I'd never given her my age. This realization spread something hot inside my chest.

"When Ollie went to Oxford, he was initiated into Pierse Gav via a circle-jerk. Everybody masturbated into a cup, and the newbies had to drink it. He asked for seconds."

Farrow gagged. "That's not funny. That's gross."

"It *is* funny on two aspects. One—that Ollie is so ostentatiously decadent. And two—that he actually holds two degrees."

He'd fucked off to England for his masters because he wanted to perform side research on European kinks for two years. In other words, he wanted more leeway to fuck around without the peskiness of pretending to hold onto a job. What little pity I was capable of, I reserved for Oliver von Bismarck's future spawns. His life's mission was to repopulate the world. One day, his children and grandchildren would wake up and realize their family tree was a wreath.

"If you have to explain the joke, it's not funny." She gave me a stern look as she copied my words. "*Next.*"

A ragged breath escaped me. No wonder comedians were always depressed. Humor exhausted me.

"I once ate a bag of oranges and suffered the consequences."

"Again, gross. *Not* funny."

I was becoming desperate, which both infuriated and thrilled me. Never in my life had I been desperate for anything.

"My aunt used to hide all her Birkins from her husband in the trunk of her G-Wagon. One time, she left the key in the ignition and someone stole the car. But they didn't know they stumbled onto a goldmine of designer bags worth over one mil, so they dumped the bags on the side of the road. The cops recovered the bags and returned them to her."

Farrow's mouth twitched, but she didn't laugh.

"Come on," I snarled. "You almost laughed."

"I also almost came when I had sex with Park Woo Bin on the roof of his dad's skyscraper at seventeen. But I didn't. *Almost* is the operative word here, Zach."

I didn't know who Park Woo Bin was.

I just knew he was a dead man walking.

"Laugh." The command escaped as a strangled whisper.

"*Make me,*" she rasped, pushing her chest out so it almost touched my partially exposed torso.

I had no choice. I had to take out the big guns. Drawing a breath, I pivoted to a drawer, pulled it open, and sifted through a few photo albums, yanking out the one I needed. I removed a photo from its slot and returned to Farrow. I dangled the photo by the tip as if it disgusted me (it did), handing it to her. She took care to grab it by the edge, remembering not to touch me.

"I've only lost a bet once." I fastened the final button on my shirt, clearing my throat. "Oliver and Romeo made me dress up in leather head to toe." *Pink* leather.

My eyes clung to her face.

"God, Zach." Her lips broke into the biggest smile I'd seen. "The pants are butt-less."

"A souvenir from Ollie's tertiary education. He returned from Europe convinced that pants are a conspiracy against buttholes everywhere."

Laughter spilled from her mouth. It hit me straight in the chest. Again. Like an adrenaline shot directly to the heart. I felt it *working*. Beating. Pumping blood. Thrashing against my sternum.

Fuck, it was addictive.

She was addictive.

Her laughter subsided, and she stared at me behind long lashes. "Happy?"

"As close as I can be," I admitted. "Point is..." I raised my hand, using my thumb to brush away a lock of hair from her eye. Hair was dead cells. Not flesh. Easier for me to handle. And yet, we both stopped breathing. Our gazes clashed. Held. Succumbed to an unrelenting trance. "You are mine now, Farrow. To protect, to corrupt, to ruin. I won't let anyone treat you badly. Least of all Brett."

A hard swallow traveled down her throat. "What do you want in return?"

Everything, I thought. *I want everything you have to give and beyond. Every inch of you. Every smile. Every laugh. Every breath. Every touch.*

For the first time in my life, I craved more than just existing.

I wanted to truly let myself *feel.*

I ignored her question. "You should move in here. Forget about staying at your house to protect the deed. Under my guard, you'll have it all. The home. The company. The keepsakes—other than the pendant. I'll make a nice coat for you out of Vera and your stepsisters' skin, if you wish."

Her breasts rose and fell, full and sensitive and begging to be touched. The peaks of her nipples dug through the cheap fabric of her uniform. "No, thank you."

"I'll buy the house off her if I must," I clarified.

"I get it, Zach. You throw money at problems, and they go away. I'm not one of them. Buying my affection won't work. You'll have to earn it."

I wanted to laugh. I'd earned so much in so little time in my life. Of all challenges, surely this was the one I was fully equipped to handle.

"I'm sorry." I brushed my thumb along her cheek, wiping away a drop of Brett's blood. Her eyes glittered as our skin touched. A shiver raced down my spine, an involuntary reaction, like cringing at the sound of a fork being dragged over a plate. "I truly am."

"For what?" She was barely breathing.

"For dragging you into my own personal hell." I kept my thumb on her cheek. "You are going to fix me, Farrow... So I can become someone else's."

Chapter Twenty-Six

Farrow

I wriggled out of Zach's touch, speed-walking out of his closet like my ass was on fire. I'd never been anything other than brave, but listening to my hotter than Hades boss tell me he planned to screw my brains out so he could overcome some mysterious trauma and be with someone else was well above my paygrade.

What the hell? I mean, seriously, *what in the actual hell?* The worst part was, my upper thighs were sticky, dripping with need for him. My face flushed, sweltering with desire. My skin tight and tingly and begging to be touched. *Empty.* I felt empty, more than anything else.

Bracing a hand along the corridor wall, I struggled to walk straight. My stomach had dropped when the pad of his finger met my cheek, and that empty, warm feeling nestled in my core, begging to be unknotted.

I needed a release. *Now.*

Dazed, I reached for the nearest door and shoved it open, stumbling inside. I pressed it shut, gluing my back to the cool wood and closing my eyes. I tried to regulate my breaths. The elegant tinge of Christian Dior candles and general cleanness prickled my nose.

Focus, Fae. My eyelids fluttered open. I examined my surroundings, realizing I'd entered Zach's art library. Unlike the ones in his office, pieces of art adorned every inch of the wall-to-wall, floor-to-ceiling maple shelves. Sculptures, paintings, ancient jewelry, and first editions.

Unfortunately, neither the Brancusi sculpture nor the first-edition *Alice in Wonderland* hardcover stopped my traitorous body from rioting. My disloyal clit throbbed, demanding to be touched, tugged, and massaged. I'd had enough.

You need to take care of this before you return to work.

I twisted the lock, jiggled it three times to double check, and shuffled to the far corner of the library, rushed by the slickness between my legs soaking my panties. Maybe I should've felt bad about desecrating Zach's antique library, but maybe *he* shouldn't have indirectly called my pussy his cure.

The shelves rattled behind me as I pushed my back against it, toppling a handwritten, limited-edition textbook from the Renaissance.

I scooted down to the carpet, pulse *whooshing* between my ears. "One last chance to stop this madness, Fae."

Too late.

My knees fell open of their own accord. Tiny sprinkles of blood peppered my thighs like freckles. I probably should've been more concerned about the mess I'd abandoned with the Bretts. There could even be police downstairs.

But I wasn't.

My pulse hummed inside my core as I reached between my legs and pushed aside my cotton panties, dipping my fingers inside myself. Normally, I went straight for the clit, but I'd never felt so empty in my entire life. Both fingers I slid inside met no resistance as they thrust into my soaking pussy.

God, my fingers alone wouldn't do. I shook my head. Desperate tears stained the corners of my eyes. I surveyed my surroundings, halting on a thick cigar holder. Scooting all the way to the desk, I grabbed it and crawled back into place, sticking it inside me as I began massaging my clit.

A shudder ripped through me. I felt filled, charged, eager to combust. It made no sense. The cigar holder was metal. Freezing to the touch. And still. *Still.* Maybe because it was *Zach's* cigar holder. In *Zach's* library. In *Zach's* mansion. But I could feel him all around me, hovering above me, whispering filthy things into my ear.

The ache between my legs intensified. I knew whatever happened here would never measure up to what I really wanted.

Zach. Pushing me against the Go board. Me splayed over it, the stones digging into my back, denting my sensitive skin as he trails his mouth down my body, his head disappearing between my thighs.

My fingers sped up against my clit. I shifted, bucking my ass up to angle the cigar holder until it hit my G-spot.

"Oh, God." My back arched like a rainbow. "*Yes.*"

I rode the cigar holder, my thighs straining, burning, desperate for more friction. Voices carried into the library from outside the door. Oliver laughing. Dallas hollering something. Romeo placating her. But I'd checked out, lost inside my own head. In another world.

Zach devouring my pussy until I come all over his tongue. Flipping me onto my belly after I'm spent, teasing his shaft along the slit of my ass before entering me from behind.

My breath caught, the pressure between my legs building. I whimpered, painting desperate circles around my clit. Pinching. Teasing. Flicking.

His name fell from my lips like a chant. "Zach, Zach, Zach."

It wasn't enough. I spread myself wider, pushing and pulling the cigar holder inside me while I worked the bundle of nerves between my legs with my other hand. The night breeze caressed my nipples, sailing in from the open window. They pebbled beneath the current. I pretended it was Zach's breath, tormenting me, demanding I submit to him.

"Make me come." My walls clenched around the thick cigar holder, desperate, begging for a release. "Please, Zach."

Please, please, please.

The voices outside the door grew louder. Merrier. It didn't matter. My muscles tightened, pulsing to the symphony inside me. Oliver stood right outside the door now, bellowing nonstop. Dallas' laughter rolled inside. Had they decided to take a spontaneous tour right when I thought it would be a good idea to get myself off? Just my luck.

And still, I didn't stop. Forever stubborn, I doubled down, forcing my entire fist inside my mouth to stifle a cry as I rode the cigar holder like a wave. I clamped my teeth around my knuckles, hips bucking back and forth. Pleasure flared through every fiber of my body like wildfire, each cell catching heat. I screamed Zach's name into my fist, the word coming out garbled and raw.

After I finished coming, I slumped against the shelves, panting, spent, and utterly boneless. I tried catching my breath as the voices drifting from the hallway grew louder.

"...the hell are they?" Dallas clucked her tongue. "That he sliced the bastard, I can understand. Relate to, even. But he needs to answer his lawyer's questions."

Footsteps echoed down the corridor. "The Bretts and Jasper just left." That came from Romeo, his voice flat. Almost bored. "Signed all the waivers and NDAs Zach's lawyer shoved down their throats. He's in the clear." A beat. "Speaking of NDAs…"

"I know, I know." Oliver sighed. "First rule of Fight Club. Do not covet thy best friend's banging hot wife."

"Oliver."

"I'm offended you'd think I'd narc."

"I'm offended you think I'm dumb enough to trust you after a bottle of Clase Azul."

"I'm offended that you're offended that…"

Their footsteps continued, clicking further from the library. Meanwhile, I remained frozen, legs still open, not daring to exhale. A gust of cold wind licked at my entrance. Finally, when the quiet persisted for a solid minute, I released the breath.

Get up, you reckless idiot. Clean yourself. Chuck that cigar holder out the window. Come to your freaking senses, Farrow Ballantine.

"Farrow."

It took me a moment to realize my name hadn't come from inside my head. Zach's husky voice bounced off the walls, sounding extra robotic this time. My eyes snapped open. They immediately darted to the corners of the ceiling. Sure enough, on the one diagonal, a camera hung from above. Pointed directly at me.

Oh my God.

He saw me masturbating in his house.

He saw my pussy wide open.

My fingers playing with it.

The cigar holder.

The cigar holder, the cigar holder, the cigar holder.

I wanted to combust right there and then.

But I refused to appear humiliated. I cleared my throat and smiled to the camera. "Yes?"

"Are you finished contaminating my library?" It came out matter-of-fact. Unfazed and unaffected. Suddenly, it drove me mad that he hadn't busted into the room as soon as he saw me spread my legs. Didn't throw me against the window and fuck me raw.

I slumped against the laden shelves, keeping my legs open. "Pretty much."

I knew he could still see everything. My swollen clit. My pink folds. The juices running down my thighs, onto his carpet. The residual blood from Brett's finger painting messy strokes on my thighs. But I refused to show him weakness.

"What about the room turned you on, exactly? Was it the Dostoevsky and Murakami hardcovers or the Degas paintings?"

I flicked a bang away from my forehead. "It was mainly the absence of you."

He chuckled on the other end of the intercom. A static noise that still managed to drip into my gut.

I dusted off my hands. "Are we done with the chitchat?" I wanted to stand up and clean myself. Then, obviously, slink under a rock and spend the rest of my life mortified by what happened.

"Almost." Silence. And then, "Suck your fingers."

I wanted to defy him. To deny him. But… I also wanted to do this for myself. My nipples had already pebbled again, my body springing to attention at his husky command.

I turned my head to grin at the camera. "Ask nicely."

He paused, considering it. "Kindly shove your fingers into your mouth and taste what my mere existence does to you."

"Cocky much?"

"Much. And all of it, root to tip, is about to fill your pussy, ass, and mouth. Soon."

A tremor of eagerness and euphoria rolled through me. I wanted that. I wanted that more than anything else in the world in this moment.

I circled my nipple with my wet finger. "Do you think you're capable of touching me?"

Another beat of silence. He answered, firm, "I *know* I can."

Slowly, I raised my fingers to my mouth and sucked, gaze still trained on the camera.

"Taste good?" It came out thick. Strained. Barely controlled.

"You have no idea."

I smirked, pulling my knees together and shimmying my ruined panties off. The dress tumbled down my legs when I rose to my feet. I crouched, collecting the panties and cigar holder, about to tuck them both into my uniform pocket.

"*Tsk, tsk.*" Something like a dark chuckle rumbled through the speakers. "No stealing, Little Octopus. This is your second strike. Shall I put up signs in each room to remind you of the rules?"

I scowled to the camera. "It's a cheap cigar holder."

I'd reached a new low. Standing in an empty room, talking to the boss I wanted to climb like a tree. And yet, somehow, it felt like a high.

"It's mine nonetheless."

"I'll buy you another."

"I'm afraid this one is utterly irreplaceable."

"You're just pulling at my leg at this point."

"Sweetheart, I want to do *so* much more if you'd just let me." He paused. Something like a hoarse chuckle tickled my ears.

I crossed my arms. "What now?"

"It's not a *cheap* cigar holder."

"How expensive can it be?"

"It's not about the price. It's about the history."

I resisted the urge to slink into the shadows, finally processing all the antiques this room held. "What?" I flipped my hair over one shoulder. "Did Winston Churchill own it?"

"Close. Thomas Jefferson. He held it in his other hand as he signed the *Declaration of Independence*."

Well, fuck. No way could I ever fix an oopsie that big. No point in trying. With more confidence than I expected, I sauntered to an empty display case, popped off the lid, and tucked the cigar holder inside, along with my panties.

I pivoted to the camera, arching a brow. "Happy?"

"Only after you're sprawled on top of my Go board, creaming on my cock. The invitation remains open."

"Are you hard?" I croaked.

"No," came his instant reply.

"You're a liar."

I strode to the door, wondering if he was. Maybe I wasn't his type. Maybe he just got off seeing me masturbate but didn't want to touch me. Maybe he always did this. Hired girls as the help and toyed with them. What did I know about this man? Only the dry facts delivered to me by Wikipedia.

His voice tickled the backs of my ears as I walked away.

"Maybe, but you can't handle my truth."

CHAPTER TWENTY-SEVEN

Zach

I didn't even bother kicking everyone out of the house. That would imply I had my shit together, which I most certainly did not. I simply locked myself in the master bedroom, launched into the shower, and turned the handle to the coldest temperature.

Didn't work.

I braced my hand over the tiles, fisting my engorged cock. It throbbed, pre-cum leaking from the crown. *Drip, drip, drip.* So hot and heavy that it turned purple.

Don't jerk off. Have a shred of self-control. You are breaking all your rules.

But I couldn't get the vision out of my head. Of her glistening pink pussy, so tight and pretty, like a half-bloomed rose, dripping for me. Waiting for me to take it.

Fuck.

I grabbed my cock by the root, squeezed it hard, and began moving my fist back and forth, gaining speed as the pressure in my balls intensified.

The way she dripped for me.

The way she arched her back.

The way she had *my* cigar holder in her pussy.

Heat swirled in my stomach, and I came within seconds. The fastest I'd ever come. Jetting further than I'd thought possible. Thick, hot cum painted my tiles. I imagined it on her ass, dipping a finger into the pool of it, smearing myself all over her cheeks. Writing my name on her smooth skin in pearly white.

I shut off the water, staggered backward, and pressed my head against the tiles, closing my eyes.

Everything was changing.

Including me.

Chapter Twenty-Eight

Ollie vB: Is it just me or did Zachary pull a Houdini after slicing Brett Junior's fingers off?

Romeo Costa: Not just you.

Ollie vB: @ZachSun, want my advice?

Zach Sun: Not keen on taking advice from a man who collects more DNA than the FBI.

Ollie vB: And the DEA, too. Why does everyone here keep downplaying my achievements?

Romeo Costa: You were saying…?

Ollie vB: Right. My advice.

Ollie vB: https://www.dicksdicksdicks.com/Condoms/Durex-Extended-Pleasure/Family-Pack

Ollie vB: Lidocaine condoms. So you don't bust your load in 0.2 seconds. Don't say I never had your back.

Chapter Twenty-Nine

Farrow

"You look happy."

The accusation rumbled past Andras' lips as we danced on the piste. I could practically *hear* him glower. His joints cracked like twigs beneath a boot. He was aggravating me, constantly beating at my sword, trying to push me into defensive mode. I refused to cower.

My eyes crinkled behind my mask. "You say that like it's a bad thing." I lunged forward, catching his shoulder.

"Very good, Fae. So, tell me, why are you happy?"

Maybe because I barely spent time at that godforsaken house anymore. The idea that it would rot and deteriorate—like the people inside it—no longer bothered me. Dad wouldn't want me to suffer to preserve a house on its last legs.

Or maybe because Zach never commented when I intruded into his domain. I'd taken a liking to napping in one of his guestrooms whenever I felt like it. Spending time in his territory—even when he wasn't there—made me feel safe. For the first time, I understood why people settled down. Put their faith in other humans and latched on tight. That sense of security did wonders to the body. Even my advances on the piste felt lighter.

Or maybe because the two-week mark was just around the corner, and that meant my first paycheck. I planned on cashing that in by asking Zach for the name of a good lawyer.

No point in keeping the good news all to myself.

I panted, twisting in place to avoid his attack. "I'm finally getting a lawyer to fight Vera."

"Posture. Extend." He corrected me, swatting my arm with his sword. While I adjusted, he pulled his mask up his forehead, even though we were mid-match. His face appeared before me, inked with confusion. "Where did you get the money?"

I straightened, sliding up from my lunge. "My new boss and I have… an arrangement."

"*Remek*. You have a new job." He yanked the mask completely off his head. "Who is the lucky boss?" He didn't smile, nor congratulate me.

Dread trickled into my gut. But I refused to let his lukewarm reaction get to me. He knew how desperately I wanted to contest the will. This man cared for me. Wanted me to fulfill my dreams. Helped me reach them, even when I could no longer pay him for his time.

"Zachary Sun."

Andras whistled low, giving me his back as he strode off the piste. "The billionaire with all the blind dates?"

I frowned. "Among other things."

"Wonder why he's willing to fund this little project of yours."

So, I guess we finished practicing for today?

I dumped my mask on the sidelines, unclipping my fencing suit from the wire I was attached to with more force than necessary. It snapped back into place.

Slinging my sword carrier over my shoulder, I jogged behind Andras. "Hey, what are you insinuating? I'm just his housekeeper."

Although, by now, I had a good idea why Zach had hired me. He'd said so out loud. He wanted me to cure him of his revulsion to humans. *If* we were to fall into bed, however, it would be completely consensual and have nothing to do with his wallet. It didn't hurt that, lately, I felt seen around him. Protected and adored under the intensity of his persistent gaze. Did I think the attention would last? Absolutely not. The man had spent his entire adult life laser-focused on hostile takeovers, jumping from company to company. He could pivot in a blink. So what?

Why shouldn't I get to experience hot sex with a handsome man? My life didn't have to revolve around practice and work. I didn't have a boyfriend. His mom still had his face plastered to the walls of every elite dating agency east of the Mississippi. Nothing would change for me except the occasional chance to unwind and earn karma points for performing a charitable act for someone who clearly needed it.

Andras punched the silver button, forcing the doors open. We treaded the country club's wide corridor, passing members in tennis and basketball gear. The golf course stretched from window to window like a green fitted sheet, pressed against artificial mounds and peppered by flags.

"I am not insinuating anything." He softened his voice. "I am just worried your head is not in the right place."

My shoulders slumped. I needed to stop assuming the worst about people. I'd forgotten his one-track mind. Andras wanted me to focus on my craft. It was all we ever spoke about.

He stopped in front of the men's lockers, turning to face me. "If you contest the will, you would put all your time, effort, and money into it, and you are already spreading yourself thin. You need to be focused." A frown deepened the wrinkles around his cheeks. "What is so hard about moving on?"

I twisted my fingers together, ping-ponging my weight from foot to foot. "It's not fair that she got half the company."

Andras rolled his eyes. "It is just a cleaning company. Open another one."

"It's not *just* a cleaning company. It's Dad's legacy. We made that name together. We chose the logo, the products, the services. We had plans, and they're gone." I tossed my hands up, heat creeping into my neck the more worked up I got. "And the keepsakes. She sold them all. I want them back."

Dad always said—*Memories are a second heart. After you're gone, they beat inside the people you've left behind.*

That woman sold Dad's second heart. I wanted it back.

"They are gone." Andras shook his head. "The jewelry. The art. They could be in Siberia for all we know. Even if you were to track them down, you would never be able to afford them."

He was right. And still, I couldn't let it go. I wanted to fight Vera with everything I had left in me, even if it wasn't much. Out of spite. Out of justice. Out of vengeance. *Out of pain.* Twenty-two years of abuse from the moment I'd landed on their steps as a newborn. Twenty-two years of fending off schemes to kick me out of the house. If I let those twenty-two years go unanswered, would I still be a human or a doormat?

That's my girl. Dad's voice came to me like a sudden storm. I wanted to weep at the sound of it. *Stand up for yourself. Even against those you love. If you find yourself alone, they never truly loved you back.*

"It's not his real will," I hissed through gritted teeth. "That's the main reason I want to contest it. She tainted his inheritance and robbed him of his last wishes."

He clutched his head like he thought it would explode. "What are you talking about?"

"She drafted this thing herself."

"How do you know?"

"Because I know my dad. That is not his will. I know it in my heart. In my *bones.*"

The will read at his will reading referred to his art collection as *miscellaneous items.* Items to be sold at auction with full profits handed over to Vera Ballantine. The painting Dad swore he'd never sell, even if the President himself got on his hands and knees to beg. The zany nose sculpture he'd insisted he'd start World War III over, since it reminded him of the one he'd passed down to me. And the pendant he promised he'd give me at my wedding after walking me down the aisle.

I didn't simply not believe the will. I *refused* to believe it, because if I did, it meant every promise Dad made me was a lie. And my father was *not* a liar.

"What does it matter?" Andras flung his arms in the air. "It's done. It's been almost two years. Focus on what you can change."

"I *can* change this." I balled my fists at my sides. "I don't have to lay down and take it."

"If you spend time with this Mr. Sun, laying down and taking it will become your main position, *te bolond,*" he snarled, unzipping his fencing suit.

Whoa. Hold up. Abort. Rewind. Pause the television. Andras had basically just called me a slut. For starters—a slut is just a woman who knows that she's allowed to do anything a man is. And secondly—I didn't need to take this.

I straightened, speaking as slow as possible, making sure my words absorbed into his skull. "What you just said isn't okay. At all."

"What I just said is the truth."

I'd never seen him so animated before. It wasn't jealousy. Andras never cared about anything but fencing. And even then, he prioritized me. Since I'd returned from Seoul, ruined and disgraced, he'd stitched together the pieces for me, doing so much behind the scenes that I knew I'd never understand the full scope of his efforts.

But he sucked with words, and some things were unacceptable to say.

I crossed my arms. "I'd like an apology."

It didn't matter that I considered Andras a second father. Or that his words probably came out of concern.

"Do you not hear the rumors?" He doubled down, gesturing in the direction of the throngs of wealthy members on the other side of the wall. "Zachary Sun and his friends only know how to take, use, and abuse. He is a playboy. He will never take you seriously. He can help you with something now, then stop when he tires of you."

He was right.

Zach said so himself. I was a Band-Aid. A cure. An antidote. Nothing more. Nothing less. A means to an end.

I tilted my chin up. "I'm a big girl."

"Ah, but you are still a *girl*." Andras tapped my nose, peering down at me. "Do yourself a favor and listen to a grown-up for once in your life. That thing with your stepmother should be buried right along with your late father. He would want you to get along with her, Fae. He would want you to start fresh. Choose peace, not war."

I wasn't the one who chose the war. I was dragged into it, kicking and screaming.

I shook my head. My next class with Zach started in ten minutes. I wondered if he'd even show up, everything considered.

"I need to go." I tightened the strap of my bag over my shoulder. "Thanks for the advice, but I'm going for it."

I twisted on my heel, marching to the women's locker room. As soon as I elbowed past the door, I collapsed onto a desolate bench and buried my face in my hands.

It's fine. You're fine. Zach Sun is your ticket to redemption, and you've never shied away from one-night stands. This isn't dirty. It isn't wrong. And this won't end with your heart splattered on the piste, a sabre speared through it.

That was the thing about growing up in an environment absent of human affection. I found it in any place I could—including, and especially, in one-night stands.

Growing up, Dad delivered scraps of love in titrated doses in hopes they'd go unnoticed by the other three Ballantine women. He did his best to keep the peace, hoping to raise all three of his daughters in harmony. And he did consider Tabby and Reggie his daughters, equal in value to me, even if they didn't share a drop of his blood. They just refused to see it.

And I? I had no problem warming my heart with cardio and the musky sheets of a man. In fact, I'd long suspected I had the exact opposite problem that Zach did. I craved the feel of another person's skin on mine. Took my pleasure in hookups and didn't look back. Relationships were high-stakes. Risky. Sex was simple. Instant gratification. And Zach was a god among men. I was at no risk of falling in love with the broody, patronizing billionaire sitting atop an ivory tower.

I produced my phone from my duffel bag, skimming through my best friend's texts.

Ari: I can't believe we won't celebrate your birthday together.
Farrow: Me, either. You're my favorite person in the whole world right now.
Farrow: (Not to sound like a stage-five clinger or anything.)
Ari: More than Keanu Reeves?
Farrow: Yes.
Ari: More than Taylor Swift?
Farrow: Yes.
Ari: More than Madonna?
Farrow: Hey, don't push it. She's the queen of pop.
Ari: Merp.
Farrow: Well, gotta go have a sword fight with the guy I'm masturbating to on the reg. Talk later.
Ari: Way to make me feel like a loser. The highlight of my day was getting my nails done.
Ari: P.S. When was the last time you got laid? Maybe trade in the sword for his, ya know, sword.

CHAPTER THIRTY

Farrow

He stood me up.

The telltale signs of disappointment looped around my ankles and tugged. It was stupid. I had no reason to be upset. After all, I'd get my paycheck for this training session either way. Now I had a rare ninety minutes of free time to do with as I pleased. And still, almost ten minutes had passed since the appointment time, yet I hovered by our piste, wrapped up in full fencing gear, my helmet clutched in my fist as I surveyed the gym.

Did I keep waiting?

Only if you're an idiot.

Hmm... debatable these days. With a huff, I plopped down on the piste, my elbows digging into my knees. Another ten minutes passed. Then fifteen. After twenty, I called it quits. He wasn't going to come.

Screw this.

I hopped up, swung my weapons carrier over my shoulder, and strode out the gym. Fencers around me battled in full force. The humming air conditioners and clinking swords assaulted my ears. Envy licked at my chest, something dark blooming within. *Anger*. He could have texted me. He *should* have texted me. I could be home. In bed. Perhaps sleeping a full four hours for the first time in two years. The more I thought about it, the angrier I got. How dare he? The last decent sleep I had was in the womb.

My feet slapped the tiles as I stomped into the locker room, traded my gear for a plain t-shirt and jeans, and bulldozed toward the exit. I marched by indoor basketball courts, Pilates studios, pickleball fields, and golf simulators. The more uber-rich assholes I passed that reminded me of Zach, the more the temperature spiked inside me. I could crack an egg in my veins right now and fry it in two seconds flat.

By the time the club's spa stretched before me, I'd added hunger to my list of reasons Zachary Sun had landed on my shit list.

Perhaps I'd begun hallucinating, because I swore that I saw Andras head inside. *Odd.* The man wouldn't recognize a Botox needle if it stabbed him in the eye. Frowning, I darted after him, diving to catch the door before it closed and planting a hand on his shoulder. "Hey, about our conversation…" The man turned, and I realized it wasn't Andras at all. "Sorry." I yanked back my hand. "Wrong person."

"Hey, Fae." Stacey, the receptionist, grinned at me from behind her station. "How're you doing?"

"Great." I smiled back. Lies tasted like nothing these days. "You?"

I crept toward the door without turning, too tired to carry on a conversation with someone I barely knew. The club employed us both, but I could count on one hand the number of times we'd spoken and still have fingers left over.

"Not bad. My boyfriend is taking me to Spain next month. I think he might pop the question." She twirled a curl around her finger, eyes sweeping over the ceiling as if the drywall had her Pinterest wedding board projected on it. "Oh. I forgot to ask… Are you sick or something? Need anything?"

Common sense, maybe, with the way I've been thinking about my asshole boss.

I frowned. "No, why?"

"No reason." She tucked her pen behind her ear. "It's just that I saw your student entering the sauna, so I figured you canceled your class."

"What do you mean you saw my student?" I scratched my temple. "He was here?"

"He *is* here." She cocked her head to the back of the spa. "In the sauna. If he hasn't evaporated by now." She giggled. "Been in there for forty minutes."

Son of a…

He'd made it to the venue but never went in? Why? I bit the corner of my cheek, cursing my foolishness. I'd forgotten rule number one in life: never expect anything from anyone. It only leads to disappointment.

"Excuse me." I ramped up my fake smile, already headed to the sauna. "I think I left something back there."

She frowned. "But you never went in—"

Her voice drifted into the distance with the speed I trotted past her. Latent anger drummed a beat against my veins. Something else intertwined with it. Excitement—at the prospect of seeing him in nothing but a towel.

Correction—at the prospect of *maiming* him in nothing but a towel.

Zach sat alone in the deserted sauna, head pressed against the shadowed wall, oblivious to the Peeping Tom before him. On my tiptoes, I peered inside through the small square window, pulse ratcheting at the sight of his carefree expression.

He rolled his neck, massaging away a knot in nothing but a white towel. His raven hair dripped sweat across his face. He looked like a bronze god, his biceps and abs bulging and glistening. The dull ache between my legs intensified, and that was when I realized it had always been there. That it had never really left since I got myself off in his library.

My backpack hit the floor with a soft thud. I pushed the door open and strolled in, still clothed.

Zach's eyes remained firmly shut, but somehow, he still said, "How did you find me?"

"Followed the stench of wealth."

"Is this the part where I'm supposed to get offended?"

"This is the part where you tell me why you stood me up."

Steam slowly seeped into me, marinating with the rage boiling in my veins. The humidity glued my hair to the nape of my neck, dampening my clothes until they clung to my body. If he opened his eyes, he'd get a front-row view of my nipples saluting him through the white fabric.

He didn't.

Zach adjusted the rolled towel behind his neck, eyes still closed. "Didn't feel like seeing your face."

"Are you serious right now?"

"I think we've established I'm not one to joke around."

Stepping forward, I shook my head. "You can't just stand me up."

"I can." His eyes snapped open, his mood shifting from nonchalant to attentive in 0.2 seconds. "Case in point—I did."

"If you'd have told me, I could've slept in."

"You couldn't have, though. You had training with Andras."

"I could've shifted things around."

"Negatory again. You have work to do, Cinderella."

"But I—"

He cut me off. "Did you know that the female octopus does not eat or clean herself after giving birth? She dies soon after she tends to her eggs. Males, too, become senescent and expire a few weeks after mating."

What?

"That's depressing." *And bizarre.* "Thanks for the not-so-fun fact. Anyway, back to the topic—"

"The female octopus can lay as many as four hundred thousand eggs. And she spends her life protecting them, night and day, shielding them with her body before perishing once they hatch."

"Are you vying for a National Geographic career?" Salty sweat leaked into my mouth. The wet air drenched my whole body from head to toe. This no longer felt like the glamorous confrontation I'd expected it to be. "What does any of this have to do with anything?"

"You seem fiercely loyal." He hitched a shoulder up. "I once knew a man like that."

I refused to let him butter me up. Especially since this marked the first time we'd spoken to each other since he saw me masturbating.

I shook my head. "I'm so angry with you."

"Don't be."

"Why?"

His nostrils flared. "Because."

"That's not an answer, Zach."

"Because…" He slapped the side of the bench, breathing fire. "The only reason I didn't show up was because you're a temptation." The heavy pants ripping out of his chest made his pecs move up and down. He was gloriously gorgeous. Lickable from head to toe. And we were all alone. His confession filled me with satisfaction.

"You find me attractive?" I asked, even though I felt about as desirable as a soiled napkin while sweating my body weight through my clothes.

He flicked lint off the towel secured around his waist. "You know I do."

"You sure have a funny way of showing it."

His lips pursed. "It's… hard."

"Hmm." I tapped my pout with my finger. "That's how it's usually supposed to be, sweetie. Unless you need Viagra."

"I'm not talking about *it*." His eyes slid down to the towel. *It* was growing beneath it, the ridge of his thick, long cock pressing against the pristine white fabric. "I'm talking about all of it. Touching. Letting go. Changing. It's one thing to try and succeed. But if I fail…" He swore, rubbing his jaw. "If I fail, it's a nail in the coffin. The final confirmation I need to fully accept that I can never have any trace of something human to enjoy."

"Zach—" My voice cracked.

"I live the life of an immortal. Nothing means anything to me, Farrow. Not living. Not dying. Not eating. Not drinking. Not laughing. I have no range of emotions for the simple reason that I possess no such thing. You are the only person I have ever come across that I want to touch. So, if this doesn't work—"

"It *will* work," I cut him off, heart pumping so fast, my chest could cave at any second. I wanted to help him. Not only because the tingling between my legs had become unbearable every time we were in the same room, but because I wanted the man who protected me to *live*. To experience normalcy. Pleasure. *Orgasms*. I pulled my shoulders back, staring him right in the eyes. "I will make sure it works."

He wet his lips, obvious wariness lurking within his pupils… but also laced with something else. *Curiosity?* Suddenly, the walls of the tiny, scorching room felt like they were inching together, closing in on us. I decided to take action. With one smooth move, I grabbed the hem of my shirt and yanked it off, dumping it on the wooden planks.

Zach didn't respond, save for the bob in his throat that told me he was paying close attention. My heart galloped in my chest. A drop of sweat rolled between my breasts and beneath my bra, journeying down to my belly button and disappearing inside it. He watched its descent with hungry eyes. I took a step toward him, releasing my hair from the clip holding it together.

Zach tilted his head up and watched in fascination.

"Tell me something interesting about yourself." I unbuttoned the first button of my jeans, stripping for him. "Distract yourself while you let your body react to this."

"I…" he started, then stopped.

I loosened another button on my jeans. Then another.

"You what?"

Was that throaty voice even mine? I didn't recognize it. I pulled my jeans down in one go and kicked them to the side. They tangled with my shirt. I was sure my white cotton panties were see-through with how wet they were.

Zach wore vulnerability like a bespoke suit, somehow complementing his high cheekbones and sharp jaw. "I'm a virgin," he admitted, his eyes searching mine. For mockery. For confusion. For pity.

He found none of those things. Because the truth was… all I felt was pain for him. Pain and a pang of possessiveness that rattled me. I had no right to feel it. I'd told myself I wouldn't get attached. But I couldn't help it. He looked like a boy in that moment, not one of the richest, most attractive men on the planet.

I am going to take his virginity.

I am going to have something no one else has ever had—Zachary Sun.

I inched toward him, unclipping my bra behind my back with one hand. "That's not something you should be ashamed of."

He released a bitter chuckle. "I'm a thirty-three-year-old virgin."

"You're a man with a traumatic past that makes it hard to touch or feel," I countered, guessing but also certain. He never spoke of it in interviews, but I'd run across articles describing his father's gruesome death—and the condition firefighters had found Zach in. If that had been me, I'd be inconsolable. Forever changed. Forever damaged.

I let my bra slide off my arms. My tits swelled, full and ready to be touched. His eyes trained on the way my nipples stood on end like two diamonds. He watched transfixed as I treaded his way.

"That thing with Eileen…" He cleared his throat. "It isn't real. It's an arrangement."

"I know."

And I still hate it, even though I have no right to.

I reached him and straddled his waist, everything bare but my panties. My knees sank to the bench on either side of him, hovering above without touching him. I propped a hand against the wall to keep my balance.

He tilted his head up, observing me through hooded, lust-drunk eyes. "How do you know?"

"Because I saw the way you look at her."

"And how did I look at her?"

"Like she's a 600-page merger guideline you need to sign."

A chuckle escaped him. It moved his neck and chest an inch closer to me. My pussy leaked in response. I felt empty. So empty.

"Bylaws aren't usually signed."

I rolled my eyes. "You know what I mean."

"I do. I like your sense of humor. If I ever develop one, it would look something like yours."

This was the oddest, most heartwarming compliment I'd ever received.

"Anyway…" I frowned, longing to touch him. "You shouldn't marry her if you don't like her."

"Liking someone has nothing to do with marrying them," he countered, his eyes dropping to my tits. His hands twitched by his sides. I knew he wanted to touch them. But I also knew that he wouldn't. He wasn't ready. Not yet. He licked his lips. "In fact, the less I like her, the better our marriage is going to be. Catching feelings is a terrible weakness. Look at what it did to Romeo."

I shook my head. "Oh, Zach."

"What?"

"What it did to Romeo is a wonderful thing—it made him happy."

I wanted to touch his face, his hair, his muscular arms, but I stopped myself. Instead, we stared at each other, breathing the same hot, humid air. Getting used to the proximity. I knew someone could walk into the sauna any minute now. That I could be banished altogether from this country club and the fencing team. And still, I didn't care.

"Farrow," he growled, finally, eyes gliding down to the triangle between my thighs. To my wet panties.

"Yes?"

"I want to see your pussy dripping for me again."

"Take them off of me, then."

His nostrils flared, and he concentrated, frowning at my panties like they had personally attacked him. I stifled a giggle.

"I might touch you if I do," he said after a beat.

"I would love that, Zach."

He reached for them, and this was my chance.

I curled my spine, withdrawing from him slightly. "On one condition."

He looked up, alert, hair dripping, face perfect. "Yes?"

"You fulfill your part of the bargain. You hire me a private investigator and a team of lawyers."

"Done."

I gave him a small nod, even though I regretted the timing of the reminder. It made this a transaction, which it wasn't. I wanted him with or without the lawyers. I just also wanted to erect a barrier. To remind myself the ugly truth. *Zachary Sun will never be mine.* I didn't know what was more tragic. That I wanted him. Or that I knew it would never happen.

He licked his lips and cracked his knuckles, like he was preparing for a fight. My emotions veered between wanting to kiss him better— his scars, his fears, his inhibitions—and amusement at how seriously he took all this.

Zach brushed his fingertips along the elastic of my panties, careful to avoid my flesh. "Seeing you touch yourself yesterday made me almost bust my load right there in my office."

"Why didn't you, then?" I bowed my back, enjoying the feel of his fingers through my panties. It felt forbidden and clandestine. Like a dirty secret only he and I shared.

His jaw clenched, his trembling hand sliding down my panties. "I didn't want to admit that I was affected by you." For a novice, he'd mastered the art of teasing, pressing his palm against me until it covered my entire pussy through my underwear. And still, his fingertips didn't brush my skin. "Fuck, you're soaking wet." He dropped his head back and hissed. "I want to nail you through the wood until you become a permanent fixture in it."

Whoa. Okay. Somebody needed to put dirty talk very slowly and very carefully on the floor and kick it toward me. But now wasn't the time to discourage him. He'd made huge progress. This was the same man who'd given himself *burns* after shaking a woman's hand.

"I need you to fuck me so bad." The confession stumbled out of my mouth. I realized that I meant it. There was nothing I wanted more than to be full of Zachary Sun's cock. His hand alone through my panties almost made me come, the pressure too delicious, too intense to ignore.

With a ragged breath, Zach curled his fingers, digging into my ass through the cotton, somewhat painfully. He pressed his other thumb to my clit. A ripple of pleasure rocked through my body, rattling my knees. My thighs burned, struggling to keep myself hovered above him.

"Is this okay?" He was breathless.

I peered down at his hand, noticing that he was rock hard between us. Completely erect, the heavy crown of his cock peeking through the slit of the towel. A drop of pre-cum glistened at the tip. I wanted to lean down and scoop it in my mouth.

"It's perfect." My nipples were so sensitive, I couldn't help myself. I grabbed one of my tits and began massaging it, tugging at the sensitive bud. "Keep going."

He dug his thumb harder into my clit, and I almost combusted right there and then, a rush of liquid heat rolling from my lower belly to my core.

I let out a cry. "Massage it, please. But… gently. In circles."

I wanted him to do to me exactly what I'd done to myself to ease the need I'd felt the other day.

He rolled his tongue along his lower lip, thumb slowly massaging my clit, teasing it with confidence. My skin burst into goosebumps, the pleasure absurdly intense. I began riding his finger, closing my eyes, slapping my own tit, pretending his finger was the tip of his cock. I'd lost it. I'd officially lost control.

"I want to touch your skin." Desperate need thickened his voice.

I opened my eyes to look between his legs. His dick was so engorged, it was purple. It had to hurt.

"Do it."

"I… I can't." His voice was pleading.

"Just distract yourself. Tell me something else."

Something that isn't about Eileen, preferably.

I knew they were just for show. That theirs would be a marriage of convenience. But I still didn't like to think of him with another woman.

The pressure between my legs intensified. My head swam, thoughts swirling in one direction like a cyclone. I was on the brink of the most intense orgasm I'd ever had, and he hadn't even touched my skin yet.

"I have not set foot in a normal civilian vehicle since... since what happened to me." His throat bobbed with a swallow, his fingertips gliding toward the junction between my ass and my thighs—to my bare flesh. "I only drive army-grade, military-protected vehicles."

What happened to you? Who did this to you? I wanted to scream, but I knew I had to keep the conversation going. To keep him distracted.

"Do you want to change that?"

A single fingertip touched my skin. It lit a fire on that spot, shooting a fuzzy buzz through my entire body. His other hand still pressed against my pussy through my panties, thumb flicking my clit.

"I don't know. Yes. No. Maybe." His pinky fully rested on my skin now. "I want to experience what being normal is like. I want to be..." He paused, peering up at me with white-hot lust in his eyes. "Human."

You are *human.*

I wanted to scream it at him. I wanted to tattoo it on his chest, right over his heart, to remind him he had blood, flesh, and bones. Just like the rest of us.

Good job, Fae. So much for keeping an emotional distance.

What did I care if Zachary Sun felt human in that dark, soulless chest of his? I was treading in dangerous waters, pretending not to see the tsunami rushing toward me.

I cleared away the errant thoughts, focusing on his pinky against my thigh. "How does it feel?"

He knew exactly what I meant. My skin.

"It feels... not awful. Foreign. Like experiencing a new texture for the first time."

"Your dirty-talk game is strong."

One corner of his lips tipped up. They were beautiful. Hand-drawn and pink. I wondered if I would ever get to kiss them. How it'd feel against my own. I wanted it, but we'd never agreed to kissing. Only sex.

He stared between us, where his finger touched me. "What do you want me to do now?"

"I feel... empty," I admitted.

His thumb on my clit stopped, and I thought I'd topple over and burst into flames. I clawed at the walls, fighting the throb between my legs. We dripped sweat over one another, exchanging breaths like they were kisses.

Then, he did the most glorious, sexy, maddening thing he could do.

He released his cock from the towel, grabbed it at the base, and guided it to my pussy, pressing it against my panties. His eyes fluttered shut. Mine did, too, the mounting pressure from his tip alone tensing my entire body. I clench around nothing, on the brink of a release, needing to be filled.

"You d-don't have to do this if you don't want to." I could barely tear the words out of my mouth.

"Farrow," he hissed, letting his head rest against the wall, his chin tipped up. His hand moved his dick up and down my slit in slow, deliberate movements. "The fucking world coming to an end couldn't stop me from making you come."

His words undid me. With a savage moan, I began riding the tip of his cock through my panties, moving my body to the rhythm of our pants. Heavy footsteps and laughter trickled into the sauna. We were too far gone to care.

Zach's hand clasped my ass now, half of it covering my skin. He tucked his pinky into my panties, teasing my tight hole.

He rolled his head back and forth against the wall, eyes shutting. "Fuck, I'm going to come."

I wanted more, but I knew he couldn't handle it. That we'd reached the edge of his capacity. The door behind me shot open. Someone padded into the sauna, slicing through the steam. My heart jolted in my chest. We had company. *Where I worked.* I swiveled my head to see who'd come in.

Zach grabbed my chin and steered it back to face him. "Eyes on me, Little Octopus. He doesn't matter."

He. There was a man there. *Jesus.*

And yet, the feeling was too good, the orgasm too close. We were both dripping wet, hot and heavy, slow-fucking through my panties. His tip teased my ass, my slit, my clit. *Everywhere.*

I trained my eyes on Zach. "Is he gone now?"

Zach shook his head, his face completely tranquil, studying me.

"No. He sat on the opposite bench. He's watching us."

My mouth dropped open. I moved to climb off of him, but Zach's hand snuck from my ass to my lower back, fingers splayed over it with force. He sank me a few inches onto his cock, stretching the fabric of my panties so thin, I could feel him throb inside me. Touching, but not touching.

I wanted to explode from pleasure.

What is wrong with you, Fae?

Too much to count. Shame, embarrassment, and desire pirouetted over my skin. I couldn't believe I was letting him dry-fuck me while someone watched. At least I now knew I hadn't done this for the money or the help. I would have slept with Zachary Sun either way.

"Zach," I choked out, wishing I could put my hands on his shoulders, to embrace him, to kiss him, to feel more of him. "I'm not going to be able to take all of you in when it's time."

"You will. You'll take every inch like a good girl."

The intruder shuffled behind me. Zach looked strained, barely in control, one hand sliding as much of his cock in and out of me as my panties would let him, the other holding me steady by my lower back.

His grip on me tightened, possessive. "He's masturbating now."

I didn't know this man.

I didn't even know what he looked like.

But I was undeniably turned on by the thought of someone stroking himself to the sight of us.

"I want to watch you as you come all over my fucking cock, Farrow," Zach growled into my face, close now—too close.

My heart picked up speed. I clamped over the tip of his cock, threw my head back, and came. Shattered. Soaked my thighs with a gush of wetness. My head fell back, eyelids fluttering open. I spotted the man on the bench opposite to ours.

He was young-ish. Unfamiliar and utterly sexy. His towel splayed open all the way, his long cock thick beneath his fist. He pumped his dick hard, increasing his pace, close to the finish line, too.

My body tightened like a bowstring. I was coming, and coming, and *coming*. Toes curled, muscles shaking, mouth dry, stars dancing all over my vision.

"*Farrow*," Zach hissed.

I couldn't stop looking at the stranger behind me. We made eye contact. I felt like he was fucking me, too.

Zach gripped my jaw—touching so much of my bare skin—and steered it back to face him. "Look at me right now before I stab this bastard right in the heart."

"You can't go around killing everyone who looks at me."

"I'm afraid I can and fucking will. Don't try me."

I believed him wholeheartedly. He'd sliced a man for less. For *almost* pinching my ass. This man was fantasizing about fucking me while I was in Zach's arms.

I stared straight into Zach's eyes, the waves of pleasure from the orgasm crashing against my skin.

"What do you care?" I taunted him with a smile, still riding his swollen crown, mixing my cum with his pre-cum. "I can do whatever I want—with whomever I want. You're going to have a fiancée in half a second. We're not exclusive. We're not even in a relationship."

His lips thinned. "The marriage won't be real."

"The ring will be and so will the paperwork." I warned, "I'm not going to sleep with a married man."

"It wouldn't be cheating. We're both free to take lovers as we please." His abs contracted as he tried to keep himself from coming. "And I'll be cured long before I put a ring on, so don't worry. Neither of you are endgame. Not her, and not you."

His words stung, but before I had a chance to let the insult fully sink in, he squeezed his cock, wincing as though he was in pain. He pulled out of my soaked underwear and came, firing thick strings of hot cum all over my stomach. We watched in fascination as he marked me, jet after jet.

Our eyes met after a few seconds.

"You touched me," I croaked.

His eyes looked angry, his mouth curled in a snarl. For a moment, I thought he'd lash out at me. That he'd run out and give himself third-degree burns washing my presence away from him. I shook with anticipation and dread.

But instead, Zach grabbed me by the waist—fingers shaking, touching my skin—and brought me up to my feet with him. Without a word, he collected the tattered clothes I'd discarded on the floor—now completely wet—and tossed the balled fabric into my arms without touching me. I stood frozen, my back still to our intruder.

"Put your bra and pants on, Octi."

I did as I was told, though I had no idea why. It defied my nature to be obedient. Maybe I really did fear that he'd put a knife between that dude's brows. I pushed my jeans up my legs with a struggle, then did my bra.

Zach twirled my hair around his fist, using it as a rope to turn me before I had a chance to toss my shirt over my head. We walked toward our intruder together, him guiding me with the makeshift leash. His sticky white cum slid down my stomach and into my jeans. Shamefully, my clit tingled again, just from the thought of it leaking into my pussy.

We stopped a couple feet from the stranger. I dragged my eyes up to meet his gaze. He looked spent, flushed and sweaty, his cock now concealed by his towel. He stared at Zach with parted lips, not expecting the man to confront him.

"See this?" Zach gestured to his cum on my stomach. "Answer me, before I put a knife in your eye."

"He will," I informed the guy breathlessly, shaking from horror and... *yes*, from thrill, too.

"Y-yes," the stranger finally coughed out. "I-I see it."

"This is *my* cum. On her." He tightened his hold on my hair, tugging deliciously. "She's mine. Understood?"

"I'm not his." My spine straightened, turning ramrod straight. I stared the man dead in the eye. "If I want to fuck you—if I want to fuck *anyone* else—I will."

It was one thing to help Zach overcome his issues. It was one thing to have *him* help overcome mine. But I refused to be his toy. His plaything.

"Okay, easy there, please." The dudebro raised his hands, his eyes ping-ponging between us, brows smashed together. "I just wanted to get into the sauna before work. I... I... you didn't stop when I entered, so I thought it was okay to watch. Next time, I'll ask."

"Next time you stare at what's mine," Zach bent forward, whispering in his ear, "your pride won't be the only thing you lose."

CHAPTER THIRTY-ONE

Ollie vB: I'm going to kill Zach.

Ollie vB: @ZachSun, I got kicked out of the country club because of you.

Romeo Costa: I thought you got kicked out because you slept with the president's wife?

Ollie vB: They got divorced and moved to Hawaii and New York, respectively, since the affair. I've been reinstated. Until Dickbag McExhibitionistson over here decided to show his willy to strangers.

Romeo Costa: You're going to have to elaborate.

Romeo Costa: [Michael Jackson Smiling and Eating Popcorn GIF]

Ollie vB: Apparently, our boy decided to screw someone in the sauna. McGrew's son walked in. Watched the whole thing. He narc'd that it was one of us three. They naturally pointed the finger at me.

Zach Sun: How do you know it's not Romeo?

Ollie vB: The woman he fucked wasn't heavily pregnant and hugging a bucket of KFC.

Zach Sun: Maybe Romeo decided to sample a disposable mistress.

Romeo Costa: @ZachSun, please, don't make me help him kill you. I have enough on my fucking conscience.

Zach Sun: I'll get you your membership back.

Ollie vB: You better. The women's tennis team is about to accept 20 new members. This was going to be my pet project for the year.

Romeo Costa: Jesus.

Ollie vB: ...died for my sins, so I might as well make them worth his while, right?

Romeo Costa: What happened to senior bingo night?

Zach Sun: Don't tell me...

Ollie vB: Gloria and I spent a lovely weekend together before she retired to Florida.

Ollie vB: The woman invented Kegels. King Arthur wouldn't be able to pull me out of her.

Zach Sun left the chat.

Ollie vB added Zach Sun to the chat.

Zach Sun: There are prisons easier to escape than this group chat.

Ollie vB: Anyway, who is the unlucky woman?

Romeo Costa: Probably a thrice Nobel Prized STEM nerd.

Ollie vB: You're off. My chips are on the new maid.

Romeo Costa: The one who annihilated him at Go?

Zach Sun: For the last time, she did not annihilate me at Go. We're still playing.

Ollie vB: And a very fun game at that. Why wasn't I invited?

Zach Sun: You don't play Go.

Ollie vB: TO THE SAUNA GAME.

Zach Sun: Because I prefer my intercourse without a side of syphilis?

Romeo Costa: Is this an official confirmation that you hooked up with her? [Smiling Face with Tear Emoji]

Ollie vB: That's the first time I've actually gotten concrete evidence that Zach's not a virgin.

Romeo Costa: Shut up, Ol.

Ollie vB: And here I thought he was about to be engaged to that doctor chick.

Zach Sun: I will be. Soon.

Romeo Costa: Are you for real?

Ollie vB: From having NO love life to becoming the Bella to Cinderella and Dr. Ulick's Edward and Jacob. Bravo, @ZachSun. Bravo.

Zach Sun: Dr. Ulick?

Romeo Costa: Eileen Ulick. [Unamused Face Emoji]

Ollie vB: [Tongue Emoji]

Ollie vB: Love triangle is my favorite trope, btw.

Romeo Costa: You don't read.

Ollie vB: What does reading have to do with anything? I'm talking about porn.

Ollie vB: Just Google two nurses one cop. Thank me later. But make sure you do it through your iPhone to avoid viruses.

Romeo Costa: For the millionth time, iPhones are not immune to viruses.

Ollie vB: Aww, shucks. That explains that $2M charge to Anita Hanjaab.

Zach Sun: There's no love involved with either of them.

Ollie vB: Keep telling yourself that while you break every single rule you've ever had for Cinderella.

Chapter Thirty-Two

Zach

The first sign that I needed to pause the brakes on the trainwreck that was my situationship with Farrow Ballantine came from Natalie, of all people.

She cornered me in the conservatory, where I sat with six laptops open, trying and failing to track multiple markets on the tiny 12-inch screens. "Did something happen to your office?"

Yeah. Farrow's in it.

I wasn't avoiding her. On the contrary, *she'd* spent the past three days since the sauna incident dodging me every time I rounded a corner. Occasionally, she'd dip into my office and revisit our Go game, moving a stone here or there, but only when I wasn't inside. Which, pathetically, forced me to set up camp in the opposite wing of the manor.

I didn't look up from the screens. "Is there a reason you're here?"

"Just concerned."

You and me both.

Since when did I rearrange my life to suit the needs of another person that wasn't blood related to me? Better yet, since when did Farrow Ballantine become someone whose thoughts, actions, and emotions I considered at all?

I shot up from the chair, startling Natalie when it pelted across the room. Her jaw almost dislodged itself after I began pacing the floor-to-ceiling windows. Back and forth. Back and forth. I was going to erupt.

Three days. Three fucking days.

Three days since Farrow confronted me in the sauna, forcing me to question my own sanity. Three days since I felt her cum drip on my fingers and kneaded her ass—her *flesh*—without coiling or vomiting. Three days since the tight walls of her wet pussy caged the tip of my cock inside them, squeezing it for dear life.

What would fucking her bareback feel like? That very question consumed my days and devoured my nights. I was a man obsessed, and I couldn't focus on anything other than relishing the feel of her. Suddenly, I couldn't remember why or when I found human skin appalling. I wanted hers on mine twenty-four seven.

Which brought me to my next problem. Farrow showed no signs of warming up the cold shoulder she'd given me since that day. I craved any sign of life from her. Any proof that she wanted my touch as much as I wanted hers. And so, I found myself taking lengthy trips in my orchid garden, meditating four times a day instead of three, and roaming the hallways of my mansion like a haunted ghost, hunting for signs of her.

She was everywhere, and yet, nowhere at all. In the random appetizer on my lunch tray that hadn't changed for seventeen years. In the extra sheet on my bed beneath the comforter when the temperatures dropped with the season change. And in my office surveillance feeds, which I checked to make sure that she'd actually come to make her Go move.

Astonishingly, she completed her job to my satisfaction. I'd gone through every maid in the DMV to the point where I dumped ludicrous investments into robotic cleaning equipment in hopes I never had to deal with human incompetence again. But under Farrow's care, the manor never looked better.

The problem? She moved things around—yet again, forcing change on me. She put flowers in vases. Shifted furniture from one place to another. Drew back all the curtains to let natural light flood in. I should've found it silly that she took pride in making my house a home. That she grinned to herself when she rearranged a fruit bowl on one of my kitchen islands or tilted a painting to the perfect angle.

She seemed completely content avoiding me, while I was on the verge of clawing my own skin off. Why weren't we talking? Teasing each other? *Touching* each other? I was like a baby who had just figured out how to walk. I wanted to do it all the time. Touch her hair. Her cheeks. Her tits. Her pussy.

On the fourth day of our radio silence, I finally cornered her. She was in my garden, of all places, eviscerating a white rose bush to fill my six-figure art vases. I figured she wouldn't take it well if I told her those roses shouldn't be placed in urns that were essentially historical treasures, some over 600 years old. The exposure to moisture alone would eviscerate their value.

The simple black-and-white maid dress clung to her curves, highlighting every arch and bend. Her hair, like molten gold, framed her shoulders and face. She wore earbuds in her ears, bobbing her head back and forth as she took scissors to my well-tended flowers. She didn't hear me coming, even when I stood about a foot away from her. Her scent drifted to my nose. She smelled of summer and sin; of the sun kissing a flower in bloom.

Since she wore clothes, I didn't think twice before tapping her shoulder to grab her attention.

She jumped a little, staggering from the bushes, and plucked her earbuds out of her ears. "Jesus, Zach. You scared me."

Right back at you. I am fucking terrified of you, Octi.

Instead of saying this, I knotted my fingers behind my back and pinned her with a dissatisfied glare. "May I ask you a question?"

"No."

"I'll ask one anyway. Why am I getting the silent treatment?"

"What silent treatment?" She dumped a pile of roses into a bucket, wiping her hands over her apron. "You have used every opportunity to tell me I'm the help. Why would I seek you out and strike a conversation?"

She was downplaying what we were, and it pissed me off. I had to take a deep breath and count to ten backwards. I never got angry. What the hell was happening?

"You and I struck a deal," I drawled, towering over her, using every ounce of my self-control not to lash out at her. I'd always pitied my colleagues and friends who succumbed to emotions at the most trivial inconvenience. "And right now, you are not fulfilling your part of the bargain."

"And you are?" She turned back to the bushes, grabbing the shears from the muddy ground and attacking the roses in full force. This wasn't cutting. This was decapitating. "I began fulfilling my end of the bargain, yet here I am, three weeks in, and I have no lawyer, no private investigator, and no lead to start fighting Vera with."

So, *this* was why she was angry and ignoring me? Because she thought I'd forgotten about my promise to her?

My jaw tensed. I had to massage it to stop myself from barking at her. "Arrangements have been made."

They were not, in fact, made. I'd planned to prolong the inevitable as much as I could.

"Uh-huh. Sure. Super secret arrangements that nobody's ever heard about." More rose-cutting. She was relentless. At this rate, she'd leave my garden completely bare. She had no idea what she was doing. "How very convenient that you kept it all under wraps."

"I'm working on it." My lips barely moved when I spoke.

Behind us, the balcony doors clicked open. Mom and Celeste Ayi, no doubt. We had lunch together every Friday. Only, this Friday, I'd forgotten on account of the fact that I'd just discovered pussy and wanted my next meal.

"I don't believ—"

I grabbed Farrow by the arms, past caring what Mom and Ayi might think, and turned her to face me. "I'm afraid you are going to have to believe me. You have no choice. We've entered a business agreement. That makes us partners right now. When I said I made arrangements, I meant it. We have a meeting with my team of lawyers and a private investigator today at four. I was waiting for the stock market to close before the meeting."

She blinked fast, her face jumping from emotion to emotion, starting with confusion and ending with hope. And then she did something completely terrible.

She smiled.

She smiled, and I felt it everywhere in my body.

"You did that?"

"Yes," I grumbled. "I told you I would. You should probably change into your normal clothes for the meeting." I did a quick once-over, angry that she'd made me explain myself. I'd never been in this situation before.

She nodded, fingering the velvety petals of a rose in her bucket. "I will." Pause. I wondered if she knew my mother was watching. Probably not. She seemed deep in thought. Farrow raised her gaze to meet mine. "Do I need to pay anything? A retainer? A…"

"I'll take care of everything." I shook my head. "You just have to show up and give us a rundown of what's happening."

She nodded. I felt desperate for something. I didn't know what. My fists balled at my sides.

Turn around, Zach. Walk away.

Instead, I just stared at her, hostility radiating off me in waves. Waiting for... What? A thank you? I didn't want her to thank me. Thanking someone was formal in Chinese culture. It signified distance between two people, and I wanted her close.

"Well?" She licked her lips, scanning my face, seeming unsure herself. "Do you need something else?"

Your attention. Your impossible words. Your sweet pussy. Especially your sweet pussy.

"For you to stop murdering my roses," I blurted out instead, prying the sheers from her fingers. "You have no idea what you're doing."

She laughed a little. "I finished cleaning the entire place and got bored. Humor me."

I said nothing. I was, in fact, humoring her. Letting her get away with things I never would anyone else.

"Zach..." Farrow frowned. "Do you want me to touch you?"

Yes. No. Jesus, I have no fucking clue.

I felt like I was regressing—Benjamin-Buttoning myself back to high school, where I didn't know how to think, feel, or act around girls.

I tossed the shears into a bucket of fresh roses she'd slaughtered. "You can touch me, I suppose." Though the kind of touching I had in mind wasn't something I necessarily wanted my immediate family to witness.

Her lips twitched, not quite a smile. "Try again."

My nostrils flared. "Please, touch me."

She raised a brow, clearly amused. "Where?"

Anywhere. Everywhere. But I had to keep it SFW, seeing as Celeste Ayi was probably ready to break out the camcorder and offer industry tips.

"Face," I hissed out, humiliated and elated all at once. My whole body trembled with the admission. "I want to feel skin on my face."

It would be the first time since the accident. Since his blood dripped into my eyes, running down my cheeks like tears.

We stared at each other, and for a moment, the world ceased to exist. Birds did not chirp. Clouds did not sail overhead. My mother did not watch us with her disapproving glare.

Farrow's chest moved with a ragged breath. She set the bucket of flowers down on the ground, her hands rising up to my face. "Tell me something to distract you," she instructed, her smile soft, her voice silk. "Something about the octopus."

I shut my eyes. "It has three hearts."

"I bet it loves big."

Her hands almost reached my face. I could feel them hovering in front of it. I stopped breathing altogether, bracing myself for it.

"It is a tragic creature," I countered, popping one eye open. "It can never love. It is programmed to consummate its reproductive purpose, procreate, then perish right after. It never stands a chance to live."

"Couldn't you call me a kitten, then?" Farrow scrunched her nose, looking annoyingly adorable. "I'd even take a bunny."

"Kittens are a generic choice. Bunnies belong in Hugh Hefner's mansion." I opened the other eye now, shaking my head, resolute. "You are an octopus. Smart. Sophisticated. Tragic."

And then it happened. Her palms clasped my face from both sides, bracketing my cheeks. I sucked in a breath and slammed my eyes shut. Her warm, damp skin pressed onto mine. I forced myself to open my eyes. To look at her. Her nails grazed my skin. A shudder thundered down my spine.

"Look at me, Zach." She smiled. *She smiled.* "You can do this. You can touch. Feel."

We stood in the garden like two trees, sturdy but fragile, swaying gently with the wind, and I couldn't bear it. How everything slammed into me all at once.

The memories. The disgust. And the guilt for wanting to feel her skin, still, even though my father was dead, and I couldn't even remember his dying words.

"What happened to you?" she croaked.

I shook my head. I couldn't tell. Couldn't repeat it for my own ears to hear, let alone hers.

"Does this feel okay?"

I thought about it. "It... *feels.*" Good. Bad. Complicated. "And that's more than I can ever ask for."

"Zachary," Mom barked from the balcony, dousing the moment with ice. "You are late, and we are hungry."

Farrow unclasped her hands from my face, darting a step back. Her neck flushed. "I'll see you at four." She turned away from me, picking up the bucket of roses and scurrying toward the front door.

"Don't leave," I croaked, the voice coming out of nowhere.

She paused but didn't turn to face me. "Don't go," she whispered, and I didn't know why, but everything felt tragic all of a sudden. Like the octopus, creating life just to end her own.

Swiveling on my heel, feeling the sting of her hands on my face, and knowing I wouldn't try to scrub it clean of her touch, I made my way to the balcony. Mom and Ayi sat on the marble banisters, staring at me like I'd just landed in a cornfield on a spaceship with a Spongebob propellor hat on my head. Perplexed did not begin to cover it. They looked like they were having an out of body experience.

"You should be careful with the staff." Mom spoke loud enough for Farrow to hear. "You don't want a sexual harassment lawsuit."

I didn't answer.

Growing up, people always told me, 'So good you survived.' But had I really survived that crash? I didn't think I did. I'd lost too many parts of me that day. Still, I lived without living. After all—survivors are pros at going through the motions with the weight of everyone left behind on their shoulders. And for twenty-one years, that was my fate.

Until now.

I was making progress. Slowly coming alive.

Lights were too bright. Food oversaturated with taste.

But I was no longer dead inside.

And that frightened me.

Chapter Thirty-Three

Zach

"You must lock the Eileen arrangement down before she comes to her senses." Mom set her chopsticks on their stand, spine straight like a sentinel's. "Your days of sneaking around with the staff should be over. You're thirty-three now."

Celeste Ayi scooped a dumpling into her mouth, eyes cutting from my face to Mom's. "Who told you they're sneaking around? That embrace was practically projected in IMAX."

"Don't be ridiculous." Mom snapped up the napkin from her lap, bringing its edge to the corner of her mouth to wipe an invisible stain. "My son knows better than to break my heart this way. An ambitionless woman is not a logical choice as a wife. Far too dangerous." I picked up a cucumber slice and shoved it into my mouth, chewing. Mom peeked my way, waiting for confirmation. When it didn't come, she continued, "He knows his Dad wouldn't have approved of her, either. Which he cares about deeply, since Lao Bo is no longer here to voice his opinions."

She said that often, and it drove me mad. Especially because sometimes, I wished it were me who died. I reached for my wine. "I am well aware, Mom."

"And since when do you drink wine at *lunch*?" Ayi drew a hand to her chest. "We could've done so many happy hours together."

She didn't need my company. She had more friends than a person should have, most of them she'd acquired after single-handedly sponsoring a local pride parade two decades ago. She'd just arrived in the States, hadn't gotten used to acronyms, and had mistaken LGBT for Let's Get Boba Tea. The rest was history.

Mom ignored her sister. "Is there a problem I should know about?"

"I think there *is* a problem." Ayi produced a pocket mirror from her purse and checked her makeup, even though it was only the three of us. "The problem is, he finds Eileen just a little less attractive than a bathroom carpet. And I'm not even talking about the fuzzy kind."

"That's not true." Mom slapped the napkin back onto her lap. She never slapped things. "He adores her, and she's stunning." She turned her head to me. "Isn't she, Zachary?"

"She looks fine." I swirled the wine in my glass, dissatisfied that my mother was, in fact, right. Pragmatically speaking, there was no reason for me to delay the inevitable. I'd made an arrangement with Eileen. She'd since written to me numerous times in emails, even texted. She expected me to take it to the next step. Why shouldn't she? We had a deal.

She was going to give me heirs. Stability. Peace of mind from my mother. And most importantly, help me fulfill my promise to Dad.

Mom pushed her plate away, losing patience. "Zachary, are you even listening?"

I snapped out of my reverie, setting my wine glass down. "Always."

She stood, her plate still full, her tea untouched. "Wrap this thing up with Eileen Yang." She slung her bag over her shoulder. "She's a good girl. Don't you dare tarnish her reputation."

Mom stormed out, leaving me with my oblivious aunt.

"Are you going to eat that skewer?" Ayi pointed at my plate with her chopsticks. "I'm on a carb-less diet these days."

She'd just had a dumpling, but the last thing I wanted was to engage in a conversation with her. "Sure." I stood, buttoning my blazer. "Go ahead."

At three-thirty, I strolled into one of my conference rooms. I'd scheduled the meeting a half hour before I asked Farrow to show up on purpose. I didn't want her to see this next part.

The minute I entered, everybody rose from their seats. Two estate and trust litigators—Dan Harlow and Bryan Di Pietro, the best in the area. My own lawyer on retainer—Deanne Tibon. And a private investigator—Tom Coates. They sat in a row on one side of the oval table.

I unbuttoned my blazer and claimed the head seat without shaking anyone's hand. Farrow aside, I still found most humans distasteful.

"So?" Bryan peered around the room, frowning. "What was so serious that you made us come together as a force?"

"And made me cut my vacation in Barbados short." Deanne reclined in her chair, rolling her neck. She was in her mid-sixties and dying to retire. In fact, I was the only client she'd kept. "Are you finally taking over Walmart?"

"Not quite." *But also not out of the question.* I laced my fingers together. "I have a task for you. Failure is not an option." I stared them down, taking my time. "No dime will be spared, no stone left unturned. By all means necessary, the four of you will win this case or face banishment from your industry of expertise."

Tom whistled. "Strong words."

Deanne knotted her arms over her chest. "Not for me. I *want* to retire."

"What is it, then?" Bryan unclipped his briefcase, fishing out a notepad. "What do you want us to do?"

I pressed a button on the intercom, summoning Natalie, who dished out pre-prepared folders. "I want you to drop everything you're working on and focus on this task."

If they ruined this, I'd ruin them.

Simple as that.

Chapter Thirty-Four

Zach

The mangled sheet of paper buried in the front pocket of my slacks burned a hole into it. I could practically feel it scorching through the fabric, searing my skin.

"For fuck's sake, this place is such a drag." Oliver breezed past the glass counters of the boutique jewelry shop, stopping in front of an antique emerald necklace that must have cost a cool ten mil. Thick glass barricaded it. "Why does all jewelry look the same?" He released a provocative yawn, his burgundy suit sewn to his body, all swagger. "It's bland."

"What more do you need?" Rom chuckled, leaning forward and squinting at a pair of earrings he was one-hundred percent going to buy for his wife. "A cock-shaped bracelet?"

"For instance." Oliver shrugged. "A little diversity wouldn't hurt."

He drummed his fingers over the display glass, surveying the luxurious jewelry store. Tiny, exclusive, and only open by appointment. It displayed some of the most expensive engagement rings in the world.

Better get it over with. I tugged out the wrinkled paper and smoothed it over my arm, trying hard to stare at the list without setting it ablaze.

Pear cut.
20 carats.
$1.8 million+.
White diamond.
Thin band.

Please, also be aware that I do not wish to have anything that is not custom-made. For further instructions, you are welcome to reach my cell.

Eileen

pleas. It could only ever come to this.

A suited, middle-aged woman approached Ollie, her hands folded together at her stomach. "Are you searching for something for that someone special, sir?"

Rom answered for him, "If Oliver had to buy jewelry for every person he saw, you'd be out of stock. The man has distributed more protein than a butcher shop."

The woman's nose scrunched up. Beside her, Oliver cackled, swinging an arm around Rom's shoulder.

I ignored them both, marching to the jeweler behind the glass counter, my Oxford shoes slapping the porcelain tiles. "I need one of these." I discarded the paper on the counter between us, hoping it would fall to the floor and spontaneously combust. No such luck.

The sweaty, stout man leveled the list to his face, squinting behind his reading glasses. "Does this say two carats?"

"Twenty," I corrected. "Between one-point-eight and two-point-two million dollars, please."

He gulped. Any other zip code, and the insurance alone on this sale would build him another house. "Ah, yes, sir." He turned toward his office. "Let me show you a few of our options…"

"No need." I waved a hand in his face, checking my Philippe Patek. "I don't need to see it. Just as long as it ticks all the boxes, you can bag it and give me the insurance paperwork." Pause. "I'll need the certificate, too."

Eileen seemed like a stickler for such things, just as much as I was. It should have made her more relatable, but it didn't. I found that trait tedious and tiresome. Was that how people—*re: Fae*—saw me?

The jeweler dropped the tweezers he was holding, his mouth agape. He blinked. "You don't want to see the two-million-dollar engagement ring you're about to purchase?"

"Did I stutter?" I scowled. "Yes, that's what I just said."

"Excuse our friend here." Ollie laughed, sliding next to me. "He's being strong-armed into marrying the human answer to a 1040 form."

I shot him a glare. "You haven't even met her."

"You said she reminds you of yourself." He pouted at me with naked pity. "One must conclude she isn't the life of the party."

One needs to ask God for forgiveness for being a manwhore, and my job is to arrange that meeting between them. Unfortunately, Buddhists didn't do violence. Buddhists that have never met Farrow Ballantine, that is.

"We're missing the Frestone Agency Art Auction." I tapped my watch, turning back to the jeweler. "Just pack up something. Do it fast."

"Why are we even going?" Romeo gestured for one of the employees in the store to wrap up the necklace he'd eyed for Dallas. "The art there is subpar. Always has been."

"And the pussy is nonexistent." Oliver ran a hand down his face. "The average age there is one hundred and two. Even I have my limits."

"You always said Frestone's art is where good taste goes to die." Romeo raised a brow. "Why the change of heart?"

I watched the perplexed jeweler slide a black velvet square into a crème satin pouch. "I have a piece I want from there." He handed it to me. In return, I slid the black Amex card his way.

Romeo paused. "A piece of what— Shit?"

"A replica of Da Vinci's *Salvator Mundi.*"

"What?" Oliver choked on his saliva, then proceeded to slap his own back. "You're buying a *replica*? Next thing you'll tell me is you buy knockoff Prada and Gucci from the back of a truck."

Now was not the time to admit Celeste Ayi owned some limited-edition Hermès bags of dubious origin. She'd bought them out of a garage run by a former luxury department store associate, who'd insisted she had a good hookup. I intended to take her secret to the grave. Spilling the beans meant entering said grave earlier than necessary.

"That painting is horrendous." Romeo collected his bag. "I'm a fan of Da Vinci, but our boy Salvi looks like he has full-blown cleavage."

Oliver put a hand to his chest. "I honestly get a little turned on every time I see this painting."

I flicked his forehead. "You get turned on every time you see *The Scream.*"

He snapped his fingers, pointing at me. "Hey. There's an O-shaped mouth in that one. Perfect for a blowie."

I rolled my eyes, plucking the card and bag from the counter. "You two know nothing about art. Let's go."

"I can't believe you are dragging us to this shithole." Oliver shook his head as he followed me out the store, Romeo utterly emotionless at his heels. "The things I do for true friendship."

CHAPTER THIRTY-FIVE

Ari: Hey, hottie.

Farrow: <Le sigh>

Farrow: I should have never told you about what happened in the sauna…

Ari: Nonsense. It's the first time you've done something fun for yourself.

Ari: And what FUN it was…

Farrow: I still have orgasmic aftershocks.

Ari: I can't believe the entire world is holding its breath to see who he'll pick, all while you're riding him like a Ferris wheel in public saunas.

Ari: Actually, I can. It's such a YOU thing to do.

Farrow: Okay. Moving on to the next subject.

Ari: So, you officially have legal representation now?

Farrow: Yes. I met with the private investigator, too. It's a dream team, Ari. They're all sharks. This kind of feels like it's too good to be true.

Ari: That's only because you haven't had good things happen to you in a very long time. I really think Zachary Sun is your guardian angel.

Farrow: Funny.

Ari: Why?

Farrow: Because I think he's the devil who just might end up killing me.

Chapter Thirty-Six

Farrow

The rest of the week flowed like a warm river against my skin.

On Monday, Zach asked that I accompany him to his lunches. *Plural.* His intentions were clear. Spend more time together. Get him used to the idea of sharing his life with a woman. In other words, I'd become his pet. An obedient companion that shadowed him everywhere he went, waiting for orders.

I told myself I went along with it because of the fancy lawyers he'd hired for me, but really, I enjoyed spending time together. Not exactly a compliment, given his competition. Vera's company could drive a nun to a dive bar. Tabby and Reggie were more suitable for black-site torture than companionship. Andras' idea of a good time included intensive training and banana-shaped bruises from his sword. And my sweet, beautiful Ari lived across the world.

Currently, we sat in Zach's office, nibbling raw fish and discussing abstract art. I couldn't bear it. Not the food, not the scenery, and not the man I spent time with.

"Why do you eat by your screens?" I fidgeted in my chair, slinging my legs over the armrest of the velvety seat and staring at my plate. Sashimi. Some kind of cucumber salad, accompanied by a green juice.

"Because work never stops." A piece of toro disappeared into his mouth, but he wasn't looking at the screens. He was staring at me.

I picked up the unagi sashimi between my fingers, glowering at it like it personally offended me. All I saw when I stared at it was an octopus. Zachary Sun had single-handedly ruined sushi for me. "If you don't take a break to enjoy all your hard work, what value does it really have?"

"You're not an animal." Zach sighed. "Use your chopsticks."

"I don't know how to." I stabbed the raw fish with a single chopstick, using the stick as a skewer to shove salmon into my mouth. "And I thought I was an octopus?"

His eyes nearly bulged out of their sockets. "You lived in Korea and never learned how to use chopsticks?"

I didn't know why, but everything this man did made me hot and bothered—even when he frowned, scowled, huffed, and berated me. Maybe I suffered from Stockholm syndrome. But that would imply that he'd kidnapped me, rather than the simple fact that I'd lost my mind and willingly agreed to be here.

"Nope." I popped the P, releasing an exasperated breath and pushing my plate away on his desk. "I always use a spoon and a fork. Ari always gives me shit for that." To be fair, everything tasted better on Korea's ultrawide metal spoons.

Zach scowled. "Am I supposed to know who Ari is?"

"My best friend from Seoul."

He arched an eyebrow. "Sex?"

Jealous? I was tempted to ask.

"No, thank you," I replied instead.

"Do not cross me, Farrow. I asked you a question."

"So? I don't work for you, Zachary Sun."

"You *literally* do." His lips barely moved when he spoke. I could tell I was dragging him to the brink of insanity.

I shrugged. "Personal tidbits cost extra."

His jaw locked. He pulled his drawer open and plucked out his wallet, tossing a Benjamin between us. "Is Ari a girl or a boy?"

"Girl." I shrugged. "But that doesn't say anything about her sexual orientation." With an eye roll, he threw me another hundred-dollar bill. I rolled the money together and tucked it into my waistband. "Straight." I smiled. "Happily engaged, too."

"Couldn't she have taught you how to use chopsticks?"

"Oh, she tried. But once I realized I couldn't vacuum food into my mouth fast enough with them, I lost all interest."

"Food is not made to be vacuumed. It's meant to be consumed over a lengthy period of time."

"Spoken like someone who doesn't hold two jobs."

He shook his head. "Constance would disown you."

"Glad I'm not her kid, then. Better no mom than one who bends you to the only shape she can love you in." I stood, gesturing to the plate I'd discarded, wondering if my words cut him as deep as I'd intended. A lot of layers of dead skin covered that heart of his. "Sorry, this is inedible."

No way could I get full off six tiny slivers of fish. I craved something decadent and bad for me. Something I had no business eating. Like Zachary Sun. *No, Fae,* the logical side of my brain chided. *Like jajangmyeon or pupusas.* The sooner I got that, the better off I'd be.

"It is perfectly nutritious." He continued chewing with his mouth shut. Thirty-two times each bite. Without fail. "The ideal fuel for your body."

"Maybe if I were a machine." Which I seriously suspected he was. "I know my body. And it wants something that will block its arteries to the point where I'll need acetone to clear them."

Andras would kill me.

Andras also isn't here.

He opened his mouth—about to scold me, no doubt—before clapping it shut, then opening it again. "Like what?"

Good question. Anything beat what I usually stole from the fridge—Vera, Reggie, and Tabby's gross gluten-free, sodium-free, carb-free, taste-free diet food. Since I doubted I could handle the consequences of requesting *him* on a platter, pupusas needed a solid fifteen minutes to reheat in the air fryer, and my favorite jajangmyeon was all the way in Rockville, I settled for the greasiest thing I could think of.

"Pizza." I felt my eyes crinkling as I smiled at the memory of wolfing slices down before entering a Broadway show with Dad. "I want a New York-style pizza. Huge, thin-crusted, with enough cheese to sculpt out a life-sized five-year-old." My mouth watered at the thought. "Actually, make it an eleven-year-old."

He looked horrified. As if I'd told him I wanted to eat an *actual* child. So, I figured—why not push the envelope a little more? Zach was so deeply offended by the pleasures of life, I wanted to make him try them. See what all the fuss was about.

I folded my arms, leaning back. "When was the last time you ate pizza?"

His brows crashed together as he sifted through the neatly organized files of his memory. "Third... no, fourth grade, I suppose.

Trevor McKee's birthday party. Flown in from Sicily, yet quite subpar."

I tried flicking through his empty desk calendar with a chopstick, shaking my head. "Oh, Zach."

"I know. Why not fly in chefs and ingredients from Italy?"

"We're ordering pizza right now. And it better be so oily, we need four towels beneath the box to soak up the stains. And…" I tossed my hands in the air, lighting up like the Rockefeller Center Christmas tree. "…and beers. Shitty, watery college beer."

"Belgian beers," he countered.

I shook my head. "Sorry, you're gonna slum it up with me today."

"Lovely." He pressed his mouth into a thin line. "What's next in my bingo card? A trip to Aldi and a fentanyl overdose?"

"Aldi is the shit."

"The *the* is silent, I suppose?"

Despite my horror at his strict lifestyle, I found myself laughing. "Oh, and you're paying, by the way."

He looked ready to vomit, his high cheekbones pale and sharp. My heart hiked up to my throat. I was sure he'd say no. After several minutes of silence, he pushed the sashimi away. "Fine. We'll have pizza."

"I'm glad you saw the light."

He raised a finger. "On one condition."

My heart galloped. "Which is…?"

Please say something dirty that I want to do anyway.

"No gross toppings."

"Just pineapple."

"*Especially* not pineapple."

"Are you always this tough a negotiator?"

"No." He submerged his hands in an oversized washing bowl. "I usually don't negotiate. I just take what I want."

"What's wrong with pineapple?"

"Nothing." He ran a towel over his palm. "Pizza is simply not its natural habitat."

"What is, then?"

"The trash can."

Rude. "Well, I like it, and you're going to accommodate me."

The idea seemed to appall him. "Why?"

"Because you want *me* to accommodate your twelve inches."

"It's not twelve inches."

"It's pretty damn close."

"You are anatomically built to push out a twelve-pound human," he pointed out.

"You're anatomically built to eat a Bromeliad flower."

He shook his head. "This is terrible."

"Welcome to the world of courtship, Zachary."

"I'm tempted to make a sharp U-turn." Zach pressed a button on his dashboard. "Natalie. Order us a large pineapple pizza."

"Extra cheese," I whispered, scurrying to the edge of my seat, forgetting to keep my distance.

A muscle twitched in his jaw. His leg kicked out, rolling my chair back a half a foot. I pouted. He sighed but added, "Extra cheese."

"Mr. Sun?" Natalie gasped. "Do you… need any help?"

"Clearly," he drawled. "That's what I'm paying you for."

"What I mean is, are you… are you okay?"

Yup. It was *that* unbelievable.

"Not by a long shot." He stared at me dispassionately, heaving a sigh. "What I am, Natalie, is pussy-whipped."

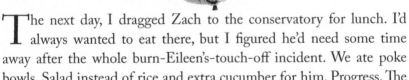

The next day, I dragged Zach to the conservatory for lunch. I'd always wanted to eat there, but I figured he'd need some time away after the whole burn-Eileen's-touch-off incident. We ate poke bowls. Salad instead of rice and extra cucumber for him. Progress. The day after, we gobbled up branzino on the balcony. This time, he let me feed him a roasted potato. He glowered, complaining about the grease the entire time. Still, before the meal ended, I spotted him swallowing another one.

And the following day, I prepared both of us banh mi thit nuong—dousing the sandwiches with extra homemade aioli. I even shoved pâté in them when he wasn't looking.

I tossed my napkin on my empty plate, reclining against my seat. "What's your favorite piece of art?"

"Don't have one."

"Seriously?" I boomeranged upright. "You collect so much art, and none is your favorite?"

"Nope. Not everything needs to be measured against something else."

"But…" I frowned. "Everyone has a favorite work of art."

"Even you?"

"Yup. The *Lobster Telephone*."

Dad used to own a replica I'd begged for. Vera had auctioned it off weeks after his death.

Zach paused, mid-bite. "By Dalí?" It drove me crazy how tiny and measured his bites were. Thirty-two chews each. At my nod, he arched a brow. "That *would* be your favorite."

"What's that supposed to mean?"

He didn't answer me, wrapping his lips around the sandwich. When his scheduled lunch hour ended, I double-checked his plate. He didn't leave a single crumb.

Every morning, I spent half an hour roaming the grounds, opening every window in the manor to let the sun enter. So Mr. Sun himself would feel warmth for the first time in his life.

I refused to eat in silence, always telling him about my life. The mother that never was. The father that was—but I could never get enough of. The loneliness. Seoul. Fencing. Olympic dreams. How I missed my old life. The one in Asia, far away from my evil stepsisters and stepmother.

He sat there and drank it all in. Like he had to endure human interaction. Sometimes, when I made myself laugh, he actually recoiled.

Zachary Sun was barely human.

For me to fix him, I had to make him real.

CHAPTER THIRTY-SEVEN

Farrow

The night before my birthday, I decided to sleep over at Zach's home. Guess I'd become addicted to the small indulgences of his many guestrooms. The sprawling firm mattress. The plush pillows. The large dressing table. And the scent of fresh flowers and decorative candles that wafted from every corner. The chef kept the fridge stocked, and lately, that somehow included things I loved to eat. Zach left me to my own devices, busy hiding from me then seeking me out spontaneously.

For the first time in nearly two years, I had a long, uninterrupted sleep. No Vera to yell at me to do the dishes. Nor Tabby and Reggie to whine for me to cook breakfast. Just… peace. I woke up to delicious silence, blinking my eyes open.

You're twenty-three. Congratulations. You made it another year. Much to your so-called family's chagrin.

I allowed myself twenty-three seconds to mourn my fencing career. Valentina Vezzali had two Olympic medals by this age. Every day, my biological clock ticked down. It probably didn't matter. Showing up at a competition would be shameless.

Next, I flicked the bridge of my nose until I smelled nothing, then spent two minutes convincing myself a waft of Dad's signature birthday confetti pancakes had drifted by. I missed them. I missed *him*.

And finally, for no logical reason whatsoever, I reached for my phone on the nightstand and checked the messages. Disappointment tickled my tear ducts when I clicked open my last messages with Dad and found no new ones. He used to leave me a long text every birthday morning, full of affirmations. By afternoon, I'd arrive to my dorm to a basket full of goodies.

I reread his last texts, though I already had them inked in my brain in permanent marker.

Dad: Remember Ms. Langer?

Farrow: My first-grade teacher?

Dad: That's the one. She finally got married. I went to her wedding last night.

Dad: Their vows were perfect. Even the cake was in tiers.

Farrow: BRB. Bleaching my eyes.

Farrow: Dad jokes are the worst.

Dad: We talked about you for a while. (Okay, I bragged about you, and she listened politely.)

Dad: I'm so proud of you, baby girl. Can't wait to see you kick ass at your competition this weekend.

Farrow: Pick a seat in the front this time. :(

Dad: Promise.

Farrow: Love you.

Dad: Love you more.

I sighed, exiting it out of the messages, double-checking that I didn't accidentally delete them. I'd grown paranoid when it came to losing tangible memories of Dad. Especially with all of his belongings pawned off. A single tear threatened to slip down my cheek. It was true what they said… The happiest memories eventually become the saddest.

Now, I only had one birthday wisher.

Ari: Happy Birthday, you kick-ass woman, you.

Ari: Don't forget how much I love you. Though I'm still here to remind you every day for the rest of your life.

Ari: Okay, that sounded hella creepy. But you know what I mean. Oh. Also, I sent you a check for cash. Not too much, but enough for you to book yourself a spa day. You know you've earned it.

Ari: Seriously, don't come at me for the money. I wasn't sure about your schedule, so I didn't want to book you anything myself.

I smiled at my phone, fighting tears of nostalgia and self-pity. I really wanted to be with her right now. Correction: I wanted to time travel to two years ago, to Seoul, to the moment Dad visited and treated me and Ari to hanwoo and soju. I swiped furiously at my eyes, texting back through a blurry curtain of tears.

Farrow: Coming at you at full force. Also, you are such a sap. Love you to pieces. – F

It would be so easy to fall back asleep. To shut my eyes and forget my troubles. Zach would let me sleep in. Andras would deal with it, in light of my birthday.

Instead, I grabbed my duffel bag and drove down to the country club for a practice session. I was on point, focused, and hungry. Andras, however, seemed a little distracted, so I didn't give him shit about forgetting my birthday. Anyway, he was my trainer, not my BFF. I had no one but myself to blame for my lack of company. Most of my friends lived in Seoul, where I'd spent my formative years. And I was too broke, chicken-shit, and disgraced to fly over there.

Once we finished practice, I retired to the locker room for a quick change before Zach's class. But when I pulled out my phone, I spotted a message from him. (He'd made a show of demanding my number after he spent Monday searching for me before our so-called lunch date, berating me for not making it on time. One—we both knew he already had my number, a byproduct of his hacking skills and utter disregard for my privacy. And two—who ate lunch at 11:30? Only people with an AARP card.)

For one pathetic second, my heart rose to my throat.

Did he remember my birthday?

Zach: Raincheck on class. Mom is throwing a party today. Apparently, I need to go over the menu details with her.

My heart crumbled into rubble, scattering all over my chest. What did I expect, though? He didn't know my birthday. Had no indication that I'd just turned twenty-three. I guess he had a copy of my ID somewhere on his servers from when he hired me, but why would he check it?

With shaky fingers, I replied.

Farrow: K. Have fun.

I drowned my sorrows in a chocolate donut from Dunkin's. The large iced coffee felt particularly glacial beneath the freezing air. I drove to Swallow Falls to watch the river flow, stuck a candle in the donut's hole, and made a wish.

"Dad, if you're up there, please give me a reason to wake up tomorrow. Anything. No matter how small. Consider it my birthday present."

A tear dropped onto the donut, painting a shimmery line down the chocolate glaze. I shut my eyes, tipping my chin toward the sky.

"If you do, I'll forgive you for breaking your promise and missing my last competition."

The chilly early winter air seared through my airpipe as I sucked in a breath, reminding myself *not* to fucking cry. I had no reason to. Pretty soon, I'd bring Vera down.

You do *have a reason to,* the lonely, bitter chunk of my soul reminded me. *You're all alone in this world. Your best friend is on the other side of the planet, and you've put all your chips on a man who wants to screw you then dump you.*

My phone pinged with a message, interrupting my pity party. I yanked it out of my back pocket, biting down on the donut.

Please, be someone who cares for me. Please.

Vera: I see you got yourself shiny new legal representation.

Vera: Just received the letter.

Vera: And who foots the bill for this entire nonsense? Do tell.

Vera: That's fine, Farrow. I'm still going to crush you. Gloves off now. Just how I like it.

I stared at the screen. Three little dots danced along the bottom. My breath hitched. Another text box appeared.

Vera: Happy Birthday, Farrow. Let's hope it's your last.

Chapter Thirty-Eight

Farrow

Any hope that Zach knew it was my birthday flew out the window when I returned to his mansion. His home resembled a snow globe, so pretty from afar, nestled in a thin blanket of ice. The inside buzzed—warm and lit, the flurry of mouthwatering scents engulfing me like rich fabric. By now, my shitty mood had sunk into my bones so deep, even a bulldozer couldn't excavate it.

It didn't help that, on my way to the kitchen, Zach's powerful voice sliced through the air from the chamber upstairs, snapping the backs of my ears. I hadn't even made it to the landing, and he'd already issued a command. "Farrow. My office. *Now.*"

He'd waited until I was one step away from the kitchen before calling me upstairs? What a prick. With a growl, I tromped up the steps, slamming the double doors to his office open. He sat behind his desk, sprawled on his seat like a big cat, playing with something in his hand.

I propped an elbow against the doorframe, refusing to cower or shrink in front of him. "Sup?" Pink bubble gum popped between my lips.

He looked abhorred. He always looked abhorred. "Is that gum you're chewing?"

I arched a brow. "Yeah. Problem?"

He shook his head, ignoring my provocation. "You need to pay extra attention to the ballroom today. The decorator and catering staff are already there, shifting things around. They're creating a mess."

Another party? *Why?* Even aliens galaxies away could see he absolutely detested large gatherings. But I knew the answer. *Constance.* Always Constance.

"Got it. Anything else?"

He spared me a glance. An odd thought struck me. *I wonder what those eyes look like when they're in love.* "You haven't made my bed yet."

"Had an early morning. Will do it now. Is that all?"

He traced his jawline with his finger, mulling it in his head. Was he *trying* to find more tasks for me? Why was he being extra tool-baggy today? "You need to clean all the windows on the first floor. We can't allow the photos with flash to show any markings of raindrops or fingerprints."

I frowned. "I did all the windows yesterday."

"Do them again."

I noticed, for the first time, that Zach held the cigar holder I'd used to play with myself. I recognized the unique metal barrel and golden cap. He toyed with it, flipping it between his fingers.

"They're squeaky clean." I threw my hands up, losing it. "Why would I redo them? It makes no sense."

"You're not here to make sense, Octi. You are here to take my orders."

Zach put the cap in his mouth. I swallowed. *This thing was inside me.* This was why he'd wanted me to leave the cigar holder behind. So he could taste me. Something simmered in my veins. Desire? Rage? I couldn't tell. All I knew was my blood bubbled, threatening to spill out.

I curled my fingers into fists. "What the hell is wrong with you?"

"Everything, I suspect."

"You're being extra insufferable today."

He turned his attention back to his screens, typing away on his keyboard, the cigar holder nestled between his straight white teeth. "Nonetheless, you have work to do. Chop, chop, Little Octopus."

I stared at him, dumbfounded. Whiplash struck me every time I spoke to him. Hot one second. Cold the next. This wasn't the same man who'd spent hours in a meeting with me and a team of lawyers, working relentlessly to drag me out of the mess Vera had pulled me into. Not the same man I had lunch with every day, whose throat bobbed whenever our eyes met. Not the same man who craved my touch so bad, sometimes I felt his eyes alone lick at my skin.

With a shake of my head, I turned away and stomped downstairs to start my workday. Tears burned the backs of my eyes as I scrubbed already clean windows. Dad did not answer my prayers this birthday, that much was certain. I shut my eyes, delivering one more message into the universe. An apology.

I'm sorry, Dad. I didn't mean it. It's not your fault you broke your promise. But it is my fault that I did something I know you'd be ashamed about.

Chapter Thirty-Nine

Farrow

The mansion had transformed into a Disney castle. White and creamy string lights draped the army of red maple trees leading up to the manor. Columns of red and gold flowers bracketed the double entry doors. In the foyer, white roses stretched across an entire wall for guests to take photos in front of. Swag bags lined up at the entrance like toy soldiers, secured by crisp velvet bows. In the ballroom, round tables framed the dance floor while LED balloons covered the tall ceiling in its entirety, lighting the room up from within.

I'd stepped into a fairytale.

A fairytale I, as usual, wasn't invited to.

I wondered what the occasion was. Hopefully Zach's belated emancipation from his overbearing mother. Though I didn't count on it. Guilt was the only emotion he was capable of feeling. Cutting the cord would be admitting to himself that he was dead inside.

The good news—and there wasn't much of it—was that I was off-duty. I'd managed to steal a box of white-and-red macarons before making my way upstairs to the guestroom. My own private birthday gift for myself. I locked the door behind me, launched myself on the pillows, and cranked the music all the way up, listening to "Water" by Tyla.

Even through my cheap earbuds, I managed to hear everything outside. Cars pulling up at the entrance. Valets. Champagne glasses clinking together. The indulgent laughter of people who didn't know how to pay their own bills. The live band. The hustle and bustle of point-one-percenters enjoying themselves.

I laid in a bed that wasn't mine and stared at the ceiling, stewing in my own anger. This time, I'd chosen the furthest guestroom from the stairs, not the one I usually occupied, hoping the sound of other people's happiness wouldn't reach me. But it did.

It did, and it seared my soul.

Alone, alone, alone.

Everything reminded me of that simple fact. Here was the thing about loneliness—there's no such thing as a loner. Only someone who has tried to give others a chance and ended up thoroughly disappointed.

Burrowing deeper under the covers, I grabbed my phone and started watching old YouTube videos of my fencing matches. Mainly to spot Dad in the first row, cheering me on. Andras always urged me to study my weaknesses. That my path to the Olympics required discipline and humility. I still didn't know if I'd ever make it. It seemed unlikely, considering my past. Yet, fencing made me truly happy. I would hate to let Andras down. Plus, the only time my mind shut off was on the piste.

And while getting impaled by a broody billionaire in a sauna.

A soft knock rapped on the door. I shot upright, the duvet rolling down my lap. Maybe I hadn't heard right? Why would Zach seek me out in the middle of his party? I stared at the door. The knock sounded again, this time louder.

I cleared my throat. "Yes?"

A sweet, feminine voice seeped through the door. "Farrow?" *Dallas Costa.*

"Yeah."

"Can I come in?"

Why?

"Sure…?"

The door crept open. Dallas waddled in, about a hundred centuries pregnant, clad in a shimmery gold A-line dress with a sweetheart neckline. Her boobs were out of control. I doubted even the US military could wrestle them into submission. She used what appeared to be a forty-thousand-dollar check to fan her face.

"Thank God, I found you." With her other hand, she shoved a tray full of enough food to feed the entire neighborhood my way, cannonballing onto the bed beside me. "I've been looking for you everywhere. I went through every single guestroom. How many are there here?"

"Thirteen." *And I'd slacked off on cleaning each and every one of them today.* "Plus, a dumbwaiter leading to a secret cellar. I don't clean that one, though. Can't run the risk of finding the remains of people Zach has killed for mispronouncing Latin words or miscalculating his tax returns."

"Oh, he does his own tax returns." She waved a hand. "It's like a hobby for him. A way to unwind. Kind of like sudoku or six-thousand-piece jigsaw puzzles."

I studied her with a tilt of my head, still confused. "Why are you here?"

Translation: If someone made a mess downstairs that needs urgent cleaning, I might strangle them.

I was off-duty. It was almost eight-thirty.

"What do you mean, why? Isn't it obvious?" She treated herself to a sponge cake off the tray, her light eyes twinkling with warmth. "Everyone else downstairs is a total bore."

I bit down a smile. I really liked Dallas, even if I felt like I shouldn't. Everyone in town knew she'd grown up rich. That she spent summers in Europe, waltzed at balls in Georgia, and rubbed elbows with people whose annual tax returns I couldn't count the zeros on. She had every opportunity to be exactly like Tabby and Reggie—a rich, spoiled brat. We shared nothing in common—no mutual interests, friends, likes, and dislikes. And yet, I knew a loyal friend when I stumbled upon one.

Dallas reached for a donut hole, popping it inside her mouth. "The way you answered that dudebro at dinner the other day? Legendary. Finding women with a spine on this side of the river is hard. It's like Air Force One flew by and sucked the personality out of everyone."

"Thanks." I regarded her with interest, still puzzled, and pointed at the tray at my hip. "Is this for me?"

Dallas released a joyous, addictive laugh. "Oh, yes."

I admired the rays of sunshine emanating from her. She struck me as the kind of person who could burn down the entire place if you rubbed her the wrong way, but also light up a room. I dug her vibe.

She snuck another pastry. "I figured I'd make you a sample platter with all the stuff worthy of eating. I took it upon myself to test everything first. True friend, or what?"

"Total bestie," I murmured.

"I'm a ride-or-die kind of chick." She grabbed her tiny Hermès purse and tugged something out of it. "Hey, I made us those friendship bracelets." A small plastic bag landed on my lap. She dangled an identical one, the beaded circle waving as she jiggled it. "No judgment, please. Being heavily pregnant is super boring. I had to cancel bungee jumping in New Zealand last week. Can you believe how overprotective Rom is?"

A small smile played on my lips. "Unheard of."

I couldn't believe she'd made me laugh on a day I felt so freaking sorry for myself. When I didn't make a move, she snatched the bag from me, pulled out the purple-green Swiftie bracelet (she'd remembered our conversation), and slid it up my wrist, thrusting hers beside me. They matched. Our names winked back at us from cheap plastic beads. It looked ridiculous among her otherwise head-to-toe luxury brands.

I snatched a spam musubi, unwrapping the film. "What are you having?"

"Probably the steak and fries." She heaved a sigh. "I mean, the sushi downstairs looks so good, it should be downright illegal, but I can't eat raw fish right now."

"I'm talking about your pregnancy."

"*Oh.* A girl, I hope." Dallas' face lit up. "Rom says he's worried about being outnumbered. But I say he's always been outnumbered. I have multiple personalities, depending on my mood and what time of the month it is."

"You're going to make an amazing mother." I meant it.

"I'm going to try my best." She smiled. "If there's one thing I learned from my own mother, it's that you need to teach your daughter to be powerful enough to protect herself."

A lick of longing tugged at my belly. I wished I had a mother. A real one. Not one that abandoned me. Or one that spent my entire life trying to kick me out.

I tilted my head, toying with my next words. "Have you noticed something about the moms here…?"

"Here as in this household, this city, this state…?"

"Here as in around us."

Not that there was an us, but Dallas felt like an actual friend. I couldn't help but latch on to her warmth.

"Hmm…" She tapped her lip, pausing. "I actually don't know much about Oliver's mom, but Romeo's leaves much to be desired. He mostly calls Constance his mom."

"*Constance?*" My jaw dropped. "As in, Zach's Constance?"

She grinned, nodding. "I know. It seems impossible, but Romeo said she wasn't always like this. That the Constance he remembered used to be warm. She packed him lunch every day because she didn't want him to eat junk, picked him up from school with Zach, and personally taught him math, which she once lectured at the collegiate level."

"Constance Sun," I repeated.

"That's the one." Dallas traced circles on her belly. "Rom told me that, after her husband died, she became a zombie. When she finally snapped out of it, she transformed into a different person. *Rigid.* Full of rules. Humorless. Rom thinks Constance is afraid that, if everything isn't perfect, something bad will happen again."

I laid on the pillow, considering Dallas' words. Losing someone tragically didn't excuse bad behavior, but it *did* explain it. Grief rewired your brain. The quiet moments became the loudest ones. The only way to shut it off was to make your life louder than your mind. I, of all people, could attest to that. Which gave me no right to judge. And still, I couldn't help but resent her for the way she made her son suffer. Even if *he* constantly made *me* suffer.

I nibbled on a corner of cieple lody without really tasting it, though it must've tasted good because Dallas' eyes rolled to the back of her head.

She nudged my arm, wiping crumbs off her chin. "Hey, what's eating at you? You were a complete firecracker the first time I met you. You look... *down.*"

"Everything's fine."

Was I convincing her or myself?

"Try again." Dallas snorted. "In this friendship, we only do honesty."

"It's my birthday today," I admitted.

"What?" She paled, jumping up to her feet in an instant. Well, as fast as she could with an entire human in her belly. "Are you kidding me? What are you doing here? We should be celebrating."

"There's nothing much to celebrate." I stared at the desserts, swallowing saliva. "I don't have any family, and all my friends are in Korea."

"Not all of them." Dallas opened the closet, saw that it was empty, and shut it. "I'm here, and I have some gorgeous clothes to lend to you for an unforgettable night. All you have to do is say yes."

"*No.*"

"The music downstairs is amazing. The food is divine. Besides, no one will recognize you. And I won't leave your side at all."

"The answer is still no."

"Oh, come on, Farrow." She bent her knees, pressing her palms together, begging. "You can't deny me. I'm pregnant and vulnerable. What if my water breaks early because of you? You'd have to move to another planet to hide from my husband, and then we can't binge eat our way through Earth together."

I couldn't afford to binge eat my way through Earth, both financially and practically if I expected to win any gold medals in this lifetime.

Dallas began panting, listing all the ways her husband and his friends tracked their enemies. She was relentless. No wonder she wore Romeo Costa down. The woman could overthrow entire regimes with one tantrum.

"Do you want that?" She didn't wait for me to answer, patting my shoulder. "You just stay here, okay?"

I wanted to say no. To tell her that I was beyond repair. But if Zach could find it in himself to push through and make a change… then, maybe I could, too.

"Okay." I forced a smile. "I'll wait."

CHAPTER FORTY

Farrow

I must have looked like the Beast after dolling up for dinner with Belle. Overdressed. Hair curled to submission. Utterly *ridiculous*. A puffy, pale-pink ballgown draped over my limbs. I felt like a pavlova.

"I bought it last week, but I can't wear it, because…" Dallas gestured to her stomach, sighing. "Isn't it so glitzy yet understated?"

So is a meringue cake, which is exactly what I look like.

But I grinned, because even though I felt absurd, I also felt… *happy*. My new friend fluttered around me, placing butterfly clips in my hair and squeezing so much gloss on my lips that it looked like a beehive exploded on my mouth. I couldn't remember the last time I'd worn makeup. I didn't even own mascara.

Dallas trapped another tight curl behind a clip and stepped back, dusting her hands as she admired her handiwork. "Girl, you look like Candice Swanepoel."

I tapered my eyes. "Was that in English?"

She laughed. "The Victoria's Secret model?"

"I don't watch TV," I mumbled.

She laughed harder. This was why Ari was my only female friend.

Dallas tugged at my hands, dragging me out of the guestroom with a proud grin. "Come." We both still wore our ridiculous bracelets. "I want everyone in the ballroom to see that you're hot shit. And then I want someone to hit on you and for Zach to go all possessive on your ass. The way he sliced that idiot…" She plastered the back of her hand to her forehead and pretended to faint. "*Swoon.*"

"I still don't know how he got away with it." I gathered the many skirts of my ballgown to avoid breaking a leg. This shit was heavy.

Dallas pressed her hand to her lips. "Oh, my sweet summer child. Zachary Sun is bigger than the law."

Fan-fucking-tastic. Where does that put me if I piss him off?

I descended each stair slowly, gripping both the wall and Dallas' arm to keep us upright. How did women wear heels? I'd have an easier time balancing on circus crutches.

She laced her arm in mine. "So...do you have many friends in Seoul?" It must've been nice being the sun personified. Chatty. Sweet. A complete natural at this whole peopling thing. I could see why Romeo was obsessed with her. She possessed the uncanny ability to make anyone feel seen. Important. Worthy.

"Not many, but some. My best friend Ari is getting married in a few months. I can't wait to see her." In fact, I'd saved up for over a year to afford the plane ticket and a small off-registry gift.

Dallas nodded. "Ari's such a pretty name."

"It's short for Arirang. She hates it, because she's named after this ancient folk song that played in the hotel room next door when her parents conceived her. The song is stunning, by the way. But every time she has to explain that her parents smashed to it, she turns pinker than a Barbie doll." I giggled into my palm. "She's gorgeous, funny, and just the best. A fencer, too. I wish you could meet her."

"I'm sure I will, one day."

We reached the ballroom. It felt forbidden to be here, almost, even though the woman beside me practically held the keys to the city. Not to mention I'd literally scrubbed this room wall-to-wall yesterday. I hesitated, fingering the glossy fabric of my gown.

Two suited staff members opened the door, and just like that, we were sucked into the vortex of the dazzling soirée. Pastel dresses swept the floor as couples waltzed. Servers weaved in and out of the crowd like black floss spinning around diamonds. Women leaned in, whispering in each other's ears as soon as we stepped inside.

Dallas' spine tensed. She burrowed closer to me, almost hugging me. In that moment, I realized Dallas and I were actually more similar than I'd ever expected. She was too colorful—too brave to fit in. And I was too poor—too unruly to want to.

"Don't mind them. Only people without love in their lives become haters." Her hand slipped into mine, tugging me inside. "I'll teach you how to waltz."

My knee-jerk reaction was to protest, but then I thought—why the heck not? It was my birthday. I deserved to dance in a pretty dress.

Dallas gathered me in her arms, one hand on my upper back, the other clasping my free palm. It felt ridiculous. I was so much taller than her, and a stomach full of baby separated us. Still, I rolled with it.

"Forward with your left foot, side with the right, close them together, then… yup." She guided me with her feet. "Backwards with your right foot. You're getting the hang of it. I forgot you're a fencer. Quick on your feet."

The music caressed the bare skin of my arms as I swayed and twirled. I closed my eyes, ignoring the heavy stares we got. *Incognito, my ass.* We flew under the radar like a marching band in a library.

"Do you believe in happy endings?" I croaked, barely audible for Dallas to hear.

"Yes." She clung onto my back tighter. "I live mine every single day. It's not always perfect, but it sure is happy. We can all write our own happy endings. That's why hope exists. It's our pen."

"I feel like mine ran out of ink."

"Oh, no." She shimmied us, lips curved up. "You just need to give it a good shake."

We laughed and twirled, like two kids playing make-believe. When the song ended, Dallas bowed to me, and I did the same. I raised my head, the grin wiping off my face in an instant.

Because behind Dallas' shoulder stood no other than my boss.

My formidable, incredibly pissed-off boss, by the looks of it.

Zach stared at me with enough ire to scorch a path straight to me. I was surprised he even recognized me with my borrowed frock and fancy hair. His eyes delivered a warning. He curled a finger to signal me to come to him. I flipped my hair, gave him my back, and headed to the bar. *Nope.* I refused to be treated like a misbehaved dog, especially on my birthday.

Halfway through my journey, a hand clasped my elbow from behind. I turned, jerking it away. "Don't you dar—"

Oh. I'd expected Zach but got Oliver von Bismarck instead. Up-close, he looked even more delectable. Eyes clearer and bluer than the Caribbean Ocean, dark blond hair swept to the side like a Tom Ford commercial. So beautiful. So depraved. I pitied the women who fell prey to his trap.

He curled his pink lips. "*You.*"

I arched a brow. "Me?"

"You're the antidote."

The antidote? I'd heard he was a player, not an alcoholic. Perhaps he was a man of many parts.

"I'm not sure what you mean."

"Of course, you don't." Oliver studied me. "We need to talk."

"I wholeheartedly disagree."

"Let's have a little chat. Dance with me."

"What's in it for me?"

"A memory to cherish." His smirk was agonizing. He dripped sin and decadence. "Something to write home about."

I slouched against the bar, waving a hand to draw a bartender's attention. "Nice ego. Do they make you pay extra for overweight luggage when you travel?"

"Is this a middle-class thing?" His brows snapped together. "I've only ever flown private." *Jesus H.*

The bartender ignored me, whizzing by with three drinks in his hands.

Oliver inched closer to be heard. "Anyway, name your price."

That was an easy one. "A round-trip ticket to Seoul. First class."

He chuckled. "Deal."

Then, he grabbed my hand without asking, dragging me back to the dancefloor before I could say *margarita.* I could practically feel Dallas' smile warming the back of my neck as the crowd parted for him. He placed us in the middle of the floor and spun me to face him. His fingers pressed against my upper back, warm and strong. In another world, in another time, I would enjoy them. In reality, however, all I cared about was survival.

The orchestra began playing. We took position—him with flawless posture and me with unpracticed rigidness—and danced.

"Mr. Sun…" Oliver twirled me. "…is broken. I'm sure you've figured it out by now."

He held me closer. It occurred to me that this looked like an intimate, clandestine moment by design. I didn't know how, but I knew Zach watched us like a hawk—and that Oliver had intended this.

I didn't respond.

"All sharp-edged shards." Oliver spun me again. "He doesn't let anyone get too close, so they don't bleed out."

Still, I said nothing, letting him spin me like a ragdoll. With the whirl, I noted a sea of women watching in envy as I clung to Oliver von Bismarck's shoulders. I ignored them, trying and failing to find Zach.

"Now, I don't know who you are..." Oliver guided each of my steps, moving just slow enough for me to concentrate on his words. "...and the way you wormed yourself into his life is questionable to say the least." That crisp, businesslike tone surprised me. Not at all like the ditzy party boy his reputation claimed him to be. "But if you hurt my best friend, who seems downright obsessed with you, I will personally drag you into the pits of hell and toss you into the fire. He's been through enough. You hear me?"

I threw my head back and laughed. It must've seemed like we were having a splendid time. "I will crush him into dust if I so wish to, von Bismarck. I don't take to being threatened very well."

I didn't tell him the truth—that I had no power over Zachary Sun. No one did. I was simply the only person he somehow found bearable enough to touch. I was a shiny new toy. Something to pass the time with.

"You have a smart mouth." He gave me an appreciative once-over. "I can see why he likes you."

"Wait till you see me with a sword."

His eyes flared, a gleam of curiosity lurking within them. Weirdly enough, his beauty did nothing to me. He reminded me of a statue. Perfectly polished, yet completely dead inside.

You once described Zach that way. What changed?

I swallowed the question, focusing on Oliver. "How do you know he likes me?"

"For starters, he no longer looks like life is pushing lemons into his rectum, two at a time, twenty-four hours a day." I stumbled over his feet. He caught me by the waist, a chuckle rolling from his throat. "God, you're adorable. All rough edges, just like him."

"It's my first waltz."

"For the sake of every pair of feet in the state, I hope it will be your last."

"Do you always find people not in your class so amusing?"

"Not at all. I usually find them completely insignificant." God help the poor girl who managed to tame this beast. What a handful.

The song came to an end. We pulled apart, about a foot.

Oliver bowed, claimed my hand, and brought it to his lips. He peered up, staring right into my eyes as his lips grazed my skin. "Remember, little Fae. No hurting Zachary's feelings. I can be a teddy bear, but make no mistake—I can also become one hell of a lion."

I mustered a smile that must have resembled a grimace. "As I said before, von Bismarck, I won't be intimidated by a fat bank account and the mediocre dick it's compensating for."

He laughed all the way to the bar. Great. Now I couldn't get a drink. Asshole would think I followed him. His ego needed its own zip code. I turned toward the kitchen instead, pushing my way through people. Everyone buzzed with excitement. Instead of ramping mine up, it suffocated me. I almost made it to the door when I heard my nickname.

"Octi."

Ugh. Couldn't catch a single break tonight.

I stopped but didn't turn to face Zach. "Asshole," I greeted back.

His footsteps barely made a sound as he placed himself right in front of me, blocking my way to the kitchen. "Enjoying my party?"

I took my time perusing him in his slick tux, settling on his bloodshot eyes. Oliver's words shotgunned to the front of my mind. For the first time, I realized that—behind the designer suit and thousand-dollar haircut—Zachary Sun was a wreck of a man. *If only I wasn't so focused on my own misery.*

"Not really." I hitched a shoulder up. "I've been trying to get a drink for an hour now, and there's always someone in the way." I raised a brow. "Currently, that someone is you. Kindly see yourself out."

"This is my house."

"I'm aware. If it were mine, I wouldn't let *Mommy* be in charge of the décor." Shit. I really was in a bad mood tonight.

He stepped toward me, his fingers twitching as he stopped himself from touching me. "What did Oliver say to you?"

He threatened my life if I hurt you, you fool. Great friends you've got there. What did you do to deserve them?

"None of your business, Zach." I arched a brow. "May I remind you we're not exclusive?"

"May *I* remind *you* I hold the purse strings?"

"Don't worry... I'm reminded of that every time I see your annoying face. It's not good will that's keeping me here."

"Watch your mouth, Miss Ballantine. I may want it wrapped around my cock, but I also won't hesitate to fire you."

My face must have betrayed my thoughts. That he was dangerously close to getting his nuts kicked.

He stepped back and released a growl, thrusting a hand into his hair. "He had no right to touch you."

"Will you cut the possessive bull crap?" I folded my arms over my chest. "You have no right."

"But I have will." His teeth slammed together. "The will to finish anyone who looks at or touches you." He curled his fist, pressing it against his thigh, and I knew he wanted contact. A hug. A skin-to-skin moment to soothe his anger. His face softened, and dammit, so did my heart. He glanced away for a moment. "I was an asshole today, wasn't I?"

"You were," I agreed. "Why?"

He opened his mouth. From the center of the room, the unmistakable *clank* of a knife against fine glass interrupted the moment. We snapped our heads in its direction. The music stopped.

Constance stood on a heavily mic'd podium, swathed in a navy gown with a cape, hair twisted back and adorned with delicate jewelry. "Ladies and gentlemen, thank you for joining us today. May I kindly have your attention?"

Her voice—pure steel, cold and sharp—grazed along my skin, giving me goosebumps. She handed the champagne glass to a server and scanned the room until her eyes landed on Zach. *Next to me.*

Her expression clouded, a flash of lightning surfacing, but she quickly smothered it with a smile. "I'd like to start by thanking you for making the time to attend such a last-minute gathering. Your support means the world. The Sun family and the Sun for Warmth Foundation are forever grateful for this community and your mutual efforts in preserving local wildlife." Oh, she saved wildlife? That seemed so fitting, considering she was a rabid bitch.

Grief, I reminded myself, *changes people.* But with her eyes drilling a hole in my temple, I struggled to conjure Dallas' description of the old Constance Sun. Packed lunches? Carpool? Tutoring? Surely, not the woman stabbing me with her eyes.

A tight smile tugged the corner of her mouth. "We have gathered here today to share exciting news. Something I'm sure a lot of you have wondered about."

My heart sank all the way to my toes. I had an inkling of what it could be. Even though it came as no surprise, my whole body revolted.

"As you are well aware, my son Zachary has been on the market for some time now, searching for the perfect bride." She laughed so gracefully, even I wanted to join her. "I do believe my search for a daughter-in-law is the worst kept secret in America."

A wave of laughter rolled through the room. An upsurge of nausea crashed into my stomach. *No, no, no.* Beside me, Zach tensed, his expression morphing into granite. His pinky touched mine.

His. Pinky. Touched. Mine.

And that was enough to ignite the entire world into flames.

"I am, therefore, delighted to inform you that the search is over. I'd like to take this opportunity to announce the official engagement of my son Zachary to the lovely Eileen Yang. Come, come, children."

At first, Zach didn't move. We both stared as Eileen glided across the room in a sparkly silver-and-olive sequin gown. The train swished against the marble floor. She wore satin gloves up to her elbows, her aura otherworldly and elegant.

A piercing pain dug through my heart. It felt like everything I'd promised myself wouldn't happen. Like my heart lay bloody on the piste, a sword straight through it. Suddenly, I couldn't breathe.

Eileen's voice boomed through the six microphones attached to the podium. "Oh, Mother." She kissed Constance's cheeks. They embraced each other's elbows, their hairdos identical. "It's such an honor to join your family. I promise I'll make Zach very happy."

Another woman—Zach's aunt, I recognized—sashayed across the dancefloor, resting a hand on Constance's shoulder. Unlike her sister, Celeste didn't seem elated. Her eyes scanned the room. "Speaking of Zach, where's the man of the hour?"

"Seconds from migrating to Denmark," Oliver coughed into his fist, eliciting a warning glare from Constance.

I felt like I was having an out-of-body experience as Zach abandoned me, drifting deeper into the ballroom, taking his place beside the most important women in his life. The four of them stood shoulder-to-shoulder without touching. Constance served as a buffer between the couple. Even through the agonizing ache that ripped through my veins, I took a little comfort in the fact that Zach wouldn't have to touch Eileen. I knew he didn't want to.

Where is all this jealousy coming from?

"Ladies and gentlemen." Constance planted her hands on Zach and Eileen's shoulders.

Zach visibly flinched, his nostrils flaring as he bit back a scream. I wanted to scream, too.

Constance's face erupted in a grin, genuine happiness radiating off her. "I'm happy to introduce to you the future Mr. and Mrs. Sun."

Claps erupted across the room, ringing between my ears. Camera flashes zinged in front of my eyes. I turned around and began speed-walking away.

"Eileen…" Constance's voice boomed through each speaker peppering the walls, loud enough to be heard through the cheers. "Show everyone your engagement ring. Do a little tour."

My legs carried me on auto-pilot, my mind reeling from what should have been obvious to me. Zach had warned me all along that he'd marry Eileen. When I reached the stairway, I collapsed on the third step like a broken swan, my ballgown surrounding me. I sobbed into my arms, realizing that, for the first time since Dad had died, I was actually crying. I didn't recognize myself in this fragility. I'd always prided myself in my strength.

"Stupid…" I sniffed, my entire face a sea of snot and tears. "You're so stupid." I yanked the stupid heels from my stupid feet. "Thinking you could somehow fit in with these people."

So much for rejecting the glitz and glamor of Maryland's elite my entire life. In one reckless night, they'd served me the reminder I'd tried to ignore—that I could be the side piece, but girls like Eileen Yang would forever be the endgame.

"Farrow." Dallas' voice erupted from behind me. I craned my neck, watching her charge toward me. "Wait up, please."

I shot up, taking the steps two at a time. I didn't want to wait. I didn't want her to see me so thoroughly humiliated, and I definitely didn't want to listen to her little white lies, designed to make me feel better.

When I reached my room, I locked the door behind me, pressing my back to the wood. I closed my eyes, sucking in a deep breath.

You're fine. You can't mourn what you've never lost. He was never yours, Farrow.

But he'd started to feel like mine.

It was like the past, the present, and the future conspired to bring me exactly what I needed, then changed their minds.

I forced my eyes open, begging the pain and humiliation to go away with each blink. And they did, replaced by shock as I realized for the first time where I was—the guestroom I usually occupied. *My* room.

I brought my fingertips to my lips. "Oh, Zach."

Presents dusted every inch of the room. Every corner. Every piece of furniture. Every thread of the carpet. A sea of fancy boxes and bags. All wrapped and tied with golden foil.

He remembered.

He remembered my birthday.

Unless… it was Ari? But it couldn't be. Ari didn't know Zach's address. And no one else in this world cared enough.

Wiping at my eyes and nose, I treaded to a mountain of boxes and picked one up, tearing the wrapper apart. A Chanel box materialized beneath the shiny paper. I opened it, discovering a pair of sneakers. White calfskin with the signature logo embroidered in black. My brows slammed together.

I picked another box and opened it. Tory Burch sneakers. Camel-hued. Another box—Prada this time. Silver Golden Goose. Pink Balenciaga running shoes. Burberry low-tops. Dior high-tops. Custom Louboutin fencing footwear. He'd filled my room with every designer shoe possible—all comfy, all shoes I'd actually wear.

It was sweet, and thoughtful, and utterly *enraging*. Because now, more than ever, I didn't want to feel like a charity case. Each box mocked me, reminding me of the gap between us. Of how poor I was in comparison to him. Of the tattered shoe I'd left behind the day of the ball.

I may be Cinderella, but Zachary Sun is not my Prince Charming.

Without further ado, I began collecting the shoe boxes and hurling them out the window.

Zachary Sun could buy his way into most places.

But not into my heart.

Chapter Forty-One

Zach

I swiped my shelf clean with my arm, sending sculptures, special editions, and paintings crashing to my office floor with a piercing smash. "What was she thinking?"

"She was thinking that you're engaged-to-be-married to someone else, and she doesn't want your fucking pity presents." Oliver sprawled over a massage table in the middle of my office, unfamiliar with the concept of boundaries. "It's called a spine, Zach. Some people have it."

"Why does one have to be on *that* woman?" I turned to my screens, ripped one from its cables, and readied to hurl it out the window before remembering my staffers were currently picking up 23 packages of designer sneakers. One for every year of her enraging existence.

"Because if she were like everyone else, you wouldn't have liked her," Oliver murmured into the face-hole of the massage table while a huge Swedish dude dug his thumbs into his shoulder blades.

I slammed the screen down, cracking the display in three. A nice new dent graced the desk. My feet thudded on the rug as I marched to the window, glaring at the mess she'd made on the lawn beneath. The worst part was, I'd thought for sure that, after Farrow realized I'd taken the time to gift her things she'd actually use (gifts that also happened to be a wink to the time we'd met), she'd seek me out. Slip into my bedroom during the night. Practice our touching.

My fingers clawed the windowsill as I hunted for a glimpse of her, knowing I wouldn't find her. I'd checked the footage of every security camera on the property, and nothing. *Nada.* Where the hell was she?

Still on my payroll, that's fucking where.

"Steam's coming out of your ears, bud." Ollie chuckled behind my back. "What did you expect?"

"A professional employee?"

"She was there for your surprise *engagement party*. Standing next to your fiancée. After you fucked her in that sauna less than a week ago."

"I didn't fuck her." *Not yet.* But I wanted to. More than anything else on this goddamn Earth, the *Mona Lisa* included.

"Well, still. Don't expect the Boss of the Year award. You acted just as unprofessional."

I turned from the window to scowl at him. "She knows it's not real."

"Seemed real to me."

"I'm marrying Eileen out of necessity. Everyone but Mom knows it."

I was going to grind my molars into dust if I wasn't careful.

"Sorry, buddy. 'Mommy made me do it' is not the compelling argument you think it is."

"You are in no position to lecture me, Oliver. Your most lengthy relationship is with your anal beads."

"I'll have you know—I replace them every other week to ensure high hygiene levels for my sexual partners." Oliver sounded scandalized. "Not that I've been getting a lot of action recently. To be honest, yesterday I found myself running with my flip-flops down the hallway just to remember what sex sounds like."

"You had someone over two days ago. You *literally* sent us pictures." Much to my chagrin.

"Time is subjective." Oliver shrugged beneath the Hulk's diligent fingers. "Point is, you earned your spot in the doghouse. Enjoy the snacks."

I shot him a look. "You're an insult to the species."

He raised his smug face from the face hole and smirked at me. "Now use this same energy to grovel your life away, Zachary."

"I do not grovel."

"You've been glancing at the Go board like a photo of a lost loved one."

That was because the little witch hadn't even bothered making a move this morning, and it was her turn. She never missed a move.

"I. Will. Not. Grovel."

What did groveling even look like? What did he expect me to do?

"Better clean that mess up." *How?*

"For the last time, I do not—"

Oliver waved me away, sticking his head back in the hole. "Natalie, hey, yoo-hoo. Please make yourself useful and bring me another cocktail."

Chapter Forty-Two

Zach

I couldn't find Farrow. She'd gone missing since last night's engagement party, not bothering to show up to work in the morning. By the time Oliver left, I'd convinced myself she'd gotten cold feet and moved back to Seoul without handing in her two-week notice. After all, irresponsibility seemed right up her alley.

I sulked, barked at Natalie to find her, reviewed the surveillance cameras again, then finally resorted to showing up at Vera's doorstep. The entire drive there, I told myself this wasn't about missing her. This was entirely about accountability. An employee of mine had taken a leave of absence without giving me notice. I refused to let her get away with it.

When I pulled up the Ballantine driveway, double-parking in front of a Mercedes, it became clear that Farrow had *not* moved to Seoul. Two shiny roadsters flanked her dirty old Prius, barely leaving room for her to slip inside.

The entry door swung open before I cut the engine. One of the sisters—for the life of me, I couldn't remember which was which—rushed to my door, gasping at the sight of me. I popped it open, using the heavy metal to force her away.

"Mr. Sun." She batted her lashes, pushing her tits out as she arched over my hood. Another thing to disinfect once I returned home. "How can I help you?" *You can vanish into the ether.*

I kicked the door shut behind me. "I'm looking for your sister."

"Reggie?" Her expression melted into a grimace. "She's in New York, shopping for the season. I don't even know why. She's too short for anything worth wearing."

"Not Reggie. The one who is not a complete waste of space."

I'd forgotten her family completely disowned her.

"Farrow?"

"That's the one."

"Can you believe the little shit disappeared on us? The house is a total mess." Tabitha pouted. "You know… we're worthy, too."

"Beg to differ."

"Don't be so harsh." She giggled. The hyena laugh screeched down my ears like nails on a blackboard, reminding me I only ever liked Octi's. "You know what you need, Zach?"

"A conversation partner who doesn't have the IQ of a dead starfish."

"Someone to complete you. A girl who's simple and easy." She flung her hair over one shoulder. "Like me." If only empty minds came with mute buttons.

"Free advice?" I locked my car, not trusting any of the Ballantine women not to steal it. "Describing yourself as low hanging fruit? Not as appealing as you think it is."

"You're not as tough as *you* think you are, you know." She followed me to the gaping front door. "You're an open book."

"And you're illiterate." I strode right past her, inviting myself in. Apparently, I could add trespassing to my list of negative influences Farrow had on me. "Where is she?"

I went from room to room, noticing the layers of filth. Every inch reeked of rotten food. The crack in the dining room wall—only a small fissure when I'd last visited—had metastasized, slashing from end to end. Dirty dishes sprouted from piles of clothes, peppering the stained carpet. Did these people do anything when Fae wasn't here to serve them?

Tabitha tailed me, shimmying her miniskirt down her thighs. "Is it true that you're engaged now?" *Unfortunately.*

I started taking the stairs to the second floor.

"I hope you don't think you have a chance with Fae." She panted, trying to keep up with me, white-knuckling the banister as I poured into the hallway. "Because you don't. No one does. She… she's incapable of emotions. She's always been like this. Unsympathetic. Unloving. Weir—"

I spun, getting so close to her I could see the pink blemishes staining her face. "Don't finish that sentence if you value your meaningless life. Farrow Ballantine's pinky nail is worth more than your entire being. Now make yourself useful."

She blinked, stunned by my reaction. "H-how?"

Good question.

Her breath fanned across my cheek. I wanted to tear the flesh off.

"Get the fuck out of here. Take a walk." I reared back, putting as much space between us as the narrow hall would allow. "I need to talk to your sis—" No, she wasn't her sister. "To Fae."

Aside from the obvious indicator of her presence, her car, I knew Octi lurked somewhere within these walls for the simple fact that she didn't have anywhere else to go.

Tabitha sniffed, her lower lip poking out. "You don't actually like her, do you?"

No, I don't like her.

I more than like her.

I'm tragically obsessed with her.

"Leave."

I gave her my back, graduating to throwing doors open. When I reached the final door in the hallway, I found it locked. *Bingo.*

I released the door. "*Farrow.*"

I could break it clean off its hinges if I wanted to. Normally, I would. Strangely, with Octi, I wanted her to let me in. To invite me into her domain.

"Jerk," she greeted from behind the wood. She sounded fine. Calm and casual. *Brave.*

I pressed my forehead to the door, closing my eyes. Her voice alone soothed my fucking soul. And that was a problem. A big one. "Open the door."

"I'm not even opening a can of tuna for you to slit your wrist with. Try again."

"Let me rephrase—open the door or I'll kick it down."

So much for wanting to worm my way back into her good graces. My body hummed—one part rage and two parts desperation. She needed to open up. *Now.*

"You can do that." The sound of a drawer opening filled the space. "I'm as good with a knife as I am with a sword." On cue, something *thunk*ed. Like a blade hitting wood. "Fuck around and find out, Sun."

Despite myself, a smile tipped my lips up. She was a one-woman army, and I admired that.

I leaned a shoulder against the door. "You threw away fifty-thousand dollars' worth of shoes, young lady."

She yawned. "You had someone put them back in my walk-in closet."

"How do you know?" Was I that predictable?

Silence met my question. Another beat passed before she answered, with obvious reluctance, "You always take care of me."

"Yet, you ran away."

"Bitch, I drove. Under the speed limit, too. Don't give yourself so much credit."

"Open up."

"Shut it down."

I fought a smile. "Tell you a fun fact about the octopus?" I bargained.

Silence. I took it as my cue. *Finally.*

"The octopus releases ink when it's in danger. The mucus and melanin cloud the predator's sense of smell, making it hard for them to find the octopus." I twisted, resting my forehead against the door again. "But the ink is so potent, if the octopus doesn't escape its own ink, it could die."

What are you doing, and when did you become Animal Fucking Planet?

Oliver and Romeo would have a field day if they heard me right now.

Still, I ran the tip of my nose along the chipped wood as my lips moved. "Sometimes, you have to take a chance. You've got too much to lose by ending this, Octi." Was this begging? Groveling? I didn't know. Didn't care, either. In fact, I only cared about one thing—getting this woman back inside my house.

I waited a minute for her to speak. One minute stretched into two. Then three. Another minute, and I swore I'd leave here with a purple-pink dent in the middle of my forehead.

Finally, Farrow took me out of my misery. "You could've told me about the engagement party."

My lungs emptied, *whooshing* against the wood. I flattened my lips together. I never explained myself to anyone other than Mom, and doing so right now felt humbling. Farrow was, of course, right. I could have. I *should* have.

"I copped out," I admitted.

MY DARK DESIRE | 219

More silence. Then a response. "Come again?" I could hear a hint of a smile in her words. *Little shit.*

"I said I copped out," I repeated, louder now. "I took the easy way out, because I'm not used to dealing with messes. And what we are is… *messy.*" To say the least. I sighed, exhaling hard. "And because I have the emotional palate of a Veggie Straw."

Her chuckle tumbled past the door, and a ten-ton rock rolled off my heart. "I still don't like you."

"You can dislike me and still love the way my cock fills your pussy, Farrow. You can even hate me and enjoy being showered with presents and legal help." I curled my fist around the doorknob, knowing it wouldn't open but wishing for it anyway. "This thing with Eileen isn't real. She will never have my kisses. My adoration. My complete and full attention. She is a checkmark in a box. She's no threat to you in the same way a lone shooting star is no threat to the sun."

"Zach…" It came out louder yet quiet—her voice just behind the door now. "Do you think of me as the sun?"

No. You're the entire fucking universe.

And I hate that most about you.

"We have a deal." I cleared my throat, trying to sound pragmatic. "And I will fulfill my end of the bargain. I'm here."

"Till when?"

"Until the very end."

I held my breath, waiting for the door to unlock, but it didn't.

"Why were you awful to me on my birthday?" Her voice rolled over my skin like velvet. I could practically feel her heat pouring through the other side of the door.

"Because," I admitted through gritted teeth, "we both need the reminder that this is only a business transaction. I enjoy you, Farrow. In more ways than I can count. If we don't make that separation… this thing could tear us both apart." My fingers curled into fists, and I bit my knuckles, drawing blood. "Now kindly open the door. I have some important information regarding your legal case I'd like to share with you."

Finally—*finally*—the door whined open. I stepped back, my breath caught in my fucking throat as I saw her for the first time in nearly twenty-four hours. Makeup free. Hair a mess. In blue sweatpants and a

USA Fencing tee. Simple. Unassuming. *Perfect.*

"Farrow." I choked on her name. *Get your shit together, Zach.* I shook my head, ridding myself of the spell she'd put me under, and trained my face to its usual callous disinterest. "I have some news."

I brushed past her, entering her room. A jolt of pleasure warmed my shoulder where we connected. I expected the tiny room to burst with personality as big as its owner's. Instead, it seemed impersonal. The bare essential furniture. No intimate belongings. No pictures. Nothing out of place. Nothing *in general.* It could've been a guestroom. Or the torture chamber of a serial killer. I raised a stack of folders I'd brought with me, depositing them on her nightstand.

Her eyes followed my movements. "What's this?"

"Bryan and Deanne ran the records in the bureau." I flipped a folder open and retrieved a document littered with highlights, handing it to her. "There's a time discrepancy with the will."

Her mouth tumbled open, her plump lower lip begging to be scooped into my mouth and sucked to oblivion. *Fuck.* I'd never kissed a woman in my entire life, but I wanted to now. Wanted to feel her heat and tongue mix with mine. For us to melt into one entity.

Farrow tucked a lock of hair behind her ear, her eyes running over the text. "What does this mean?"

"It means the executed will doesn't match the one officially filed three years prior." I studied her face, searching for a reaction. "Vera's will has no legal standing."

As she read, her eyes became shinier, glistening with tears she refused to shed. Something feral reared its head inside my chest. I wanted to hug her. To tuck her into my side. To shield her from a world that always failed her.

"Zach." She snapped her head up, smiling. "This is amazing. It's proof Vera faked the will. We can contest it."

"Not yet." I plucked the sheet from her fingers, tucking it back into the file. "Dan, Bryan, and Deanne want more time."

"What?" Her smile dropped. "Why?"

"The stronger our case is, the easier it will be to win it. We want timelines, hard evidence, a play-by-play of how she did it, when she did it, and who assisted her. There's a witness on the original will we need to speak with. We can't half-ass this, Octi. It needs to be bulletproof.

You have to be patient."

"Ugh." She flung herself at me, wrapping her arms around my neck, her lips kissing my skin as she spoke. "But I don't want to be patient."

For a second, I froze in my spot, fighting my instinct to pull away. *What the fuck, what the fuck, what the fuck.*

I slammed my eyes shut, counting down from ten. *10, 9, 8...* I popped an eye open, realizing I didn't feel like pouring acid over my head. *7, 6...* My shoulders rolled back, relaxing a bit, easing into her touch. *5, 4...* I breathed through my nose, familiar with each and every delicious scent coming from Farrow. *3...* I stopped counting, letting myself enjoy it.

Our skin felt like velvet against each other. Hers glided along mine like silk, squeezing me to her. It was... pleasant. And marked the first time I'd ever seen her let go. She dropped the warrior act, utterly radiating without the heavy armor in the way.

A thread of pride stitched itself into my chest. She'd chosen *me* to drop her guard around. The cold, cruel villain in her *Cinderella* story. The worst part—I doubted she even realized what she'd done.

I weaved my fingers through her hair, unsure what to do with them. Did I stroke her waves? Run my fingers through the strands? Pat her head like she'd just returned from kindergarten with a gold star on her workbook? My fingers trembled. I almost stepped back with how overwhelmed the options made me.

This is happening. It is happening, and I don't want it to end.

I pressed my cheek to hers, relishing the fact that I could. "Time will fly."

"How do you know?" Her breath tickled my ear.

I didn't cower. Didn't shiver. Didn't retreat.

"Because it always does when you have fun."

"You are a lot of things, Zachary Sun, but fun is not one of them."

"Your pussy is in complete disagreement."

"My pussy doesn't call the shots."

"Perhaps it should. Lovely creature. I'm its number-one fan."

Her fingers slid up my neck, cupping my cheeks. She drew away from our embrace, tipping her chin up at me, eyes dilating as she soaked in our position. The proximity. The *touch*. Our eyes met. Hers gleamed like the sparkling Mediterranean, so impossibly blue I couldn't look away. Her lips parted. I dropped my gaze, tracing them with my eyes.

"Just once…" She let her thumb drift to my lips, hovering over them. "Just once, can I kiss you? I mean *really* kiss you."

"Farrow." Her name tore out of my throat, guttural and raw.

"Do you think you're ready for a kiss, Zach?"

No. Yes.

I feigned confidence, digging my fingers into her sides. "Sweetheart, I've been ready since you sat at that Go table in a flimsy nightgown and tried to pretend you belong."

"I never tried to pretend, you fool. I knew I'd stand out—and was proud of it."

She beamed, and in that moment, I'd never seen anything so miraculous, and stunning, and *fuck it.* I erased the rest of the space between us, searing my lips to hers.

For a moment, we just breathed each other in. The air crackled between us like fireworks. Her lips were soft and warm, pliant in contrast with the rest of her. Every cell in my body tingled. It felt like we were fusing together, and I craved more.

Slowly—so damn slowly—I pried her mouth open and glided my tongue along her lower lip. She let out a tiny moan, and I remembered what Tabitha told me before I sent her to hell—Farrow didn't do love. Was incapable of feelings. There'd be nothing to worry about for her. Her heart wouldn't break. But mine?

Farrow's tongue found mine and slid into my mouth, chasing away my thoughts. The sensation felt awkward—even uncomfortable. Having someone else's organ in my body made the skin on the back of my neck crawl.

I froze in place, but Farrow didn't relent. She slid her fingernails along my scalp, sending blissful shivers down my spine. She took her time withdrawing her tongue from my mouth. It was only after she retreated that I realized I fucking loved having a part of her inside me.

I took over, clutching her shoulders and kissing her with abandon. Our mouths fought, nipping and biting and kissing and growling. I swallowed every groan and whimper she produced, holding her by her hair and backing her against the wall. We both stumbled over discarded blankets and strewn pillows, laughing into our kiss. I wanted to devour her. To eat her whole and lick my fingers afterwards.

"Heaven," I decided, my tongue chasing hers inside her mouth, swirling and caressing, reaching every corner. "You taste like heaven."

My fingers moved from her hair, hands bracketing her delicate throat. I tilted her head up, kissing my way down her neck. She felt so fragile in my arms, bucking her hips to meet my hard cock. I shook with anticipation, ready to fuck her through the wall and into another dimension, I was so horny for her. Her mouth found mine, and again, we kissed like our lives depended on it.

"Clothes." She clawed at my shirt, breathless. "We don't need them."

I happened to be in complete agreement. She began tearing at my button-down when the door downstairs kicked open and slammed against the wall.

"I'm baaaack." Regina had returned. *Great.*

In an instant, Octi pushed me away. I staggered back, frustrated and horny and on goddamn edge. "We can't do this." Fae wiped her swollen, bruised lips. "No one can know I'm messing around with an engaged man."

"The engagement is bullshit," I reminded her. Eileen had informed me just yesterday that she'd like to return to New York as soon as our schedule allowed.

"No, your *relationship* is bullshit. The engagement, however, is very real." She was right.

I stared at her, frustrated and annoyed. The hushed voices downstairs left no room for doubt—Tabitha had filled Regina in.

Farrow rubbed her face, growling. "What do you want, Zach?"

I want to soak in your warmth just a little longer, so when I return to my cold, numbing life, I don't freeze over.

"I want us to honor each other's promises." I kissed the top of her head, halting for a moment to let the secret scent of her body crawl into my system. "Fix me, Farrow."

Each second she got closer to unchaining herself from Vera and her stepsisters was a second that brought us further apart. The moment she didn't need me anymore, she'd leave.

So what if she does?

I would return to my peaceful, quiet existence.

Structured, ruthless, and solitary.

Lifeless.

CHAPTER FORTY-THREE

Farrow: We have a breakthrough regarding Dad's will.

Farrow: I'll definitely be able to contest it.

Farrow: Ari?

Farrow: You there?

Farrow: You're fired as my best friend.

Farrow: Okay, you're not. But come back. I need you.

Chapter Forty-Four

Farrow

Two days after my birthday, I was back to scrubbing toilets and wiping windows. My knees scraped the tiles of the bathroom in Zach's guestroom as I poured bleach into the toilet nobody had used for at least a decade. The fumes tickled my nose, burning my eyes.

Zach roamed the house like an unhinged phantom, barking orders and casting a dark, formidable shadow on Natalie and the rest of his staffers. He'd done zero work since morning, instead popping his head into the various rooms I floated between and demanding to know what I wanted to eat for lunch, what my plans were after work hours, and if it were possible to spend time together.

I assumed 'spend time together' was code for rubbing our genitals until fire ignited. Shamefully, I did not find the prospect too off-putting. Yes, he was engaged, but I'd read the thick contract with Eileen on his desk. Neither of them wanted to share a room, touch one another, or even cohabitate in the same state. I'd even been privy to their conversations. They sounded like elderly siblings barely managing to tolerate one another through the mutual interest of dividing a fat inheritance.

Still, something ate at my inner organs, devouring me inside and out, one bite at a time.

I traded the bleach spray for beeswax and cleaning wipes, moving on to the wooden cabinets. Behind me, the door creaked open. I used my elbow to wipe my sweaty forehead, not bothering to look at the intruder.

"I already told you… I want mac n' cheese balls and a burger for lunch." I sighed. "Yes, I know I'm not five. No, I don't car—"

"Get your ass up, Cinderella. We're out of here."

I whipped my head around to find Dallas filling the doorway, clad in a huge faux leopard coat, a pink cowgirl hat, diamond-studded sunglasses, and enough makeup to repaint the Sistine Chapel. She looked… *unhinged.*

But also extremely freaking adorable.

I was still on my knees, trying not to get an epileptic episode from watching her alone. "What are you doing here?"

"Celebrating your birthday, silly." Dallas ripped the shades from her eyes, grinning at me. "Sorry it took me over a day to organize. I was ironing out the kinks." She bulldozed inside, protecting her nose (and baby) from the fumes with pinched fingers. "Come on, now. Our flight leaves in thirty minutes."

"Our *flight?*" I jumped to my feet, eyes flaring in horror. "What do you mean, our flight? I don't even have my passport on me."

She waved me off. "Don't worry, it's domestic."

I let her drag me out of the bathroom by the wrist for the sole fact that I refused to be responsible for harming her baby. "I didn't even pack."

"I packed for you." Her voice practically radiated cheer as she all but skipped her way out to the hall. "Hope you like thongs and leather nipple warmers."

I honestly didn't know whether she was joking or preparing me for what was to come.

"My ID…" I trailed off.

"We're flying private. You don't need anything."

Private. Holy shit. Dallas wasn't playing. We were almost at the front door when Zach materialized like a bat from hell, blocking our way. He was the epitome of tall, dark, handsome, and psychotic. Darkness rolled off his shoulders like smoke crawling into my lungs. A black cashmere sweater and charcoal slacks wrapped around his body, paired with a chunky wristwatch.

He crossed his arms, attention pinned on Dallas. "Where do you think you're taking her?"

"She's not your living room vase, Zach. She's a person." Dallas tilted her chin up. "*I'm* not taking her anywhere. We're both leaving."

He closed his eyes. Took a deep breath. Opened them—and still looked ready to burst into angry flames. "Where are you two going?"

"To have some fun." Dallas tipped her cowgirl hat and winked at him, all good vibes. "It's this thing where you laugh and have a good time and don't plot the mass murder of people you disagree with. Look it up on Google. I swear it exists."

"We have plans together." His nostrils flared, and he got so deep in her face, I feared he'd accidentally touch her, then projectile vomit all over the floor. I'd just polished it an hour ago.

"Yes." She draped her arms over her pregnant belly. "I saw what you had in store for her. Another day of work. She's coming with me."

Zach stepped even deeper into her face. "Absolutely not."

"Nice caveman impression, Zach." I laced my arm through Dallas', our friendship bracelets clinking together. "Now go ooga-booga in front of someone else."

"I volunteer as tribute." Romeo's nonchalant drawl came from behind Zach's back as he approached us. "By the way, Sun, you better get out of my wife's face unless you're eager to find out what pissing into a bag for the rest of your life feels like."

Zach didn't budge. "Farrow has plans."

"Farrow has a *mouth*." Romeo jerked him back by his collar. "If she wants to stay, she can say so."

Zach's eyes glided to my face, searching for help. The truth was, I wanted to stay with him. But it was exactly why I *shouldn't* stay. He was never mine to have, only to borrow. I needed to put my emotional chips on other people. And Dallas? A solid bet if I'd ever seen one.

I shook my head. "See you later." I shouldered past him with Dallas close behind. "Enjoy your raw fish and overcooked neurons."

Romeo rested a hand on the small of Dallas' back, leading us to a sleek black limo. "You heard the lady."

"You can't just leave." Zach tailed me, ignoring the two of them. "You're on a shift."

The cold burrowed into my bones, but I ignored it. "Fire me."

I'd reached the limo now. The driver stood at the door, opening it for me. I smiled at him, about to slide inside when Zach grabbed the back of my arm over my shirt, trying to tug me to him.

I jerked my arm back and swiveled. "Don't you dare ruin this for me."

Dallas settled into the backseat with Romeo kissing her through the window, whispering his goodbyes against her temple.

I gestured to them. "This, right here, is my Cinderella moment. Spending time with a new friend. Going somewhere fun. Feeling like a full-fledged human and not just someone's housekeeper for a day. I don't care what you have planned for me, Zach. You threw an engagement party on my birthday. I work ridiculous hours for you. I'm allowed to have this."

His eyes ran in their sockets, drinking my face in. "I don't want you sitting in an unprotected vehicle. At least take mine."

My shoulders sagged. Some of my anger dissipated. I pressed a hand to his chest, met by the wild gallop of his heart, the thuds so intense they hurt my palm. "I always drive my Prius."

"And I always have a small heart attack when you do." He looked downright annoyed by the fact. Then, realizing what it sounded like, he added, "You're my shot at normalcy. I'm fully invested in your life until I discard you."

"Extremely romantic."

"Sadly, it's probably the most romantic thing I've ever said."

"I'll be okay."

He grabbed my elbows, and I fought the urge to kiss him. "Promise."

"I promise."

He threaded his fingers into my hair, cupping my head. My breath caught in my throat when I realized he was about to kiss me. I wanted to be kissed by him more than I wanted to survive the remainder of our contract. Which was exactly why I needed to put a stop to it. For me, Zachary Sun would break all his rules. But for *him*, I'd break my own heart.

I turned my head at the last second.

His lips landed on my cheek, brushing a lone tear that escaped my eye. "Have fun," he croaked out.

"Thank you."

Chapter Forty-Five

Farrow

"Here. Try this one. Duck jianbing." Dallas ripped open a bag of mantecaditos, popping one into her mouth. "How were the Scottish teacakes, by the way?"

I nibbled on a biltong jerky, one of about two thousand snacks that splayed in front of us. "Oral orgasm perfection."

We hadn't even taken off yet, and Dallas had already sampled the majority of food Romeo stocked his plane with. Her favorites from every country. Evidently, she'd visited all of them. I stared at her with a mixture of alarm and awe. How could she fit all of this food into her body?

Frankie kicked her feet on the couch across from us. I couldn't take my eyes off Dallas' younger sister. She was the kind of beautiful that defied both nature and logic. With feline green eyes, pouty lips, and lush brown locks that cascaded all the way to her butt.

"Don't look at my sister that way." Frankie's eyes narrowed. "She's eating for two."

I slanted my head to one side. "Sumo wrestlers?"

She burst into laughter.

Dallas leaned over to swat her arm. "I told you she was fun."

"You also told me she can kill me with a toothpick." Frankie fanned herself, wriggling her brows. "Is this true?"

"A very slight exaggeration." I picked up my cocktail, taking a sip. "But I know how to inflict serious damage with sharp objects. Why?"

"I have some names and addresses." Frankie released a hard candy from cellophane wrap, popping it into her mouth. "But whatever. We'll talk about work some other time. Now let's celebrate your birthday."

I frowned. "How can you celebrate a person you don't know?"

"You're certified by my sister. Anyone who passes her bar is worthy of being celebrated."

The plane began rolling before it took off, slicing through dense silvery clouds. I didn't even ask them where we were going. Destination was of little importance when you had good company. And these girls were prime BFF material.

"Anyway." Dallas sucked her thumb clean of crumbs, grabbing a duffel bag from a seat and hurling it into my arms. "Go take a shower and change. We'll be landing in New York soon."

New York. One of my favorite cities. My heart sang. I slung the duffel over my shoulder and walked to the bathroom, opening the door.

Then, I dropped the bag. A squeal tore past my lips. "Ari."

My best friend stood at the threshold, glowing and beautiful and smiling like a loon. "Finally. I've been hiding here for *ages.*"

We jumped into each other's arms, squealing so loud, a raccoon would be jealous. She hugged me tight enough to grind my bones together.

I rocked her side to side. "What are you doing here?"

"Your new bestie called me to surprise you." She laughed into my ear. "She's a keeper."

"Bestie? That was the fastest promotion I've ever gotten." Dallas popped in the doorway, propping a shoulder over the frame. "Then again, it's also my first ever job position."

Ari peeled herself from me, giving Dallas a once-over. "Girl, I'm sure you've experienced *plenty* of positions to get to where you are today."

Dallas ran a palm over her very pregnant belly. "You have no idea."

"No, but I want to hear all about it."

After more squealing and giggling, Ari and Dallas retired to the cabin while I took a lengthy shower, washed and blow-dried my hair, and shrugged on skintight jeans and a designer hoodie Dallas had picked out for me. The clothes came with a note:

Not every girl wants a dress to feel pretty.
Some dazzle with combat boots and a sword.
One of them has even become my dear friend.
Happy Birthday. F. <3
Dal

When I finished, the plane was already preparing for landing. Soon enough, the girls and I spilled out onto the tarmac, where a uniformed driver ushered us to Angelo's.

"Only the best Italian restaurant in NYC." Dallas kicked her feet up in the back of the limo. "And I've been to all of them."

Ari and Frankie laughed.

Dallas didn't, staring at my best friend, serious as a heart attack. "I'm not joking. Did you know there are twenty-four hundred? And that doesn't include the underground ones."

Ari's smile disappeared. She elbowed me on a whisper, "Where did you find this chick?"

"At a dinner party." I shrugged, grinning at Dallas. "Where else?"

After a seven-course meal, during which I ate enough for the entire nation of Belgium, we grabbed cocktails at a nearby bar. Frankie flashed her fake ID and bought us five rounds.

"How can you afford this?" Dallas stared her sister down. "I thought Daddy confiscated your credit card after you bought a small island for service dogs to retire on."

"Can you believe the lack of altruism from him?" Frankie rolled her eyes, knocking back a fruity cocktail. "Those dogs have done more for our country than most politicians."

"I'll ask again, Sis. How can you afford this?"

"Oh, Oliver gave me two of his Amex cards. Such a gem."

Dallas choked on her mocktail. "You two are in contact?"

"No." Frankie giggled, like the answer was obvious. "I texted him that I need to borrow a card or two, and he sent them to me with a courier."

"Frankie, credit cards are not a cocktail dress. You can't borrow them."

"Of course, I can. How do you think I've been funding my life for the past three weeks?"

By the time we reached Broadway to catch a show, we weren't pleasantly drunk—we were completely hammered.

"What are we watching?" I hiccupped, swaying inside Dallas' arms.

She'd knocked back non-alcoholic margaritas while we got sloshed, periodically glaring at her mocktails and hissing out, "How ironic it is that pregnant women can only have virgin drinks?"

"Cinderella." Frankie spun around, her '50s dress blooming like a flower. "It's a limited four-week run. Isn't it great?"

Isn't it fitting? I corrected to myself.

No matter how hard I tried to run away from the comparison, it always boomeranged back to me. Ari pulled me from Dallas to make sure I didn't squash her, coiling my arm over her shoulder to carry me into the hall. Theater-goers weaved in and out of the building.

We found our seats and fell into them in fits of unexplained snickers. Frankie and Ari even produced a small tiara from a designer bag and placed it on my head. The show was incredible. I had to keep myself from crying through most of it. And when we escaped into the prickly early winter night, all I could think about was that Dallas was right. *Sometimes you have to write your own story to get your happy ending.*

"So." Ari pressed her shoulder to mine, deliberately walking faster than the Townsend sisters to lose them. "What's going on with Zach?"

"We're fooling around while he's engaged." I barely mustered the energy to tip a shoulder up. "So, you know, pretty messed up."

"Dallas says he's your puppy." Ari scanned my face. "That he follows you around and stabs anyone who dares to get near you."

"Ha."

"Does this mean he pees himself a little every time he sees you?"

"Hope not. I'm in charge of his laundry, too."

I had no idea where we were going, and I was beginning to understand that it didn't matter. Sooner or later, a limo would appear out of thin air and scoop us all to a boutique airport, where we'd fly back home on a luxurious plane that looked like a Manhattan bachelor pad. That was the reality of Dallas Costa, the most charmed girl in all of America.

"He wants me," I admitted, feeling my throat squeezing around a ball of anxiety. "But he wants to please his mother even more. This has no legs."

But it had a heart and a soul, and that scared me. I didn't tell my best friend why Zachary Sun was so enchanted with me. That something had made him a human-fearing heathen. That I was his only shot at salvation, even though I had no idea what had made him this way.

"And if he wanted you more than pleasing his mother?" Ari looped her arm around my elbow. "What would you have done?"

We stopped at a crosswalk, Dallas and Frankie now joining us. I swallowed. I'd been avoiding asking myself this question for a while now.

Finally, I said, "If I allow myself to hope, I'll allow myself to break. And I have never had the privilege to do that."

A limo rolled in front of us, double-parking and stopping at our feet. The driver slid out and opened the door for us.

I slipped in, knowing I hadn't told Ari the entire truth.

Because a part of me had already cracked.

And every day that passed, Zach pried the fissure open even more.

Chapter Forty-Six

Farrow

The Sun manor resembled a gingerbread house in my tipsy state. Snow swirled together on the windowsills like thick frosting. I swayed back and forth in Dallas' heels, flinching when the limo door slammed shut behind me. The silly plastic tiara toppled off my head.

I crouched to pick it up, stumbling back when Natalie stormed out before I could touch it, clutching manila files to her chest.

"Oh." Her lips curved down. "You're back." As always, she seemed impeccably put-together and freakishly unhappy.

I returned the tiara to my head, tossing the duffel bag Dallas gifted me over my shoulder. "You sound disappointed."

Natalie had given me shit since my first shift. Usually, I let it roll off my shoulders, even when she *accidentally* and habitually spilled her drinks for me to clean.

"I *am* disappointed." She pivoted, following me back into the house. "Before you came along, we were getting to know each other."

I dropped the duffel at the stairs, heading to the kitchen for a glass of water, only half-listening to her.

She shadowed me, uncomfortably close to my heels. "We were forming something until you confused him with your… your…" She sucked in a breath, giving me a once-over, trying to figure out what Zach saw in me.

Whoa. Déjà vu.

"Did Constance raise you, too?" I kicked my heels off in the hall, brain a bit fuzzy, but vaguely remembering Zach loathed shoes in the house.

Natalie ignored me, stomping her feet at the kitchen's entrance, gesturing up and down my body. "I don't even know what he sees."

I snatched a tall glass from the dishwasher and filled it with tap water, bringing the rim to my lips. "Very mature."

"You need to get lost. He's engaged. She will never let him keep you around."

Ha. If only Natalie knew that neither I nor Zach planned on seeing much of each other after the next few weeks. Not that it mattered much to Eileen. She'd been the one to request a clause that allowed extramarital dating, just in case she ever got over *her* aversion to people.

"Thanks for the advice, Natalie, but Zach doesn't like randos here after hours." I wiggled my fingers her way. "Toodles."

"Wait… You don't actually think he's into you, do you?"

No. Yes. Maybe a little.

I knew his body liked me. And that his mind enjoyed my company. But I also knew the same could be said about sex toys.

I didn't answer her question, dumping the leftover water and soaping up the glass.

"You know you're just a toy for him." She observed me with a crescent smile, trying to gauge if her poisonous arrow hit anything vital. "I see you guys sneaking around the house. You're just his plaything. Eileen's the real deal."

I kept my expression neutral, rinsing off the suds, telling myself what I always told myself whenever Reggie informed me that she needed to bleach her eyes after looking at me.

Hatred isn't about what you lack. It's about someone finding something they want in you and realizing they can't take it.

"Still don't believe me?" She hissed out a laugh. "Look at him with you, then look at him with Eileen. That's all the answer you need."

I set the glass down in the sink with too much force. It cracked, a tiny shard tunneling its way into my palm. I was bleeding. Inside and out.

Why, Fae? Why? It's just an arrangement.

But it wasn't. And it was time I admitted it.

I kept my hand in the sink so Natalie couldn't see it. Forever an injured animal fighting to save face.

I feigned a smile, the buzz wearing off. "Is that all?"

"Maybe check the dining room." Natalie hitched a shoulder up, dissatisfied I didn't burst into tears. "It'll wipe that smug look off your face."

I did not, in fact, check the dining room.

First, I checked Zach's office, taking the stairs two at a time, itching to end the magical night with him. The doors swung against the stoppers as I burst into the room. He'd installed them there a few weeks ago, after the first time he'd witnessed me rattle the shelves bracketing the doorframe.

I ambled into the room, barefoot, checking left and right, stopping to stroke a Go stone.

Not here.

Next, I strolled to his bedroom, knocking first. No answer. I cracked the door open, peeking my head in to glance at his bed. Still made. With a huff, I began moving room to room, coming up empty. I trudged downstairs, headed to the one room I didn't want to check on principle. But as I approached the dining room, the soft *clink* of utensils drifted my way.

I twisted my wrist to check my watch. Ten. Zach always ate dinner at seven. My legs carried me forward. Soft light spilled into the hallway. Live music caressed my ears. Violins. Flutes. A freakin' harp. A tidal wave of delectable scents crashed into me. Lasagna. Cinnamon pudding. Candied bacon. All my favorites.

Zach knew this. I'd once told him after he caught me moving a stone in our never-ending Go game. *Anything that tastes like somebody else's family. So, I can close my eyes and pretend I have one, too.*

A seed of excitement planted in my belly, sprouting roots.

No way. Did he...?

I skipped to the doorway, the tiara clinging on for dear life. It tumbled to the rug when I rounded the corner, coming to a halt. My heart crashed to my ribs with it. It was a wonder how something so painful could be so silent.

Zach sat at the long table, his back to me, eating dinner with Eileen. A lovely pale-pink gown draped over her lithe frame. The room spun, a blur of red. Roses. Everywhere. Choking the room like a bloodbath. And the candles. God, the candles—lighting up every inch of the place.

I froze, unable to move. Natalie's words bounced between my ears.

Look at him with you, then look at him with her.

They were sharing a romantic dinner.

He was courting her.

Courting was never part of the contract. I'd read the entire thing. Even peeked behind his back at the track changes on the Word doc.

Eileen leaned over the table, whispering something to Zach, who sat ramrod straight. I could see the moment she noticed me. A small grin played on her lips. She maintained eye contact with me as she threw her head back and laughed at something he said.

Now I got it. Natalie's smugness. Her warning. She knew what I was stepping into.

I treaded backward, bumping into a lamp. The thud rang in the air, just as the ensemble played its last note of Beethoven. I caught the lamp at the last minute before it fell to the floor.

Zach's head snapped up. "Farrow."

Our eyes met. I didn't know why, but I couldn't move. I couldn't even bear the thought of facing him. Not now.

Back away. Leave. Abort mission.

And still, my feet remained rooted to the hardwood. He stood, rushing to me. The sudden movement spurred me into motion. I ran. Sprinted faster than I'd ever run. Straight toward my beatdown Prius.

As I burst out of the mansion, I realized I had nowhere to go. My so-called family wouldn't have me. I didn't want them, either.

Dallas. Her name shotgunned through my head. Dallas would give me shelter.

Zach sauntered behind me as I changed direction, making my way to the Costa mansion. "Farrow." He picked up pace, probably realizing I had a target now. "Where do you think you're going?"

It began to drizzle, the rain tap-tapping my face.

His footsteps paused, hesitated a beat, then continued to crunch behind me. "I'm talking to you."

I flipped him the bird without turning, picking up speed toward the Costa mansion. "I know. I just wish you wouldn't."

"What, pray tell, have I done now to piss you off?"

Is this dude serious?

I could hear his teeth grind together as he tried to catch my shoulder. I dodged, always faster. The rain intensified. Icy water seeped into my clothes.

"Go back to your date."

"Farrow, come here."

Screw this. I refused to let him treat me like a dog. I reached Dallas' door and banged on it loud enough to wake the dead. Zach clawed at my shoulder, turning me around. I saw him through a curtain of raindrops, hair slicked back and wet, face dark as thunder. His designer suit clung to his powerful body, and for a second, I found myself jealous of fabric.

"We need to return to the house." He shivered, but I wasn't sure if it was from the cold. "*Now.*"

"I'm not your business."

"You literally *are.*"

Ugh. *Dammit.*

"I'm off hours," I amended. "I can do whatever I want. And what I want is to not be within stabbing distance of you."

Footsteps approached from the other side of the door. Zach squinted up to the sky, flinched at the rain, then lowered his eyes to me again. "I can explain, if you just let me—"

The door swung open. Romeo Costa filled the frame, approximately the size of a T-54 tank. "What's going on here?"

"Nothing." Zach clasped my arm, his fingers frozen. "Farrow and I were just leaving."

"I'd like to spend the night in your house," I blurted out.

Romeo's expression shifted from irritation to confusion. "Ah, fuck." He ran a hand over his face. "Shortbread collecting strays again. She promised to stop after the fourth kitty."

"She's no stray, and she isn't staying, either." Zach tugged me again. "Come on, Farrow."

I kept my attention on Romeo, standing my ground. "Can you call Dal?"

I knew I wasn't being fair. Zach and I had a deal, and so far, only I had broken it. But I couldn't help it. Did he have to court Eileen in his house? He had the means to take her to the moon if he wanted to. He didn't have to throw her in my face time and time again.

Why do you care? And how could he possibly know that you care?

God, I really needed to confront these pesky feelings head-on. One day. Just not now.

Romeo turned to Zach, brow raised.

238 | *HUNTINGTON & SHEN*

I frowned. "Did you really just ask your friend for permission? Are you five?"

"Not helping your case," Romeo said at the same time Zach drawled out, "No."

I jerked my arm away. "*Yes.*"

Zach glared at Romeo. "I'll short your new pharmaceutical company."

"I can't, man." He seemed genuinely apologetic. "Shortbread will make caviar out of my sperm, and we're not done having children."

"Farrow, *please.*" Zach spat out the word like it was acid in his mouth. "We need to get back inside."

I finally turned to face him. "Why?"

"Because." Zach sent a quick glance to Romeo, his ears turning a little a pink, hidden by the fast pellets of rain.

I popped a brow. "Yes?"

"Because I cannot fucking stand the rain." He threw his hands in the air. "Happy, now? I'm triggered. PTSD'd. Whatever you want to call it. I have never—in the past twenty-one years—been out when it rained."

The rain turned into hail, striking every inch of our skin. I couldn't believe what I'd just heard.

Romeo cleared his throat. "I'm going to leave you two to it…" He slid the door shut, pausing before the click. "Farrow, let me know if you still need a place to crash."

Zach and I remained standing before one another. We were both panting hard. I had an idea. A terrible idea. But one that needed to be executed, nonetheless.

I reached into my pocket, checking for the metal object. "You want to explain yourself?"

He stuck his hand in his hair and tugged, flinging raindrops everywhere. "Desperately."

"Let's run to my Prius. I'll drive."

"I don't—" He clamped his mouth shut.

"You're ready, Zach. It's time." I grabbed his arms. "I'm here to heal you, right? So heal."

He closed his eyes, screwing his fingers into their sockets. "This deal has a lot of strings attached to it."

"We're one big messy knot, Mr. Sun. Deal with it."

Chapter Forty-Seven

Zach

The Prius cruised through Potomac, fending rain off its windshield. It seemed so light. So insubstantial against nature. *A deathtrap.* I gripped the armrest, sinking my fingernails into it until I ripped the cheap fabric, ignoring the way my heart beat at 10,000 pulses a second.

His blood. His face. The scent of burned flesh. The memories washed over me with rain, just as they always did. But denying Farrow this request meant continuing our earlier argument, and I didn't want to risk it.

So... you'd rather risk perishing in this deathtrap?

Not my finest act of logic, but I'd quickly discovered logic didn't exist when it came to Farrow Ballantine.

I double-checked my seatbelt, half-expecting it to split if I tugged too hard. "Must you drive like a maniac who just binged on four kilograms of coke?"

She sped toward the outskirts of town. "I'm driving below city limits."

I wanted to throttle her and kiss her at the same time. We both dripped salty water into her seats, our clothes heavy and sticking to our bodies.

"Where are we going?"

"You'll see."

"No, you'll tell me," I snapped. Then, realizing I was being an asshole again, I cleared my throat. "I need at least some sort of control over the situation. This is triggering me."

She pressed her lips together, mulling this over. "I'm taking you to my hideout place. I used to go there whenever I returned home from Seoul. I'd spend my entire summers locked up in a treehouse I built for myself."

I believed her. Believed this woman built an entire fort for herself because life didn't give her a kingdom of her own. I stared at the tears in the car roof, welcoming the distraction. "Where?"

"Gold Mine Trail."

"Great place to hide bodies."

"Kept my options open." She shrugged, her wrist slung on the steering wheel as she accelerated, ignoring the pounding rain. "I *did* live with Vera, Reggie, and Tabby."

"Your father should've divorced her."

Better yet—dump her the minute he saw Farrow was unwelcome in that house. I secretly harbored some pretty fucked-up feelings toward the man. He was dead now, but not dead enough to atone for his sins.

Fae nibbled on her lower lip, considering my words. "He was like me. He really wanted a family, at all costs. And... I guess it blinded him. The possibility of being welcomed into one." She paused. "This is why I don't do relationships. I don't want to make the same mistake. To give too much of myself to the wrong person."

The car slammed to a stop. Farrow pulled the handbrake in front of the park regulations sign. I gripped the doorhandle, stifling a growl. The place was deserted, the Prius the only car in sight in the pitch-black night. I watched her profile while my pulse slid back to normal. The way her eyelashes stuck together from the rain.

My phone buzzed in my pocket, text after text. No doubt from Eileen. I couldn't bring myself to care. For a woman who claimed to not want romance, she sought me out far too many times for my liking.

Farrow turned to face me. "Look at you."

She gathered my hands in hers. Mine shook so bad, they jerked around, hitting the center console. Heat crept up my neck, warming up my cheeks and ears. I was embarrassed, and terrified, and furious, and *alive*. So fucking alive I choked on too much oxygen. I'd never veered so far out of my comfort zone before. To me, entering an unsecured car was the equivalent of jumping off a plane without a parachute. And entering one in the rain? Might as well ask me to slit my wrists first.

"Who hurt you?" She stared at me with angel eyes that saw good where there was none. "Who did this to you? Why are you like this?"

I stared at the trees ahead, watching as they swayed like praying people at a vigil. "I'm not the talk-about-your-feelings type."

"I'm not the fuck-your-engaged-boss type." She squeezed my hand, reassuring me in her own way. "We're both out of our depths here. *Talk.*"

And in that moment, when it felt like the woods would swallow my secret and take it to its grave, I decided to make a tactical error for no other reason than to please this woman. I moved the wrong stone.

"When I was 12, Dad and I picked up his anniversary gift for Mom. The pendant."

Her eyes widened. "The other pendant in the set."

I nodded. "On our way back, a truck slammed into our car and flipped it over. Dad shielded me with his body and died."

I'm the only Sun in the world that brings darkness.

"*Zach*—"

I interrupted her, speaking with flat vowels. "But he didn't have the privilege of dying instantly. Neither did I. A rake pierced through his body, turning his death into a slow and agonizing ordeal. The entire time, he watched me, his eyes turning redder as his face became bluer."

Farrow sucked in a breath but didn't say anything.

I carried on. "I watched him lose his life in real time."

Even now, I could still see him dying before me. It didn't take much to conjure the image. Bile hiked up my throat. I swallowed it down, forcing myself to spit out the rest of what happened.

"Because of the way the car tipped, gas leaked into the engine. They had to take the car apart piece by piece before they got me out. For hours, my father's dead body laid on top of mine, his blood dripping onto me."

Farrow squeezed my hand tighter, encouraging me to continue.

"At first, the blood poured on top of me like a current. But eventually, it slowed to drips—splashing onto my face every now and then. I don't even remember Dad's last words." I swallowed, pressing my eyes shut, knowing it wouldn't erase the memory but wishing it could. "It rained that day. So goddamn cold, Dad must've felt it in his bones as he took his last breath."

The air left her lungs in a *whoosh*. I knew she pitied me. That most people would. Which was why I refused to tell anyone this. Not even the therapist Celeste Ayi sent me to until I turned sixteen. Even Romeo and Oliver only heard about what had happened through the media and Mom.

Farrow whispered, not releasing my hand, "Was the driver drunk?"

"No." I rolled my head over the headrest, salt seeping into my body through my drenched clothes. "That's the worst part. He wasn't drunk at all. He wasn't a villain. Just an overworked father of five, who reached for his coffee in his cupholder and lost control of his vehicle."

Farrow's thumb stroked the back of my hand, moving in tiny circles.

I curled my free hand into a fist, digging my nails into my palm. "He drove over the limit to finish his last job early. His kid had a recital. He pleaded guilty immediately. Then proceeded to write us an apology letter."

It occurred to me that Farrow had lost her father in an accident, too. I glanced at her, wondering if hearing about Dad's death triggered anything for her. I found my answer immediately. She had her eyes fixed on me, her full attention focused on nothing but me.

I rolled my lower lip into my mouth. "The case never made it to court—he took a plea deal. Granted his wife a speedy divorce, so she could move on and find someone else to take care of the family. My mother still pays for her kids' tuition."

Fae buried her face in her hands. "Jesus."

I wondered if this changed her perception of Constance. For all of her negative traits—and there were many—Mom wasn't a terrible human. Just deeply misguided, chained by grief, and struggling to exist without total control over every aspect of her life—and mine.

"I was left with all this rage and no one to direct it at." I stared down at my lap. "And so, I turned my rage into guilt."

I'd never said these words to anyone before. Or aloud, for that matter. The truth of them pierced my chest like a bullet. I'd gone so long without feeling anything at all, that ever since Farrow entered my life, I'd been on sensory overload. She was living proof that angels existed in hell.

"I am so sorry." Her voice drifted into my ears, soothing me where I burned. "I'm sorry the world was so cruel to you. And I'm sorry you had to carry this experience alone." Her fingers interlaced with mine. "Most of all, I'm sorry no one taught you that it's okay not to be okay. Healing is like treading water. You drown as much as you float. You need a shoulder to cry on, Zach. Not a bride."

"Speaking of my bride…" I unknotted our fingers, still unused to being touched so much. "What happened tonight—"

"Is none of my business," Farrow finished for me. "We have a deal. I know you're engaged. I should've—"

"Let me finish." I faced her. "I had this entire thing planned for you tonight. Dinner. Candlelight. Flowers… All those pesky things in movies."

"You watch romance movies?" She looked unconvinced.

"Involuntarily. And only to come up with ideas to make you feel… *unused.*" I grimaced. "Just because ours is a clinical arrangement does not mean you should feel taken advantage of." I paused. "Ollie gave me a list."

She pressed her lips together. "What did you watch?"

"God-awful things." I wrung my sleeve dry, making her laugh even harder. "*When Harry Met Sally*, which sucked."

"It's a classic," Farrow protested. "What's wrong with it?"

"In my opinion, two people with such unfortunate hair should not procreate. Only bad can come out of that."

She tossed her head back, bellowing. "What else did you hate?"

"*Titanic*. There was room on that door, Farrow. In fact, there was room for a party of three if they squeezed in tight."

The car shook with her laughter. I didn't understand why. I didn't find facts funny. She managed to wave between cackles. "Continue."

I sighed. "*Dirty Dancing* should be called Creepy Dancing—Swayze was considerably older than her. And *Call Me By Your Name* is basically *American Pie*, but with a peach. Look, point is, I went through extreme discomfort to apologize for your birthday."

Her smile dazzled, so big it warmed me. "You made dinner for me?"

"All your favorites."

"And bought roses and candles?"

"It *was* your birthday. And you did make a big stink about my gift, although I maintain that it was a nice gesture."

"You asked your friends for advice?" She slapped a hand over her mouth, howling behind it.

I couldn't help it—I smiled, too. Her happiness was contagious.

"Stop looking so smug," I ordered.

"Did you at least like one or two?" She wiggled her brows. "Movies."

"Octi, they were objectively terrible."

Her giggles trickled into my bloodstream, making me feel lighter. "Call me that again."

"Octi?"

"Yes."

"Octi."

She grinned. "Such an unusual nickname."

I smiled. "Such an unusual girl." I peeled my jacket off my shoulders. "At any rate, as I sat there, surrounded by roses and a home-cooked meal I made myself, I realized how pathetic I was. You weren't there. What's more, you looked so happy going away, even when I begged you to stay."

"I thought it was a power flex." Her eyes softened, and I believed her. "How did Eileen end up where I should've sat?"

I gave her a blank, dispassionate stare. "She appeared at my doorway. She came to visit my mother across the street, and I suppose she figured we could go through our checklist while she was in town."

Mom had appeared behind Eileen before I could turn her away, dragging her into my den and insisting we should all have dinner together. Then, she'd fled before the champagne even made it into a glass.

"*You know how my headaches are.*" Perhaps the least convincing excuse in existence. She hadn't had a headache in three decades.

Farrow appeared deep in thought, tapping her lips. "Why don't you tell your mom you don't want to marry her?"

"Because I don't only owe a good marriage to Mom. I owe it to Dad, too."

"And you're willing to sacrifice your happiness for your mother's?"

"Yes," I said without missing a beat. "I'm used to feeling unhappy. In fact, I'm used to not feeling anything at all. At least Mom still has a shot at happiness." Not many things got to me, but those six or so years that Mom had zoned out of life scared the shit out of me. A repeat would ruin her. Celeste Ayi and I did everything possible to prevent it.

Farrow looked miserable, which made *me* feel miserable. I loathed that her mood seemed to seep into mine, like we were connected by an invisible chain.

"I can respect that." She nodded. "All I ever wanted was a family. Somewhere to belong. I can see why you'd make one up, even if it's not organic." Farrow's chills had graduated to violent shivering. I noticed her teeth chattered, too.

"We should get naked," I blurted out.

She swatted my chest. "Very convenient."

I licked my lips. "To prevent pneumonia."

"I'm not that cold."

"Well, in that case, do it for me."

"You want me undressed?"

"I want you any way, anyhow," I admitted, knowing she'd never misinterpret my intentions for her. "But especially naked, and specifically on top of me."

She reached for the hem of her hoodie, pulling it off in one go.

And just like that, I went under, drowned by desire.

Chapter Forty-Eight

Farrow

Zach's cock shot up at the sight of me without a bra. My nipples begged for attention, extra taut and sensitive. He ignored them, reclining in his seat, his erection sticking to his thigh through his wet slacks. He stroked his cock lazily through his pants while his other hand unbuttoned his dress shirt.

I arched my back, shimmying off my jeans to my knees, still maintaining eye contact. "How many?"

His shirt fell open. "How many what?" He shook the fabric off his shoulders—ripped, bronze, and perfect.

I leaned against the driver's door and kicked my boots off with my pants, leaving my underwear on, so he could take it off with his teeth. "How many movies have you watched for me?"

Zach toed off his shoes and unbuckled his belt, not taking his eyes off my tits. "Too many."

Of everyone I'd ever met, no one made me feel as stunning as Zachary Sun did, simply by staring at me the way he stared at me. In fact, he was the first man to make me feel beautiful.

He pushed off his pants and briefs in one go. His dick sprung out, the shaft as silky as velvet. Thick, long, and complemented by smooth veins and a prominent crown. The mere sight of it made my mouth water.

Zach tossed his pants to the backseat, his hand halting on something. "What's this?" He pulled it from the backseat. A Chanel shoe box.

Heat shot to my cheeks. "Your gift to me."

"Part of it," he corrected, hooking his finger at the bottom of the satin bow and untying it until it loosened into a long cream-white string. "The best part of your gift is yet to come. Put your wrists together and press them to your headrest."

Normally, I would tell the person asking me to respectfully go fuck himself. But with Zach, I wanted to relinquish some of my control. Wanted to feel helpless before a man for once in my life. To let go. He feared touching, so I vowed to let him do all of it.

Slowly, I raised my arms and pressed my wrists to the metal connecting the headrest and the seat. I expected my body to react with something other than anticipation. Fear. Reluctance. Regret. But it didn't. I realized, for the first time, that I trusted Zachary Sun. With my life. With my safety. With my quest for vengeance... Just not with my heart.

Zach leaned over the center console, fisting the white Chanel ribbon in his hand. "That's a good girl." He tilted the backrest all the way down until I laid almost flat, straddled me with his muscular thighs, and gathered my wrists together, quickly tying me up. "Who knew you could be so obedient when a long, hard cock is your incentive?"

He stole a quick kiss, double and triple knotting my wrists. The dull bite of the satin digging into my skin shot an arrow of adrenaline through my spine. A rush of liquid heat tickled under my navel, and I knew he'd find my underwear completely drenched. I yanked the restraints, just to test them out, finding myself securely fastened to the seat. Completely helpless and at his mercy.

I tapered my eyes. "You're suspiciously good at tying people."

"You would be, too, if your best friend constantly finds himself in compromising positions."

"Oliver?"

"Romeo."

I bookmarked this conversation for a later time. *This* I had to know.

Zach straightened as much as he could in the small car, still straddling me, admiring his handiwork. He grabbed my chin and tilted my face up so our eyes met. "You're always beautiful, Farrow Ballantine, but you are especially beautiful when you're at my mercy."

He used his knuckle to brush my right nipple, a feathery soft touch. My body convulsed, my hips bucking, my pussy begging to be filled with him. "More," I whimpered.

"More?" He toyed with the edge of my panties, snapping it at my skin. "More what?"

I stared him in the eyes, reminding myself that this wasn't easy for him. The whole touching thing. "More of whatever you're willing to give."

"I'm starting to realize I'm willing to give almost all I have." His knuckles traveled from my right nipple to the left one. "Where should I kiss you now?"

My eyes trekked down to my underwear. But I knew, practically, that the car was too small for him to scoot to the floor.

"Ah, I see." He nodded. "Don't worry, sweetheart. You're coming on my tongue tonight."

My throat bobbed with a swallow. He leaned against the steering wheel, gathered my thighs in one hand, and pulled my legs upward, so they propped on his shoulders.

"We don't have to if you don't want to," I felt compelled to say, even though an inferno of need blazed through me, singeing every cell of my skin.

"Don't want to? I intend to make your pussy my new home. I want to live inside you. To devour you from head to toe." He dragged my panties to one side, sinking his lips onto my pussy and breathing me in. His nose massaged my clit, sending me to the verge of combustion. His full, hot lips moved against my pussy as he spoke, "You're a drug, Farrow Ballantine. And you're already in my veins."

My thighs crushed together, knees wrapped around his neck as he ran his tongue from my tight hole up to my slit, then sucked my entire pussy into his mouth. I arched, desire morphing into desperate pain, needing to give his wet tongue more access to my greedy pussy.

His tongue found my clit. The tip of it circled around the tight nub at a teasing, torturous pace. He sank his middle finger deep into my pussy. Shamelessly, my walls clasped onto it for dear life, begging for more.

"Look how soaked you are," he murmured, tonguing my clit faster, a depraved grunt rolling from the back of his mouth. "How fucking tight you are. I've never fucked a hole this small in my life."

His finger started working my pussy, and I couldn't help it. I blurted, "How many holes have you fucked?"

How does a man appalled by human touch lose his virginity? Alcohol? Drugs? Sheer suffering? These questions had consumed me for weeks.

Zach added another finger, driving into me with punishing force, almost to the point of discomfort but not quite. "Promise not to laugh?" he growled into my pussy, devouring my clit, my slit, my inner thighs with the hunger of a starved man.

"Promise."

"Sex dolls." His mouth paused over my skin, his labored breaths bumping his chest into the backs of my thighs. "Plastic. Synthetic. Cold. I needed to take care of my needs."

"That's it?"

My heart grew, expanding to the size of Zach's misery, wanting to gulp every drop of anguish he'd ever felt and carry it myself.

"That's it." He unfastened the Chanel ribbon to release me and pressed a hot kiss to the back of my knee, closing his eyes at the admission. "I am otherwise a complete and utter virgin."

I reached between us to put my hand on his knuckles, where he still fingered me. "Well."

He stopped, staring up at me through lust-heavy eyes. His face was so boyish, so absurdly stunning, I found it hard to keep my tears at bay.

"There is nothing pathetic about you." I traced his jaw with a single fingertip. "I'd be so honored to take your virginity, Mr. Sun, if you would give it to me."

He offered a crooked grin. "It's all yours, Miss Ballantine."

I glanced between us at his hand that hovered beside my pussy. "Can I teach you a few tricks?"

His Adam's apple rolled with his nod. "Usually…" He paused. "My *partners* aren't very good at giving me pointers. None of them have had mouths."

I rolled my eyes, trying not to giggle. "Let me show you."

I guided his index finger back into my pussy. "Now curl it when you reach the end. Yeah, like that." I shifted, my juices coating both our fingers. A frisson of pleasure swelled inside me. "Here. In and out. When you twist it like that, it hits my G-spot." I threw my head back, moaning. "*Yes.*"

His gaze clung to my face as he worked my pussy, his lips swollen from eating me out. I couldn't bear it. His desire to make it good for me. This childlike eagerness for approval. I clasped his cheeks and pulled him to me, kissing him savagely, tasting my juices on his tongue, the rain on his skin.

Condensation fogged the windows. He continued fingering me, his dick pressed to the back of my thigh, hot and ready, the crown damp. The scent of sex filled my car, and I knew I'd never be able to get rid of it. Every time I drove, I'd think about this moment.

My orgasm began building, swirling under my belly button.

Zach scooped one of my nipples into his mouth, sucking and grazing it with his upper teeth. He paused to stare up at me, resting his chin on the valley between my breasts. "How can a creature be so perfect?" His finger moved faster inside me, his saliva smeared over my tit. He shifted from my left breast to the right one, sucking it into his mouth. "How come I can't stop touching you?"

I reached for his cock on my thigh, rubbing it. "Keep going. Faster."

"No. I need to fuck you," he growled, lips moving back to my mouth, kissing me with frantic, animalistic need. "*Now.*"

"Do you have a condom?"

His mouth slipped to my throat, kissing and nibbling. "I'll pull out."

The orgasm built between my legs. It felt like floating off a cliff, waiting for gravity to catch up.

"*Zachary.* I'm not letting you fuck me bareback."

His lips returned to my nipple. "Even if I ask really nicely?"

"Even so."

"Even if I'm willing to gift you every piece of art I own other than the pendants?"

"Y-you would do that?" I gasped, my muscles shaking as a climax rumbled through my body.

"I'm a desperate man, and you're a hardheaded woman."

But I was too busy falling apart into a trillion pieces to answer him. As soon as I began coming, he stopped fingering me, cupping my pussy and pressing it hard with the base of his palm. I moaned so loud, whales in the Pacific Ocean must've taken it as a distress signal.

"I can feel your cum. Fuck. It's coating my palm." Zach buried his face in my shoulder, rubbing his dick over the back of my thigh. "This is beautiful. *You* are beautiful."

He rose to his knees, slowly unfastening my legs from his shoulders, raising the palm that held my pussy between us. It was covered with my juices. I bit my lower lip, refusing to feel embarrassed. I panted hard from the orgasm, our sweat mixing together.

Zach brought his hand to my face. "See what you did?"

I nodded.

"Now lick it."

I did. With a level of enthusiasm that should've been reserved for saving the entire nation from alien invasion. There was something so incredibly hot about licking my own desire for him. When I finished, he inspected his palm through hooded eyes, grinned, then dove down to kiss the hell out of me.

Our tongues tangled together. We moaned into the kiss, holding each other for dear life. My entire body was wrecked, both with the orgasm and the position I'd had it in, but I still wanted to return the favor. To give him the release he desperately needed. He was human, after all—no matter how much he denied it to himself.

I pushed him off me. He rolled back to the passenger seat, following my movements through thirsty eyes.

I unlocked the door, rounded the car, and opened the passenger side, hooking a finger. "Get up."

"Are you ditching me in the woods?" Zach clasped his cock, trying to tame his erection, fishing for his boxer briefs in the dark. "Because let me assure you, Little Octi, I'm already suffering here."

"We're going to take care of your problem without having sex," I announced, grabbing his hand and tugging him out.

He seemed fine with touching—with touching *me*, anyway. Pride filled my chest at how far he'd come. Through the faint glow of the headlights, I noticed the skepticism in his raised brow, but he still humored me.

I shut the door behind him and pushed him against it, kissing him. We were both still naked—down to our underwear. At any second, someone could catch us. The mere idea of being seen thrilled me. But I was different from Zach—I flirted with danger all the time. I knew I was pushing his limits. What I didn't understand was why he let me.

Zach glanced around as I lowered myself to my knees. Gravel dug into my skin. I pushed his black Calvin Kleins further down. His hot dick pulsed in my hand, so big I couldn't even hold it still.

"I'd strongly prefer not to be caught with my dick in my housekeeper's mouth," he muttered, running his fingers through my hair, tugging me closer, contrary to his words. "This is a level of depraved only middle-aged white politicians can afford, Octi. Stand up. We'll do this some other tim—"

But before he finished the sentence, I grabbed the base of his cock and guided it into my mouth, licking all the way to the tip.

"Never mind." He dragged a hand over his face, hissing out, "It appears I'm going to destroy my reputation, along with every other principle I've ever held. It's truly astounding how *your* mouth is getting *me* into trouble."

A giggle bubbled up my throat, but I tamed it, sucking half his cock into my mouth. I wanted more, but he'd never fit.

He wrapped my wild locks around his fist twice-over, sloping my head just so as he began thrusting into my mouth. "Fuck, Octi, you feel so good."

I watched his face through a curtain of lashes as I bobbed my head back and forth, relishing his taste—earthy and citrusy.

"More, Farrow. That's it." He pushed his hips forward, begging me to take more of his dick in my mouth. "Such a good girl."

I grinned around his cock. No one had ever accused me of *that* before.

"You're too big," I managed to mumble. "It'll never fit."

"We'll make it fit. I promise."

"It's huge."

"Let's try one inch at a time."

Easy for him to say. He wasn't the one who had to accommodate so many inches. I opened my mouth wider, tilting my chin up as he gripped his cock and guided himself deeper into my mouth. His tip hit the back of my throat. My eyes stung with tears, my gag reflex activating. I tamped it down, desperate to make him feel good.

He stopped all of a sudden, his body tensing. His six-pack was crazy. Every time he breathed, it contracted.

He pet my head, almost reverently. "Are you okay to take some more?"

I nodded.

Why are you nodding? He's going to push your tonsils down your lungs.

"Are you sure?"

Since I couldn't talk around his cock, I flipped him the bird rather than answering. Zach chuckled, his gruff voice trickling into my system, warming me on such a cold night. He pressed even deeper. His cock curled to the shape of my throat. I breathed through my nostrils and tried to regulate my breath. I was literally choking on his cock.

"You feel so warm," he cooed, and my entire heart melted into a pool of goo in my stomach. "I want to fuck your mouth so hard, you'll never be able to close it again."

I cupped his balls, a warning for him to fix his dirty talk. He groaned, letting his head fall back as he inched further. He was all the way inside my mouth now. We took a beat to adjust to the situation.

He toyed with the hair at the nape of my neck. "Can I thrust?"

I felt him leaking pre-cum into my throat, one drop at a time. His whole body trembled. I gave him a faint nod, as much as I could. He began thrusting, fucking my mouth mercilessly while holding me by the hair. I propped one hand against the passenger door behind him, delirious with desire.

With my spare hand, I reached between my legs, swirling my clit with my index finger as I sucked and nibbled and spat on his cock while it filled my mouth. Zach's thrusts became jerkier, his hold on my hair tighter as I rubbed my clit faster and harder.

"I'm going to come fucking buckets." Zach groaned. "I need to pull out now."

I shook my head frantically, releasing the door and clutching his iron ass cheeks in my hand, whimpering as I felt myself coming. I wanted him to come inside my mouth.

"I'm not a believing man, Farrow." Zach buried both his hands into my hair, tipping my head slightly up to look at him. "But I find it hard to believe nature is capable of flawlessness as radical as you."

His cum washed over my mouth. I gurgled on the thick, hot liquid. It stuck to the walls of my throat like honey. He brought me up to my feet, unsteady himself. I struggled to stand, knees like jelly beneath the weight of my own climax.

I was riding the mid-orgasm euphoria when he righted me and grabbed the back of my head. "I want to do filthy things to you, with you, and *for* you. And I'm going to start with this."

He tongued me hard, kissing the breath out of me, my mouth still full of his cum. It dripped from the corners of my lips as we kissed, bit, and nipped, moaning into each other's mouths. Down our chins, sticking to our skin like glue in the ice-cold night.

We were tangled everywhere—limbs, fingers, hair, tongues. I couldn't stop this trainwreck even if I wanted to. This dark, tortured man had trapped me under his spell, and I was going to let him use me.

Only this wasn't any spell.

It was dark magic.

CHAPTER FORTY-NINE

Romeo Costa: So? Did you guys make up?

Ollie vB: Was there makeup sex involved?

Ollie vB: (Also: who are we talking about?)

Romeo Costa: Housekeeper Hot Stuff showed up at my door last night, drenched like an abandoned kitty, asking for shelter.

Zach Sun: We had a mild disagreement. We figured it out.

Ollie vB: Did you ask for your balls back?

Romeo Costa: Don't be ridiculous, Oliver.

Zach Sun: Thank you, Rom.

Romeo Costa: He doesn't have the balls to make such a request.

Zach Sun: You are both mentally five.

Ollie vB: Lies. I am clearly at the height of my hormone-filled adolescence.

Ollie vB: Probably somewhere between thirteen and nineteen.

Ollie vB: I still cannot get over the fact that you are screwing the help.

Zach Sun: I still cannot get over the fact that you gave a woman you literally do not know two of your five Amex cards.

Romeo Costa: COME AGAIN?

Ollie vB: I did. Three times. Today alone. To Frankie's IG pictures. She's in Costa Rica, basking in the sun, wearing tiny bikinis. Best money I've ever spent.

Ollie vB: Also, how'd you find out?

Zach Sun: Farrow has a mouth.

Ollie vB: She should use it to suck your dick more and talk about my business less.

Zach Sun: Don't you need a job to have a 'business'?

Ollie vB: How does Farrow know Frankie?

Romeo Costa: Dallas and Frankie took Farrow out for a birthday celebration.

Ollie vB: Wow. Okay. Not going to pretend not to be hurt by the lack of requests for me to be the stripper jumping out of the cake.

Zach Sun: The last thing your criminal record needs is you jumping out of places completely naked.

Ollie vB: My probation is over, and that was completely consensual, thankyouverymuch. I already told you. She was mad because I forgot her name.

Romeo Costa: Pin this conversation for a second.

Ollie vB: Why? You've got something important to tell us?

Romeo Costa: No. I'm making some popcorn for this.

Ollie vB: [Eye roll Emoji]

Ollie vB: So… where is she now?

Romeo Costa: Frankie? Probably Kindergarten, learning letters and colors.

Ollie vB: Farrow, you swine.

Romeo Costa: In my living room with Shortbread. They appear to be making voodoo dolls.

Romeo Costa: My bad. I was just informed they've taken up crocheting. Shit, they're really bad at it.

Romeo Costa: Dallas just finished a beanie, and it looks like a cock warmer.

Zach Sun: I sincerely hope by 'cock' you mean a rooster.

Romeo Costa: Listen, Dallas likes skiing. This is a no-judgment zone.

Ollie vB: Isn't three o'clock a work hour for Farrow?

Romeo Costa: Doubt her job description currently includes anything beyond taking Zach's dick in every available hole in her body.

Zach Sun: Objectify her one more time, and you will find yourself with a knife in your hand like Brett Junior.

Ollie vB: Aw. Zachy Boy, you're not supposed to get attached. You're ENGAGED.

Romeo Costa: This engagement is going to be shorter than Vanilla Ice's career.

Zach Sun: Vanilla who?

Romeo Costa: Exactly.

Ollie vB: Can you stop saying the word vanilla? It is very triggering to me.

Romeo Costa: Why?

Ollie vB: Reminds me of missionary sex.

Zach Sun: I'm carrying through with the marriage.

Romeo Costa: Didn't you just put a 100k retainer down for Dan? For Farrow's legal fees?

Zach Sun: This is beside the point.

Ollie vB: Okay, @RomeoCosta, who's gonna tell him?

Romeo Costa: Not me. Imagine how hilarious it's going to be when he finds out.

Zach Sun: @RomeoCosta, can you tell Farrow to come back home?

Romeo Costa: Hold.

Romeo Costa: She said she doesn't have a home, that she lives in her employer's guestroom, and that she is having too much fun with my wife to come back today. Try again tomorrow.

Ollie vB: This relationship is the best thing to happen to this world since sliced bread.

Zach Sun: I don't eat carbs.

Ollie vB: You really should. You are moody AF.

Zach Sun: I hate all of you.

Romeo Costa: Not all.

Romeo Costa: Not Farrow.

CHAPTER FIFTY

Zach

Up until now, I never understood why the Greeks invaded Troy over Helen. I woke up ready to justify a war or two if it meant sinking my dick past Farrow's full lips again. I started my morning early, spending half of it wondering when I could go for round two. After my workout, I set out for my office in my best suit. It was pathetic, wearing a bespoke three-piece while working at home to impress my fucking *housekeeper*, but I'd long passed pride. (I was past a lot of things since I'd tasted Fae's pussy.) I swiped a finger over my phone, spotting missed calls. Three from Mom. Two from Eileen. Irritation swept over me. We'd included a clause in our agreement that limited conversations. I made a mental note to send her an annotated copy of the contract.

I ignored the calls, replied to a chain of emails from the lawyers, and followed up with the PI. This needed to be an all-hands-on-deck operation. Octi deserved to annihilate Vera, and I intended to ensure my legacy with Farrow. Her full inheritance, the house, the cleaning company, and a severance package to help her elevate her business to a monstrous scale. Or, preferably, retire. The thought of her cleaning another asshole's home in her hot little uniform made me want to set fire to the entire city.

"Mr. Sun." Natalie emerged from the bathroom, heels stabbing the floor as she hurtled toward me. "Good morning." Since I took business meetings in this wing, I allowed shoes in this zone of the manor.

"Debatable." I kept my pace. "What do you have for me?"

I continued scrolling on my phone, idiotically hoping that... What? Farrow would decide she wanted a quickie in the laundry room? I needed to get my expectations in order. Two nights ago, I'd begged to fuck her bareback. What would've happened if I'd gotten her pregnant?

For starters, you'd be released from the chain that is your marriage to Eileen.

I shook my head, not letting my thoughts stray so far from reality.

Eileen was a fact, not an option. She'd make Mom happy. She'd fulfill my promise to Dad. All of these aside, she was safe. With her, I'd never run the risk of getting a blowie naked in the woods like a horny teen. Would never stab someone because he dared *think* about touching her. Would never be consumed by every breath she took, every smile she smiled, every tiny quirk she picked up.

"You have a 10 o'clock Zoom meeting with CIRPE Corp, an eleven-thirty brunch downtown with the TechT shareholders, and a two o'clock domestic flight to Chicago to sign a contract finalizing the GoProBono deal. Other than that, you have a question-marked dinner with Constance and Celeste at that new Indonesian restaurant at Rockville Pike if you can make it." Natalie managed to rapid-fire my list in one breath.

"I won't make it. Send them my apologies. Pick up the bill on my card." I hadn't seen Farrow in 24 hours. Getting into her pants was of utmost importance. Prior to breathing and other mandatory functions. I'd purchased enough condoms to last the entire red-light district for a decade. I pushed the doors to my office open. "Make sure you're done with my filing, dry cleaning, and shopping before five. I want the house to myself."

Translation: I want to peacefully hump Farrow's leg in various places of the house without being doxed to the world as a pervert.

Natalie scrunched her nose. "What if I don't have time to finish?"

"Finish tomorrow."

"But I—"

"I'm not asking, Natalie. I'm commanding." I paused at the threshold. "If you don't like the terms of your employment, I can always offer your position to someone equally incompetent."

She pouted. "You never seem to care when Farrow talks back."

That's because she runs the show, and you're merely an extra in it.

In lieu of a response, I shut the door in her face. Before settling into my executive chair, I made a pit-stop at my never-ending Go game with Fae. She'd moved a stone last night, which meant that she'd returned home at some point. The knowledge that she slept across the hall from me oddly satisfied me. I plucked a stone from my bowl and set it on the board. I harbored two prisoners of hers. I'd win the game in the coming days, after all.

"Silly, Octi. At this rate, I'm going to conquer your entire kingdom." I fought a bitter smile, knowing deep down I was the one being captured.

CHAPTER FIFTY-ONE

Zach

Like all gusts of hope, mine died a slow, cruel death. I'd *hoped* for another blowjob from Farrow before lunch. Instead, I received numerous interruptions from Natalie, impeding my scheduled video conferences and business calls.

Then, Mom dropped by to complain about my lack of response, urging me to download a tracking app in case I ended up in a ditch somewhere. Genuine tears leaked from her eyes, and I knew the latent anxiety from learning of the crash never actually left her.

Oliver came next with an absurd request to borrow my home for an orgy. I kicked him out, literally, but he only pivoted, asking me to do it again—harder.

And *still*, no sign of Octi.

I checked the surveillance cameras. Hallways. Kitchens. Living areas. Nowhere.

Stop with this obsession. Concentrate on your work.

Two hours in, that proved impossible. I tried to feed myself the excuse that I was checking in on an unruly employee as I rose from my seat and made my way to her room. I knocked on her door, feeling like a certified idiot. It was *my* house. She was under *my* payroll. Why did I feel so out of control?

"Farrow. I know you're in there." No answer. I pressed my elbow to the door, my nostrils flaring. "Your car's parked out front—where *I* should be parking, by the fucking way—and all my healthy snacks have been raided overnight."

Finally, her unapologetic voice came from the other side of the wood. "Those cashew energy balls are the bomb. You need to buy more of them."

She'd spoken with her signature sass, yet I picked up on something fragile. Brittle, even. My hackles rose all the way to the sky.

"Octi?" I replayed the last forty-eight hours, sifting through my memories. "Did I do something wrong?"

"Shockingly, no. It's not you."

"Can I open the door?"

"I'd rather you didn't see me like this."

"Like what?"

"Vulnerable."

"Farrow." I closed my eyes, drawing a breath. "I've shown you the darkest, most depraved sides of me. I bared my soul to you. All I'm asking is to catch a glimpse of yours."

The world tilted on its axis as I waited for her answer.

Finally, she said, "You can come in."

I pushed the door open and stepped inside, closing it behind me. Natalie lurked somewhere in the house—Constance, too, maybe—and I felt protective of Octi's privacy. She laid in bed, her long legs tangled in the satin sheets, her face buried in a pillow. She wore nothing but an oversized sweatshirt, somehow looking lovelier than any girl I'd ever seen in a ballgown. Her golden hair splayed across the pillowcase like liquid sunrays.

Something tightened in my chest at the sight of her.

This better be a heart attack, Zachary, Mom's voice warned inside my head.

I rushed to her bedside. "What happened?"

I'd never seen her cry or anything close to it. In fact, one of the reasons this woman appealed to me so much was the fact that she was stronger than tungsten.

"Who did this to you?" I demanded. My hands found her back, rubbing it back and forth as I sat on the edge of the mattress.

Face still buried in the pillow, she fished her phone out from under her chest and tossed it in the general vicinity of my hand. "This is what I woke up to."

A *New York Times* article popped on the screen, the headline bolded. *Farrow Ballantine: Prodigy, Talent, CHEAT.*

"Check out the news tab under my name." The silk muffled her moan—not quite a cry but a sign of her obvious misery. "Just have a bucket ready in case you need to vomit."

Dozens of scandalous headlines graced all of the leading sites.

Farrow Ballantine Officially Kicked off the Olympics for Throwing Match.

Fencer Farrow Ballantine Lost on Purpose—Should Team USA give her another chance?

Farrow Ballantine 'Cheated' the System: A report.

Nothing about these headlines surprised me. I'd dug all this up in my deep-dive prior to hiring her. Shortly before returning to the States, Farrow had thrown her last match in Seoul. The little cheat somehow managed to keep it under wraps, handling this internally with USA Fencing and the Olympic Committee. *That* I didn't know how she'd pulled off. The woman had less connections than a prepaid phone.

"My future as a fencer is done. I'm toast." She shifted, hugging her pillow to her chest. "I'm never going to make it to the Olympics now."

I checked her cheek for wetness. Nothing. Still, she sniffled, fighting a fresh wave of tears.

"You need to tell me what happened, Octi. From the beginning." I brushed her hair away from her face, mainly as an excuse to touch her. "Think you can do that?"

She rolled on her back. I got a full glimpse of her face now. Nose pink, eyes bloodshot, hair a tousled mess. I balled my hands into fists to stop myself from breaking something.

Farrow licked her lips. "Promise not to judge?"

The one who needs judgment is me. Much to my horror, you could set the entire world aflame and I'd hold your fucking earrings and cheer you on from the sidelines.

"Pinky promise."

She scooted up, plastering her back against the headboard as she peeked at me. Her teeth sank into her lower lip. "My last day in Seoul, I did something... bad."

"Elaborate."

"I'd just received a phone call that Dad died in a freak accident. A distant aunt told me. Not Vera. Not Reggie or Tabby." Her gaze dropped to her lap. "I tried reaching Vera via email and phone. I even sent a neighbor to knock on her door, but she dodged me."

I swore, looped an arm around Fae's waist, and carried her onto my lap, her hair spilling down my leg like a golden waterfall.

Fae blinked up at me, relaxing into my thighs. "Later that day, I found out that she'd canceled the card Dad set up for me to use in Korea. She emptied my joint bank account, too, including my personal savings I kept there. She knew I wouldn't be able to buy a plane ticket home without that money."

I ran my fingertips down her head, massaging her scalp, mostly to distract myself from the rage stewing inside me.

Fae rested her cheek against my abs. "She didn't want me at Dad's funeral. Probably to hurt me, but with the added bonus of convincing people that I didn't care when she presented his will." Her pink-rimmed eyes glistened with unshed tears.

Lucky for me, Vera was nowhere near our vicinity. Spending the rest of my life on death row sounded like a depressing existence.

I kneaded a knot out of her neck, gliding my thumb down its column, hoping to ease her tension. "Everyone who knows you knows you love your dad."

"No one here really knows me except you." She scrunched her nose, rubbing away tears that refused to spill. "I had options. I won't pretend that I didn't. Ari's a chaebol. Heiress to a ginormous fortune. I could have gone to her for a loan. She wouldn't even ask me to pay it back. And my other fencing friends would've chipped in for a plane ticket if I'd told them I needed the money."

My hand drifted up her nape to her jaw now, just touching her. Marveling at the fact that it could. Marveling at the fact that she let me. And knowing I needed to do something with it, or I'd hunt Vera Ballantine down.

"But I was so dang... *proud*." Fae's expression darkened, her gaze fixed on an invisible spot on the ceiling. "My pride wouldn't let me beg for money. Not even to attend Dad's funeral."

She curled to her side, burying her nose into my stomach. "I spent my entire life helpless against Vera, Reggie, and Tabby. But this marked my first fight against them without Dad behind me. I wanted to show them I could hold my own."

Shame oozed from her pores. "I wasn't thinking straight." The fabric of my dress shirt muffled her voice. "I'd just lost my dad. I was broke, all the way across the world, with two days to get a ticket home. I couldn't see the future. Not my fencing career. Not the Olympics."

Farrow's fingers curled into tight fists against my thigh. "The day Dad died, he was supposed to fly to Korea on a red-eye. To watch me at my competition. My last bout before I returned to the US for Olympic qualifiers. Enter Laura Müller. Rich, young, and talented, but nowhere near the skill level required to beat me."

She sucked in a breath, the tips of her ears turning pink. "Her dad approached me weeks before, insinuating he wanted to strike a deal. That the competition meant nothing to me, since I'd still make it to the North American qualifiers, beat everyone there, and cinch my spot on Team USA."

I uncurled her fists, soothing away the nail marks on her palm.

"But for Laura… winning against a fencer like me would give her the confidence to compete in the European qualifiers." Fae's shoulders tensed. "Of course, I said no. Then, I went on with my life as if nothing had happened."

"But that morning of the competition, I suited up, mere days from Dad's funeral with no way to get there." She gulped, closing her eyes. "I sat in the locker room and thought… *What could it hurt?* So, I struck a deal…"

A lone tear rolled out of her right eye, cascading down her cheek and disappearing inside her sweatshirt.

"I agreed to lose the match in exchange for a ticket to D.C. and unlimited legal fees." Fae's jaw set. "I knew Vera would do something fishy with the will. That I'd need to lawyer up. It seemed so easy. So harmless. No one was supposed to find out."

I traced the bridge of her nose. "How *did* they find out?"

I'd watched that match several times on YouTube after Tom had given me Farrow's full background report. Obvious grief lined her bloodshot eyes. The announcer even noted the recent passing of Fae's father. For all intents and purposes, any performance she gave—good or bad—should've been believable. I still hadn't figured out this missing piece of the puzzle. How Farrow got caught.

"Vera." Farrow snorted. "How else?"

I am going to kill this woman.

Slowly. Painfully. Enthusiastically.

"I made it to Dad's funeral in the nick of time." A shaky breath rattled Fae's chest. "Just as they started lowering his casket into the ground. I flung myself over it and hugged it hard, crying on top of it."

A bitter chuckle crept up her throat. "It was a big scene. And the last time I cried." She paused, deep in thought. "Before now. Before *you.*"

Cruel thoughts trickled into my head. Useless, unrealistic thoughts. *Let me be your shelter, Farrow Ballantine. Let me redeem you as you redeem me.*

I bundled her hand in mine, squeezing hard. "What did Vera do?"

"Made a huge scene, of course. She tore me straight from the casket and onto the ground. Her relatives had to scrape her off of me. Then she started yelling at me. That I had no right to show up there. That I wasn't invited."

A small grin played on Farrow's lips. "I clapped back, like I always did. Which was how I landed across the world in the first place. She'd gotten sick of my 'unruly' ways. I always refused to let Vera, Reggie, and Tabby bully me around."

A ribbon of pride looped around my chest. It used to frustrate me that Farrow refused to take shit—particularly from me. But I'd grown to look forward to her sass, seeking it out every day.

You are so royally fucked.

As if she could hear my thoughts, Farrow sighed. "Tabby screeched loud enough to burst my eardrums. *But how did she even get here, Mom?* And Reggie gave up the gig. *I thought you said you emptied her bank account.* Enough people heard her to send gasps across the crowd."

"Then, what happened?"

"Vera dragged me behind a tree and told me she'd spoken to Laura's mom. That she admitted to the bribe. They must have let it slip because they considered her my de-facto mother. They definitely didn't think Vera would go running to the Olympic committee with the info."

"What happened after?"

"They fined me out of my ass. Overnight, my reputation crumbled into ruins among officials. Team USA dropped me from the qualifiers. The only reason it didn't escalate was because of Andras. Everyone reveres him."

"He's never won a medal." I ran a hand down my jaw, remembering the dossier I'd read on him. "Never had a fencer who's won an Olympic gold."

"He's rough around the edges. Has the personality of a traffic jam. Only I've ever managed to stick with him. It doesn't matter though. There's an urban legend around the community that all you need is one session with him to medal. It's true. The last four women's medalists trained with Andras. They just didn't take him as a coach, because he's a raging asshole."

"And Vera? She just went along with sweeping everything under the rug?"

"Vera agreed not to run to the media if I stayed in my lane and did all her dirty work."

The rest of the puzzle clicked into place. Why Farrow became Cinderella 2.0. Why she still practiced fencing with hopes of competing in the Olympics. And why she'd spent the morning in tears with her chance officially gone.

"I'll never be able to do this professionally." Fae shook her head, hopping to her feet and ambling toward the window. "That dream is gone. Dead. Just like my father."

"Why did Vera leak it?"

Fae hugged herself as she looked out at the rose bushes. "Vera found out I have a private investigator and a herd of lawyers sniffing around. She found Tom going through her trash in the middle of the night."

Motherfucker.

"How do you know?"

"She texted me."

Guilt rocketed through me. I'd brought Tom into her life. I killed her fencing dream.

Farrow's shoulders caved as she hugged herself tighter. "I'm not even sure Andras will still work with me. I was his shot at an Olympic gold."

"Has he reached out to you yet?"

I picked up her phone, scrolling through the nasty articles. This story had legs, picking up speed as we spoke. Blasted on every news outlet. Trending on all social media platforms. No shot in hell Andras hadn't seen this. Unless he'd taken a lengthy vacation on Mars.

Octi shook her head, turning to face me. Full-blown tears coated her cheeks now.

Sheer fury simmered at my heels, heating me from head to toe. "Farrow, stop crying," I bit out. The command smeared the walls like sticky tar.

I wasn't used to this. To... *feeling*. And with Farrow, I felt. All the damn time. How terribly inconvenient. I loathed it.

To my horror, Fae's sob grew louder. Her wails clawed at my chest, ripping the flesh to shreds.

"You don't understand." She fell to her knees, tilting her head down so I couldn't see her face. "My entire life, I didn't have much to my name. Not a family. Not a home. I had one thing—a dream. A destination. An Olympic piste."

Her body vibrated with her sobs. "I pledged my whole being to that moment. I dreamed about it every night. Wished for it every morning. Read all the books, studied all the techniques..." She wrapped her arms around her knees, burying her face into them. "Without this goal, I don't know who I am anymore."

I strode to her, sinking to the rug as well, holding her shoulders. It didn't even register that I touched her with ease now. That I let her lay on my lap—not to help me, but to help *her*.

And I wanted to touch her again. Often.

"Listen to me, Farrow." I nudged her chin up with my fingertip. "Fencing is only one of many layers in you. You're not reduced to a single dream. You're a fighter. A businesswoman. A daughter. A moralist."

Her eyes clung to me, shiny with tears like two polished sapphires.

I rolled my eyes. "A somewhat decent Go player."

She snorted, a tiny grin playing with her lips now.

"Fencing never defined you, Octi." I brushed away her tears with my thumb. "It gave you a home when you needed one."

But you don't anymore. You have mine.

Jesus. Where had that come from?

I drowned that thought as fast as it came, gripping Farrow's shoulders. "You're not a helpless child anymore. You're capable. Competent. Infuriatingly smart. Soon, you'll destroy Vera. And she knows it. Ratting you out to the press? It's a show of weakness. She blinked first, Octi."

Farrow fell to her back, grabbing her stomach. I frowned, wondering what about my words she found funny. Something strange happened.

A wisp of air from the vent tickled my ear, sending a chill down my neck. It felt... *cold?* I hadn't felt cold in years. I hadn't felt much of *anything* in years. This—tasting the cold while Farrow raced through every emotion under the sun—felt like the highlight of my existence.

Farrow began hiccupping, managing to stop for a second to say, "Who would have thought *you* would be the one to deliver a pep talk?" She clutched her sweatshirt, her shoulders shaking. "Seriously, I've been waiting for Ari to wake up for hours."

I flattened my lips, unamused. Still, she couldn't stop laughing. I ambled to the door, taking my sweet time, giving her the opportunity to stop me.

She did. "Wait." More giggles. "Has anyone ever told you that you can be a real gentleman when you want to be?"

"God, no." I spun, raising a brow at her. "And don't tell the others. This won't be a reoccurrence."

"Zach?"

"Yes, Octi?"

"Tell me something interesting about the octopus."

I didn't have to think hard. I'd stored these fun facts in my brain especially for her, because I knew she liked them. "Octopuses are such intelligent, cerebrally superior creatures that, when devoid of mental stimulation, they become so distressed, they resort to autophagy and eat their own appendages."

She blinked, staring at me with her head cocked. "I'll ask again— couldn't I be a kitten?"

"No."

"Why?"

"Because you are spectacular, intelligent, and different. Not a cliché."

She tucked her lower lip in her mouth, delicious pink creeping up her cheeks. Her breaths came out heavier. We were treading deep into something that would end in utter destruction.

"Zach?" she asked again.

"Yes, Octi?" I replied again.

"What happens next?"

"For my next act..." I grabbed her hand and helped her up. "I'm going to burn down the world for you."

Chapter Fifty-Two

Zach

I broke protocol.

The protocol? Do not engage with humans unless absolutely necessary.

Simple enough. Yet, I found myself cornering Vera Ballantine in a dark alleyway like a mobster cliché. I told myself she'd practically invited me, since she'd made herself easy to find. With geo-tagged selfies plastered on three different social media platforms and backup reservations under each of her subpar daughters' names.

They'd chosen to dine at one of those god-awful genre-confused "oriental" restaurants that managed to convince influencers their food didn't suck. The type that served sushi, pad thai, and pho under the same roof.

I hid in a narrow passageway, waiting for them to finish. The last thing I needed was to be plastered on a gossip rag. About an hour after I'd arrived, Regina and Tabitha hung back inside the restaurant while their mother poured outside to ask the valet for her Mercedes.

Vera slipped into the alleyway, producing a cigarette from her Gucci purse. The second the orange embers of her cancer stick glowed, I pressed the tip of my knife to her lower back, still hiding in the shadows.

She gasped, trying to turn. "What the—"

I burrowed the blade deeper into her back, forcing her body to slam against the wall face-first. "No need to turn, Vera. I'd like to eat dinner tonight, and your face is a prescription-grade appetite suppressant."

She gulped, her cheek digging into the rough bricks. "Zachary Sun?"

"Listen carefully." I ignored her question, knowing she couldn't see me, especially in the dark. "Your existence is currently a terrible inconvenience for me. Stop messing with your stepdaughter."

"Farrow?" She leaned back before remembering the knife. "That girl ruined my life. She's trying to take me dow—"

"I didn't ask for a TED talk. I gave you specific instructions. Don't you dare mess with her. Not now. Not in the future. No matter the outcome of your dispute." I slanted the knife, taunting her with its blade. "Farrow Ballantine is under my protection. You know who I am. You know what I'm capable of."

Farrow will come out of this victorious if it's the last thing I do with my life.

I needed to ensure Vera didn't attack her afterwards. I didn't intend on sticking around my maid to find out.

Vera tried to turn again, seconds from stomping her feet. "You don't understand."

In the background, the valet asked his coworker where she'd gone.

Her cigarette fell from her shaky fingers to the pavement. "I'm going to be penniless—"

"I do understand. Perfectly so. I just couldn't care less. Farrow Ballantine is officially off-limits to you. Tamper with her life one more time, and I assure you, I will take yours."

"You'll never kill me." A wretched laugh tumbled out of her throat. She tried to turn again, but this time, I curved the knife to the side of her throat, losing patience. "You won't risk your life for that white trash."

"You and I are not the same, Vera. I don't answer to the law. Ruining you is as easy as ordering takeout."

"Mr. Sun—"

I cut her off, refusing to confirm my identity, knowing she could never prove her suspicions. "I consider myself a thorough person. When I'm done with you, I'll move on to your daughters."

"Please—"

"They'll live in utter poverty, unable to marry anyone respectable. We both know they're incapable of making it on their own." I dug my heel into her cigarette, grinding it beneath my sole. It died with a hiss. "By the time I'm finished with your family, you'll be sorry for the day you decided to form one and exclude Farrow from it."

She sobbed, tears beginning to leak from her eyes. "You're evil."

The valet boys got impatient, calling out her name. One of them asked the other to run into the restaurant and fetch her daughters. I needed to wrap this up.

"I am," I confirmed, completely at ease with her observation. "You'll be better off if you remember this simple fact. Not only am I more evil than you, I'm also more capable. Consider this your first and final warning, Vera. Leave Farrow alone."

She burst into a fresh bout of tears, nodding.

"Now turn around and walk back to the restaurant. Look behind you, and the last thing you'll see before you die is the flash of my blade."

I had no intention of wasting a perfectly good knife on her, but she didn't know that.

She nodded, faster than a bobblehead. "Okay, *okay.*"

I pushed her toward the street with the hilt of my knife. She stumbled over her own feet, weeping and choking.

"Mom. Ugh, where were you?" One of Vera's spawns clung to her arm as soon as she neared. "We had to wait in the cold."

"Not to worry, sweetie," Vera purred, her voice business as usual. "Just went on a little cigarette break."

"You should really give them up, you know. It's eating at our inheritance, and it's not like there's much left."

Chapter Fifty-Three

Romeo Costa: @ZachSun, what's with the never-ending traffic of lawyers and private investigators spilling into your house?

Romeo Costa: Are you planning a coup?

Ollie vB: If you are, can I be in charge of the Economic Development Administration? I love not having a job.

Ollie vB: Scratch that. Is the Social Security Administration available? Two birds. One stone. I'm nothing if not efficient.

Zach Sun: Hilarious. I'm helping Farrow out with her legal case.

Ollie vB: All day, every day? You seem to be solely focused on this.

Zach Sun: May I suggest a hobby? And a fucking life, while you're at it?

Romeo Costa: Do you even work on your own shit?

Ollie vB: Or, you know, plan your own wedding for that matter?

Ollie vB: (Your hobby suggestion is too ridiculous to entertain. Your shit show of a life is much more amusing.)

Zach Sun: My life is a well-oiled machine.

Ollie vB: Lube is a godsend. I love it, too.

Romeo Costa: Is everything about sex to you, @OllievB?

Ollie vB: Of course, not.

Ollie vB: Some things are about watching you two succumb to the monogamous grind. This brings me a lot of joy, believe it or not.

Romeo Costa: I believe it.

Ollie vB: I'm officially the last one standing.

Romeo Costa: Unless one of your STIs spreads to your limbs.

Zach Sun: I'm not married just yet.

Ollie vB: I'm not talking about Dr. Ulick. She doesn't count. I'm talking about your little sword-yielding housekeeper.

Zach Sun: Her name is Farrow, and she and I are strictly casual.

Ollie vB: Respectfully, you are strictly delusional.

Romeo Costa: I second Oliver.

Zach Sun: Nonsense. She's a calculated risk.

Romeo Costa: If so, you seriously suck at math.

Zach Sun: You are both useless.

Ollie vB: False. Wait until your heart breaks. My shoulder will be your best place to cry on.

Romeo Costa: Aw. Where'd you learn that, Ol? Outer Banks?

Ollie vB: It's called culture, gentlemen. You should try it sometime.

Ollie vB: #JusticeForSarahCameron.

Chapter Fifty-Four

Farrow

Natalie must've whacked Zach over the head with the amnesia stick, because he spent the next couple days pretending the moment we shared in my room—where we clutched onto each other for dear life—never happened. She caught on to my mood, too, winking at me every time our paths crossed. As for Zach, I couldn't be mad. Not like he gave me the asshole treatment he served to everyone else—with second and third helpings. Unlike with Natalie and his staff, he still paused to talk to me every time we met in the halls.

He showed up when Dan, Bryan, Deanne, and Tom arrived with legal briefs—skimming the documents, guiding me, asking the tough questions I didn't necessarily know how to ask. And he quietly hired cleaners to pick up the work I stopped doing as I focused my energy on the case, digging through all the paperwork.

In lieu of winning a gold medal, I decided to laser-focus on winning my case. The more I thought about it, the more I realized I never wanted to return to the competitive stage. I loved the sport, yes. But I'd known from the moment I committed the crime that I deserved to be punished and only managed to skirt it through Andras' deep-rooted connections to the fencing world. I needed to face the music. Vera didn't rob me of my last chance at the Olympics. I'd done that to myself.

But that didn't mean I'd let her take everything Dad had left behind.

After annotating a legal brief, I roamed Zach's house, looking for something to do. The place shined thanks to my joint efforts with the new cleaning service and Dallas had an OB appointment, so I couldn't pass time binge-shopping for the baby online and watching in horror as she DoorDash'd from seven different restaurants to satisfy her cravings.

I sauntered down the hall, passing by open doors, when I heard my name being called from the sunroom. "Miss Ballantine?"

Constance Sun. I stopped dead in my tracks, my shoulders squaring into a stiff knot. *Don't let her push you around. You have every right to be here. Life makes you strong so you can protect yourself.*

I rerouted with a sigh, stopping at the sight before me. Constance and Eileen sat at a grand driftwood table, brochures fanned all over. Sun spilled behind their shoulders, making them look like two fallen angels. Zach had left hours ago. They must've shown themselves in. Still, the idea of Eileen in his proximity—in his *house*—made my skin crawl. So much for safeguarding my heart.

I plastered on a carefree smile. "Yes?"

Constance poured herself another cup of tea. "Could you be an absolute doll and help us out?"

"Sure." My teeth slammed together, but I kept my smile intact. "How can I be of service?"

"My vision isn't what it used to be. Could you help me organize these wedding venues in alphabetical order?"

My eyes darted to the reading glasses on her nose. A frown creased my brows. Her intentions were obvious. She wanted me to see what the future had in store for her son, Eileen, and most importantly—*not* me. If I let her get to me, her claws would sink straight into my bones. As subtle as I could, I coiled every muscle in my body, aware they both watched me like hyenas.

Eileen sucked in a quick breath. "Constance…"

She, too, couldn't believe the pettiness. But I could. I jeopardized the most important thing in the world to Constance—her son's future. Nothing mattered more to her than keeping Zach safe under her watchful eye. She refused to introduce dangerous, unknown elements into his life, lest he end up like his father. I understood it, but I didn't have to like it.

"Oh, not you, too, Eileen." Constance emphasized the word *too*. "These people are here to help."

"These people?" Eileen nearly shrank into her seat to the point of disappearance.

Constance snapped her fingers at me. "Dear, do hurry, please. We have a cake tasting in an hour."

Screw this. I refused to let her see me break.

I flashed her my brightest, happiest smile. "Coming right up."

As I gathered the brochures, I decided not to tell Zach about this.

What was the point? She would stay after I left. As much as I hated Constance, I couldn't deny the fact that she adored her son in her own warped way. She dropped off batches of his favorite cucumber salad every three days, celebrated his every professional win, and (according to Dallas) even pulled strings to have the strip of road her husband had died on redone, so Zach wouldn't recognize it. I didn't question her devotion to him.

Eileen shot me an embarrassed smile without meeting my eyes, helping me sort through a stack of brochures. A reluctant pang of respect dragged through me.

The Maldives. The Amalfi Coast. Southamptons.

The destinations didn't matter. Neither did the wedding itself. The simple reminder that Zachary Sun would no longer need a reason for me was enough to send a wave of despair spiraling through me.

"Oh, Eileen." Constance frowned at the silent—and shocking—act of resistance but accepted a stack of pamphlets from her future daughter-in-law. "There's such a thing as a heart too pure. Unsavory people will take advantage of it."

I caught her underlying meaning. She must've seen me in the worst way possible. Could I blame her? I'd barged into her son's life, broken into his home, tried to steal from him, and traded orgasms with him in exchange for legal help and a boatload of money. Hardly a beacon of altruism. All the while, I vowed to follow through on my lifelong promise to never engage in a relationship. To never become Dad and Vera.

Constance held the booklet to the light. "Isn't this venue lovely?"

It took me a moment to realize she'd spoken to me. I couldn't help it. Even though I knew it would hurt, I glanced at the photo. The Botanica. A lush haven of soaring trees, hundreds of thousands of rare flowers, and hand-carved outdoor furnishings. It hit like a bullet to the gut.

What is wrong with you, Fae? Weddings make you cringe. You've always called them a waste of a down payment.

"Stunning," I agreed, meaning it. With the fake smile still plastered on my face, I deposited the remaining brochures onto the table and offered a little bow, bending my knees with flourish. "How else may I be of service to you, Mrs. Sun?"

It worked. Constance looked completely devastated by my good mood. "Actually…Eileen, darling, why don't you show Miss Ballantine the gowns that are our frontrunners? I'm sure she'll have some interesting input."

Eileen's eyes widened. She looked horrified by the idea. I couldn't blame her. I no longer bothered wearing my maid uniform, so my fashion style—or lack thereof—was evident to the naked eye. I wore black leggings paired with a fuzzy green and yellow sweater.

"I'm sure Miss Ballantine has things to do…" Eileen trailed off.

Time wasn't my problem. The thought that I wanted to curl into a ball and cry until I died of dehydration was. Because choosing a wedding dress for Zach's bride was the height of angst for me. I had a literal physical reaction to it. Like scorpions were crawling all over my skin.

But again, I couldn't let Constance win. "I'd love to take a look."

With a sigh, Eileen clasped a stack of glossy brochures tabbed with Post-it notes, sifting through three of them until she flipped to the right pages. She fanned the options before me. Classic A-line dresses with extensive tulle and enough lace to open a French bordel.

Zach would absolutely hate them. He enjoyed contemporary, artsy things. Grecian silk. Pleated cuts. Maybe something diamond-embellished. It frightened me that I knew his likes and dislikes so well.

I swallowed down a desperate scream, shrugging as I tapped one of the pictures. They all looked the same to me, anyway. "This one is gorgeous."

Eileen brightened. "This one is my favorite."

For a moment, I pitied her. For suffering the same phobia as Zach. For entering a loveless marriage. For having no one to help navigate her fears. At least Zach would leave our arrangement cured. I swore to it.

Constance searched my face for any trace of emotion—sadness, disappointment, jealousy—but found none. Little did she know, she'd stumbled upon a veteran when it came to emotional abuse, courtesy of Vera's twenty-three-year bootcamp.

"Very well, Miss Ballantine." She nodded to the door. "Please, leave."

"If you need anything else…" I jerked a thumb toward the hallway. "I'll be in the living room, watching a movie." I deliberately antagonized Constance, resenting her for controlling Zach, knowing she didn't have the balls to cry to him.

She glowered. "Hadn't realize this was your day off."

"It isn't." I drew a hand to my chest. "My, my. How *unsavory* of me."

Humming, I strolled out, not letting the first tear fall until I was absolutely positive it couldn't be heard.

Chapter Fifty-Five

Farrow

Zach never arrived home.

I produced my phone, checked the time (ten-thirty—*the fuck?*), and stopped myself from texting him for the sole reason that he didn't owe me anything. In fact, I'd chanted this to myself on the regular since Constance and Eileen left three hours ago.

He is not your boyfriend. Not your husband. Not yours. Period. Soon, he'll promise his forevers to someone else in a fluffy dress on a field of pollen.

You are temporary and insignificant. A feather in the wind.

I paced my room, a lioness in a rusty cage. The irony wasn't lost on me. While Dallas' now-husband had imprisoned her in a golden cage as she fought tooth and nail to break free, I'd slipped into my own gilded prison voluntarily and didn't want to leave. It would be easier if the glitz and glamor attracted me. I could find that elsewhere. No, I craved the soft smiles we shared across the room, the fleeting touches, and his addictive words of comfort, each of them carved onto my skin like a tattoo.

I curled my fingers over my windowsill, staring at the gleaming pool. The clear water twinkled back at me under the moon.

What you need is a dip. Cool off those raging hormones and red-hot jealousy.

I slipped into a tiny yellow two piece from Dallas ("since I now look like bologna stuffed into a rubber band in it"), grabbed a towel, and made my way downstairs despite the freezing weather. Steam rolled from the pool's surface in thick white clouds.

I dove in headfirst, slicing through the surface to the bottom and doing an entire lap before I resurfaced on the other end. I sucked in a greedy breath and tilted my head skyward. Stars danced across my vision, melting into one another, whirling in a puddle of tears.

Stop with the weird pity party. Those are reserved for your birthday. Just swim.

I did. Until my muscles strained and burned. Until I thought my limbs would fall off and float away. Lap after painful lap. Until finally, my mind cleared. When I finished, I hopped onto an in-pool lounger, closing my eyes, not bothering to dry off. The unforgiving wind licked my body. My nipples hardened to the point of numb. A pool of water dripped from my hair to the deck. I shaped my lips around a line of a song I listened to every night in my bunk bed in Seoul.

The ribs aren't a cage. They're the walls to your home.

I drew a shaky breath, pushing aside the melancholy.

You're living on borrowed time, Fae.

I refused to give Constance the pleasure of ruining this for me.

But what if she's right? a tiny voice in my conscience asked. *What if you're hurting him?*

The seed sprouted in my mind, planting roots in my chest.

And what of yourself? This man will inflict carnage on your heart. A victory against your evil stepmother isn't worth that.

Just the idea of Eileen in one of those poofy wedding dresses churned acid in my stomach. How would I cope when the time came to part ways with my personal demon?

"Octi." His soothing voice draped over me like a cashmere blanket.

Every muscle in my body tightened, but I kept my eyes closed. His steady footsteps neared, clapping against the heavy granite deck. Beneath my bikini top, my nipples strained and my heart missed a dozen beats. The mere sound of him made heat swirl inside my stomach. Still, I refused to show him how happy I was that he'd returned.

"What are you doing out here? It's freezing."

Is it? I can't feel much of anything other than my desire for you.

"Do you want to catch pneumonia?" he growled.

"You're not my parent."

"No, but I'm the closest thing to a family you have right now." His voice softened. "Look at me."

I opened my eyes. He was painful to look at. Too beautiful, with his raven hair and tar eyes and devastating bone structure.

"Where have you been?" I couldn't keep the bite out of my voice.

Zach treaded toward me, dripping power and wealth in dark gray slacks and a navy cashmere sweater tucked under a black peacoat. "I had some meetings in D.C." He shoved his hands deep inside his pockets, his eyes roaming my body.

"At eleven at night?"

Not your business, I reminded myself.

I had to stop. I *needed* to stop. Since when was I a clingy girlfriend?

"Spent the rest of my time driving around," Zach admitted, stopping when he got to the edge of the pool, only a few feet away. I'd expected hunger in his eyes. Instead, I saw concern. A dangerous emotion that had no place in our arrangement.

I arched a brow, trying to remain unaffected. "In your secured car?"

His lips quirked a little. "In a normal BMW."

"Living on the edge."

"Yes, whenever I'm certain you aren't there to push me off the cliff." He paused. "I had to think."

"Oh?" Foolish, idiotic hope flowered in my chest. I wanted him to say, *about you, about us.* "That's a new concept. You know you can do it anywhere, right? Even from the comfort of your home."

"Octi," he warned.

"Tell me what you thought about."

"Mainly about the timeline of my impending marriage. How it fits with my business schedule. I'm currently acquiring a few tech companies that will demand my attention as I reconstruct their boards."

I nodded, pretending his answer didn't cut through flesh and bone. "Time management is important. You're lucky to have Natalie."

"I don't wish to talk about Natalie or any other woman in my life." He looked so miserable, and for a single moment, I actually welcomed his pain. Why should I be the only one to suffer?

"What do you wish for, then?"

"For you to come upstairs, take a hot bath, and get into at least three layers of clothes before I lose my fucking mind."

"I think I'm good here." I knew I was punishing no one but myself, and still, I wanted to act out. To flip him the bird.

His fingers twitched by his side, his patience melting away. "Your lips are blue."

"Your heart is black."

"*Farrow*," he growled, baring his teeth at me. "Come here right this minute. It's *winter*. You're going to end up in the hospital at this rate."

"What a terrible inconvenience."

"*Farrow.*"

"If you care so much, come pick me up."

To my surprise, Zach's face didn't even twitch. He stepped onto the first pool stair, ankle-deep in water, and began treading toward the lounger. When he reached me, he shouldered off his coat and picked me up bridal style, wrapping the heavy fabric around me. Woodsy citrus swarmed me, warming up my body in an instant. On instinct, I wanted to wind my arms around his neck. Instead, I pretended to stare at something behind him, feigning a yawn.

To my chagrin, his lips twitched.

"What's so funny?"

He strode out of the pool, pushing through the weight of the water as he carried me toward the house. "*You.*" His eyes didn't waver from mine for one second.

"I entertain you?"

"You *please* me."

"Well, you happen to *dis*please me."

Telltale heat swept up my cheeks. I looked away, toward the house lights, to stop myself from kissing him.

"Did you know that the octopus perishes after it mates? The species exercises external fertilization." He tightened his grip on me. "Several males either insert their spermatophores into the female or hand her the sperm. Then, the males leave to die. The female lays the eggs. Once those hatch, her body suffers 'cellular suicide,' starting from the optic glands."

I almost snorted. "Zachary Sun."

"Yes, Farrow Ballantine?"

"Your dirty talk is one of the worst I've encountered."

He laughed, his chest vibrating and rumbling against me.

I rested my cheek against him. "So, what you're saying is that consummating our attraction will end in death?"

He pushed the balcony doors open and took the stairway to the second floor. "What I'm saying is—desire is a messy business, especially for intelligent creatures."

"But?"

"But it's worth it."

He carried me to his bedroom, where he laid me on the bed before proceeding to his bathroom. The sound of water hitting his massive claw tub traveled toward me. Lavender filled the air. *A bath bomb.* He hated scented products.

Zach turned off the faucet and approached me, his slacks still drenched with pool water.

I licked my lips as he picked me up again. "You should join me in the bath."

What a screwed-up relationship we had, always ping-ponging from enemies to lovers. Zach didn't answer, placing me on the edge of the tub and loosening the string holding my bikini top together. The top fell to the floor with a wet smack. He drank in an eyeful before hooking his thumbs on either side of my bikini bottom, sliding it down my legs.

He sank my naked body into the bathtub, spilling my hair over the edge. I could barely feel the water. My body had gone numb from the cold. Slowly, my nerve-endings defrosted, regaining sensation. I tipped my head back against the edge and stared at him, drunk with desire. My frustration dissolved into pleasure, uncurling as my body blossomed with yearning. He still stood to the side, watching me like a hawk, his cock erect and plastered to his thigh.

I arched a brow. "See something you like?"

"Like is an understatement." He ran a hand down his slacks, pretending to smooth an invisible wrinkle, squeezing his cock in the process. "And therein lies the problem."

"What problem?" I batted my lashes. "I thought this was just a temporary agreement."

"It is. I've always had issues parting ways with my favorite toys."

I arched my back, reaching between my thighs and finding my clit. My stomach dipped as his jaw tightened, his brows drawing together. The peaks of my nipples cut through the water's surface, pink and erect and begging to be touched.

He swore, turning his head for a moment. "*Farrow.*"

"Come on, Zach. After all, I'm just a toy." I picked up the pace between my legs, letting out a moan. "And you, too, are my favorite game."

He watched without blinking as I flung one leg over the tub, spreading my pussy, feeling the heated water penetrate me. "Fuck, fuck, fuck."

He ripped his sweater from his shoulders, dumping it on the floor. His socks came off next, followed by his pants and briefs in one move.

His cock sprung out, thick and long, the crown glazed with a pearl of pre-cum. For a moment, I feared it wouldn't fit inside me.

He slipped into the bath with a splash, circling my ankles and tugging me toward him. I gripped the tub's edges to regain my balance. My tight hole collided with his cock, eliciting a groan from him. He splayed one hand on the small of my back, using his free one to grab my jaw and kiss me long and hard and messily.

I whimpered into our kiss, his tongue meeting mine. He fisted his cock, guiding it into my pussy.

"Condom." I swallowed his moans, gasping. "We need a condom."

"Please, Farrow." His mouth glided down the side of my neck, teeth scraping my sensitive flesh. "I'll give you anything and everything in this world to let me fuck you bare. I need to feel you. All of you. No barriers. I beg you."

I rubbed my pussy up and down his length, our eyes locked in a battle of wills. "Anything?"

"*Anything.*"

He plastered his forehead to mine, closing his eyes, raw agony painting his face. For a cruel moment, I thought about asking for the pendant. But it wouldn't be fair. Psychological warfare aside, I wanted him to give it to me because he knew I deserved it, not as part of a blackmail scheme.

"I want you to tell me why you kept your distance from me for the past few days."

He reared his head back, staring into my eyes. "You really want to know why?" I nodded. "Because you terrify me, Farrow." He looked aside, paused, and turned back to me, throat bobbing with a swallow. "You remind me that I'm human. That I can, in fact, be destroyed by a simple touch. I should banish you, Fae."

"Why?"

"You make me want to enjoy my life, not just survive it."

His words ran down my spine like a shiver. I raised my pelvis, knotting my arms over his neck and sinking onto his cock.

He dug his fingers in my back, guiding himself deeper. "*Fuck.*"

A groan tore from my throat when he reached about halfway in. My eyes flared. Even wet and ready, there was too much of him.

"It's okay." He caught me by the waist, kissing my cheeks, my nose, my eyes. "We'll make it fit. Trust me."

I didn't know why I was putting my trust in a literal *virgin* with a dick the size of an AR-15, but I nodded, swallowing down a cry of pain as he reached between us. His thumb played with my clit as his fingers dug into my hips. He wedged another half an inch inside me. I tipped my head back, hissing as he kissed every corner of my face and neck. My fingers squeezed the bathtub walls.

"My beautiful, brave girl." He filled my pussy, mouth traveling to my breasts, licking at my nipples. "Look how good you take my cock. Such a good girl. Do you think you can come on my dick for me?" He nibbled the side of my jaw. "Think you can make my first time special?"

I nodded, holding my breath as he slid in another inch. He was almost all the way in, so big it felt like his cock was squishing my organs, ripping me to shreds. And still, I couldn't deny the intense pleasure. Bit by bit, I uncoiled, accepting the foreign object inside of me.

"That's it. Now ride my cock."

The walls of my pussy clutched his cock in a death grip. His eyes rolled back, the pleasure so intense he stopped playing with my clit and simply shuddered inside me. Each time I rose and sank back onto his cock, riding him like a cowgirl, his hard abs crashed into my midriff.

My tits bounced between us, heavy and full. He tried to catch them between his lips, sucking on them and releasing them with a pop.

"Slower." He cupped one of my breasts, slid his gaze from mine, and hissed out, "I'm about to come, and I don't want to. Fuck, I want to live inside your pussy. I'll pay rent with interest."

I teased him, picking up speed, enjoying the way a vein bulged at his neck with the effort to stop himself. "Ask nicely."

"Please..." His forehead fell to mine. "I need more."

He tugged my hair, kissing the living hell out of me. Ravenous, and earth-shattering, and full of desperation I'd never felt before. He refused to unglue his lips from mine as he cupped my tits, his tongue swirling inside my mouth. We kissed and we kissed until we ran out of saliva.

He grabbed the back of my neck, claiming my mouth once again, growling into it. "Mine. You will always be mine, you hear me?"

Passionate words that would mean nothing when we managed to tear apart. I turned my head away, refusing to answer.

He gripped my chin, forcing me to look down between our bodies as his cock slid in and out of me, thick and glistening with my juices. "Look at us," he instructed. "At *this*. Right here. The height of my existence. *Nothing* feels as good as your pussy clenching around me."

I slowed my movements to watch his thick cock enter me, giving him time to wind down, but neither of us could stop this freight train of pleasure. In no time, we both panted hard again, sweat glistening over our shoulders. I rode him harder, faster, angling my hips so he slid in deeper. He clutched my waist, guiding me with frantic movements.

The entire world fizzled out, leaving only the two of us. Zach—with undiluted, raw pleasure stamped on his face. And me—climbing higher up the orgasm ladder. My thighs shook from the strain as an avalanche tumbled down my limbs. My climax washed over me like a storm, tearing a cry from my lips.

"I'm coming. Fuck, I'm coming." He cursed, gripping my chin and meeting my eyes. "I need to come inside you."

"Zach…"

"I beg you." His voice cracked. "Please."

I clenched around him at his words, turned on all over again, knowing how reckless we were being. *What the hell is wrong with you, Fae? What the hell is wrong with you both?* But we'd become prisoners to our desire. Unable to think clearly. *Unwilling to.* I barely managed to calculate my cycle, confirming I'd hit a safe day, just moments before my period.

"Please." Zach's eyes glazed over, barely coherent, reminding me I'd taken his virginity. I owned a piece of him that would forever be mine.

I swallowed, almost coming again at the idea of him filling me. "Come in me."

At my words, his cock throbbed and swelled. Then, I felt it. The rush of heat spreading in my pussy as his seed spilled into me. Our orgasms clashed together. We clutched onto one another, my nails sinking into his flesh, his mouth fusing into mine like we were one entity trying to brace a hurricane. We flew high in the sky, reaching our peaks together.

After, we stayed curled against one another, shuddering into each other's skin until the water turned lukewarm. Zach kissed my shoulder. His nose nuzzled into my neck every once in a while. I didn't want to leave. Didn't want this moment to end. His dick began softening inside me, and I wanted to cry, because there was something so pathetic about us. Me, desperate to fight for my survival and refusing to admit I was falling for this man. Him, finally finding happiness and rejecting it to appease his guilt.

Zach clasped my face, turning it to look at him. "Octi…"

I set my expression to neutral, even though my heart rioted in my chest. I let him fuck me without a condom. I let him come inside me. I let him into my body, into my mind, into my *soul*. Now the only space he hadn't conquered was my heart—and he was fast-approaching it.

"I'm sorry I asked to fuck you without a condom. It was a scumbag move." His eyes crinkled with regret. He was still inside me. "A terrible error in judgment. If something happens…" He swallowed. "I promise I—"

I rushed to cut him off, not wanting to hear a promise he couldn't keep. "Nothing will happen, because I'm going to get the morning-after pill right now."

I stood. We both watched as his cock slid out of me, inch by inch. I towered over him, wet and vulnerable. Shivering. His semen trickled down my inner thigh.

"You don't have to." He clasped the back of my knees, closed his eyes, and kissed my pussy, breathing me in. "I would never do you wrong. Never turn my back on a child of mine."

A lash of panic whipped my back. I snorted to hide the ball of tears in my throat and stepped over him. "Trust me, no part of me wants to be an elaborate oopsie that snowballed into a scandal."

He stood, following me. "You're not a mistake, and you're not a scandal."

"Are you going to tuck me and the baby somewhere far away?" I wrapped myself in one of his lush towels. "Send us a check every month?"

He scowled, drying off. "That's not what I meant."

But I didn't stick around to find out.

"Farrow." His footsteps came from behind me, gaining speed. "Don't run away from me."

Then, convince me to stay. End your engagement. Tell me I matter.

He did no such thing.

I stumbled into the hallway, rushing to my room. If he saw my face, he'd see the tears. The pain. The confusion. Because what happened in his bathtub didn't feel like sex. It felt like making love.

"Farrow, *wait*."

I slammed the door in his face.

Hoping my heart could lock, too.

Chapter Fifty-Six

Farrow

The next morning, the universe showed off its twisted sense of humor. I returned home from Walgreens, popping Plan B onto my tongue and guzzling it down with clearance orange juice, a day from its expiration. But as soon as I stepped out of my Prius, the telltale trickle of my period slid down my thigh.

"Goddammit."

By the time I finished showering away the blood, my mood had taken a nosedive. I descended the stairs, ready to raid the kitchen for something sweet and decadent. Zach drifted down the halls somewhere, surely marching like a demon looking for his pound of flesh. I'd managed to dodge him all morning and planned to do so into the evening. My phone buzzed with another text, probably from Zach. Still, I checked it just in case, frowning at the name that flashed.

Andras: Tomorrow. Same time.

I careened to a stop, wondering how to reply. This marked our first contact since the news broke about my cheating scandal. I figured he needed time to process the news before unceremoniously dumping me, along with his dreams of fostering an Olympic gold medalist. In the end, I settled for something simple.

Farrow: K.

I slipped into the pantry without bothering with the lights, rummaging through the snack baskets when the door shut behind me. Darkness blanketed the room. I fisted a bag of cookies and sighed, turning for the knob. I crashed against a muscular chest, gasping.

"You're avoiding me." Zach's voice seeped straight between my thighs, an area he apparently had on speed dial. I hated how my traitorous body never seemed in sync with the rest of my opinion of him.

I flipped my hair over my shoulder. "This seems to be a recurring theme in our relationship."

"Another thing that seems reoccurring in our relationship is my willingness to spend all my time, effort, and resources on you, while you completely disregard me."

"Your Boss of the Year award is on its way." I sighed. "What do you want, Zach?"

"Your company. Your attention. Your pussy. Just to name a few." He paused, consuming the tiny space with his presence. "We have a deal."

Ah. Our deal. Our stupid, cursed deal. "We have a deal that we'll fool around when time permits. We *don't* have a deal that I'm at your beck and call. Your 'pussy for hire.'" I air-quoted the crass words, though he couldn't see it in the dark. "I'm not your whore, Zachary."

He crowded me against the shelves, his hand finding my cheek with eerie precision. "I never said you were." Zach lowered his head to get a taste of me.

I turned my face away on instinct. "Can't right now. Just got my period. No hanky panky."

"I don't mind if you're okay with it."

"Well, I'm not okay with it. And actually, I have to go."

Not a lie, per se. I *did* have to go. To my room. To decompress from all the feelings haunting me since we had sex.

His breaths came out faster. "Go where?"

"A date," I blurted out, cursing myself for such a stupid lie.

"A *date?*" His hands slammed on the shelves behind me.

"Nice hearing, Zach. Yes. A date." I licked my lips. "I told you— we're not exclusive."

"Name your price for exclusivity." It occurred to me that he didn't ask for the date's name for one simple reason—he'd find out himself anyway. His fingertips grazed my collarbone. "Is it the pendant that you want?"

More than I want revenge. That pendant brought me here in the first place. It forever lurked in the back of my mind. I never failed to glance at it when I stopped by his office. But now that I knew him, I refused to resort to theft or blackmail. Somewhere along the way, I'd decided to win the pendant back, fair and square.

"My freedom is not negotiable." I flicked his finger off me. "I'll date whether you like it or not. And if it pisses you off, just remember—you have a fiancée."

Rather than answer me, he swooped down, drawing my lower lip inside his mouth, sucking hard, stealing my breath away. The kiss was different this time. Cruel and demanding, teetering on the brink of frenzy. "I want to fuck you right here. Right now." His tongue stroked the roof of my mouth. "I don't give a fuck that you're on your period."

I was still raw from yesterday, a dull pain coating the walls of my pussy, and I couldn't think of anything more horrifying than sex while on my period. At the same time, I wanted this. Wanted to fill this emptiness with him.

He sucked my tongue into his mouth. I whimpered when he dared, "Tell me to stop, Octi."

But I couldn't. Not when his mouth sliding down my chin felt like bliss. His hands clawed my pajama top, ripping it clean of buttons. They flew everywhere, wheeling at our feet. He picked up my breast and squeezed the underside, bringing my soft flesh to his lips.

"This means nothing." The words ripped out from the back of my throat. He sucked my entire breast into his mouth, licking away the pain every time I moaned, running his teeth over my sensitive skin.

"Yes or no?" He sounded cold. So, so cold.

I groaned. "Yes." He didn't play fair. My hands roamed his body, fingers disappearing inside his hair, greedily clutching his smooth skin and bulging muscles. I barely managed to add, "Condom."

This time, he didn't argue. He produced one from his pocket—did the jerk walk around with it, just in case?—and ripped the wrapper with his teeth, shoving my sweatpants and panties down. A shiver bolted up my spine when he pushed my bra to my neck, his tongue lapping circles on my skin as it traveled south.

"I hate this so much," I informed him, still driving his head down to my pussy.

He used his thumb to stroke the slit of my dripping pussy, his mouth fastening on my clit. I released a desperate moan, arching my ass up, chasing his touch.

"Poor baby." His breath fanned my clit. "I'm so sorry you have to suffer through another orgasm."

He darted his tongue out, rolling the tip of it from my ass crack to my clit. My entire body spasmed with pleasure.

"I feel so empty." The strangled confession tumbled past my lips. "I need you inside me."

I didn't even care that this was wrong, and out of control, and even sinful. Didn't care that my body hadn't recovered from last night. That delicious bruises still peppered my skin. I wanted him where he belonged—inside me.

"I know, baby. I'm about to fuck you so deep, you'll feel my cock every time you walk."

I didn't doubt it. Last time, his dick seemed to reach my heart. Slowly, he withdrew the tampon and dumped it on the floor. As soon as the tampon was out, Zach was in. He didn't ease into me this time. He thrust home with his sheathed cock all at once, filling me to the brim. The sensation was so intense I felt like I was climaxing and giving birth at the same time. My muscles squeezed around him, milking his erection as his upper body hovered above mine.

Our foreheads met. "Hello, Octi."

I imagined his hungry gaze. He must have looked like a lion after a good feast. I waited for my embarrassment to kick in, but all I could feel was desire. So much desire.

"Hold onto my shoulders, Farrow."

"Why?"

"Because I'm about to fuck the soul out of you."

He squeezed my throat between his elegant fingers, pulled out of me, then started fucking me mercilessly. A grunt punctuated each thrust, followed by a swirl of his waist and a tilt of his body to hit my G-spot. He released my throat, dipped his head down, and ravished my mouth. Our tongues fought and molded into one another, neither of us gaining dominance.

Behind us, the door whined open. Light seeped in, inch by inch.

"Hello? Anyone there?" Natalie's head popped in. "I wanted some pretzel—"

"*Out.*" Zach kicked the door shut with his foot without even looking back, still kissing and fucking me. He must've caught her finger, because I heard her yelp.

Zach shifted, lowering us to the floor. Each time he speared into me, my back slid against the glossy tiles. The friction, pain, and vibrations brought me to heights I didn't know my climax could reach.

Everything in my body felt electrified, swollen, and alive.

I tightened my walls around his cock, feeling his skin humming against mine. "I'm going to come."

My eyes rolled back. An avalanche of warmth swept over me. I rocked back and forth as my climax grabbed me by the throat.

Zach didn't slow, fucking me even harder, wilder, like he intended to nail me to the floor. "I'm going to mark you until there's no doubt who you belong to."

"I belong to no one," I groaned out, letting him devour my breasts, tease my nipples, lick every inch of my chest. Snacks tumbled from the shelves, joining the buttons on the floor.

"Have fun on your date, Octi." He released my skin with a pop, no doubt leaving a love bite tattooed to my skin. "You can pretend to enjoy another man's company, but we both know that no one will ever come close to me." Zach rubbed his mark with his thumb, letting it soak into my skin. "Coming now."

"Me, too."

Only with Zach did I ever have orgasms so close together. I couldn't help it. He overloaded my senses. It was all too much. The scenery. The sensation. The man. His cocked jerked inside me. He released a guttural groan, pushing his face into my shoulder blade. I felt the heat of his cum inside his condom and the drip of my juices leaking onto the tiles. Within seconds, he returned to his feet before I could regulate my breaths, tucking his dick back into his pants. He opened the door, letting a sliver of light in as he knotted the full condom. I still laid on the floor, panting, wet, and naked.

"Admit it, Octi. No one else will ever chart. I'm it for you. I'm the only man you'll ever desire."

"How do you know?"

He stepped back, frowning. "Because you're it for me, too."

Every ounce of defiance I'd managed to muster knocked out of me in one swoop. Before I could answer him, he turned and walked away, making sure to flip on the lights, so I could take a good look at the gift he'd left behind.

My discarded tampon, drenched from my juices and coated pink with diluted blood. Proof I would always and forever be his little slut.

Chapter Fifty-Seven

Zach: Don't forget not to clean the pantry.

Farrow: Your autocorrect sucks. And yes, I'll clean the pantry when I'm back.

Zach: It wasn't autocorrect.

Zach: Don't you dare touch it.

Farrow: ?

Zach: Until I have the chance to make you lick the fucking floor clean while I take you from behind.

Farrow: You cannot be serious.

Zach: I said don't touch it.

Farrow: You're sick.

Zach: Yes, I am. And you are the antidote, Octi.

Chapter Fifty-Eight

Farrow

It occurred to me that Andras' invitation to train could be punishment before my execution. After all, he'd reached new levels of cranky today. A miracle, considering his narrow range of emotions rivaled a psychopath's.

Andras ripped his mask from his face. "Az lsten verje meg."

He stomped off the piste, halfway through our training session. I didn't even know what I'd done wrong this time—other than show up early, focused and alert, annihilating his every attempt at catching me with his épée.

I unclipped myself from the wire, charging behind him. "Hey, we still have forty minutes left."

He ignored me, storming into his office.

I managed to slip inside before the door slammed shut. "What's going on?"

Hair clung to my forehead, glued by sweat. I swiped it away, bouncing from foot to foot. We'd managed to ignore the elephant in the room all morning, but I had a feeling said elephant was about to crush the little hope I had into dust.

"There is no point, Fae." Andras collapsed into his seat, lighting up a cigarette despite the no-smoking zone. "*Vege.* Your career is in an existential crisis. No matter how talented and motivated you are, you have no future in fencing." He reclined in his seat. "Pretending otherwise is cruel to you and a waste of my own precious time."

I remained standing, frowning. "Then, why did you wait three-quarters of our session to tell me this?" Heat set my cheeks ablaze.

Andras hitched a shoulder up. "I tried to spare you my thoughts."

"You've never done that before."

He sucked on the cigarette, releasing a plume of smoke between his thin lips. "I wanted to take one last look at your craft before giving you my decision."

"Oh, yeah?" I crossed my arms. "What's the verdict?"

"You're ready for the Olympics." He tapped his cigarette on his ashtray, a deep frown still marring his face. "Remember my friend on the IOC?"

He had many friends high up on the International Olympic Committee. His reputation as Andras Horvath preceded him, after all.

I nodded, though it could be anyone. "Sure."

"We discussed you all week."

I inched forward. "And?"

"He went back to the committee. They are willing to give you a second chance if you pay the rest of your fee upfront."

My heart rioted against my ribcage. I could do that. Now that Zach footed my legal bill, I could actually *do* it.

Hope cluttered my throat, thickening my voice. "Do you think there's a chance?"

"Can't promise anything." Two columns of gray smoke shot from his nostrils. "But it is a possibility."

"We should try." I splayed my fingers on his desk, leaning in. *So much for accepting my retirement.* "I'll do whatever it takes. We'll practice twice a day. I'll pay the rest of the fee upfront—"

"There are strings attached."

I blinked at him, waiting.

He used the lit ember of his cigarette to erect a small mountain of ash on the tray. "You drop that silly lawsuit against your stepmother and leave your father's family alone."

His words knocked the wind out of me. I stumbled back from their force. *Your father's family.* What was I to him? A Christmas decoration? Why wouldn't I fight against injustice? Vera fabricated the will and robbed Dad of his last wishes. Retiring at our company had always been my endgame. Fencing was the dream—but it wasn't a long-term career. And I refused to be shamed into submission. After all, a rose doesn't survive without its thorns.

"She made up a whole will." I tossed my hands up. "She stole my father's art collection, sold his entire—"

Andras crashed a fist onto his desk, shaking its contents with the force. "*Enough.*"

I shut my mouth, but I refused to move an inch.

He stood, panting, screwing the cigarette butt inside the ashtray. "I do not care about your family drama. I do not care about this Vera woman. Or about your sisters. Your mind is off the piste when you are busy fighting them. Either you are all in, or you are all out. I am not going to let you waste my time while you spread yourself thin."

I didn't understand why training for the Olympics and bringing Vera down were mutually exclusive.

"I'm not spreading myself thin." I shook my head, rushing words out. "Fencing takes top priority. The Vera thing is handled by the lawyers and a private investiga—"

"Private investigator?" Andras' face splotched like strawberry ice cream. He jabbed his finger at me. "You have lost whatever mind you had. Consider this my ultimatum. Either you leave this nonsense alone and move on with your life, or I am done training you."

"This isn't fair." I curled my hands into fists, shaking so hard I practically vibrated. "This has nothing to do with fencing."

"Everything has to do with fencing." Andras rounded the desk, sloping against it. He folded his arms over his belly, regulating his tone. "If I bring you to the Olympics, you must listen to me. You will let things go when I tell you to. You will eat from the menu I give you. You will obey my every request." His nostrils flared. "And my first request is for you to drop it all. The private investigators. The lawyers. The nonsense. Stop living in the past, Farrow. Start working for the future."

Neither of us backed down. Our eyes refused to budge. There was so much I wanted to say. Plea, beg, explain, bargain. He towered over me in height and build. I stood in the shadow of *the* Andras Horvath. Legendary instructor. Urban myth. But at the end of the day, he hadn't only pushed me to give up on justice. He wanted me to give up on who I was.

"If it's all or nothing…" I stepped back. "I'd rather have nothing."

I turned, storming out of his office. A litany of Hungarian profanities blasted through the door. Glass shattered. Furniture knocked to the ground.

I grazed a fingertip over his name plate fastened on the wall. "Goodbye, Andras."

CHAPTER FIFTY-NINE

Farrow: Is the pantry clean enough for you now?

Zach: Yes.

Zach: But now we need to take care of the laundry room.

Farrow: We didn't do anything in the laundry room.

Zach: Yet.

Ollie vB: Neat, Zach. You should totally take her for a spin.

Zach: WTF ARE YOU DOING IN THIS CHAT?

Ollie vB: I told you my tech guy is great.

Farrow: Consider me thoroughly disturbed.

Ollie vB: Oh, come on. It was funny. For a SPIN. Get it? Because you'll be doing it on a laundry machine during a load.

Ollie vB is typing…

Zach: Quick, Fae. Block his number before he makes a load joke.

Farrow left the chat.

Zach left the chat.

Ollie vB: And what a load it is going to be…

Ollie vB: Goddammit.

Chapter Sixty

Zach

A thousand-page thesis could be written on the marvels of discovering sex for the first time. Every time I exited Farrow's tight pussy, the thirty-three years I'd spent outside of it felt like a total waste. Unfortunately, she had things to do. Vera to ruin. A medal to earn. Romeo's needy wife to shave. (Ollie walked in on them and managed to send pics before Rom tossed his phone down the garbage disposal.)

So, I found myself at the country club, working out my frustrations on the tennis court. Solo, as always. Whacking every ball the machine launched my way. When I stopped to rehydrate, I spotted Mom at the edge of the court. She wore a full-blown business suit, confirming my suspicion that we hadn't bumped into each other by chance.

"Zachary." She squeezed my cheeks, pushing her Hermès up her arm. "My one and only son."

I dislodged my face from her paws. "Mom."

Oh, Constance. Never one to take a hint, even if it was thicker than a tree trunk. I'd made myself scarce at the estate the past week, opting instead to whisk Farrow away to The Grand Regent and getaway spots that reminded her of Korea.

"You're harder to find than a matte alligator Birkin." She fussed over my sweat, producing an XL sunblock stick from her bag. "Where have you been?" *Inside Farrow Ballantine's dripping pussy.*

"Hell and back." I slung the racket over my shoulder, wiping the sweat from my forehead. "Why? What do you need?" I was in no mood to entertain her wants and needs. In fact, all *I* wanted was to get back home in hopes of burying myself inside Farrow. No wonder the system stressed abstinence. One taste, and I couldn't think of anything else.

Mom huffed. "This is no way to talk to your mother."

"But it *is* a way to talk to a woman who is forcing me to marry someone against my will."

We both froze in the middle of the parking lot. Her, stunned. Me, relieved. This marked the first time I'd flat-out told her I did not want to marry Eileen. Didn't want to marry *at all*. With the truth in the open, I couldn't suppress the urge to push back.

"What are you talking about? She's perfect for you." Mom began ticking off Eileen's achievements with her fingers. "Beautiful. Kind. Smart. A doctor. To top all that, she comes from a great family. The Yangs are protective, charitable, and obscenely rich—"

"I don't care." I slammed the racket on the concrete road. "*I'm* obscenely rich, and you know what? My fat bank account and even fatter portfolio hasn't made me happy. Far from it. I've wasted my life trying to achieve more, earn more, own more. I chase safe thrills to fill the void inside me. I don't need another prize to show the world I've made it."

Mom's whole body trembled inside that wrinkleless suit. "What are you saying?"

I knew I'd treaded deep into troubled water. Yet, I took a leap, ready to drown. It was now or never. Forever was a long time to spend with someone you didn't love.

"I don't want to marry Eileen."

"*Zachary.* You cannot say that." Mom clutched the Buccellati necklace Dad gifted her on their wedding night. "We already announced it. There was an engagement party."

"People call off engagements all the time. Oliver and Romeo have a running bet on how long mine will last."

"What about poor Eileen? You made a promise to her. She'll become a laughingstock. No one will take her seriously. Or you, for that matter."

This hit a nerve. She wasn't wrong. Both Eileen and I would take huge blows to our reputations if we canned this engagement. Me, I didn't care about so much. The only person whose opinion mattered to me never succumbed to societal pressure. But it wouldn't be fair to Eileen. Not after I'd committed to our arrangement. Still, what would hurt more? Entering a marriage where neither of us could stand one another or a temporary blow to the ego?

"For the longest time, I let you and Celeste Ayi manage my personal life by proxy—simply because I never cared to develop one. I know better now than to let this snowball into a situation that will be disastrous for both me and Eileen. I'll speak to her and let her know my decision."

"*Shh.*" Mom peered around at the club members roaming the grounds in their cushioned golf carts. "They'll hear us."

She grabbed my arm, leading me to the back of a private cabin. Her touch seared through my skin but didn't make me want to spew vomit. Laughter tickled my throat. If I weren't so furious, I'd be elated. Farrow *was* fixing me. One touch at a time, she made other people's touches less revolting. Mom crowded me against a wall, flipping her Birkin open. She snatched an inhaler, wedged it between her lips, and took three hits.

I frowned. "What are you doing?"

"I'm having..." Her lower lip curled in disgust. "...anxiety. Dr. Shahi also gave me pills, which *of course* I won't take." She shoved the inhaler back into her bag, shaking her head. "Oh, it's fine. Don't look at me like that, Zachary. We both know my life hasn't been worth much since your father passed away."

Cheap psychological warfare, but it worked like a charm. Guilt slithered into my gut, spilling over like lava. Mom meant it, though. I knew it. She had one purpose in life. *Me.* Whenever I forgot that, it took all of two seconds to conjure the words Ayi once shouted that jerked Mom out of her zombie state.

What if your son dies, too? Are you going to let that happen as you wallow in grief? I can't protect Zach by myself.

"Do you think I don't know that you don't love Eileen?" Mom's eyes filled with tears. She yanked a handkerchief from her bag, patting her eyes dry. "I know that, Son. Believe me."

Forcing myself to endure the touch, I guided her to a nearby bench by the crook of her elbow. Her shoulders shook so hard, she didn't even notice that I'd touched her for the first time in over twenty years. I wondered what she saw when she looked at me. So smart. So cold. So incapable of filling the cracks in her soul. I couldn't even tell her the last words her husband ever said. In the end, for every fact I knew, the one thing I didn't know mattered most.

Mom sniffled, caving my heart inward. "But Dad and I always wanted you to experience the things that made our lives worth living. A beautiful house. Children. Someone to come home to. The emptiness you've been feeling? A family will fill it with so much joy. How do you think I survived after your father died?"

Mom blinked, her eyes red. "You and your auntie are my lifelines. Some days, you're the only things that get me up in the morning. I want you to have that with someone responsible. Someone dependable. Someone safe." She sighed, toying with her handkerchief. "Eileen is capable of weathering every storm life throws your way. She's resilient and considerate. She'll never go against her morals. Never cheat or steal. I handpicked her for you. She's similar to you in every way."

Mom was right. But the truth of the matter was—Eileen wasn't the one I wanted. "And that girl… *Farrow*." Mom's mouth twisted downward. "The one you brought to live with you…" She raised a finger, stopping me preemptively. "I refuse to pretend she's your housekeeper. We both know what she is."

I worked my thumb down my tense jaw. "She's off-topic."

"But she isn't." Mom patted her nose with the handkerchief. "I know she's your mistress. It's fine. There's nothing wrong with fulfilling your urges. We all have needs." If I could cringe myself into oblivion, I would. She continued, "But she's not wife material. You know this, too. You've seen the news. She cheated for financial gain. How do you know she isn't with you for your money and power?"

I didn't respond, mostly because Farrow *had* agreed to our arrangement for legal fees (money) and revenge (power).

Mom shook her head. "You're a trophy to her. If you were poor, would you have met? Would you have begun a relationship together?"

I remained silent, knowing this to be the truth. Not because I found Farrow to be a gold digger—if anything, she treated people with money *worse*—but because I understood the circumstances of how we met. What it looked like to the outside world and why a parent would be concerned.

Mom continued, sensing a crack in my shield. "I'm not telling you to cut her loose. You can keep her for vacations and the occasional treat." Her throat rolled with a swallow. "I've spoken to Eileen. She's happy to accommodate you. She mentioned neither of you intend to pursue a physical relationship."

"What's the point of being together if neither of us want to *actually* be together?"

"Oh, Zach. Relationships aren't about sex. Relationships are about mutual values, goals, and friendship." Mom quaked beside me, frail and small, spewing out her argument like she was on death row. "Your relationship with this Farrow girl is a hoax. You built it on an unstable foundation. Attraction fades. Desire evaporates. Cravings come and go. But friendships? They stay."

Against all will and odds, I tried to see her perspective. Her logic hinged on the mutual exclusivity of friendship and attraction. Had it occurred to her that I could consider Farrow my friend while also wanting to fuck her?

Has it even occurred to you? *If it had, you wouldn't have thrown the agreement in her face every time things got uncomfortable.*

Mom smoothed my shirt, testing the waters. I tried not to flinch. "Eileen will be good for you. You're not a means to an end for her. You're a long-term investment."

Perhaps she was right. Not about falling in love with Eileen—that could never happen. But maybe I'd let my time with Farrow cloud my judgment. Eileen offered me everything I needed to tick off on my list. Farrow offered me a countdown, and even that came with a hefty price tag.

"Mom." I placed my hands on her arms, guiding her away, marveling at the fact that I could touch anyone without my knife as a barrier. "I'm sorry, but it would be unfair of me to give Eileen any hope that we can be anything more than acquaintances."

"Please." She pressed her hands together. Her bag flew to the floor, its contents spilling onto the ground like guts. She didn't even notice. "Please, Zachary. Just give it one more chance. For your mom. For your auntie. For your *father.* He would have told you to at least try. You know he would."

Tears spilled from her eyes. She seemed fragile in that moment— the same woman who'd bawled over my hospital bed before time mended my physical wounds and she'd slowly slipped away.

Mom hovered a palm over my cheek. I closed my eyes, fighting the disgust it ignited. The intense nausea was now a dull discomfort, thanks to Farrow. "Please, give Eileen a chance." Mom squeezed my shoulder through my shirt. "I've booked you a weekend in the Hamptons. The house is ready. She'll be there, waiting for you. Just try for me."

I closed my eyes, realizing I needed Eileen to break this off first. Fine. I'd do the Hamptons. But it wouldn't end in wedding bells.

"If I do this," I growled, "will you set me free?"

"Yes." Mom clutched her handkerchief. "Yes, I promise."

"Very well. The Hamptons it is."

Chapter Sixty-One

Ari: Earth to Fae—please, send a sign of life.

Dallas: Low-key tempted to hurl ass over there and see if she's okay. I haven't heard from her in a while.

Ari: Define a while.

Dallas: Three hours.

Ari: Hmm. I've had arguments about the best Milkis flavor that have lasted longer than that.

Dallas: We're kind of co-dependent right now.

Dallas: She even helped me shave my legs the other day.

Farrow: I'm alive.

Farrow: (Unfortunately.)

Dallas: How do we know it's really you and not someone else pretending you're alive so they can sell off your internal organs on the black market?

Ari: DALLAS WHATEVER-YOUR-MIDDLE-NAME-IS COSTA. Step away from the true-crime category on Netflix.

Dallas: I'm just being a worried citizen. Ari, ask her something only Farrow would know.

Ari: Who did I kiss in the tenth grade that I swore you to secrecy about because he had a mullet and snacked on raw onion in public?

Farrow: Lee Ji-sub.

Ari: WHY DID YOU TELL?

Farrow: YOU LITERALLY ASKED.

Ari: You're fired as my BFF.

Ari: Just kidding. I could never replace you… and not for my lack of trying.

Farrow: Lol.

Dallas: Okay, this lol was weak AF. Are you okay?

Farrow: Andras just dumped my ass because I wouldn't give up on my lawsuit with Vera.

Dallas: Dafuq does he have to do with it?

Ari: I second Dallas' question.

Farrow: I don't know, but I'm officially without a coach and without an Olympic medal. After the media scandal Vera has treated me to, I'm toast. I can't believe it's over.

Dallas: Shit, Fae. I'm sorry. Hold on. I'm coming with margaritas and all the snacks.

Ari: FaceTime me when you get to her.

Farrow: I'll be fine. It was only a dream.

Dallas: You can't get what you want without dreaming it first. Otherwise, how would you even know you want it?

Chapter Sixty-Two

Farrow

It shouldn't have surprised me that Zach owned an armored vehicle in every state. His personal driver zipped past lush golf courses and gigantic beach houses stretched across acres of white sand.

I stared outside, hugging my bag to my chest, my face undoubtedly bone-white. I didn't care. Nothing mattered much after my conversation with Andras. The gray skies cracked like an egg, rain pounding on the windows in thick sheets. Mother Nature was bawling her eyes out. I wanted to do the same, struggling to keep my stoic expression intact.

Zach flicked the A/C vent, so it didn't blow on my bare arms. "Is there anything you'd like to see in the Hamptons, Octi?" He'd made it a point to sit as close to me as possible. Still, I'd ignored him the entire duration of the trip, plane ride included.

"Yes," I hissed out. "I'd like to see your mansion from the rearview of my Prius after this is all done and dusted."

If the rain bothered him, he didn't show it.

He is healing, day by day, while your dreams slip further and further away.

Zach reclined in his seat, stretching out his legs. "What did I do now?"

"Bringing your side piece to a vacation with your fiancée is low, even by your standards."

"You're not my side piece." His eyes clung to my face in a way that made me happy and miserable at the same time. "And you need to stop with the Eileen thing."

"Why?"

"Because… it's complicated."

"Seems pretty simple to me."

"I need time."

I snorted, whipping my head to look at him. "For what?"

"To figure things out." He tugged the silky strands of his hair.

"With you by my side."

I averted my gaze to the window, shaking my head. I wasn't even mad at Zach. He'd made the rules clear from the start, and I'd agreed to them. No. The object of my anger currently sat 300+ miles away in Potomac. *Andras*. Andras Horvath with his ridiculous, bizarre ultimatum.

"Octi." Zach grabbed my hand and deposited it in his lap, toying with my fingers. The gesture hurt more than it soothed me. It reminded me this would all be over in a few weeks, maybe even days. "What's eating at you? Is it Andras? I can find you a better coach."

"No. I sobered up from that fantasy," I admitted as the car pulled past towering hedges and approached a French-limestone mansion. "I'm going to continue fencing for the fun of it, but that's it."

"And coaching?" His fingers curled over mine in his lap as the car rolled along the pebbled path to the front door. "Would you still consider coaching me? You're wonderful at it."

His compliment licked my skin like a ray of sun.

"I suppose you need the practice."

"Brat." He brought the back of my hand to his lips, giving it a lingering kiss. "Stay close to me, okay?"

Eileen stood at the doorway in an impeccable burgundy dress and matching coat, her hands gloved and clasped before her.

I swallowed, slipping my hand from his. "Okay."

Staying close to Zach proved impossible as the day progressed. I resorted to sweating out my frustrations in the basement gym while Eileen dragged him venue hopping across Southamptons. She hadn't wasted any time when we stumbled out of the car. Her smile had vanished when she noticed me, but she bounced back quickly, perky and polite.

"Miss Ballantine, what a darling surprise." She glanced at Zach as we made our way inside. "I thought you'd bring Natalie, if anything."

You and me both. I'd only agreed to come to keep track of the case. Zach regularly communicated with the dream team via teleconference. I couldn't risk missing any news. Not with victory over Vera so close.

Zach opened the door for us. "Farrow is my right hand."

I almost cackled, whispering under my breath, "All puns intended?" Our shoulders brushed in the hall. We trailed about two feet behind Eileen. He smirked, his pinky touching mine ever so briefly. "That depends on whether you found it funny or cringy."

I loosened my shoulders, thawing. "A bit of both."

"In that case, yes. Pun intended."

We embarked on a courtesy tour of the fourteen-bedroom mansion, during which Zach shamelessly assigned me the bedroom next to his and Eileen one in the furthest corner. While his staff took our luggage to our rooms, Eileen announced their appointment with a wedding planner to scout venues. Of course, I snatched up the chance to redeem myself.

I spun to him. "You should go."

The more I thought about it, the more resolute I became. Zach needed an Eileen. I wouldn't be around forever. Once I cured him and we parted ways, it would reassure me if he had someone steady and unwavering in his life. Zach's eyes ping-ponged between us, the corner of his lips curling down at the idea.

"Really, Zach." I smiled, nodding. "You should go. I'll be fine."

And by fine, I meant stewing in green, gooey jealousy I had no right to feel. I sweated my ass off on the stepper. The machine buzzed when I hit the sixty-minute mark. I hopped off, snatching a water bottle from the holder and chugging the entire thing. During my shower, I thought of all the ways I'd laugh in Vera's face when this ended. For two years, I'd imagined this moment a thousand different ways. But today, for some reason, the thought of taking things from Vera no longer thrilled me. The thought of *giving* things to Zach did.

I slipped into sweatpants and a sweater and padded downstairs when shards of a conversation between Zach and Eileen seeped into my ears. I halted, pressing my back to the wall to stay hidden.

"...just think that we should honor your mother's wishes in attending the dinner." Eileen poured herself a glass of chardonnay on one of the double islands. "It takes six months to secure reservations at The Winstonian."

"It could take an eternity, and I still wouldn't want to dine there. Besides, I'm not hungry." Zach spoke in his signature detached tone. "I have paperwork to sift through. You should go, though. You'll have fun."

If it were me, I would've picked a fight by now. Which was exactly why Eileen suited him better.

"I hear the food is divine." She set her glass down, the picture of patience. "It would be such a waste to give up the reservation. Plus, doesn't your friend Romeo co-own the place? I'm sure he wouldn't appreciate you wasting a two-person table."

My heart lodged in my throat as I waited for his answer. Selfishly, I wanted him to stay home. To turn his back on her. In fact, for one outlandish moment, I wanted to yell, "I'm better for you. Why won't you choose me?" Instead, I said nothing, my entire body rigid in the silence.

"Fine." He checked his wristwatch. "We'll go."

I closed my eyes, inhaling a ragged breath.

"Great." Eileen dumped her wine in the sink. "I'll call your driver and put on something sexy. It'll be a good idea to draw attention. Show people we're a power couple. This could be great for our careers."

Her heels tap-tapped on the hardwood, moving in my direction. I bolted up the stairs to my room, closing the door behind me. Eileen's voice flooded inside from the hall.

"…taking me to dinner now." She sighed into her phone, like she'd just come back from a five-mile run. "I had to work my magic, but I made it happen." Silence. Then, she groaned, giggling. "I know. I cannot wait to ride this man. He's so grumpy and hot. He's defrosting, though. You should have seen him when we went venue hunting. Not a single woman managed to rip her gaze off of him. Once I show him how good I am in the sack, it's game over for this brainiac."

Sharp, rusty claws clung to my throat. I couldn't take it anymore. Her words should have rung warning bells, but I couldn't see past the constant reminder that he'd soon become someone else's.

Eileen slipped into her room, leaving a trail of laughter and perfume behind her. I kept my ears to the door, listening as she exited again, whistling to herself. Her heels pounded down the steps.

The whole time, Zach didn't come to my room to check on me.

He didn't even text me.

An hour after Zach and Eileen left, I stood at the doorway of his mansion, clad in a metallic minidress Dallas told me she'd left here last summer.

"Are you sure this is the right way to deal with my raging jealousy?" I clutched onto her designer purse, my phone glued to my ear, waiting for my Uber. "Because I thought sexting with a stranger would do the job."

"Positive." Dallas munched on something crunchy on the other line. "Trust me, I'm a relationship engineer."

"That's not a thing."

"Zach is just letting his mother play at his heartstrings." Dallas ignored my skepticism. "It's you that he wants."

"But Eileen's good for him." The sarcasm dripping from me could've cured a drought. "She's the rational choice."

The more I thought about it, the more of a trainwreck I knew it would be. A marriage between the two would be like holding an Addicts Anonymous meeting in a pharmacy. How could two people with the same phobia cure each other?

"Ain't nothing rational about love, babe." Dallas giggled her church-bells laugh. "I'm a Fackery stan."

"Fackery is a terrible shipping name." I winced. "Too close to fuckery."

"How about Zarrow?"

"No." I shivered in the tiny dress, already regretting this night before it started. "I told you—Zach and I aren't even an option."

"Of course, you are. I mean, hello? Kate Beckinsale and Pete Davidson, anyone? There are no rules in love and war."

I shifted my weight from leg to leg, fighting the cold burrowing into my bones as the headlights of a Toyota Camry flashed in the distance, coming toward me.

"I can't believe I'm going on a date with someone else."

"Hey, you aren't exclusive." Something rustled. Probably another bag of snacks. "And I happened to set you up with a really great guy. Who knows? Maybe something real can blossom out of it."

Dallas had insisted on setting me up with a date at The Winstonian—finding me last-minute seats courtesy of a wary Romeo—so I could remind Zach that our lack of exclusiveness went both ways. It was petty, but I wasn't in a position to turn it down. One—because I hadn't eaten since morning. And two—because I really did need to prove to both Zach and myself that I wasn't all-in in this relationship.

"Set your expectations way low." I shimmied my minidress down over my thighs. The thing was shorter than Romeo's fuse. "Zach marked me with love bites all over my boobs and stomach the other day."

"Ugh. That is so hot." Dallas sighed. "And he is so screwed."

I flashed the Uber driver a smile, muttering, "So am I."

CHAPTER SIXTY-THREE

Farrow

A nderson Stause was not a man capable of stealing my heart.
Quite frankly, he was not a man capable of stealing the pepper grinder sitting between us on the candlelit table.

There was nothing overtly wrong with him (other than the fact that his jawline reminded me of Bob Belcher). There was nothing overtly right with him, either. To be completely frank, he was blander than unseasoned oatmeal. Nice, but not kind. Well-read, but not intelligent. Aesthetically pleasing, but not handsome. He didn't possess the same powerful magnetism Zach did, nor the boyish, enthusiastic passion that lit a fire in his eyes.

"I'm so pumped we get to eat here." Anderson splayed a napkin on his lap, grinning. "I've always wanted to try this place, but I could never get a table."

I surveyed the room. We'd settled at the table not even a minute ago, and already he'd polished off all the complimentary bread, chugged down two cocktails, and pocketed the fine utensils. Where did Dallas find this guy?

I offered a polite smile, still scanning the restaurant, only half-paying attention. "Hmm."

My eyes landed on Zach and Eileen three tables over. As if sensing my gaze, Zach twisted his head, zeroing in on me with uncanny precision. As soon as he drank in the dress, his expression darkened, brows pinched together. A tingle zapped down my spine. I swallowed my saliva. I'd never seen him like this. So... *uncontained*.

Eileen sat across from him, talking a mile a minute as she toyed with the stick in her cocktail. I brought my cherry drink to my lips, refocusing my attention on my date, giving him an honest chance. Anderson appeared to be deep in discussion with me.

"...father wanted me to go to public school. You know, so he wouldn't have to pay tuition. All because of that so-called 'sexual harassment' case while I temped for Senator Hurton. Like, am I not allowed to make any mistakes? Where's the compassion?"

Where, indeed? Not anywhere with me, that was for sure. The guy was a bore and a chauvinist. *Relationship engineer*, my ass. I quickly caught on to the fact that Dallas had put us together purely for the purpose of pissing Zach off. Anderson was as charmless as an overflowed trash can. As if reading my mind, her name flashed on my phone in my lap.

Dallas: Sorry I told you he's cute.

Dallas: I knew you wouldn't have said yes if you realized he's a dud.

Dallas: FYI, he was also accused of sending unsolicited nudes, but I know you can make dumplings out of his nuts if he oversteps.

I sighed inwardly, making a mental note to get back at Dallas. Meanwhile, Zach and I had engaged in a stare-off. Neither of us turned. Neither of us picked up our utensils. Neither of us *moved*.

Eileen tried to draw Zach's attention back to her, her behavior at odds with my initial impression. She flipped her hair, pushing her tits together in her gown, giggling like a schoolgirl. My body hummed with jealousy, barely catching the ping of another text. Anderson didn't even notice when I checked my phone as he droned on.

"...barely graduated because I was too busy helping my mom set up her new Hamptons house after my parents divorced, so he had the *audacity* to cut me off the inheritance..."

I kept my phone in my lap, swiping my finger across the screen.

Zach: What are you doing here?

I answered quick.

Farrow: Eating. Drinking. Flirting.

I looked up. Zach was reading my text. Eileen had finally noticed something amiss. With a pout, she peered around, spotting me. Her lips pressed into a hard line. She guzzled down half her drink.

Zach: You're not flirting with this guy. He's not your type.

Farrow: How do you know?

We were now openly ignoring our dates.

Zach: Because he looks like a clump of talc powder and is probably just as riveting.

I hated that he was right. And I hated that he was giving me crap for dating someone when he was literally doing the same.

Farrow: For your information, he's fascinating and nice. Might take him home.

Zach: Don't you dare even joke about it. You're mine.

He was unapologetically possessive, when he had no right to be. White-hot anger coursed through my veins. Before me, Anderson had moved on to discussing whether unsolicited nudes could even be considered harassment. Without thinking, I reached across the table and clasped his hand in mine. He gasped, but his surprise morphed into cockiness quick. With a grin, he kissed the back of my hand. Bile hit the edge of my throat.

He scooted his seat closer. "I see I'm not the only one who noticed our chemistry."

Bitch, the only chemistry going on here is the botulinum toxin I want to feed you.

"The chemistry is there." I tried to keep my wince in check. "I feel it, too."

The phone in my lap pinged in quick succession.

Zach: You're letting him TOUCH you?

Zach: Are you fucking kidding me?

Zach: Meet you out front in two minutes. We're leaving.

Farrow: You are not the boss of me.

Zach: FOR THE LAST FUCKING TIME, I LITERALLY FUCKING AM.

But it was too late. I'd made up my mind. And what I needed right now was to get out of here. The food, the cocktails, and the glitz weren't worth it. Dallas was wrong. I didn't need this at all. I knew I should've stayed in bed with hot cocoa and my Kindle.

"Would you mind if we go somewhere else?" I pried my hand away from Anderson's, wiping it on my dress beneath the table. He'd guarded it like a Venus flytrap. I needed a whole battalion to uncurl my fingers from his. "I…" *Can't face my boss and his fiancée for fear I'd combust.* "… need to get out of here."

"You sure?" His forehead creased. "Because Mr. Costa mentioned the meal will be free…"

"Positive."

I stood, wondering if Anderson could be any *less* appealing, when he snatched a bamboo skewer from the hors d'oeuvres and used it as a toothpick. *Yup. A new rock bottom.*

I set my napkin on the table. "Excuse me while I go freshen up. I'll be right back."

Anderson saluted me. "Take your time. I'll work on the entrées in the meantime. No reason they should go to waste."

Suppressing a headshake, I weaved through the sea of tables, slipping into the women's restroom. I clutched the edge of the shell-shaped sink, staring at myself in the mirror. "Get yourself together, Fae. He's just a guy."

"A pissed off one at that."

Zach slipped inside, locking the door behind him. I swiveled, my lower back pressed against the damp vanity top. He strolled toward me, a dusky mist of wrath purring around him. My heart stumbled to a screech, missing a beat. Every muscle spasmed at the mere sight of him.

He pressed against me, his entire body covering mine. "What are you doing here?"

Losing my mind. But on instinct, I tilted my head back, feeling the hot bulge of his cock against my thigh. "Enjoying a meal and a handsome man." I desperately needed to remind him—and myself—that I was a free agent. "I told you we're not exclusive. There's nothing you can do about it."

His cock jolted between us, digging harder into my thigh. "I can think of one thing I can do about it."

Liquid desire flooded the bottom of my stomach. My nipples sharpened into little pink diamonds. "What would that be?"

"*You.*"

He fisted my hair, bringing my face to his and crashing his lips over mine. The kiss seared through my lips, evaporating my anger, confusion, and doubt. He bracketed my cheeks with his palms, drawing me closer, like he wanted to devour me whole, swallow my entire body, and leave nothing of me to anyone else.

"Mine," he growled into our kiss, biting my bottom lip, his hands roaming, fingers curling around my body. Now *he* was the octopus, trying to take over every cell of my being. "Mine, mine, mine," he repeated, deepening our kiss, hand snaking between my thighs.

Zach's fingers traveled along my slit through my panties. A moan escaped me. I decided I'd hate him properly *after* we screwed each other's brains out. His lips journeyed south, along my body, hiking the minidress up my thighs in rough jerks.

His mouth was everywhere—covering my nipples through my dress, biting the sensitive flesh of my waist, licking and sucking every inch of bare skin peeking through my outfit. He lowered himself to his knees and tugged my underwear aside, penetrating me with his tongue.

I arched my back, opening my legs for him, one hand propped on the sink and the other clasping his hair. "*Zach.*"

He fucked me cruelly with his tongue, clutching my ass cheeks with punishing force. His pinky teased my tight hole through my underwear as he ate me out like a starved man. I lolled my head, the pleasure building inside me too intense, too much.

His fingers sank deeper into my ass. "This dripping pussy is mine."

I clenched his tongue in a death grip, already close to the edge.

"This ass is mine," he continued, biting the junction between my ass and inner thigh, swirling my clit with the tip of his nose. "Every single breath you take belongs to me."

I rocked back and forth against his greedy mouth.

He rolled down his zipper, shoving his pants off as an orgasm ripped through my body. "You can flaunt your dates all you want, but you will never escape me."

He rose to his feet, hoisted me over the marbled sink, and pushed my knees apart. With a snap, he tore my panties, thrusting into me like a man possessed. I felt him stretching me to the max, the scent of latex mixing with sex.

Someone tried to wiggle the doorknob from the outside. My heart jolted as Zach slammed into me, withdrawing, then pressing home again. In the past two weeks, we'd gone through two super packs of condoms. I should've been more accustomed to his size by now. But I wasn't.

I panted, pretending to care about anything other than being fucked by him as I wrapped my arms around his neck. "They're going to catch us."

My fingernails dragged through his biceps, refusing to heed my own warning. I propped my chin down, watching as his cock disappeared inside me and reappeared again, gleaming with my juices. Through the thin layer of rubber, I could still make out the thick, veiny ridge.

The door handle stopped rattling, the sound replaced by loud knocks. "Oh, come on. I have to pee." Laughter leaked from my throat.

"Shh." Zach pressed his palm against my lips, shutting me up as he picked up the pace, fucking me deeper and faster. "Be a good girl and take my cock quietly. Yes. Just like that. You're doing such a good job."

With his free hand, he peeled off one of my shoulder straps, releasing my breast. It was full and engorged, begging to be touched. He lowered his head to take my nipple in his mouth. Every nerve ending in my body blossomed into goosebumps.

I cried into his fist, clutching onto him harder. My second climax rushed like a current along my body. Each time he entered me, the tip of his cock hit my G-spot. Stars filled the back of my eyelids. The knocking on the door intensified.

"Please tell me you're close." His mouth moved over my nipple, his thrusts becoming jerkier and less controlled. "I can't fucking take it anymore. Your pussy is milking my cum one drop at a time."

The door rattled with force now. "Hey." Someone drank their twelve glasses of water today.

"I'm close," I whimpered.

He removed his hand from my lips, swallowing my moans as we kissed. His warm cum filled the condom as he came inside of me. We both trembled in each other's arms, sweaty and shattered by our orgasms. For a long moment, we just held each other, his forehead resting atop of my shoulder. His hard breaths shot down my spine.

Neither of us wanted to move. To return to the real world.

"I'm going to combust here." Pee Lady smacked the door again. "That's it. If you don't open up right now, I swear I'm calling the manager."

Zach and I stared at each other. He withdrew from me slowly, dick half-mast, knotted the used condom, and flung it into the trash can. I clutched the counter behind me, struggling to catch my breath.

He pressed a soft kiss to my lips before a polite, distant smile took over his face. "Remember, Octi. You can date whomever you want and sell yourself stories about moving on from me, but I will always be the one to fuck you. The one to make you cum. The one to own every inch of you."

He zipped up and strolled to the door, unlocking it. The blonde twenty-something on the other side backed up, flustered in her smart business suit. "Hush money." Zach produced a wad of cash from his pocket, tossing it in her general direction. "Run your mouth, and I'll run your life to the ground."

Ever so casually, he walked back to his date with Eileen.

Leaving me thoroughly fucked, both physically and mentally.

CHAPTER SIXTY-FOUR

Zach

Eileen's eyes clung to me as I stopped by Farrow's table on my way back to mine. The fact that our union was an ongoing farce of Monty Python proportions was becoming more and more apparent. Unnecessary pain must be avoided. In fact, the only reason I'd agreed to this dinner was to cancel the engagement and map out damage control.

The dudebro in the Lacoste polo peered up at me from his pasta dish, grinning with tomato-stained teeth.

"Shit. It's *you*." His eyes lit up. "Man, I've been following your career for a decade. Tried to get an internship with your company when I graduated. I'm a true fan."

I towered above him, cataloging his face and reassuring myself that Octi could never find a man like this truly desirable. "Unfortunately, I cannot say the same."

The linguine noodle fell from his lips.

I buttoned my blazer with one hand. "Now, let me tell you how the rest of your night is going to unfold if you wish to conduct business in the state of New York. Your date will return, and you will take her home, driving below the maximum speed limit. You will walk her to her door but won't go inside. You will shake her hand—*briefly*— and tell her she looks lovely and is the most enthralling date you've ever had, but due to the fact that she is severely out of your league, you will bow out and make way for someone who actually deserves her. Then, you will disappear from her life permanently. Now, do you need me to write that down for you?"

His fork fell from his fist to the plate with a clatter. He opened his lips but couldn't manage to speak, confirming my suspicion that nothing existed between his ears other than get-rich-fast Bitcoin schemes and fetish porn.

I snapped my fingers in front of his eyes, losing my patience. Eileen was staring, and I didn't want to prolong this more than needed. Now that I'd discovered the pleasures of sex, I figured I'd be doing her a disservice by trapping her in a marriage without it. She could find her own Octi to cure her (best of luck—mine was one of a kind).

"Am. I. Clear?" I repeated.

He gulped. "Y-yes."

"Good." I brushed lint off my shoulder, a cold smile playing on my face. "Remember, Oatmeal—if you hurt her, if you offend her, if you try to hit on her, I'll know, and I'll retaliate." I adjusted the collar of his shirt without touching him. "Enjoy your baked pasta dish."

CHAPTER SIXTY-FIVE

Farrow

Being waited on, I decided, was even worse than being the actual housekeeper. The entire weekend at the Hamptons, Zach sent his staff to coddle me. I found myself being chased by people begging to make me another smoothie, draw me a bath, fetch me Starbucks, and drive me around for a shopping spree.

"I have legs, a driver's license, and agency," I'd growl at them to the backtrack of Zach's amused chuckle somewhere in the distance. "Please, for the love of God, take a break. Watch a movie. Treat yourself to something from the pantry. Leave me alone."

With Eileen gone, a weight lifted off me. She'd rushed off to an emergency patient in the middle of her dinner with Zach and hadn't returned.

The entire weekend, Andras blew up my phone with texts, begging me to reconsider my position on Vera. I called him once, demanding to know why he felt so strongly about it. He dodged my question, insisting he was looking after me and my interests. I was frustrated and confused, but mostly disappointed. I'd thought Andras was on my side.

Zach and I acted recklessly, slipping to the rose garden to steal kisses and orgasms. Guilt sat in my stomach like a brick, sinking me down, and yet—I was a willing participant.

At night, he'd crawl into my bed, wringing emotions and sensations out of me I didn't know existed. He worshiped every part of my body, and for the first time in my life, I felt like someone's choice, not default. To the extent that I realized we needed a frank conversation about where we were headed.

This didn't feel like a project anymore.

It felt like forever.

316 | *HUNTINGTON & SHEN*

A few hours before our flight home, Zach left a note on my
nightstand.

Two p.m. at the rose garden.

The butterfly wings caressing the walls of my belly told a tale as
old as time.

Zachary Sun wasn't my boss and my fling—he was my everything.
It was time to have the talk I'd put off for months.

I arrived at the bench in the garden a few minutes early. Lush red-
and-white flowers and thorns cradled the swan-shaped stone, twisting
into one another like swords. I busied myself with my phone, skimming
emails from my lawyers. I'd never been a coward, but telling Zach my
feelings gave me cold sweats.

The rustle of leaves swished behind my back. I glanced up from
my phone, surprised to see Eileen trudging in my direction. Her heels
dug into the damp soil. A brown maxi dress swayed as she walked,
paired with a thin Hermès belt. She wore minimal makeup, a placid
expression, and her hair gathered into a flawless, elaborate bun.

I stiffened, finding it hard to meet her penetrating gaze. She was
privy to my indiscretions with her fiancé. It didn't matter that both of
us had agreements with him—and neither of us had technically broken
them. Up until this moment, I'd managed to avoid her in the sprawling
mansion. Now, she was like a mirror, forcing me to look my sins in the
eye.

I stood.

"Oh, please, Miss Ballantine." Eileen waved a hand. "You're not an
employee of mine. You can sit back down."

"I'm an employee of your *fiancé's*." The word scorched a path up my
throat, burning my tongue.

"Even so, I come to you today as a woman speaking to another
woman."

My heart spiraled downward dangerously fast.

Eileen slid beside me, forcing me to scoot to the edge of the bench.
She propped her bag on her lap. "I appreciate you for coming here."

"I don't appreciate you tricking me into thinking it was Zach who
invited me here."

"Perhaps you don't appreciate it, but surely you can understand it."
Eileen nodded. "That's why I kept it vague. I couldn't risk you refusing

my request. Time is not on my side in this matter."

I clung to my mask of indifference, feeling a looming catastrophe barreling straight into my life. "How can I help you?"

"I think we both know how you can help me." She rummaged for something in her bag, lips pinched together. "Stop fucking my fiancé."

Her demand sliced my chest, reached deep into my heart, and grabbed it. There was no point denying the obvious, even if it was my knee-jerk reaction. If nothing else, Eileen deserved the truth.

I retreated into my jacket, forcing words out of my mouth. "It's not serious." Not a lie. For Zach, at least. He repeatedly reminded me—and himself—that we were just a temporary arrangement. Still, it felt dirty to say. Like a white lie.

Eileen's eyes explored my face. Behind them, I saw so much of the same emotions I'd been drowning in. Agony, jealousy, and desperation. Raw self-pity that made it hard to breathe. Her eyes glossed-over with tears, but I knew she wouldn't let them fall. Eileen, like me, viewed vulnerability as weakness. She didn't allow herself to break.

"It might not be serious for you, but it's serious to me." She flattened her dress, smoothing out a wrinkle. "My dream has always been to marry him."

I reared my head back, brows pinched together. "I thought you didn't even know each other until a few months ago?"

She rubbed her red nose, shaking her head. "Goodness gracious, aren't you naïve?"

Shoving her hand inside her bag again, she retrieved a tiny old-school photo album, handing it to me. I flipped it open. My heart sank further when my eyes landed on the first two pictures. Two squishy babies with thigh rolls and matching mullets grinned at me.

No. No, no, no.

"This is Zach and me as babies." She pointed to the second photo. "And this one is us at two years old. Our dads were good friends."

"Zach never mentioned this."

"He doesn't remember it. When Constance reunited us, I didn't want to embarrass him by bringing it up. I've waited for this for a long time. I…" She closed her eyes, her cheeks flushing pink. A beat later, she shook her head. "Oh, never mind."

"Tell me," I insisted, swiveling my body to face hers.

Eileen had quietly endured my presence in Zach's life for months. Did she truly not mind or did she fear rocking the boat until she secured her place? Her phone call the other night zipped through my mind. Zach viewed this arrangement as business only. But did she?

"I've loved him my entire life."

Oh, my God.

Never once had it occurred to me that she wanted him as more than a status symbol. She'd fooled me with her constant suggestions to add no-touching and pro-dating clauses to their contract.

Eileen opened her eyes, her lower lip unsteady. "I've spent thirty-three years designing myself to be what Zachary Sun needs in a wife. I sculpted myself like Play-Doh to his wishes and wants."

That's not how to love, I wanted to scream. Instead, I sunk further into my jacket, listening to her speak.

"As kids, he used to protect me when my older brothers bullied me. He was smart, wild, and brave. He loved sculpting mud, so I'd sculpt mud. He loved swinging on ropes, so I swung on ropes. He goofed around on the jungle gym, so I did, too. Anything to be near him. And he let me… until my family moved away."

I wanted to cry. For Young Zach, who should've stayed carefree and playful. And for Adult Zach, who struggled to shoulder the burden of his trauma. And most of all, I envied Eileen Yang for meeting both versions of him. Suddenly, I couldn't help but curse the unfairness of it all. People who met their soulmate young never had to feel like they'd started a book on the wrong chapter and needed to read the beginning to appreciate the end.

Eileen fingered one of the photos, biting down on her lip. "One day, Dad told us his friend from college died. My siblings barely remembered him, but I did. I showed up at the funeral and offered my condolences. Zach didn't even recognize me. He barely even recognized his school friends."

Oh, Zach. My heart broke for him all over again.

Eileen continued, unaware that pieces of me had shattered across the rose garden. "I decided then that I'd take the opportunity to become everything he needed and return to him as the perfect woman. The medical degree, the smart dresses, and the charities. All designed to please Constance and draw Zach in. I tailored my personality to suit his—calm, collected, cold, and elegant."

A desperate, devious, deranged piece of me wondered... *Is that truly what he needs? Or does he need his opposite? To break him out of his shell and give him a dose of the playfulness he used to have.*

Eileen's teeth scraped her lower lip as she stared into the distance. "Meanwhile, I drank up every tidbit I heard of him from my parents, collecting any info I could about him off social media—from the feeds of his friends, his classmates, his aunt."

Were we really so different? I'd done my research on him, too, prior to meeting. We'd both met Zach under a guise, both entered contracts with him, and both fell fast, hard, and deep.

Eileen flipped through the photo album without really looking. "By the time I met Zach again, I'd morphed into the version of myself he required. I showed him everything I needed to show. A woman that is intelligent, cold, and uninterested in touching men. Someone who would give him a family without ruining his current lifestyle. I knew we'd hit it off, and we did."

A small, sad smile stretched across her lips. My heart broke for her—and for myself, too. Because I finally understood what it felt like to love someone who could never be truly and wholly yours.

"We struck up an engagement the same day we met. I ran home satisfied that I could help him, knowing how relieved he must have felt to find someone who could give him everything he needs without compromising any part of himself."

She gutted me one word at a time. I felt nauseous with guilt and pain and horror. I couldn't even speak.

"His mother loves me. His aunt adores me. I am willing to abide by his rules. If he wants me close—I will be. If he wants me to stay away—I can do that, too. I will be there for every version of him, regardless of whether he stays this way or changes. I will mold myself into anything he needs. Can you say that about yourself? Can you give up all your dreams for him?"

I flashed back to Andras' office. To me, trembling with rage, unable to back down from my quest for vengeance. And him, ordering me to let it go to chase our mutual dream.

But, I realized, *the idea of taking from Vera no longer thrills me. I may not be able to give up revenge for fencing, but I can give it up for Zach.*

Eileen took my silence as agreement, snapping the photo album shut on her lap. "My life is stable. I have a real job, a proper schedule, and the ability to raise a family—emotionally, physically, and financially. And I have *never* stolen or cheated in my life."

But you lied to Zach, I wanted to point out, swallowing the words because I had no ground to stand on. *You lied about who you are, about knowing him, about sharing phobias.*

"Farrow, I'm telling you this because I think you're a good person with a clear mind. You must see that I'm more suited for him. That your troubles will only be a burden. If you truly care for him—and I actually think you do—you'll let him go."

"What are you asking me to do?"

On the fringes of my mind, a giant warning signal went off. I forced myself to push away my emotions and think logically.

Everything about her is a lie. And the phone call. She laughed about tricking Zach into a dinner date. Don't trust her.

Eileen gathered a stray hair behind her ear. "I'm asking you to get on a flight, move out of my fiancé's home, and never come back. And if you do, I'll take over the legal fees for your court case—"

I reeled back, wondering how she even knew about this. "I don't need your charity."

Did she snoop? Did Zach tell her? But I knew he wouldn't.

She toyed with the oversized engagement ring on her finger. "It's not charity. It's an agreement. No different from the one you share with Zach."

Except it *was* different. I wanted to help Zach. Eileen merely wanted to exist beside him. How could she love someone she hadn't seen since childhood? Did she even know him? That he hated rain yet loved the cold. That he pretended to be disgusted by hot Cheetos but scarfed them down by the dozen if a bag neared him. That he only seemed detached but possessed fierce loyalty when it came to friends and family.

I kept my voice level, carefully crafting my expression into neutral. "My agreement with him ends soon."

"Your agreement with him ends *now*." She dumped the album into her bag, rising to her feet. "I think I've been patient enough."

"I'm not the one you need to speak with. Actually, from what I remember, you're the one who requested stricter no-touching clauses and suggested allowing outside relationships." I doubted she'd be content to keep *those* forever. In fact, I'd put money on the fact that she'd suggested them proactively to lower his guard.

As if she'd heard my thoughts, she giggled into her fingertips. "Do you think he would've agreed to marry me if I hadn't?"

"So, you tricked him?"

"It's just a white lie."

"A white lie is telling a five-year-old their hamster went to the farm after it dies. It is *not* making up an entire phobia as the premise of an engagement." I always wondered why my hamsters needed fresh air on that address-less farm.

"Does it matter? It worked. I'm engaged to him. You're just the help. Know your place." She spun her ring until the giant diamond faced me. "Your arrangement with my fiancé ends now."

I tipped my chin up. "Zach is a big boy." *Ain't that the truth.* "He can make up his own mind."

"Asking you to leave is no more than a courtesy." Eileen towered over me, so close, I could smell the mint on her breath. Not a muscle in her face twitched. "Make no mistake—I will get rid of you one way or another. What I lack in imagination, I make up for in ambition."

Oddly, I relaxed at her words. This was my comfort zone, thanks to Vera. The corners of my mouth tugged up. "Are you threatening me?"

"No, Farrow, I'm *telling* you." She flicked a rose thorn from my sleeve. "You're not worthy of Zachary Sun's love. Step aside for someone who is. Or I'll make you step aside."

I didn't know what life had in store for me and Zach, but I did know that I no longer believed he'd ever be able to experience happiness with this manipulative woman.

"I'm glad we had this talk, Eileen." With a smile, I rose to my feet, feeling lighter than I had in days. "Good luck convincing Zach to fall in love with you. You never know…" I paused, remembering her words on the call and tossing them back at her. "…Once you show him how good you are in the sack, it's game over for that brainiac."

I pivoted with a spring in my step, headed back to my room.

"You've messed with the wrong bitch." Eileen latched onto my arm, stopping me. "I'm about to unleash every circle of Dante's inferno on you."

CHAPTER SIXTY-SIX

Zach

If Farrow moaned the word *porn* one more time, I'd fuck her on this jet and create our own, audience be damned.

"Hold up." Her tongue poked out of her mouth as she struggled to angle the camera at her chilaquiles without them resembling baby food. "Dallas and Ari want food porn pics."

I relaxed against the leather, annoyed by the constant distractions. Octi's friends from Korea had decided today would be the perfect day to hit her up and tell her to stay strong through the media bloodbath. She'd finally hopped off a call, only for Dallas to hound her about the in-flight snacks in their group chat.

"Mr. Sun?" From the couch, Natalie raised her phone. "Your lawyers are on the line."

She'd crashed in Manhattan over the weekend to check on my properties there, hitching a ride back to Maryland with us. Eileen, however, stayed in the city. I couldn't wait to tell Mom I took a stab at my engagement and accidentally killed all chances of it ever forming a relationship. There was nothing wrong with Eileen. In fact, she only had one shortcoming—she wasn't Farrow. But that was enough to kill the deal.

"Lawyers?" My brows knitted together. "*Plural?*" Normally, they called me one at a time.

"Yes, sir. All three." Natalie unplastered herself from her seat, patting off cracker crumbs from her suit as she handed me her phone. "Tom is on the call, too. I think it might be important."

"Do you now, Einstein? I wonder what gave it away."

Farrow's head flew up from her phone. She shot me a worried look. I inwardly cursed, abhorred by the unwelcome diversion. For starters, I'd planned to use the plane ride to talk to Octi about us.

More specifically, if 'us' could ever exist beyond the scope of tearing each other's clothes off and engaging in endless verbal foreplay. And secondly, on the car ride here, Fae had mentioned she had something to tell me about Eileen.

Farrow twisted her golden hair into a high bun, untucking her legs from under her ass. "What are they saying?"

I took the phone from my assistant, who continued to hover. She bounced from heel to heel, just staring at me.

"Natalie?"

"Yes, Mr. Sun?"

"Kindly fuck off."

She nodded, albeit with visible displeasure, stuffing her laptop under her armpit and moving to the cockpit. Farrow clutched my sleeve.

I interlaced our fingers, squeezing. "Everything will be fine."

Her eyes clung to mine. "How do you know?"

"Because..." I traced the beauty mark beneath her eye with my free hand. "If you lose this case, what I have in store for Vera will be infinitely worse than whatever punishment the law can deliver."

"It's a marvel you haven't ended up in jail."

"Only to those naïve enough to believe in the legal system." I leaned Natalie's phone against the snack box, switching it to video conference. "Talk to us."

Deanne's face popped up first. "Miss Ballantine?"

"Yes." Fae raised her hand like we were in preschool. "I'm here."

"Do you consent to Mr. Sun hearing this conversation? It contains some sensitive information."

"Yes." Farrow nodded. "Go ahead."

A lick of pride prodded me, confirming what I already knew. I was Fucked with a capital F.

"We might be better off having this conversation in person." Tom pulled out a notepad. "A lot of delicate evidence to go over."

"I literally don't have the self-control to turn down dairy-free dessert." Fae scooted halfway into my seat to get a better angle. "What makes you think I can wait the entire plane ride to hear your news?"

Our elbows brushed, and that alone ignited something possessively depraved inside me.

Tom brought a pencil to his lips. "Hmm..."

"You heard her." I rubbed circles on her thigh with my thumb, relaxing against the backrest. "Spill the beans before I spill out your guts."

"I'm just trying to make sure nobody falls apart here."

"I'm already in pieces." Farrow waved. "Please, just continue."

"We found out something alarming." Tom paused. "As in, criminally disturbing."

Farrow licked her lips. "Has Vera committed a crime?"

"It appears so. An egregious one at that." He hesitated. "Miss Ballantine…"

"Yes?"

"Are you sitting down?"

"No." Fae bared her teeth, eliciting a grin from me. "I'm up on both feet, dancing the Copacabana." She jerked her thumb to the leather upholstery behind us. "What do you think?"

Guess she hadn't forgiven him for blowing her cover and triggering the media storm.

Tom shrugged, going for the kill. "Vera hired someone to kill your father." Silence. Utter silence. The kind that penetrated through eardrums. "I'm sorry," Tom added, as an afterthought.

The words floated in the air, choking us like nerve gas. I searched Fae for signs of pain, recognition, agony. All I could find was bitterness.

Tom scratched his temple. "Are we good to continue?"

Deanne stopped typing. "Let's give her a minute."

But Fae didn't need a minute. She shot up, pacing. "That's impossible. Dad died in an accident. The valet—"

"Knew exactly what he was doing." Tom reached for a folder, flipping it open. "A man by the name of Eugene Thomas. He was the valet involved in the alleged accident, as I'm sure you know."

"Alleged?" Fae closed her eyes. "He didn't even know Dad or Vera. His foot got stuck on the accelerator."

Tom flipped through pages, yanking out a sheet. "I found a burner phone Vera purchased two months prior to the incident." He held up the paper as if we could make out the tiny print. "These are records I pulled from it."

Fae stopped pacing. "What do they say?"

"Vera withdrew 200k from a secret savings account. She also

shared multiple brief conversations with a number that tracked back to Thomas' wife."

Farrow squeezed the bridge of her nose. "What does his wife have to do with this?"

"Nothing. She had stage 4 cancer. Needed a pricey experimental drug." He set the paper down. "Gene did it for the fast cash."

"He was counting on being charged with involuntary manslaughter." Farrow planted her fists on the table, piecing the rest together. "He knew they'd give him a light sentence in minimum security. Why wouldn't they? He has a baby and a wife with cancer. It was an 'accident.'"

"Precisely." Dan's face popped up. "Records show Mrs. Thomas made a full recovery after the treatment. While her husband is locked up, various charities help her with bills, groceries, and childcare. She even has a new house."

Tom whistled. "Five years is a small price to pay for all that."

Bryan adjusted his camera, finally giving us his face. "We have all the evidence. The receipts. The written communication. Vera thought using a burner phone and VPN would cover her tracks. Turns out, she still missed a few steps."

The six of us simmered on the info.

Fae broke the silence with a whisper. "But… why?"

"Insurance money." Tom waved his folder. "I looked through Vera's joint tax returns with your dad, along with their financial statements. They spent more than they made." He paused. "Vera liked to buy pretty things."

Farrow plopped onto the seat opposite me, staring at the ceiling without really looking. "She still does."

"That may be true, but right now she can only afford them at Walmart." Deanne produced another document. "Vera spent the insurance money as soon as it hit her bank account."

"Eugene Thomas." Farrow rubbed her forehead. "Can you tell me a bit about his background? His family?"

Tom flipped through pages. "Sure."

As we waited for him to find whatever he was searching for, the plane began its descent. A flurry of texts dropped from the top of Natalie's screen in quick succession.

Jilly Bean: Is your boss still playing hard to get?

Jilly Bean: Or is he getting too hard… [Smirking Emoji]

Jilly Bean: You have to figure out what the housekeeper did to make him screw her.

Jilly Bean: This is your way in.

Jilly Bean: Get knocked up, and we're gold. We can finally open the company.

I made a mental note to fire Natalie—and not drink anything she handed me—while Tom answered Octi.

"Eugene Thomas. Twenty-Eight. Parents never married. His mom registered him under her last name. He grew up without a dad, since he traveled around the world for work. They reconnected during his court case. Both his parents visit him once a week in prison."

She edged forward, hungry for more. "What are their names?"

She had an angle. Farrow always had an angle. I enjoyed this side of her most. It reminded me of our first official encounter. Her—hot as hell in lingerie, setting down Go pieces like a savant. And me—soaking up the view as her tongue swiped across her lips. Any other time, and I'd be rock hard.

"Mom is Paula Thomas. Dad is… wait, let me find it." Tom clucked his tongue. "Ah, there it is. Dad's name is Andras Horvath."

Farrow closed her eyes.

And all I saw was red.

Andras.

Everything clicked into place. My temperature hiked up to a level more suitable for an oven. Farrow's nostrils flared. I suspected the same thought ran through both our minds. How we'd deliver punishment to Andras and Vera. Another thing I enjoyed about Farrow—we shared the same thirst for vengeance.

"I know this is a lot to take in." Deanne collected her phone, holding it to her face. "But there *is* a silver lining to all of this."

Fae plopped against the backrest. "Must've missed it."

"Justice, Miss Ballantine. Forget about the lawsuit. Our next step is to bring this to the authorities—"

Farrow waved her off. "Do whatever you need, but I'm confronting Vera as soon as we land."

"Miss Ballantine." Bryan shot forward. "That is *highly* unadvisable. Anything you do or say may hinder our—"

"Cope," Fae interjected, and I could've kissed her then. Beneath the eye. On her beauty mark. I'd wanted to kiss there for a while now. "I'm going to hunt Vera down."

"The best revenge is justice." Deanne raised both hands, like she was corralling a wild animal. "Trust me."

"You're a lawyer. I would never trust you."

This time, I did kiss Farrow—on her beauty mark, then down her jaw.

"But—"

"She made up her mind." I finally intervened, over this. "Any mess this creates is yours to clean."

Dan collapsed against his seat. "I'm not Superman."

"For the money I pay you, you fucking should be."

Deanne sighed. "I liked you better when you weren't wrapped around a woman's finger."

Yes, but I liked myself less.

"See how you like unemployment if you continue to overstep."

She grinned. "It's called retirement—"

I hung up and tossed the phone on the couch, tucking my chin on Farrow's shoulder. "Are you okay?"

"I will be." She leaned her head back, resting it on my neck. "I think." The amount of strength this woman had in her fingernail alone could detonate a nuclear bomb.

"Of course, you will. You're the strongest person I know."

"And I intend to deliver the cruelest blow." Her gaze caught mine. "But first, I need to break."

"Break?"

"You know—fall apart. Cry like a baby. Let myself break for all the times I refused to."

"Break." I pressed a kiss to her shoulder, cheek, temple. "I'll put all the pieces back together."

Even if it's the last thing I do.

CHAPTER SIXTY-SEVEN

Farrow

I had a one-track mind, and it begged for blood.

First, I called Andras, my hands choking the steering wheel of my Prius as it zinged through familiar streets.

He picked up on the first ring. "I see you have come to your senses."

Yes, and all five of them want to feast on your blood.

"I texted you an address. Meet me there."

"It's ten—"

I hung up, knowing he'd come. Even the prospect of a longer jail sentence for his son must've made him tremble. *So stupid, Fae. You should've known it was too good to be true when The Andras Horvath showed up the day you landed back from Seoul and offered to take you under his wing.*

I let a snake into my garden. A spy. Time after time, he convinced me to focus on fencing. Random training sessions that interfered with lawyer meetings. Tears in my training gear that required money to replace. Distraction after distraction. *Stupid, stupid, stupid.*

Twenty minutes later, I pulled up in front of my childhood home. I stood on the very step I'd been abandoned on as an infant. Suddenly, I couldn't fathom why I ever wanted to live here. A sliver of regret collided into me. Maybe I shouldn't have rejected Zach's invitation to join me, but I needed to stick up for myself. If I didn't learn now, I'd rely on him forever. I shoved my key into the hole and jiggled it, only to discover Vera had changed the locks. A cloud of cold condensation rushed past my lips as I laughed to myself.

"Of course. Doesn't matter." I dumped the key onto the mat, pounding my fist on the door until it rattled. "It's only your house on paper. You were never welcome here."

The pitter-patter of slippers dragged across the hardwood. "Someone woke up today and chose violence." Tabby groaned on the other side of the door. "Hell-oooo, tone it down. I'm on my way."

"Did you DoorDash without asking me what I want?" Reggie's voice came from above, probably up in her room. "What's all that noise? Who died? Ugh, please say Farrow."

Not that I needed any more reason to be mad, but I just got it.

Tabby swung the door open, only to find me standing on the porch, alive and well, waving back at her. Her nose scrunched, my mere presence apparently stinking up the place. "Speak of the devil."

"I'll take being a devil over being a common bitch." I shouldered past her, striding into the house. "Where's your mother?"

The sour tinge of decaying food slipped into my nostrils. A thick layer of dust coated the entryway bench. Something smelled like wet fur, though the Ballantine women only liked animals on their plates and coats. As expected, nobody had bothered to clean up since I'd left.

Tabby chased me into the living room, breathless as she tried to keep up with my pace. "Mom changed the locks." *No shit.*

Footsteps hammered down the stairs.

Reggie rounded the corner seconds later. "You have no right to be here." She yanked the sleeve of my jacket, but I pushed her off. "You ruined our lives. You quit the company, and now we're poor."

"*And* you're suing us?" Tabby splayed her arms out, trying to stop me from crossing. "You should sue whoever cuts your hair first, you horrible witch. Is it even straight?"

For starters, I cut my own hair with one of those haircutting clips that promised a straight cut. I supposed I had a case against them, too.

I stepped around the giant gap between Tabby's outstretched arm and the television. "You wanted me to be your maid."

"It's called paying off your debts."

"Debts? I'm not the one dripping in Prada." I tilted my head, eyeing her blouse. "Well, I suppose it's Frada now."

"Yes, debts." Reggie tossed her hands up. "Daddy and Mommy footed the bill for your little trip to Korea. He practically bled out for you. You know how much money that school cost? We couldn't even afford to keep my horses."

"Nothing."

"Huh?"

"It cost nothing, because I had a full scholarship." I dipped into the dining room after finding the living room empty. "And the horses went to an equine therapy center because *you* never fed them."

"I had school."

"So did I." I spun, getting in Tabby's face. "I only left for Korea because you spent every waking moment reminding me that I'm not part of this family." She and Reggie followed me into the kitchen. I surveyed the room, discovering mountains of cardboard boxes piled up in the pantry. I swiveled to them. "You're moving?"

"We can't afford this house anymore, can we?" To prove her point, Reggie pushed past me and taped up a half-empty box with enough toxic energy to light up Vegas. "The HOA alone is 800 bucks a month."

Tabby joined her, closing up boxes with barely anything in them. "We're renting it out and moving to an apartment so we can afford groceries. Happy now?" *No, actually.*

I didn't take any pleasure in their misfortune. I only ever wanted them to stop screwing around with my life. Vera, on the other hand...

I snatched up a free box, stuffing it with my belongings. "Where's your mother?" While they had no right to kick me out of a home I owned, I didn't trust them not to toss out my stuff.

"She's not home," Tabby lied at the exact same time Vera burst in from the garage, sweating in her skintight zebra-print bodysuit. The fumes from her hair spray alone made me dizzy.

"Girls, you have to help me out here with the boxes—" Her words died in her throat the minute she spotted me. "What are you doing here, you little shit?" Guess the gloves were officially off.

"Grabbing my stuff." I flipped open the cabinet above the sink, fetching my favorite Mickey Mouse plate that Dad had kept because he knew I loved eating grilled cheese on it. "Oh, and delivering some news."

"Let me guess—should I expect the sheriff here any time soon?" Vera folded her arms, eyes squinting at me like she was cocking a gun. "Because I obtained my own legal counse—"

"I know you killed him."

The silence that followed soaked into the walls. Vera turned the same shade as her bodysuit. Tabby and Reggie glanced at each other, whisper-shouting nonsense. Tabby scratched her temple. Reggie's head reared back. Neither looked particularly in-the-know. The panic on their faces said it all. They had no clue what Vera had done.

"W-what are you talking about?" Vera stormed to the sink, barely managing to fill up a glass with her shaking hands. "Killed who?"

"You're so bad at this. Always were." I moved toward the stairs with my box. "That's why Dad sent me away. To spare me your so-called parenting." The three of them chased me up the steps.

"Your father was killed by a valet." Vera stomped her heels on the hardwood, no doubt leaving dents. "I had nothing to do with it."

"Other than paying said valet 200k for his troubles, you mean." I swiveled, sending her a sweet smile in the hall. "Yeah, that's not going to fly in a court of law."

"You have no way of proving this nonsense."

I zipped down the corridor to my room, swinging the door open, momentarily taken aback by what I saw. "Where is everything?" I hated that my voice cracked.

Vera, Reggie, and Tabby filled the doorway like bouncers. Not leaving me an inch to escape. A satisfied smirk pulled at Tabby's lips. "Oh, we thought it was all trash, so we threw it out."

"Sorry, Fae." Reggie examined her coffin-shaped nails. "There's a difference between vintage and garbage."

"Your stuff smells." Tabby jerked a thumb behind her. "Like, all the way from across the hall. Bleach." She shivered. "Made me gag."

First-degree murder is a lifetime jail sentence, I reminded myself, edging away from them in case I did something stupid. *Drop it to ten years, and I might weigh the pros and cons.*

These vultures had left nothing. Not even a speck of lint. All of my memories—gone. The display full of fencing medals. The épées I'd competed with as a kid. The box of Broadway tickets I saved from trips to New York with Dad. Gone, gone, gone. In every version of revenge I'd conjured, I'd always intended to take only what Dad wanted me to have. I would never do anything like this to them. Heat stormed up my cheeks, so hot I feared my head would combust on the spot.

"You have no proof." Vera stepped past the doorframe, crowding me. "To these lies you're spewing under my own roof."

I met her in the middle, standing my ground. "*My* roof." *Gloves off, indeed.* Without the threat of blackmail looming over my head, I no longer needed to roll over whenever she bullied me. I had truth on my side. And a spine as strong as the Lotte Tower. Even with her heels on,

I stared down my nose at her. "I own fifty percent of this house."

Dad had transferred his share of the deed to me as soon as I'd turned eighteen. His way of making me feel welcome.

This place is yours, just as much as it is theirs, baby girl.

Vera closed the gap, bumping me with her chest. Her mouth opened, but the front door crashed against the wall, interrupting her.

"Vera? Are you here, drágám?"

Andras. His voice felt like cyanide running through my bloodstream. Then, I registered what he'd said. Drágám. *Babe.*

The word painted a more gruesome reality. I reared back, lips parted. "How long have you been having an affair with Andras?"

It was the last piece that clicked everything into place. How else would Vera, Andras, and his son be connected? He hadn't met her through his son. His son had met her through *him.*

"This has nothing to do with your father." Vera's cheeks reddened beneath three pounds of makeup. "Andras and I got to know each other after your father's passing. I was a mess." *Still are.*

Andras burst past Tabby and Reggie, leaving them stumbling face-first onto the carpet. Sweat soaked his bare chest, gluing thick hairs flat to his skin. He wore plaid pajama pants, hotel slippers, and a grimace that would put Steve Carell out of business.

Not his first time here, I noted. He'd gone straight up.

"Oh, hey, Andras." I leaned against my dresser, tipping my chin at him. "Glad you could make it."

He glanced between me and Vera. "Farrow—"

I held up a hand. "Vera was just telling me this thing between you is brand new. Which is so very fascinating, considering she somehow got to know your son *before* you two hit it off. I wonder how they met. It couldn't possibly be through an affair between Vera and his father, could it?"

Andras' face turned paper white, his hands curling into fists. "Leave Eugene out of this."

"Did you know she helped with his wife's medical treatment? There's a word for this." I pretended to think, snapping my fingers. "Blood money? No. Conspiracy to commit murder? Definitely not. Sounds so serious." I tapped my lip with a finger. "Hmm…"

Reggie gasped. Tabby hid behind her sister. And Vera?

Vera decided now would be a good time to launch herself at me.

Chapter Sixty-Eight

Farrow

Ironically, it was Andras' coaching that helped me dodge Vera.
 I dipped, retreating toward the wall, my footwork Olympic worthy. Without space on my side, it didn't matter. I'd cornered myself. Vera grabbed me by the neck, digging her acrylic nails into the tender flesh. I staggered back. My shoulder blades hit the window with a *smack*. I raised my arms to loosen her grip, then twisted, landing a roundhouse kick to her stomach. She flew back with a yelp, falling straight into Andras' arms.

Thank you, Ari, for forcing me to take self-defense lessons.

"Such a weird coincidence." I pointed between them. "That you two hooked up just after Eugene was incarcerated."

Tabby ran to her mom, patting her stomach, making her wince. She pointed at me. "You have no proof."

Meanwhile, Reggie sidestepped Andras, rushing toward me, trying to pin me to the wall. A useless endeavor. Not only was she out of shape, she'd also never fought for anything in her life.

I clasped her arm, twisted it behind her back, and bent it just before breaking point, leaning into her ear. "I suggest you stop trying to hurt me if you don't want more charges to be brought against you."

With Reggie as a human shield, I advanced. Andras, Vera, and Tabby took collective steps back, watching me in horror.

Reggie thrashed and kicked, trying to break free. "Don't let her hurt me."

"She doesn't *really* need her hands, does she?" I used my free hand to pet her head. "It's not like she does anything with them. And no, handing credit cards to cashiers and texting friends don't count." I knew I sounded like a villain. I also knew I didn't give a fuck.

Still on the carpet, Vera shook a finger at me, holding my gaze. "If you touch one hair on her head."

I couldn't remember the last time she'd looked at me. *Really* looked at me. As a kid, I'd always wanted her to. I wish I'd known then what I knew now. That seeking love from people incapable of giving it would only burn a hole through my heart. And there was no Band-Aid in the universe that could fix that.

I tossed my head back and laughed, tightening my hold on Reggie. "Read the room, Vera. You're in no place to threaten me. Your cover is blown. Eugene is about to rot in prison for a lot more years than he planned, and you and Andras will join him."

Thin rivers of sweat trickled down her temple. "Good luck proving it."

"Don't need luck. My private investigator did all the work." I offered her a serene smile. "Word of advice, Vera. Next time you plan a murder, don't leave a digital trail." I frowned. "Though I'm not sure what cell access is like behind bars."

I reached behind me, untucked a rolled-up folder from the back of my jeans, and tossed it at her knees. Evidence I'd printed on the plane. The contents scattered around her, flashes of her sins blanketing the carpet. Her eyes soaked in the proof of her crimes, one by one. She flew through all stages of grief in less than a minute, then circled back from acceptance to anger.

"You filthy little roach." Vera's nostrils flared. "It's your fault. You know that?" A vicious grin hiked up her cheeks. "Your dad died because of you."

I couldn't help it. I shrunk back behind Reggie, knowing she could feel it but unable to stop the tiny quivers.

Get your shit together, Fae. Milk the truth out of her now. Worry about the rest later.

"He changed his will." Vera clawed Andras' thigh, using it as leverage to stumble to her feet, almost taking his pants down with the momentum. "You were set to inherit the entire company, his car, most of his properties, and all the crappy old junk he kept around."

"He had every right to. It's *his* will."

"You expect me to just sit back and watch you take everything me and my girls worked for?"

It took all my self-control not to yell. Instead, I remained deathly still, clutching onto Reggie, my voice eerily level. "I expect you to be a reasonable person and not murder your husband over bullshit."

"Bullshit? *Bullshit?*" She scoffed, peeling off an errant false eyelash from her cheek. "You fucked off to Seoul. And us? We were the ones who DoorDash'd his breakfasts, dropped his laundry off at the dry cleaners, and supervised maids as they cleaned up the house. You were off living a fairytale, while we put blood, sweat, and tears into pretending to be a happy family."

Vera yanked off the other eyelash pair, tugging some skin with it. "How did that bastard thank us?" She pointed to the ceiling. "With a will that barely gave us a roof above our heads."

"Has it ever occurred to you that he left all he legally could to me because he didn't feel valued by you? He had to ship his daughter across the ocean to spare her abuse from his wife. He chose *you* while he was alive. So, he chose *me* in death. Fair enough for you?"

I didn't bother telling her I'd trade places any day. That I'd give every penny up if it meant he'd chosen me while he was still here. *Why didn't he choose me?*

"Fair? We'd be left with nothing." Vera's chest heaved up and down with her shouts. "What were we supposed to do?"

"*Work.*"

"I have." Vera unclasped a gold earring. "Since I was five, stealing wallets at malls. Never again."

"Because you've graduated to murdering men for their money."

"You can't see past your privilege. You didn't drop out at twelve to make money for your mom and brothers. You never had to sell your body for a bag of groceries. Work? I've done it all. My *body* has done it all." She gestured to Reggie and Tabby. "How do you think I ended up with them?"

I believed her. I believed her, and I pitied her, and still—and *still*—I hated her. She had no right to kill my dad.

"Mom." Reggie stomped her shoe. "You said my daddy died in the war."

Tabby scratched her temple. "You said my daddy drowned saving an injured dolphin."

Vera ignored them, unclasping her other earring. "Before I was twenty-two, I had a toddler and another baby on the way. Diapers, formula, hospital bills. I was so sick of it all. Then, your dad moved in next door to my pimp. I knew I'd hit the jackpot."

She shoved the baseball-sized hoop earrings into Tabby's palm. "I had an OB appointment for Reggie, so I asked him to watch Tabby. I had a fever that wouldn't go away. Your dad let me stay at his place. He spent the entire night up, watching over me until the fever broke. Two months later, I moved in permanently."

Beside her, Andras' eyes never left Vera, glued to her lips as if hearing her past for the first time.

"My pimp moved out from next door after your dad paid him off." Vera stepped forward. "For once in my life, I had it all. Two kids. A home. A hot husband. Then, *you* showed up. So needy. So greedy for his time. Always crying for a bottle or to be held."

"I was a baby. I did what babies do."

"What about Reggie? She was just a baby, too. He even dared to ask me for my breast milk for you, too. You're not even my kid." She kept advancing toward me, her steps slow and measured. "The minute he saw you bundled in that box, I knew you ruined everything. Because the way he looked at you... Tabby, Reggie, and I had his sympathy. You had his love."

My grip on Reggie tightened as I realized how close Vera had gotten. I could see the green flecks swimming in her dead eyes.

"Bullshit." I shook my head, refusing to believe it. "Dad chose you. He sent me away. He—"

"Boohoo. You went to an exclusive international school with all those rich kids, while he couldn't even afford your fencing equipment. You know he dug into our savings? He sold our stocks, dipped into our 401(k)."

Oh, Dad. No matter how wrong he was for this, it still didn't give Vera the right to harm us.

I wanted the earth to swallow me whole. To bury me beneath the house until it decayed. "That doesn't excuse how you treated me."

I released Reggie, pushing her away. She collapsed into Vera's arms, sobbing into her chest.

I watched the two of them embrace, shaking my head. "You never gave me a chance. You never loved me."

This set Vera off.

She shoved Reggie into Andras' arms and closed our distance, coming toe to toe with me. "Love?" She scoffed. "At least you have someone to take care of you. You bagged a billionaire. Don't pretend you would've caught us without his help."

Maybe. But that didn't mean I couldn't fight my own battles.

"I can fight my own wars." I straightened to my full height, staring down my nose at Vera. "Consider this your front-row seat. Game over, Vera. Eugene, too."

Andras shoved Reggie into Tabby, elbowing Vera away. "You leave my son out of this."

He seized my arms, rattling my entire frame. Unlike Vera, he beat me in strength. I slammed against the wall, yelping. Sharp, all-consuming pain zipped up my spine. My phone fell from its pocket, tumbling to the carpet. The recording app flashed on the screen. I tried to grab it, panicked that he'd see it.

But Andras had shoved his face into mine, saliva painting my cheek with each word he spoke. "I will not let you ruin Gene's life. You hear me? I have had it with your crusade."

His hands hiked up to my shoulders, and he started shaking me. My bones turned into Jell-O. I tried to fight, making use of my quick feet. I kicked. Stepped. Slid. Nothing worked. Andras was rabid. Completely void of pain.

"Gene did nothing wrong." Andras shook me harder. "Your father was a loser. He didn't deserve Vera. He didn't deserve her girls. I had to put up with your shit for two straight years to stop you from making trouble again. Vera is right. You are a rat. Sooner or later, you will eat your way into destruction."

My head began to swim. I'd stopped registering his words a while ago, drifting in and out of consciousness. With each jerk, my bones knocked against one another. Suddenly, it stopped. I collapsed to the carpet, barely registering the commotion.

Focus, Fae.

A sharp noise. Something smashed. All I knew was, I no longer flailed like a rag doll.

Then, Zach's voice filled the room like pure oxygen. "You fucking touched my girl? Grave mistake." I blinked away the haziness, just in time to see Andras fly across the room. "I hope you're okay with cremation, because there will be nothing left of you to bury."

Tabby screeched, huddled against my empty mattress with Vera and Reggie. Andras smashed against the far wall. He collapsed onto the floor, covering his face with his fists. Zach stalked to him, kicking him in the stomach as he laid in a fetal position. The pointy tips of Zach's loafers cracked Andras' bones, one rib at a time. They popped like knuckles, punctuated by Andras' agonized screams.

"You."

Zach stomped on his chest.

"Can't."

A rib this time.

"Touch."

The ankle.

"Her."

His throat.

"If."

His wrist.

"You're."

And finally, his face.

"Dead."

Blood gushed from Andras' nose, spurting across the carpet. His bare chest bore matching stains and the early beginnings of nasty bruises.

Oliver stormed into the room, peeling his best friend off my ex-fencing coach. "*Zach.*"

Rom joined him, clutching onto his opposite shoulder. "Jesus Christ."

Andras had stopped talking. Possibly even stopped breathing. It was hard to tell. He resembled a red bean bag. A lump that used to be a person.

Thud. Thud, thud. Thud. I flinched before realizing the sound had come from my chest. My heart thrashed against its cage. Zach shrugged off his friends, swatting them away like flies.

He rushed to me, scooping me into his arms. "Where does it hurt?"

Everywhere.

But I didn't think Andras could survive another round of Zach's fists and legs. Not that I cared. He just wasn't worth the jailtime.

Zach held me close to his chest. I wished I could melt into him.

I dug my nose into his skin, inhaling, not caring that my words came out garbled against him. "You came."

"I don't listen well." He stroked my hair, gliding his fingers everywhere Andras had touched, replacing it with *him*. "Oliver and Romeo tagged along because they were afraid I'd kill someone."

Oliver clapped Zach on the back. "Multiple someones." He raised his loafer, wincing when he realized Andras' blood had caked the sole.

I leaned against Zach's chest, nuzzling my cheek into his neck. "Tell me about the octopus."

"Octopus arms have minds of their own. Most of an octopus' neurons are in its arms. They can perform tasks without the mind of their owner. They can even move when the arm is chopped off."

I scrunched my nose. "That's morbid."

I'd had enough morbidity for the day, thank you very much.

Zach began carrying me down the stairs into the living room. Blue and red lights swirled across the window glass, casting different shades on his beautiful face.

"I recorded everything." I pulled my head back, staring up at him. "Upstairs."

Oliver strolled into the room, holding up my phone. "Already have it."

Rom guided him outside by the collar to greet the cops, giving us some time alone.

Zach sat on the couch, keeping me in his arms. "We're lucky you're the octopus and not me."

"Why?"

"If I had eight limbs, Andras would be dead by now."

I giggled, finally letting myself relax. My smile faded at the sight of an officer leading Vera outside in cuffs. "It's really over. Why don't I feel better?"

Four paramedics carried Andras away in a stretcher.

Zach swept his thumb under my eye. "Because none of this brings your dad back."

"I miss him."

"I know, baby."

"Thank you for coming."

"Always. You're safe now, Farrow." Zach kissed my temple. "You are safe *always*."

But my heart wasn't.

Because it had finally realized something dangerous.

CHAPTER SIXTY-NINE

Zach

I'd developed a sixth sense after the car accident. The ability to recognize catastrophe before it hit. I sensed it with Farrow's family confrontation. And I sensed it now, driving her home as she gazed out the windshield, lost in her own thoughts.

The stench of goodbye hung in the air like cheap perfume. According to the terms of our agreement, this was over. Done and finished. I could touch human flesh. Farrow sorted out her family issues. The lawyers would wrap the rest up in a neat bow.

And still, neither of us dared to broach the subject.

Fuck it.

I swerved, pulling over just before we hit Dark Prince Road. She didn't react, still studying the tree line in silence.

"Farrow."

Still nothing.

I unbuckled my seatbelt, hopped out of the car, and rounded to her side, swinging open the door. She stared at my shoulder, not really focused on anything, giving me my second heart attack of the night. The first happened at the sight of Andras manhandling her. If Ollie and Rom hadn't pulled me off him, I'd be in a cell right now, and he'd be in a morgue.

Finally, *finally*, she peered up at me as I gathered her into my arms and moved us both to the spacious trunk, flipping the rear seat down until it turned into a flat cabin.

"What's going on in that head of yours, Octi?"

"Nothing good."

"Impossible." I set her down, switching on the overhead light. "Where does it hurt?"

"Everywhere."

Hovered over her, I thumbed her shoulder, ever so slightly, right where I saw Andras grip her. "Here?"

A tiny, reluctant tear leaked out, trudging down her cheek. She didn't sob. Didn't make a sound. Just nodded. I leaned in, kissing the exact spot. She shut her eyes as I rolled my tongue over it, wiping away any trace of that bastard.

I traced the nape of her neck, where it slammed against the wall. "And here?"

"My elbow, too."

She stared at the roof as I washed away Andras' touch from her neck, her hip, her back, the crook of her elbow. All the while, she didn't say another word.

"Beautiful." When I finished, I pulled back and simply stared at her as she sprawled across the trunk, her wild sunshine hair splayed in every direction. "So fucking beautiful."

Farrow's fingers marked a path on the nylon lining. "What do you think about Monowi?"

"Never heard of it."

"It's in Nebraska."

"Sounds about right."

"Population of one."

"Where are you going with this?"

Please, don't say Monowi.

"Just thinking of Monowi."

I wanted to laugh. Maybe even scream. Definitely go for round two versus Andras. Farrow and I had so much to talk about, and we'd settled on Monowi. She still never told me whatever she needed to about Eileen. I still hadn't asked about our future. Except, instinct—along with the remaining cells in my brain that hadn't been fried by Andras-induced rage—told me the conversation would go differently this time than if we'd had it on the plane *before* completing our arrangement.

Farrow rested a hand on her ribs. "I couldn't have beaten Andras and Vera without you."

I plopped down on my ass and stretched my legs out as much as I could, setting Farrow's thighs on them. "You would've."

"No, I wouldn't have. Vera pointed it out. At the time, I told her I could fight my own wars. But I was wrong."

"You were right. You've been a fighter all your life."

"Maybe. But I also relied on my dad without realizing it." Her eyes found mine. "He cashed out his savings to fund my fencing career. A fencing career that no longer exists."

"Public opinion shifted to your side. Your academy friends spoke to the media about the circumstances. Once news breaks about Vera and Andras, no way will anyone hold you accountable for throwing an unimportant match."

"They should, though. I was wrong for it."

"If you want to quit, quit. Sometimes quitting is braver than persisting." I tipped her chin up, forcing her to look at me. "But if you're quitting because you're afraid of what others think, that's bullshit, and you're stronger than that, Farrow Ballantine."

"I'm not quitting. Well, I don't know yet." She sighed, pulling at the fuzzy nylon threads on the trunk flooring. "I guess my point is, I thought I was independent, living on my own, fighting Vera my own way. In reality, I had Dad's help—more than I thought I did—and yours."

Ask me for help, Farrow. You're not alone. I'm your one-man army.

Before I could reply, she sat up, dusting off her hands. "Can we head home?"

I studied her face, unable to get a read of her and hating it. "Of course."

"I think it's time to finish our Go game."

CHAPTER SEVENTY

Farrow

I decided I'd miss the naked French woman preparing for a bath most. Almost enough to ask for her as a keepsake, but I supposed that would defeat the purpose of my plans. I memorized the row of paintings in Zach's office as a doctor tended to my nonexistent wounds. The real wounds couldn't be cured with a stethoscope and first aid kit. I needed time, but I'd heal. I knew I would.

Zach orbited around us, fussing over every burgeoning bruise as if I'd picked a fight with a honey badger.

"She's fine. A little scratched up." Dr. Sullivan set down his cotton swab. "Nothing major." He paused a beat. "Not nearly as serious as a sliced finger."

Ah. I knew I recognized him. Oliver's family doctor. The one who had tended to Brett Junior after the kitchen incident. When he finished tidying up, Zach ushered him out the door, returning a few minutes later.

I nodded to the Go table. "We should continue our game now." No point in putting it off.

"Rushing off to somewhere?"

"And if I say yes?" I raised a brow, dipping a toe into the water, feeling the knot in my stomach tightening.

"Depends. Where?" He paused. "And for the love of God, do not say Monowi."

"You don't believe in God."

"No, but I *do* believe someone out in the universe is messing with me." He claimed his usual seat at the table. "Seriously, though. If you say Monowi, I might nuke the city."

I slid into the plush upholstery, lifting the lid off my bowl. "How?"

It wasn't lost on me how light our conversation had gotten. As if both of us wanted to shy away from the obvious trouble looming.

As always, he picked up a stone with perfect etiquette. "Have you forgotten that our neighbor is an arms dealer?"

I countered his move with the most ruthless one I could think of. "Right. Well, I guess I better spare the sole resident of Monowi."

He frowned at the board. "This could last all night."

"I have good stamina."

"That may well be, but I plan to wear you out nice and good."

"We're still talking about the game, of course."

"Of course."

Four hours later, he gained control over the board. Neither of us had said a word the entire duration, instead concentrating on the stones. He seemed deep in thought by the time I finally gathered the courage to broach the subject.

I reclined in my seat, linking my fingers together on my lap. "I resign."

His eyes darted up from the stones. "Excuse me?"

"I have no moves left." I unlinked my fingers, gesturing to the board. "Congratulations. You won."

"I won?"

"Yep." I nodded, doing my best not to melt into oblivion. "You won the pendant. Fair and square."

Sorry, Dad. Are you disappointed in me? Somewhere along the line, Zach and I had agreed to leverage the pendant as the award. Over time, the game had become foreplay rather than competition. I didn't think either of us really realized what we'd done. Judging by Zach's tense shoulders, he must've forgotten what we were playing on.

"Farrow."

I shook my head, shooting up. Wanting to say goodbye to the pendant one last time. But a few steps in, I realized only one of the pendants sat in the glass case. *Not* mine. My mild reaction startled me. I thought I'd break down, pivot, demand an explanation. But the confrontation with Vera had sucker punched me in the skull, rewiring my brain.

Vera, Reggie, and Tabby spent their lives amassing material items, unable to satiate their thirst. They committed crimes, ruined lives, and never understood the harm they caused. I didn't want to turn into them. Would I love everything Vera had pawned back? With every fiber of my being. But I refused to let their absence dictate my emotions. If I focused on what I didn't have, I would never appreciate what I did have.

"Talk to me, Farrow."

"Drink?" I detoured to the whiskey cart, poured two glasses, and sat on top of Zach's desk, swinging my legs. "I think we'll need them."

He padded to me, ignored the proffered drink, and stepped between my legs, resting his chin on my shoulder. A few months ago, he couldn't even lay a pinky on me. "What's going on in that chaotic head of yours?"

Everything I thought I knew about my past is wrong. I don't know who I am. Nor what my goals are now that fencing is gone and justice will be served. I'm scared of turning into Vera, prioritizing all the wrong things. I believe, with every ounce of my soul, that I'm better for you than Eileen. But I don't want to dive into a relationship without knowing who I am first.

Instead, I settled for a simple, "I'm afraid what I'm about to ask you is selfish."

"I want you to be selfish." He circled my wrist with his fingers and raised the drink to his lips, taking a sip exactly where I'd left a ChapStick mark. "Consider me your personal genie. Your wish is my command."

"Tell me something about octopuses," I blurted out, getting last-minute cold feet. *Just do it already, you chicken.*

"Hmm…" Zach buried his nose in my hair, inhaling my shampoo—which, in true mooch fashion, happened to be his. "If that's your idea of a selfish request, we'll have to revisit the dictionary."

"Please."

He closed his eyes, sobering up, and I wondered if he thought this would be the last time he gave me an octopus fun fact. His eyes shot open. "Octopuses have eight tentacles."

"Wow. Who would have thought?" I rapped a knuckle on his forehead. "No wonder you're famous for that 200-something IQ."

"I'm not done, brat." He tapped the tip of my nose. "I'm surprised you managed to survive twenty-three years with all that patience."

"Sorry." With my free hand, I mocked a zipper, sliding it across my lips and tossing the key.

"Excuse me, missy, but absolutely not." He picked up the imaginary key from the floor and used it to unlock my mouth. "I have a lot of plans for that mouth of yours, and it needs to be open for all of them."

I rubbed my knuckles against my cheek, fighting the heat. "Carry on."

"In Mandarin, the word for *four* sounds like the word for *death*, which is why four is the unluckiest number in Chinese culture. I was born on the fourth day of the fourth month of the year. Eight, on the other hand? It's the luckiest number." He pulled back until we faced each other, nose to nose, mere inches apart. "You're my good luck charm, Farrow Ballantine. Even the universe knows I need you."

It was the closest he had ever gotten to saying he loved me. My heart rebelled against my brain, threatening to tear out of its arteries and jump onto him. *Don't do it*, it begged with each thump. *Stop this.*

"I want a consolation prize." I jerked my thumb at the Go board. "For losing the game."

He arched a brow. "Is this the selfish request?"

I nodded, diving in. "Promise me—"

"I promise."

"I haven't even told you what the promise is."

"Whatever you want from me, it's yours."

I sighed, sparing a glance at the empty glass container where my pendant should have sat beside his.

What is meant for you cannot be taken away.

I lowered my chin, staring at the floor, rushing out my request in one breath. "Promise me you won't contact me for one entire month."

"Excuse me?" He went eerily still. "And if I can't live without you?"

"You did for thirty-three years."

"That was before. And it was hardly living."

"We're not even dating."

"Then, let's start."

"You're engaged."

"I'm breaking up wi—"

I held up a hand, stopping him. "Can I explain?"

"Yes." His reluctance rivaled a toddler's in the face of Brussel sprouts.

"These hands used to hold swords and slay dreams." I stared at my open palms. "Now they're just... *empty.*"

"I can get you an Olympic spot."

"Even *if* you could, I don't know if I want it. I don't know what I want in general, now that Vera and Andras are locked up, my reputation is ruined, and I learned that Dad gave up everything for me."

Zach tugged the edge of my sleeve. "His death isn't your fault."

"I know that logically, but I need time to accept it. Time, Zach.

It's what I'm asking for. To heal, to figure out who I am, and to know myself well enough to know what I want. I am so scared of turning into Vera, chasing all the wrong things."

"You are nothing like Vera."

"And yet, every ounce of me fears becoming her."

I pressed a hand to his chest, studying him. He looked so frustrated, and angry, and confused, I wanted to abort mission, make a U-turn, and leap into his arms. But I couldn't.

"I love you, Zachary Sun."

My first. My only. My always.

I knew, even before I said it, that it was true. I fell in love with him like the snow. The more I fell, the colder it became.

"Farrow—"

I held up a hand again, wanting to lower it when it looked like he'd combust on the spot. "I don't expect you to say it back. In fact, I don't *want* you to. Not now, at least. I just want you to know that I love you."

"Why?"

"I don't know." Heat crept up my cheeks, trekking to the tips of my ears. "I don't want to say it's because you help me, because you make me feel good, or even because you're all I think about these days. These reasons feel so shallow." I shook my head, grabbing the back of my neck. "If you asked me right now, I couldn't give you a real answer. Just that… I love you because I love you. Nothing more. Nothing less."

"I'll take it."

"But *I* won't. I don't know myself well enough to explain what it is I love about you. I just know I do. More than I've ever loved anything in my life. Shouldn't I at least figure that out?"

All I remembered of my life was fighting—fighting Vera, fighting Tabby and Reggie, fighting in fencing, fighting *Zach*. I didn't know who I was without that. I stared down at my Prada sneakers—one of my birthday gifts from him. It squeaked against the wooden desk as I kicked my feet back and forth. I needed to do some soul searching, to put myself first before I could love anyone else. And he had a big mess that required cleaning. Initially, I'd planned on telling him about Eileen, but he needed to hear it from her. And if he didn't, if he stayed with her, then we were never meant to be.

"Let's take a month apart. To deal with the things we need to deal with." I leaned over his desk, grabbed a red Sharpie, and snatched the tiny calendar he never used, circling the date a month from today. "If you love me as much as I love you, you'll come back to me, Zachary Sun. I'll be waiting."

He looked ready to hand me over to Dr. Sullivan to check out my brain. Finally, he managed to grumble, "If this is what you want."

I mustered a grin. "Can't wait to get rid of me, huh?" Inside, my heart crumbled like a stale cookie. After a moment of silence, I hopped off the desk, sliding my hands in my pockets, unsure of how to exit. "I guess this is it."

He didn't say anything. I waited a few more seconds. *Say something. Anything.* He didn't. With a sigh, I trudged out the office and down the steps. It wasn't until my hand hit the front door that I heard him approach from behind.

"Wait."

I paused but didn't turn, holding my breath, tensing when something slipped into my hand. An electronic key.

I flipped it in my palm. "What is this?"

"For the garage."

I still didn't turn. "Why?"

"I moved your stuff into there earlier."

Oh, God. I felt like a total idiot. Here I was, telling him I loved him, and he'd moved my things into his garage? We'd only been apart one hour since we'd landed—the time it took me to get from the airport to my childhood home and confront Vera and Andras.

I tried not to toss the key at him, studying the doorknob without really seeing anything. "Oh."

"Text me when you plan to check it out, and I'll leave."

"Thanks."

I needed to get out of here before I cried. Without another word, I swung open the front door and sprinted into the frosty winter night, not sure where I'd go from here. I made it halfway down the driveway— headed toward Dallas' house—when I pivoted, ran back to Zach's front door, and planted a kiss on the frosted window beside it.

I could've sworn, as I straightened up, a shadow jerked back from the other side.

"Bye, Zachary Sun. I hope I see you a month from now."

CHAPTER SEVENTY-ONE

Zach
T-Minus 30 Days.

Nothing said rock bottom more than crying over a girl less than eight hours after she'd left. *Fine.* There were no tears involved. But I barely managed to drag myself out of bed in time to bitch at Natalie for arriving to work a minute early.

"But you always expect me to show up early." She pouted, bouncing from heel to heel. "Last time I arrived on time, you docked my bonus."

I arched a brow, pulling up my email account. "Are you wearing shoes in my home?"

"You always let people wear shoes in your business wing."

I began typing out a draft, requesting Eileen's presence for a lunch meeting at The Grand Regent, during which I fully intended to call our wedding off. Speaking of…

I turned to Natalie. "Where's my lunch?"

Unshed tears rimmed her eyes. "But it's not even ten."

She surveyed the room, as if she expected to spot hidden cameras.

Me, too, Natalie. Me, too. Maybe this is all one elaborate prank and Octi will waltz through the double doors, strut to the Go board, and make a move.

I pressed send on the email. Now all I needed was to inform Mom that I: one) had gone to the Hamptons as she wished, two) fucked up any possibility of a future with her bridal candidate by *literally* fucking Farrow during dinner with Eileen, and three) expected her to honor her agreement to cancel the engagement.

I closed my eyes, spinning my chair around, so I didn't have to look at the Go board.

Chill the fuck out, Zach. It's just thirty days.
You survived thirty-three years without Farrow.
But did I?

CHAPTER SEVENTY-TWO

T-minus 28 Days.

Ari: Excuse me???

Ari: Why am I hearing it from @DallasCosta that Vera is in jail on 900k bail she cannot pay and Reggie and Tabby are living in a Motel 6?!

Ari: YOU DID IT. YOU WON. THE HOUSE IS YOURS. THE COMPANY IS YOURS. CELEBRATE.

Dallas: Bestie, are you illiterate?

Ari: No, why?

Dallas: Because you cannot read the room. Fae is heartbroken. She just moved out of Zach's house. She doesn't care about those beeshes.

Ari: What?

Ari: I am so not in the loop.

Ari: Why???

Farrow: We had a deal. We both got what we wanted out of it.

Ari: Wait, what did HE get out of the deal?

Dallas: [Peach Emojis x 3]

Dallas: [Eggplant Emoji, Hot Dog Emoji, Kitten Emoji, and Donuts Emoji]

Dallas: Subtle, but I thought this might explain it.

Farrow: You're literally the female version of Oliver.

Dallas: It's the pregnancy hormones. I think about sex ALL the time.

Ari: And Zach just let you walk away?

Ari: (Sorry to change the subject, Dal.)

Farrow: You guys never let me finish before you bombarded me with sex emojis. Pervs.

Farrow: [Eyeroll Emoji]

Farrow: I asked for some time apart (TEMPORARILY!!!).

Farrow: He wanted me to stick around. Which is even worse.

Ari: Where do you live now?

Dallas: Casa de Costa. Woot woot.

Dallas sent an attachment.

Ari: All I see is food…?

Dallas: My bad.

Dallas: She's there behind the stash of snacks that was just delivered. See her ear on the left-hand side?

Ari: A gorgeous ear. Enough to make van Gogh weep.

Farrow: Ha. Ha. Very funny.

Ari: Love you.

Ari: You know I'm always one phone call away—and a flight, in case someone's ass needs whooping.

Farrow: Appreciate it. <3

CHAPTER SEVENTY-THREE

T-Minus 27 Days.

Ollie vB: Is Zach alive?

Ollie vB: Haven't seen or heard from him in three days.

Romeo Costa: Oliver… is that concern I detect in your otherwise completely corrupted soul?

Romeo Costa: May I suggest checking your temperature?

Ollie vB: Not concern for Zach, but for the future of this exclusive neighborhood. Housing prices will tank if people discover it's the site of a gory crime scene.

Ollie vB: Should we check that he's not rotting somewhere in his house with a blunt object smashed into his head?

Ollie vB: Let's admit it, nobody will be surprised if we find out that he finally pissed off someone to death.

Ollie vB: The man's idea of seduction is calling a woman an octopus.

Romeo Costa: Zach is alive. In the technical sense of the word, at least.

Romeo Costa: He's just butthurt because Farrow moved in with me and Dallas and broke up with his ass.

Ollie vB: Aw. Butt pain is no fun.

Ollie vB: If only he'd only asked… I would've pointed him in the direction of great organic lube.

Romeo Costa: You're a fountain of knowledge, von Bismarck. A true renaissance man.

Ollie vB: So, she finally moved out.

Ollie vB: What happened? Did she find out he's a psychopath?

Romeo Costa: Nah, she was on board with that part.

Romeo Costa: She refused to be the side piece.

Ollie vB: Rookie mistake. The side piece gets all the perks and none of the drama and familial obligations.

Romeo Costa: Thank you for the moral clarity. Also, something about needing to discover herself.

Ollie vB: Sigh. It's always the 20- and 50-year-olds. Nothing in between.

Romeo Costa: Constance is pressuring him and Eileen to choose a date.

Ollie vB: Would have been nice if they went on one before getting engaged.

Romeo Costa: You're not wrong.

Romeo Costa: Either way, Eileen is MIA. Probably gone missing to avoid the break up.

Ollie vB: Should we check in on him?

Romeo Costa: I think that's what good friends do. So... no?

Ollie vB: Lmfao. Zach, we're on our way. Open up this time.

Zach Sun: I'm busy.

Zach Sun: Also, Farrow did not break up with me.

Romeo Costa: Right. That would require having been together.

Zach Sun: Fuck off, Costa.

Ollie vB: What's with the attitude? Who shat down your chimney?

Zach Sun: YOU did. Almost broke your nose for it.

Ollie vB: Okay, we were seventeen at the time, and that was a very sophisticated practical joke, mind you.

Zach Sun: Do not come to my house.

Ollie vB: We'll break down the door.

Zach Sun: You won't get past security.

Romeo Costa: I'll set Farrow up with a date if you don't open up.

Zach Sun: The only thing that'll be open, if you set her up with a date, is your body as I extract your internal organs with a chainsaw. One at a time.

Romeo Costa: ...

Zach Sun: Fine. I'll open up.

Ollie vB: Such a good boy.

Zach Sun: Shut up.

Ollie vB: Only with a silicone ball gag, baby.

Chapter Seventy-Four

Zach

T-Minus 26 Days.

The sound of a fifty-plus orchestra woke me up from my sixteenth consecutive hour of sleep. I couldn't even be miserable in peace. I shoved a pillow over my head. A saxophone blasted past the plush feathers, followed by the most useless instrument on Earth. The triangle.

"Goddammit."

I shot out of bed and stormed downstairs, not bothering to throw on a shirt.

"Oh, baby, you're awake." Mom lit up at the sight of me, perched on a barstool at one of my islands. "Help me choose the music piece for the wedding."

Dozens of musicians crammed into the open kitchen. They lowered their oversized instruments, nodding to me.

I ignored them, glaring at Mom. "Has this become your second home?"

"Are you complaining that I'm here too often?"

"Sounds like a cry for help." Celeste Ayi waltzed into the room, holding a mimosa, and squeezed my cheek. "Oh, Zachy, we'll absolutely come every day, since you asked so nicely."

"There's no wedding anymore, Mom. I told you this." I stared down the orchestra until they began packing up. "I went to the Hamptons and royally screwed up the engagement."

"Oh, nonsense." Mom waved a hand. "Eileen confirmed the date with me in person just yesterday."

How convenient, considering Eileen hadn't returned any of my thousand or so texts, emails, or voicemails. She obviously wanted this farce of an engagement to remain intact. Never knew her dodging skills rivaled White Goodman's. It was, in fact, the only interesting thing about her.

"Now that you're here, I would love your input on the cake." Mom lugged a five-hundred-page catalog from her bag, pounding it onto the counter. "I'm thinking a floor-to-ceiling lemon cake in ivory. Not too sweet, of course."

"I'll order you one for your birthday." I waited until every musician shuffled out, heads tucked down, before turning back to Mom. "Because I'm not getting married."

In my pocket, Tom's last text taunted me. I'd let it go unanswered.

Tom: Do you want me to follow her or not? Because you are not hot enough for me to put up with your mixed signals, man.

My nostrils flared. I had made myself a promise to respect Farrow's privacy, not to hunt her down.

Be good, Sun. It's just 30 days. Farrow will be back where she belongs in no time.

Problem was, being good didn't *feel* good. In fact, it felt the opposite.

Celeste Ayi flipped through the catalog, frowning. "Are you sure we want a spring wedding? I don't think my hair can handle the heat." She snapped her fingers. "I suppose I could hire a personal hairstylist to follow me during the reception. What a phenomenal investment."

"Xiao Ting, we get fitted for our dresses in one week." Mom tsked at the sight of her sister downing her drink in one go. "We need to keep a stable weight. At least until after the wedding."

I sighed, trudging back to my bed.

It didn't matter what I said. Mom wouldn't listen.

I needed to track down Eileen.

Chapter Seventy-Five

T–Minus 26 Days.

Zach Sun: 6:00 p.m. The Grand Regent Lobby.

Zach Sun: Is there a reason you stood me up, Miss Yang?

Zach Sun: I know you're in Potomac, Eileen. My mother informed me.

CHAPTER SEVENTY-SIX

Farrow

T-Minus 25 Days.

On day five of my liberation from Zachary Sun, Dallas called in reinforcements.

I groaned at the hanger she tossed at me, sitting on the edge of her duvet. "For the last time, I'm not depressed."

Truly, I wasn't.

Since I left Zach's, I'd vowed to focus on myself. To use these thirty days to sort out my mind and screw my head on straight. At thirty-three, he had ten more years on this earth to figure out who he was and what he wanted with life. I deserved an extra thirty days. Plus, now that I knew Eileen loved Zach—way, *way* more than she let on—my old arrangement with him felt icky. (Though I did find her manipulations to be as charming as one-ply toilet paper.)

Dallas shoved a hanger at Frankie this time. "That's what all depressed people say."

Fair enough.

"Why do we need reinforcements?" I shimmied on the fluffy tulle skirt. "We're not The Avengers."

"Speak for yourself. I feel like Tony Stark." Hettie—the head chef at the Costa Estate and the coolest person to grace this forsaken planet—frowned at the boxy red-and-gold tutu Dallas had crammed her into. "We're going to the club, not a ballet recital."

"My sister never got a bachelorette party." Frankie slung an arm around Dallas' shoulder. "If she wants us to wear these, we're wearing these."

"Thank you, Frankie." Dallas slipped into a white dress that barely fit over her stomach. "Nothing cures depression like a trip to the club."

I collapsed onto her mattress, covering my face with both palms.

"Not. Depressed."

But she'd already moved onto our shirts, assigning us identical ones to wear. She swiped on cherry-red, pregnancy-safe lipstick, spinning to face us. "Well? How do I look?"

Honestly, like a jilted runaway bride.

But also… "Adorable."

After the four of us finished dressing, we charged down the stairs two-by-two, arms looped at the elbows. From the kitchen island, Oliver dropped his spoon at the sight of us. He threw his head back and howled, not bothering to comment.

Romeo frowned, tugging the edge of Dallas' dress. "Where are you going?"

She stood on her tiptoes for a forehead kiss. "The club."

"In *that?*"

While Dallas wore a mini wedding dress and veil, Hettie, Frankie, and I donned bright tutus with hot-pink tank tops that read: I'M WITH THE BRIDE.

Dallas smoothed down her shirt. "What's wrong with our clothes?"

"Doesn't seem appropriate."

"It's just Costco. Wait." She cocked her head. "Did you think I meant a nightclub?"

"No one refers to Costco when they say club."

She whipped out her executive card and flashed it at him as proof. "I have a membership, therefore it's a club."

As always, Romeo succumbed to his wife's shenanigans, arranging for his driver to take us. A pang of envy zapped through me. I wanted what Dallas and Romeo shared. Would I get my happily ever after? The possibility that the thirty days would end and Zach would stand me up licked at the fringes of my brain the entire car ride. That was the thing about giving someone your heart. There was always a chance you'd never be whole again.

At Costco, we sampled every cart, then went around for seconds, thirds, and fourths until security kicked us out.

Dallas was right. Nothing cured depression like a trip to the club.

Maybe I *was* a little down.

After all, I carried the key inside my bra, right above my heart.

The organ that would shatter the second I used it.

Chapter Seventy-Seven

T-Minus 23 Days.

To: dreileenyang@sapphireclinic.com
Fr: zacharysun@suninternational.com

Subject: Breach of Contract

Miss Yang,

You have failed to respond to countless attempts of contact, which has resulted in a dire breach of contract of Article XVII, section 8, subsection m, paragraph 2. I've attached an annotated copy of our contract below with the relevant portion highlighted. To avoid a severe penalty, I suggest you contact me for further discussion. Future breaches of contract will result in immediate legal action.

Regards,
Zachary Sun

CEO, Sun International Inc.

CHAPTER SEVENTY-EIGHT

Farrow

T-Minus 22 Days.

I survived my first week without Zach.

During that week, I met with cops and lawyers to discuss the case, hung around the Costa house with Dallas and occasionally Frankie (much to Romeo's displeasure), and avoided staring at the key, which I finally shoved deep into one of the birthday shoes from Zach.

Today, Dallas had managed to convince me to watch a local youth fencing tournament. Paranoia tingled up and down my limbs as I speed-walked to the bleachers, chin down.

"Slow down. My belly bounces against my thighs each time I take a step." Dallas latched onto my arm. "You know, everyone's looking at you *because* of what you're wearing."

I wore my waves tucked into a cap, black-out sunglasses blocking my eyes, and the striped uniform of a bowling alley I'd recently picked up a shift for a little pocket money until the house sold. Vera had agreed to put it on the market, since she needed money for her mounting legal fees.

Dallas and I settled into a seat for two seconds before she turned her nose up, sniffing. "What's that scent?"

"Puke." I groaned, shaking out my uniform. "The con of women's suffrage. We girls have girl-bossed too close to the sun, and now we're spending our weekends cleaning up puke instead of reading books in the hot tub."

"Speak for yourself." She scrunched her nose. "I binge-watched all seasons of *One Tree Hill* this week while you worked."

The scent of acid wafted up from my shirt. I stood, slinging my bag over my shoulder. "I'm gonna wash up and change."

Dallas waved me off, already lost in the competition. The familiar symphony of swords clashing tickled my ears. I wanted to stand near the piste, close to the action, but I didn't feel the urge to suit up. *Odd.*

On my way back from the bathroom, I ran into a fencer, practicing her lunges in the hall. I'd spotted her warming up earlier with the other under-14 girls. I hesitated near the entrance back into the gym, still in my glasses and hat. "You're an épéeist, right?"

She nodded, her face screaming *stranger danger.* "I'm up next."

"I noticed you practicing." I bounced from foot to foot, wondering if I was overstepping. "You're focusing too much on fancy moves instead of distance and timing. Focus on your basic footwork, and you'll end up seconds ahead of your opponent."

"Really?"

I shrugged, realizing I'd only ever taught Zach, who was a natural. "Just food for thought."

And yet, I found myself leaning forward when the announcer called out her name and the match began. Anna lost the first two touches, too hellbent on making snappy moves.

Footwork, kid. Focus on your advances and retreats.

"Ow." Dallas jerked her arm out beneath my grip. Whoops. "You need a chill pill. You don't even know her."

"I know, but…" But what?

But you still love the sport. You love analyzing fencers. You love the thrill of the game. You just… don't want to compete anymore.

I reeled back at the realization, lost in my thoughts. Not for long.

Anna lost another point, a step behind her opponent. I shot up and cupped my hands around my mouth. "Focus on your footwork."

"Oh my God." Dallas shrunk in her seat as much as she could with her pregnant belly. "Is this how Romeo feels when I debate cheese versus no cheese at fast food drive-thru windows and there are cars behind us?"

But I didn't care. It worked. Anna won three points back-to-back, catching up on the scoreboard. And when she finished her bout 15-11, I jumped into the air, cheering as if I'd coached her myself.

The black sunglasses toppled off my face with the movement. I froze, realizing my hat had fallen off my face sometime during the bout. Whispers floated across the benches. Some people pointed at me, obviously recognizing me. I waited for someone to get up and yell at me. To call me a fraud. Instead, they mostly ignored me. A few smiled. Someone even asked for a selfie. At the end of the tournament, Dallas and I made our way down the bleachers.

"Hey."

Dallas pointed to me. "Is she talking to you?"

I spun, catching sight of a woman dressed head to toe in Lululemon. She began marching to us from across the gym. "Did you tell my daughter something before her match?"

"Oh, shit." Dallas nudged me. "She looks mad. Does she look mad?"

I backed up a step, dragging her with me. "Maybe we should run."

We pivoted to make a break for it, but Anna ran up to me, clutching my stomach in a hug. "That was awesome. I did exactly as you said. Can you coach me? Please?" She pressed her palms together, waiting for the moment the lady caught up to us to say, "My mom coaches me right now, and she has no clue what she's doing."

Anna's mom nodded, rubbing the back of her neck. "It's true. We just moved here. I haven't had the chance to find her a coach. Are you open to new students?"

"Oh, um." I toed a circle on the gym floor. "I…"

"She's available." Dallas beamed, lacing her fingers with mine. "She's totally free."

I rocked on my feet, not sure how to say this. "You know I…"

"Yeah. You're Farrow Ballantine. We recognize you." Anna's mom offered a soft smile. "Everyone in the fencing world knows about the match in Korea."

"Oh." I wanted to make like Homer Simpson and disappear into the hedges.

"We all support you, by the way." She offered a thumbs up. "Even before the news about your family stuff came out."

I stared down at Anna, embarrassed, flattered, and a little weirded out by total strangers discussing my life like it was some Netflix true-crime documentary.

I mean, you never know. Tabby always wanted a shot at Hollywood.

Anna nodded, grinning. "If I knew that it was Farrow Ballantine under the weird glasses and hat, I would've listened to your advice sooner." She turned to Dallas. "You let your friend leave the house like that?"

Just like that, on a sleepy weekday evening, I ended up the coach of a sassy thirteen-year-old.

CHAPTER SEVENTY-NINE

Zach

T-Minus 20 Days.

Today's lethal dose of misery came from the usual suspects—Celeste Ayi, Mom, and their delusions that the wedding would continue as planned. (Mom still refused to accept defeat. Celeste Ayi considered the prospect of returning her custom-made dress a national travesty.)

Mom sat at the island, before a massive binder that contained the names of every member of our family—past and present. "Zachary, are you not worried about finalizing the guest list?"

"Is someone getting married?" I stabbed into an egg yolk, just to watch it bleed, and moved on to the mango. "Certainly not me. My engagement was canceled."

I sipped my espresso, wondering what Farrow was doing right now. Working? Practicing on the piste? Causing trouble with Dallas? The fact that she lived across the street yet still managed to avoid me could be used as a CIA case study. Even as I channeled my inner Joe Goldberg. Working in front of the window. Fucking up all my calculations. Glancing up every ten seconds to see if she'd passed by. Not my finest moment.

"Don't be silly." Mom flipped a page in the binder, stamping a tab onto the outer margin. "Eileen forwarded me her guest list."

"Speaking of Eileen, I filed a missing persons case for her this morning." Well, tried to. Apparently, one could not file a missing persons case for the sole reason that they responded to everyone but you.

Mom stared at me as if I'd joined the Moonies and wanted to fork over my net worth. "She's busy working hard on creating the wedding of our dreams. It's best not to bother her for the next few months."

"I would love to not bother her for the next few *lifetimes.*"

"*Oh.*" Celeste Ayi dove forward, jabbing a finger at a name. "Let's invite Xiao Bai to the tea ceremony. Maybe she'll finally cough up the recipe for her dan dan noodles."

"Don't bother. You'll get the ingredients but not the measurements." Mom swatted her hand away, pausing at a name. "How about Olivia? She's darling."

"A darling bitch." Ayi took a butter knife to the page, scratching her out of the Zhao family records. "So condescending just because she spoke better English than me. So what if I didn't know slang when I first came? *Fuck you* was easy enough to learn."

Shards of their conversation slashed through my consciousness. Something hot and violent stirred inside me. I downed the espresso like a shot, discarding it on the island before tugging my phone out of my pocket. My knuckle brushed my dick along the way. That was enough to elicit a hiss from my lips.

No one told me I'd be reduced to animalistic needs after losing my virginity. With Octi away, I'd gone from fucking three to four times a day to zero. Suddenly, Oliver von Bismarck's entire existence made infinitely more sense. I hadn't even jerked off since she'd waltzed out of my life, leaving me in chaos. Not for lack of effort. Last night, when I pulled up random porn, I couldn't even get hard.

Fine. I missed Farrow. Sue me. Farrow Ballantine and her flowing hair, perfect length for fisting. And her lean thighs, so skilled at riding my cock. And her tight pussy, so sweet and soft like the mango on my plate.

"*Out.*"

It took a moment for the three of us to realize the harsh growl had come from me. Mom frowned, padding to me.

She placed her hand over my forehead, then retreated before it made contact, remembering that I hated touching. "Are you okay?"

"Please. *Leave.*"

I sliced the mango in half, just before the pit, forcing myself to look somewhat normal. Sensing my mood, Ayi chose self-preservation, leading Mom out of my mansion by force. As soon as the door closed, I gripped the edge of the countertop with my free hand, squeezing hard. My eyes slammed shut. I conjured Farrow into my mind, naked and spread-eagle across the island. With her pink nipples and glistening pussy, waiting just for me.

"Octi," I choked out, hardening in my slacks.

In my imagination, she invited me closer, writhing on the counter as she trailed one hand between her legs, swirling her finger around her swollen clit. My cock strained against my pants as my mouth watered. I imagined myself leaning down, getting a taste of her delicious, soaked pussy. I took a greedy bite out of the mango. Juices flowed down my chin. The fruity scent filled my nostrils as I tasted her. Sugary and earthy. Perfect, perfect, perfect.

A growl ripped from my throat as I feasted on the mango, faster and harder now, envisioning myself eating her out. I stood, pushing my cock against the cabinet, welcoming the friction, humping my own kitchen like a dog as I ate. Without her, I'd lost my mind, my dignity, my grip on reality.

"*Octi.*"

I hollowed out the mango, coming inside my own pants. The milky, hot cum shot into the fabric, refusing to end. I tossed the mango flesh into the sink and dropped my head between my shoulders in frustration. My entire body convulsed, shuddering as if going through intense withdrawals. I couldn't take another minute without her.

Fuck it.

I plucked my phone out and pressed call on the first speed dial. Then promptly hung up before it even rang, because I was officially, completely, and utterly pussy-whipped. Pathetic and doomed, I repeated the process again and again. Call. End. Green. Red. A glutton for punishment.

I wanted her touch.

I. Wanted. Her. Touch.

Cum stained my Kiton slacks, crusting against my skin. Untamed strands of hair stuck to my temples. I hadn't done any grooming in days. I glanced up, staring at my reflection in the shiny sink, not recognizing myself.

Sweat crept down my cheeks. A red flush stretched forehead-to-chin, ear-to-ear. I flicked on the faucet and lowered my face beneath the current, releasing an anguished roar.

When I lifted my head up, Mom stared at me from across the island, reaching for her forgotten purse. She clutched it to her chest, her voice small. "Are you sick, Zachary?"

I'm not sick, I thought wretchedly. *Just in love.*

CHAPTER EIGHTY

Zach
T-Minus 17 Days.

"Hello, you've reached Eileen Yang. I'm either on call or away from my desk. Please leave your name, number, and a brief message, and I'll get back to you as soon as possible. Thank you."

"This is your ex-fiancé calling for the thousandth time. You would know we've progressed into *ex* territory if you'd—I don't know—pick up the damn phone, answer your emails and texts, or perhaps even—and I know this is a wild suggestion—*not* stand me up for five fucking hours at The Grand Regent lobby. As you can see, it is of utmost importance that we speak face-to-face in order to confirm that you understand our entanglement has officially ended. If you'd like to un-fuck me anytime soon, I'll be waiting, doing my damnedest not to destroy every piece of your overprivileged life in the process. Talk soon."

Chapter Eighty-One

Zach
T-Minus 13 Days.

When it came to my future demise, I always wondered when it would happen. Not if. Not how. But *when*. It seemed inevitable. In April, I would turn thirty-four, the age Dad had been when he passed away. How could he—larger than life, a pillar of the community, my idol—be outlived by me?

The answer—impossible.

And so, I no longer bothered trying to pretend to be an upstanding citizen of society. Or even a *participant* in civilization. I succumbed to my demise, hopping restaurant to restaurant, hotel to hotel, hunting down the bane of my existence—Eileen Yang. Problem was, I knew nothing about her. Didn't know her likes and dislikes. Where she drank her coffee and went to pass time. All I knew was she'd actually taken that sabbatical and fucked off into the unknown.

I'd hacked into all I could. Her credit cards—unused. Social media accounts—crickets. Emails—all answered, except mine.

Tom reclined on my sofa, kicking his feet up on the armrest. "She's off the grid."

"Are you amused?"

He tossed a stress ball up and caught it. "Are you even Zachary Sun?"

My knuckles grazed my jaw, where a solid quarter-inch of hair greeted me. "I'm in between shaves."

"What you're in between is a mid-life crisis." He let the ball roll onto the rug. "What the fuck, man?"

What the fuck, indeed. Six days ago, I'd given up on normalcy, canceling all plans, meetings, and appointments. Not to mention Oliver and Romeo, whom I avoided like the plague. I spent my days staring out the window, hoping to catch a glimpse of Farrow in her Prius. (It

368 | *HUNTINGTON & SHEN*

happened once. Didn't see her face, but I knew that ass like the back of my hand.) At night, I roamed the halls of my mansion, desperate for a waft of her scent that still lingered in the air.

And in between, I pursued my future ex-fiancé like a man unhinged, desperate to put a stop to this madness. *Enough.* I shot up.

Tom spun to his feet, sitting upright. "Where are you going?"

"Her condo." I stormed into the hall, taking the steps two at a time.

"In New York?" He jogged to catch up to me, heaving out pants. "She won't be there. I had a friend check."

Still, I had to do something. Anything to straighten up this mess I should've dealt with ages ago. Tom gave up chasing me as I rounded the corner, escaping into my second garage. I must've given poor Ian a jump scare with my unshaven face, because he brandished his keys before him as a weapon.

It took my driver a moment to recognize his own boss, a solid twenty seconds passing before he lowered the keys. "Mr. Sun?"

"The airport." I slid into the car, snatching up a glass from the minibar. "ASAP."

I planned on drowning in my own misery and enough scotch to fill up an Olympic pool. Through the divider, the clock glared at me. I told myself drinking before nine a.m. made me a pirate not an alcoholic and that dubious sobriety was a feature not a bug when you were a mostly retired billionaire.

By the time I landed in New York and showed up at Eileen's building, I couldn't stand straight.

A foot away, some kid white-knuckled a dog leash. He struggled to keep the labradoodle still as it barked at me. "Mommy, Smithy won't stop."

His mother leaned down and shushed the pup, shaking her head. "He always does this around strange men."

Rock, meet Bottom.

And yet… Somehow, I knew I had a long way to go before I hit *real* rock bottom. 13 days, to be exact.

I should've done a better job imagining my future demise.

Because it did not, in fact, manifest in a fiery crash.

It manifested in a beat-up heart.

In the pathetic attempts of a deranged man to piece it back together.

CHAPTER EIGHTY-TWO

Farrow
T-Minus 10 Days.

Change. The word sat on the tip of my tongue like a weight, waiting to drop. I could count every major life event of mine in one hand.

When I thought of each moment, I realized I'd never done a single thing for myself. Not intentionally. Maybe moving to Seoul could be considered an act of self-love, but I'd made the decision after years of begging from Vera, Reggie, and Tabby.

Which brought me to my new apartment. A tiny studio in Gaithersburg. Safe. Picturesque. With flowerpots overflowing with peonies, dahlias, and daisies. They spilled out onto the roof of the Italian bakery underneath. The red-bricked building brought me a piece of calm in the chaos of my life. It was cozy. Nostalgic. And my first real gift to myself.

I missed Zach. Every damn day. Sometimes, I even hopped on YouTube to watch his old interviews, clinging to the huskiness of his voice. The way his square jaw set when he received a tough question. And the lopsided, contemptuous grin he offered when people expected actual smiles. And yet, I felt happy in my new home. In the same way I'd fallen in love with a man, I fell in love with the life I realized I could build for myself. *The only thing missing now is him.*

"Well, girlie." Dallas patted a cardboard box on the coffee table. A satisfied grin lit up her face. "This one's the last of it."

Oliver plopped on the couch. "You act as if you carried anything."

"I *did.*" She stroked her stomach. "My child."

I'd moved most of my stuff a week ago in between practices with Anna, while Dallas helped me with the rest today. I'd refused her hand-me-downs, though I found them beautiful. I just wanted to make this place my own. An antique dining table for two. A secondhand curtain made in Paris. My first new mattress. Ever. Naturally, the place looked like IKEA and Goodwill vomited on it. I freaking loved it. Electric excitement zipped up and down my spine. Now I understood why people wanted to have things completely of their own. It was exhilarating.

From outside the front door, footsteps pounded up the narrow staircase. "You forgot one more thing." *Romeo.*

I picked up my phone while Dallas got up to let him in, answering Ari's call with a frown. "Is everything okay? Isn't it super late over there?"

"Tell me you're headed home."

"I'm already here." I gnawed on my lip, fighting a fresh wave of panic. *An emergency, perhaps?* "Why? Did something happen?"

"Nothing bad." In fact, she sounded excited. "But I need you to sign off on a delivery."

"A delivery?" I groaned. "Dude, please, no more candles. Dallas and Frankie gave me enough scented candles for an Easter vigil."

Ari's laughter filled the other line—and my chest. "It's not candles."

"Well, what is—"

Dallas swung the door open, cutting me off with the sight of Romeo lugging something behind him. He wore a massive frown, unsatisfied with being relegated to delivery man.

"You still there?" Ari whined. "I want you to open it before I go to bed."

Romeo set the giant box in the center of the studio. Tiny holes peppered most of the surface area. I inched toward it, tugging the ribbon off. "I'm opening it," I declared, just when my gift decided to introduce itself to me with a shrill *woof.* Oh. My. God.

I tore the lid off, squealing while Ari laughed in the background. More barks jumped at me. I collected a crate from the box and flipped it open. A pair of huge black eyes stared back at me, surrounded by a ball of tar-black curls. If it weren't for the bright-pink tongue lolling out of its mouth, I would've thought she'd gifted me a giant hairball.

"That is…" I squinted, pulling the puppy out of the crate.

"A Cockapoo. Part cocker spaniel, part poodle. A shelter baby. Can you believe he hasn't found a home in almost a month?"

"What?" I pressed his wet nose against mine and gave him an Eskimo kiss. "Silly people. He's perfect."

"I thought you'd say that." I could hear the smile on Ari's face. "Now that Vera isn't there to bitch about the mess and shedding, your dream dog is yours."

"I can't believe you remembered."

"Of course, I remembered. You're my best friend."

Dallas let the pup nibble her finger. "Welcome to the family."

"Zach is gonna shit his pants. The dude loathes messes." Oliver hopped off the couch. "You should name it Dogstoevsky. Soothe the burn when you run back into his arms."

"She is not naming it Dogstoevsky." She elbowed Ollie out of the way. "How about Mary Puppins?" Genuinely, I feared for their future kids.

I pressed a kiss to the top of the puppy's head. "Allow me to introduce Vezzali. The greatest fencer of all time."

As if on cue, he tucked his head under my chin, staring up at me with adoration, confirming we'd be each other's ride or die for life. I was not going to cry. I wasn't. But then Vezzali started licking my face, wagging his tail in my arms so hard it swatted me like a baseball bat. His whole body swayed from side to side. He was so light, so tiny, and so incredibly furry. The perfect bedmate.

"Nuh-uh. What's that face?" Dallas stuck her lower lip out. "Like you're about to cry. You're not about to cry, are you? Because I'm too hormonal not to bawl my eyes out right along with you."

"I'm not about to cry." Tears hung for dear life on my lower lashes. *Dammit.* But these were good, cleansing tears. Of someone who finally had a home. My eyes bounced from Dallas to Vezzali to Oliver and even to Romeo. After twenty-three years, I had finally learned that a home didn't have to be a place. It could be a person.

"Oh, no." Dallas cupped her mouth, tears leaking out of her eyes, too. Unlike me, she started wailing and drowning her cheeks without even trying to stop the flood. She flung her arms over my shoulders, gathering me into a hug.

"Why are we crying?" She jumped up and down, bumping Vezzali with her belly. "Do I have to kill Zach? I hear prison food is so bad. But I love you too much not to."

I detangled myself from her, wiping both of our eyes with my sleeves. "These are happy tears."

Vezzali barked his agreement. And I was happy. So, so happy. The only piece missing sat on Dark Prince Road, probably brooding as he always did, hopefully counting down the days until our reunion.

"Oh, Fae." A fresh wave of tears rushed down Dallas' cheeks.

I feared she'd go into early labor. Already, Romeo looked ready to hang me from the rooftop. He swept her into his arms, rubbing her back.

"Thank God you're not sad-crying." She disconnected from Romeo, clutched her purse from my kitchen island—just the thought made me want to break into a dance, *my* kitchen island—and grabbed an unopened pack of dish towels, patting her eyes dry. "The food truck downstairs closes in less than an hour. I thought I wouldn't make it. Did you know they sell fresh fettuccine cooked in a wheel of Parmesan cheese? Is there anything else you need from us?"

I laughed, shaking my head, wondering whether she'd cried over my tears or the thought of missing food. "Enjoy the bowl of fettuccine, babe."

"A bowl?" She rolled her eyes. "I plan on buying the entire wheel. I've been craving carbs so badly this trimester." Then, she and the boys took off in a flurry of air kisses, grumbles, and dirty jokes. Dallas Costa, ladies and gentlemen. The human answer to the sweetest summer day.

With a sigh, I locked the door, padded over to my new fridge, and cracked open a soda can, settling on my hideous yet adorable yellow-and-purple checkered couch. My favorite thrift find. I scrolled through my old laptop, checking emails.

First—Reggie and Tabby begged me to accept a low-ball offer on the home. They'd moved from the motel to a distant aunt's in West Virginia and wanted out ASAP. Next—I accepted an easy job with an old client under Maid in Maryland. The two employees Vera hadn't fired needed steady work, so I kept the company while I figured out what I wanted to do. And finally—I opened an email from a stranger. An unranked fencer, who wanted to compete nationally. He'd heard through the grapevine that Anna had topped her bracket in her last competition and figured it wouldn't hurt to ask for help. I grinned, flattered, typing out my reply. A big, fat, bolded, italicized *YES*.

I was beginning a new life. One I'd started on my own from scratch. One I loved. And yet, the shoe box stacked in the corner haunted me. Weeks ago, Romeo and Oliver had gathered my things from Zach's, noting he'd kept them in my room. Which meant he hadn't meant what I'd thought he'd meant when he said he'd left my stuff in the garage.

And still… I feared what secrets the key held.

Because I'd given Zach a key, too. The one to my heart.

CHAPTER EIGHTY-THREE

Zach

T-Minus 5 Days.

The countdown loomed over me like a guillotine. Each day I couldn't find Eileen brought me further from the calm, collected, and ruthless man I once prided myself in being. I'd exhausted all my options. The four private investigators I'd hired had come up short. All of Eileen's relatives refused to give up her location (despite numerous threats). And Mom? Guantanamo wouldn't stand a chance at prying info from her lips.

On the twenty-fifth day without Farrow, I decided I'd had enough of being miserable in the comfort of my thermostat-controlled home and dragged my pathetic self into the cryochamber, where I could be comfortable with half-frozen balls.

Did Farrow even cure you? I started to reason with myself. *Surely, she is not St. Anthony, capable of miracles. Nor Bian Que. Or even Fu Xing.*

No. A sit-down in the ice room would deliver cognitive clarity. *And* prove that I hadn't changed. That I still felt absolutely nothing. Not even the cold. I hadn't entered the chamber in almost four weeks, but I still notched the temperature to advanced. I stepped inside in my robe, immediately hit with the sharp bite of frost eating at my skin.

Well, shit. "What on earth…" I hissed, closing the door behind me as white smoke curled around my limbs, climbing up my body like ivy.

My vision fogged. I turned around to the overhead digital clock to see how much time had passed. *One second.* One fucking second. Was this a joke? I shivered, realizing to my dismay that I was feeling cold. That I was *feeling*, period. My nose became numb, too frozen to properly inhale. I had to cup it with my palms, quivering violently as I shuffled from leg to leg. I felt cold. In pain. *Alive.*

The seconds ticked by at an excruciating pace. I started jumping up and down, doing a few squats to fight the freeze. I finally understood why Romeo and Oliver became restless as soon as they entered.

Finally, when the buzzer sounded after the three minutes passed, I staggered to the door and pushed. It did not open. I gave it a good shove with my shoulder, using momentum that would usually send it hurling, knocking over the wall. It didn't budge. Potent, hot panic sliced into me. The human body wasn't designed to endure this temperature for longer than nine—maybe ten—minutes. I'd already reached four.

I walked backwards, gaining momentum, ran toward the door, and delivered a roundhouse kick. Still nothing. Terror and alarm swirled inside me. *You're going to die without ever seeing Octi again. Good going, doofus.*

"Think." I paced, trying to gather heat. "Think, think, think." The door had no locks on it—purposefully so. To ensure no accidents happened. That meant...I banged my fist on the door. "Who's out there?" Whomever it was, they knew my lair by heart. Had open access to my home. I pounded my fist, trying to thrash my way through it. "Let me out."

I would kill whatever sturdy psychopath stood on the other side of this thing. In fact, I racked my brain for any suspects, hoping to at least witness his death in my head before I croaked. Unfortunately, I didn't have enough time to shortlist the top twenty. My desperation grew, clawing at my chest. *Five minutes and counting.*

I punched the door. "Let." *Kick.* "Me." *Shove.* "Out!"

Ice crusted my body. White-gray fuzz clouded my eyesight. I began to lose clarity when the door whined open. Two fiery hands grabbed me with force, dragging me out of the chamber. My eyes rolled in their sockets. Darkness blanketed my vision as the hands tugged me onto the horizontal shower in my home gym. Warm water sloshed over my skin as he turned on all six showerheads, shooting water at my back at full blast. I spasmed, my body trying to acclimate to normal temperature again. Piece by piece, my sight returned, like a camera adjusting into focus.

Oliver sat on the heated lounger, wearing a gold satin robe paired with a shit-eating grin. I launched myself at him at a sluggish pace. He yawned, hopped off the spa chair, and pushed me back with a careless shove. I couldn't fight back, my body too weak from being locked in sub-Antarctic temperatures. He wagged his fingers at me.

I punched the marble tile, regretting the idiotic decision immediately. "You psycho." Little by little, my nerves began to defrost.

Just in time for pain to shoot through my knuckles. "I could've died."

"You could've." Oliver leaned in to check the water temp. "And judging by the last three weeks, you wanted to, too. You've completely lost your desire to live, Zachary boy. I had to remind you that life is a precious gift. It's my moral duty as your friend."

"I'm going to kill you," I spat out, my body still thawing under a torrent of water, slowly coming alive. I didn't remember him undressing me before he threw me under the spray, and yet I was completely naked.

"I hear this on an hourly basis. You love me, and you know it."

"I don't—"

"Problem is, you love her, too, and you are unwilling to get your head out of your ass and do what needs to be done."

"Which is?" I narrowed my eyes, gripping the edges of the shower.

Oliver crossed one leg over the other, cupping his knee. "Cancel that sham wedding, to start with. You know I hate bad investments. I'm not sending a check or buying a registry gift only to watch you get divorced faster than Britney Spears and Jason Alexander."

"The *Seinfeld* guy?"

"One would think, but no. A different one." Ollie stood, trekking toward my robe. He retrieved it from the floor and flung it toward me.

I collapsed in the bed, done resisting. "I canceled the wedding."

"And yet, I received the Save the Date yesterday."

"And I'm hunting down Eileen."

"We both know who your best bet at finding her is."

"Mom would never spill the beans."

"Hmm… I wonder what *other* woman practically lives at your side." He reclaimed his seat on the heated lounger, kicking one leg over the other. "Some would call her a second mother."

"Celeste Ayi—" Oh. *Oh.* For years, I'd gotten used to assuming she knew nothing about anything that it hadn't even occurred to me that she had eyes, ears, and the inability to keep a secret when pressed.

Oliver tsked at the sight of me darting out of the shower and shrugging into the robe. "Eileen should've never happened. Having everything with someone who means nothing to you takes the sting out of the accomplishment. If only you—"

He'd have to finish his monologue before his audience of submissives. I had one chaotic aunt to track down.

Chapter Eighty-Four

Farrow
T-Minus 4 Days.

"Do you think he'll come in four days, guys?" I sat before the men in my life, perched on the grass beside Dad's grave. Vezzali sprawled beside me, his head on my knee, even as it raised half his little body into the air.

"I mean, realistically, it's only thirty days. I've drunk cheap wine that took longer to make." I popped open a box of flashcards onto my lap, fishing in my backpack for a pen. "Oops. I don't mean to give you a bad impression of him, Dad. Zach is great. Rough around the edges, a little *odd*, but that's what I like most about him."

Stop putting this off, Farrow.

I sighed. Sure, I wanted to talk to Dad about Zach, but mostly, it was an excuse to avoid the real conversation we needed to have.

"I guess it's time to get serious." I brought my knees to my chin, setting Vezzali onto my discarded jacket. "I'm sorry I haven't visited you. I have a lot to say, and every word of it scares me."

The breeze picked up, extra chilly in the winter morning.

"I'm sorry you made all these sacrifices that I never knew about. I'm sorry you gave up so much for me to become a fencer. And I'm sorry I ruined that fencing career in spectacular fashion. Are you ashamed of me?"

A gust of wind slammed into me, sending my pen half a foot away.

"Okay, okay. No more wallowing in self-pity. I get it." I didn't know whether to grin or cry, so I cleared my throat instead. "I'm sorry I didn't see you before you died. I'm sorry that I didn't come in time to stop you from being buried. I know you always wanted to be cremated with your ashes scattered at the ice-cream shop where we picked our company name. I'm sorry I no longer want to run Maid in Maryland. And most of all, I'm sorry about how much I resent you right now."

I worked my jaw with my thumb, buying time, wondering how to say the next part. It was odd how Dad chose this exact moment to speak in my head. *After* I'd finally realized how mad I was at him.

That's okay, Fae. Being angry isn't a bad thing. It means you've accepted that you deserve more.

I huffed out a breath, digging my fingers into my temples. "I'm mad at you. Okay, Dad?" *So, so mad, it's hard to breathe sometimes.*

I shot up, beginning to pace. "I'm mad that you knew from the start that Vera didn't want me, and you stayed with her anyway. I'm mad that you didn't protect me when they abused me, even when you had to have known how bad it had gotten."

Snow toppled from a bare tree, sending Vezzali into my arms.

"*Rude.*" I stroked his head and carried him as I marched back and forth, as if Dad had been the one to almost douse him in snow. "I have every right to be mad about these things. You should've protected me. No matter how much you wanted that family, I'm your family, too. I loved you, too. I deserved to be protected."

I wanted to cry. To laugh. To scream. But mostly, my energy plummeted. I sank to the ground, sick of being mad, wanting to get everything off my chest so I could bury my anger with him.

"I'm mad that your idea of keeping me safe was shipping me across the world. Which is why I blame you for the fact that I couldn't see you before you died. I'm mad that you broke your promise and missed my last match. And that the match ruined my life, and it never would've happened if you left Vera in the first place."

My hand curled into a fist at my side. Vezzali barked, sensing my mood, lapping his tongue on my cheek.

"I'm just so freaking mad. Any time I think about it. Why didn't you put me first when you were alive? Why did you wait until you died? Now all I have left are the memories, and they're *gone*. Your belongings? Pawned. What I remember in my head? It'll slip away with time, and I'm so scared."

When my memories of you are gone, will I even remember what it's like being loved unconditionally?

This was the problem with giving someone a piece of yourself. Once they left, you could never get it back.

I choked on my tears, realizing something I'd never noticed before.

"And most of all, I'm sorry you must have felt so alone. With a wife who hates you, stepdaughters who only wanted to use you, and the only person who loved you all the way across the world."

The first snow of the day made landfall on my cheek. It melted against the heat of my emotions, falling to my chin like a teardrop. I swiped it away, grabbed the flashcards and backpack, and rushed to the car with Vezzali before he froze.

In my Prius, I drove straight to Happy Swirls, setting Vezzali on top of an outdoor table. I sat on the bench. The same one Dad and I once sat on over a decade ago, coming up with a list of potential names for the cleaning company. *Dusty Divas* and *Minty Fresh* (me). *Crystal Clear* and *New Beginnings* (him).

At just five in the morning, the shop hadn't opened. A few cars whizzed by, but overall, Vezzali and I enjoyed peace, quiet, and the beginnings of the sun cresting over the horizon. I pulled out the flashcards and a matchbook, staring at the words I'd written on them at Dad's grave.

> **Our first fencing competition together. You were so proud, you almost started a fight with another fencing dad. He took offense to how hard you cheered for his daughter's loss.**

> **When Ms. Drake called you into a parent-teacher conference because I told her you're always high, but I meant you were taller than me. You took me to a movie after, and we ate two whole large tubs of popcorn.**

> **That time I asked you if babies come from bellies. You said yes, and you let me assume I came out of your belly for years because you didn't want me to know my birth mother abandoned me.**

Memory after memory, I seared them into my brain. One by one. All my favorite pieces of Dad. And then I set them into the tin I'd brought, lit a match, and burned them to ashes. They flew up with the wind, pieces of Dad scattering all over Happy Swirls—his ashes spread exactly where he wanted them.

I poured the tiny teaspoon of ashes left in the tin into the locket of a bracelet I'd bought with my first coaching earnings, keeping a piece of Dad with me forever.

"If there's an afterlife and we have another chance to do it all over again, I'd still want you as my dad."

CHAPTER EIGHTY-FIVE

Zach

T-Minus 4 Days.

Time slithered like a sewer monster. One day seemed like three winters. All I wanted to do was claw at the walls that constantly seemed like they were closing in on me. Even with the sudden epiphany to fleece the info out of Celeste Ayi—also, who knew emotions could cloud logic to the point of stupidity? Not my favorite scientific discovery—it didn't matter if I couldn't find the damn woman, either.

I'd spent all of yesterday and this morning tracking her, only for Natalie, of all people, to be the one to strike gold.

"SHE'S FUCKING *WHERE?*" I roared into my phone, partly to be heard over Natalie's gum chewing and also because Celeste Ayi *would* choose the one time I needed her near me to run off to a spa in the furthest place possible.

"Celeste is in Chiang Mai with Constance." Natalie bore the canned voice of a Kardashian, and I genuinely hoped she became the trillionth sister, so she could fuck off to L.A. and away from me. "It's a city in Thailand."

"I know where it is." I tore my coat from my shoulders, kicking my front door shut like a tractor-sized baby. It seemed suspiciously convenient for Ayi and Mom to be elsewhere as I ramped up my search for Eileen. "What is she doing there?"

"She said she's meditating." Something crunched between her teeth. So much for maintaining professionalism.

"She doesn't meditate." In fact, my only memories at temple were the days our cook took off, and Mom wanted me to eat there.

"She said you'd say that… And to tell you that she decided to give it a try. That there was no point in staying home, anyway, since she doesn't celebrate Christmas."

I flung my shoes off. "When did you talk to her?"

"Hmm." I could practically envision Natalie twisting an invisible phone cord around her finger as she pondered my question. "Right before I clocked out. Maybe, like, twelve hours ago?"

Right after I cornered one of Eileen's star-athlete cousins, threatening to inflict damage on his leg that would ruin his Premier League future. Mom must know I'm seconds from losing my shit.

I stormed upstairs to my bedroom. "And you didn't tell me?"

"I'm telling you now."

I squeezed the bridge of my nose. "What hotel is she staying at?"

"I don't—"

"Yes, you do. Enough with the bullshit. I know she pays you extra to book her personal travel arrangements."

Natalie groaned. The woman was about as endearing as a head-sized hemorrhoid. "Fine. I'll send you the hotel link."

"Get my plane ready. I'm going there."

It would take about 36 hours roundtrip on my private jet, which would leave me about two days to bargain with her then return to Farrow on time. Cutting it tight, but it had to happen.

I'd started gathering luggage and the essentials for a speedy trip when I was met with unwelcome silence. My favorite sound, usually. Unless it was accompanied by the feeling of premature defeat.

I stopped dead in front of my suit rack. "Natalie?"

"Uh…"

"Spit it out."

"They took your plane."

"THEY TOOK MY PLANE?"

"Yeah." At least she had the manners to seem embarrassed by it. "They said you won't need it."

"Bold of them to make that assumption."

I saw right through Mom's plan. She wanted to ensure I had no way of reaching her, assuming I thought myself to be above commercial flights. I lowered my phone, shooting a text.

Zach Sun: Need a plane. ASAP.

Romeo Costa: Dallas took mine. She and Frankie are on a cheese-tasting tour in Italy, courtesy of Constance.

Ollie vB: Someone's feeling charitable this Christmas…

Ollie vB: She got me tickets to an exclusive sex show in Berlin. Of course, I had to go.

How expectedly thorough of my mother. A commercial flight would add another two hours each way. Four if it included a short layover.

I raised my phone back to my ear. "Natalie."

"Yes?"

"Book me a flight to Chiang Mai. The earliest available."

"On Christmas *Day?* That's going to be a mission." She was already clicking away on her computer. "The earliest one doesn't have any business seats left. Just economy."

"Book it."

An audible gasp penetrated my ear from the other line. Was I really that far removed from general society?

"Are you sure?"

"I am positive," I answered in the exact same tone.

"Okay. Booking right now."

"Thank you. Oh, and Natalie?"

"Yes, Mr. Sun?"

"This is your notice that you've been fired. Your two weeks start now."

"You can't do this to me." She screeched, not even asking why. Blissfully unaware that she had breezed by the past few weeks, lucky I was too fucked up to remember to fire her.

"I can. You tried to steal my sperm."

"Unsuccessfull—" But she didn't get to finish her sentence.

"Merry fucking Christmas. Don't come back to work."

CHAPTER EIGHTY-SIX

T-Minus 3 Days.

Ollie vB: I have tea.

Romeo Costa: No, thank you. I decline any type of liquid you might be offering to me on the grounds that it is probably gross.

Ollie vB: Tea as in gossip. Your Southern wife would be so ashamed of you right now.

Romeo Costa: What's the scoop?

Ollie vB: Our good friend Zachary was spotted by a B-grade socialite sailing through BWI wheeling a trolley behind him like some commoner without his own private plane.

Romeo Costa: Are you sure it was Zach?

Romeo Costa: Because he is about as down to Earth as Neptune.

Ollie vB: She took pictures.

Zach Sun: That's not creepy at all.

Romeo Costa: @ZachSun, do you confirm this report by Mr. von Buttered Bun?

Zach Sun: My mother stole my airplane.

Ollie vB: [Okay Hand Emoji] That is actually the best homework excuse I've ever heard.

Romeo Costa: Are you currently INSIDE a commercial plane?

Zach Sun: Unfortunately.

Ollie vB: When was the last time that happened?

Zach Sun: First grade.

Ollie vB: My God, what is it like? Tell us everything. I've seen a few in movies, but I've never actually been on one.

Zach Sun: Busy. Loud. Food smells like it has been previously digested by an elderly family dog and vomited onto your plate.

Ollie vB: I think I just died a little inside just from reading this. How is business class? Is it like glamping?

Zach Sun: There were no business-class tickets left. I'm flying coach.

Ollie vB: You're fucking with us.

Romeo Costa: Please, Ollie. No one is getting anywhere near your dick without a hazmat suit.

Zach Sun sent an attachment.

Ollie vB: Sweet Jesus. He really is flying coach.

Zach Sun: It's a connecting flight, too.

Romeo Costa: @ZachSun, care to tell us what and where was so urgent? We're on pins and needles.

Zach Sun: Thailand, to pry Eileen's location from my mother and aunt.

Romeo Costa: They're both going to kill you.

Zach Sun: I am well aware.

Ollie vB: If they do, can I have the cryochamber? This particular model is out of stock.

Romeo Costa: Since you've been MIA all month, I'm asking here…

Romeo Costa: What made you realize you can't follow through with the wedding?

Zach Sun: Farrow.

Ollie vB: What about the cryochamber? Is that a no?

Romeo Costa: Fight for her, bro. She's worth it.

Zach Sun: I am. And I know.

Ollie vB: Guess I'll have to drag it home myself after your mother throws you into the Mekong River, sans floatie.

Romeo Costa: Good to know something managed to get its way into your heart.

Zach Sun: She's not just in my heart. She's in my fucking veins.

Chapter Eighty-Seven

Zach

T-Minus 3 Days.

I never expected people to bend to my will.

All my life, my peers naturally did it, as if I'd issued an unbreakable command merely by existing. After the accident, when Mom changed, I considered her one-eighty the universe's way of counterbalancing a blessed life.

Until now.

As everything went to shit.

And *no one* seemed to care about a goddamn thing I said.

I stalked into the four-bedroomed grand pool villa, swatting away the residential assistant Mom had hired for the duration of her stay at the Four Seasons Chiang Mai. "Where are they?"

She floundered, torn between chasing after me and running for help. "I don't know what you mean."

"Yes, you do. Sun Yu Wen and Zhao Yu Ting. What room?"

My loafers pounded the dark hardwood. Straight to the open balcony door overlooking the private sundeck. A wall of lotuses and lush tropical trees obscured the rectangular pool from view. Celeste Ayi sprawled across an oversized canopy bed. A sunhat with a brim wide enough to umbrella an entire building hid her face. She sipped a tropical cocktail, turning a page of the *Vogue* in her lap.

I descended one of the double stairs from the balcony, stopping a foot shy of her. The assistant raced after me, but I was taller, faster, and fueled by enough fury to last a lifetime.

"Zhao Yu Ting."

She peered up from the magazine, not even remotely surprised to see me. "Zachary. My favorite nephew."

"Your *only* nephew."

She waved her hand, flipping a page. "Don't remind me. You know I love the variety. How was the flight here?"

She didn't even ask how I knew they were there. These women knew I'd hunt them down to get the information I wanted. I considered hounding Ayi for it, but now that I'd arrived, my bloodthirst wanted it straight from the horse's mouth.

My jaw ticked. "Where's Mom?" I was dog-tired, jet-lagged, and hadn't spoken to Farrow in almost a month.

With a sigh, Celeste Ayi unfastened the satin knot holding her hat, depositing it beside her. She tilted her sunglasses down, catching my gaze. "You do not want to speak to your mother right now."

"Why not?"

"Why?" She huffed, slapping a hand to her throat. "Well, isn't the answer obvious? She thinks you're about to make the worst mistake of your life."

"Is this about embarrassing the family? Because my entire family consists of three people. Myself included."

"Nonsense. We have extended family. There are at least two hundred of us." She shot up, side-eyeing the poor assistant behind me as if she'd expected her to fight me off with fists. "And no. She thinks you'll die a gruesome death if you don't marry someone willing to listen to every safety instruction she provides. Remember when Natalie's brain short-circuited, and she bought your Stefano Riccis from the mall instead of straight from the flagship? Your mom slipped red ginseng into your tea for a week. She feared you'd die of complications from hand, foot, and mouth disease."

I followed her inside to the kitchen. "You're shitting me."

For the most part, I always figured her anxiety stemmed from the sudden violent death of her husband... but Mom genuinely thought I'd croak if I wore the wrong shoes?

"Would I lie to you?"

"Yes. All the damn time."

I'd spent every year of preschool believing all the toy stores in Potomac had gone up in flames, just because my aunt preferred spending time at the mall than babysitting me.

"Maybe." Ayi shrugged. She didn't actually care. "But I'm not lying about this, Zachary. Falling in love is like swimming too far from the shore. The moment you realize the danger you're in, it's too late. It's safer not to swim at all."

"Mom thinks this?"

"Ask her yourself. You never bothered."

I froze, realizing she had a point. The idea of discussing anything serious with Mom made me want to change my name and move to Alaska. Not as if I felt the cold anyway. Well, pre-Farrow. "Forcing me into a loveless marriage isn't about our legacy?"

"Legacy? Reputation?" Ayi waved a hand, flicking on the espresso machine. "I'm impressive enough to carry on the legacies of every family in Chiang Mai. We don't need a Fortune 100 CEO to do that. Anyone ever tell you you're a bit boring? If anything, *that's* dragging down our reputation."

"You're stalling." I snatched the cup from her, sloshing brown liquid all over the counter as I set it down. "And I'm not leaving. May as well tell me where Mom is."

"*Ugh.*" She rolled her eyes, debating between the jackfruit, longan, and lychee on the counter. "Getting a facial in the master. Don't tell her I pointed you in her direction."

"Thank you, Ayi."

"You're welcome, sha haizi."

I treaded down the vast corridor, knocking on the master bedroom door. No response. I rattled it louder this time. A sigh came from the other side.

"If it's my son, I'm not here. If it's room service, leave it at the door."

She was about to get served, all right. A nice dose of reality. I pushed the heavy door open, coming face-to-face with my mother. She laid flat on her stomach on a massage table as two young female masseuses served her. A towel shielded her—thankfully—as she typed on her laptop in front of her. *Meditation, my ass.* This woman sought peace like I sought more sex-addicted friends (sorry, Ollie).

To the sight of her only child, Mom snapped her laptop shut with a frown. "Oh." She rose to a sitting position, shooing away the women. "It's you."

"Mom." I opened my arms, feigning a smile. Meanwhile, my anger spiked at her impromptu trip while my life was crumbling to ashes. "So happy to see you."

She crossed her legs, bringing her glass to her lips and sipping through a straw. "It wounds me to the core that you aren't happy to see your mother."

I circled the massage table, zeroing in on her face. "It wounds me to the core that you've chosen to ruin any chance of happiness in my life."

She choked on the water, coughing as her eyes snapped up to meet mine. I never confronted her before. I was always cordial, understanding, and obedient. My way of apologizing for killing her husband.

Mom set her cup down. "Excuse me?"

"You are, in fact, not excused." I sat on a bench under the window overlooking the pool. This would be a long talk. "Since Dad died, I've tried to be the perfect son to compensate for killing him."

"You didn't kill him—"

"I did, and we know it. His side of the car remained mostly undamaged after the accident. If he stayed there, he'd be alive. That rake should've pierced my chest, not his."

She swallowed, turning away. Nothing she could say in the face of the ugly truth.

"After you snapped out of your grief—"

"I haven't." She shrugged her robe on, staring off into the wall. "I haven't snapped out of my grief."

"Fair enough." I believed it, because neither had I. "After you became functional again," I corrected, "Ayi and I agreed not to rock the boat. We didn't want to trigger a relapse."

"I'm not broken." She crossed her arms, still too stubborn to admit what had happened. "There's nothing wrong with me."

I ignored her, edging forward toward the nightstand. "At the time, I didn't know that signing this unwritten contract would condemn me to a life of following unreasonable demand after unreasonable demand. Not because I agreed with them, but because I needed to atone for my sin."

"You're not a sinner." She brought her index fingers to her temples, massaging. "There's no sin to atone for."

"There is, but I'm done atoning for it. I'm not marrying Eileen."

Mom hopped off the massage table. "Eileen is safe."

"Eileen isn't for me."

In fact, Eileen is more suitable for a career in Witness Protection.

"And *that* woman is?" Mom rounded on me and stubbed her finger in her chest. "Since the accident, I rearranged my entire life to make sure you're safe. That nothing like the crash ever happens again. That you ate the safest food, spent time with the safest crowds, drove the safest cars. And look at you now. You're alive."

"Yes, I'm alive. But I'm also miserable."

Well, before Farrow...

"Where is this coming from?" Mom scrunched her nose as if I was a service provider she no longer wished to deal with. But I saw through her. I'd hit a nerve. "This is just pre-wedding jitters. They'll subside after the wedding."

I raised my palm to stop her, shaking my head. We stood face-to-face. So close I could smell the faint perfume that always clung to her skin. Of coconut oil and cherry blossom.

"I'm breaking off the engagement. End of discussion. That's not why I gave this little speech. I just didn't want you to feel blindsided."

She pressed her lips into a hard line. "Blindsided by what?"

I had never seen her like this. So completely red, the skin on her neck jagged, like she was having an allergic reaction to our conversation.

"By the fact that I'm cutting ties with you, should you refuse to accept the end of my engagement."

"*What?*" Her eyes bulged out of their sockets. "You can't do that. I'm your mother."

She put her hand on my shoulder. I tore it off me. I genuinely hoped that she'd come to her senses. It brought me no pleasure to sever our relationship. At the end of the day, she did what she did because her husband died, just as I'd shied away from skin, rain, and cars after losing Dad.

"You forfeited the right to identify yourself as such when you emotionally blackmailed me into marrying someone you knew I didn't love. I accept my responsibility in letting you do that, but make no mistake—I will never let your fears dictate my happiness again."

Or my own trauma, for that matter.

Mom floundered, searching for words to say and coming up short.

I collected her phone off the nightstand and waved it, certain Eileen's location resided inside. "Oh, and *that woman's* name is Farrow. And I plan on making her my wife."

Since I'd said what I had come to say, I pivoted, headed to the door. The thud of my loafers echoed in the eerie silence. Suddenly, a set of feet joined them.

"You can't cut ties with me." Mom tried to grip the sleeve of my shirt. Sweat seeped into the fabric from her clammy paws. "And you certainly cannot marry that woman."

I swiveled in the corridor, baring my teeth at her. "I've made my decision."

This time, I picked up pace. She yelped, running after me. We passed by Celeste Ayi in the living room, who cocked her head, curious. I flung the exit open and started down the stairs when I heard my mother squeak behind me.

"Wait."

Nothing in me wanted to turn and give her the time of day, especially considering the looming deadline. Still, I swiveled on my feet, anyway, watching her at the top of the stairs. She clutched the lapels of her robe, her other hand braced against the doorframe. As if she couldn't keep herself up on her feet.

I tightened my grip on her stolen phone. "What?"

"I can't…" She closed her eyes. Then, silence.

I glanced at my watch. "Can't what?" I needed to end the engagement with Eileen as soon as possible.

"Can't…" Mom's eyes shot open. Wide and bulging. She looked surprised for a second, as though she'd seen something she hadn't expected to see.

"Out with it, Mom."

But instead of answering me, she collapsed on top of her legs, like a fawn trying to take its first step, tumbled down to the floor, and died.

CHAPTER EIGHTY-EIGHT

Zach

T-Minus 3 Days.

There was good news and bad news.

The good news was that my mother did not die. Good for my conscience, good for her health, positive all the way around.

The bad news was that I currently sat in a Chiang Mai hospital with a canceled ticket back to the States, waiting for Mom to wake up after a heart attack she'd experienced, courtesy of yours truly.

"I told you not to confront her about Eileen. You almost killed her." Celeste Ayi paced the small room, wearing Chanel head to toe, online shopping on the phone in her hand. "Aw, I think I just found a pair of Moda Operandi Louboutins. No one will know they're secondhand, right?"

I sat by Mom's bed, staring at my phone screen. "The doctors said it was a mini heart attack."

I'd found Eileen's location on Mom's phone a couple hours ago and booked a seat on every flight back for the next week, just in case. Just in case Mom took her time waking up. And in case I couldn't find a private charter. There was no way in hell I'd go through the unique experience of economy again.

"Well, yes, but who's going to stay with her until she gets discharged?" Celeste Ayi stopped in front of the window, still hunting for designer steals. "*Me*. And I have a busy Christmas season. I was invited to lots of events."

"No, you weren't."

"Fine, I wasn't. But I was invited as people's plus one."

I set my phone on the stand next to the hospital bed, tapping it with my finger. To say I did not care about my aunt's social commitments was putting it mildly. The more I thought about it, the harder I found it to regret confronting Mom about marriage. Sure, I didn't want her here. And sure, it was easy to think that when I knew her life was not in actual danger. But I'd finally ended the cycle. We could move on from here. Maybe even return to our old relationship. Before Dad died.

Celeste Ayi stopped pacing and turned to me. "Zachary?"

"Yes?"

"Do you think I should go bring myself a bag? I'll be staying here for a long time, after all."

"That's a good idea. I expect to leave here in the next five hours."

I needed to, in fact, if I wanted to catch Farrow.

"Do you want anything from the hotel?" Celeste slid her phone into her Birkin. "Snacks? Toiletries? Manners?"

"I'm good on all fronts." I waved her off, staring at my screen, waiting for a call back from the private charter company. "Other than manners. But frankly, I simply cannot bring myself to care."

Celeste Ayi twisted one corner of her mouth, stopping at the door before she walked off. She gave me a long, hard stare. "You've changed."

"How so?"

"You became..." She contemplated the right word. "*Human*."

"Okay."

She shrugged. "I don't hate it, you know."

"I don't care."

CHAPTER EIGHTY-NINE

Zach
T-Minus 2 Days.

Two hours.

My flight would take off in two hours. Straight to Italy, where Eileen resided in a luxurious estate owned by Celeste Ayi's second ex-husband. I intended to break off the engagement with her, taking no more than seven minutes, then hopping on the jet back to Potomac with a little under twenty-four hours left to spare.

I stared at the still vision of Mom, her eyes closed, her skin pale and lusterless. She looked like she'd aged a couple centuries. And yet, she also seemed at peace. Finally relaxed, unburdened by the weight of our loss.

Mom's eyes moved left and right beneath their lids. I leaned forward, elbows on my knees as I watched her. The nurses had pumped her with drugs, full to the brim with painkillers to combat the broken rib the paramedic on site had given her. She was probably higher than inflation.

Her eyes fluttered open in the dark room. The machine hooked up to her continued its steady beats. I didn't know what a good son would do in this moment. I didn't have much experience in that department. If the roles were reversed and Farrow hovered over my hospital bed, I'd want her to hold my hand.

Still, I kept mine to my side. After all, I'd *just* threatened to cut Mom off, should she contest my relationship with Octi.

"You're in the hospital." I sat back, realizing I did, indeed, feel a substantial amount of relief to see her wake up. "How are you feeling?"

Mom darted her tongue to lick her lips. A grunt escaped instead, the movement too tasking for her current state. She squeezed her eyes shut. "Been better." I didn't say anything. Mom inhaled, as if trying to make sure she could. "What happened to me?"

"A mini heart attack." I slipped my hands into my pockets. "Very mild, according to the doctors. You're currently at Chiang Mai's best private health institution with around-the-clock supervision. Celeste Ayi is at the hotel, packing up a bag. They want you to stay for five days to monitor your heart rate and put you through some general checkups."

"Then why do I feel so... *woozy*?" She swallowed and winced, like the mere movement delivered excruciating pain. "And in terrible pain?"

"The medics performed CPR at the villa. The chest compressions broke a rib. It's more painful than dangerous. In fact, it's not dangerous at all. Just a discomfort. You can pump more painkillers with this button if you'd like." I took her hand and guided it to a white remote tucked in the corner of her bed.

Mom gasped a little. Her mouth tumbled open. She almost squealed when I touched her.

"Sorry." I drew back. "Did it hurt?"

"N-no." She shook her head, staring at me, mesmerized. "I just... you touched me, Zach. You never touch anyone. Not since your father passed away."

"Farrow taught me skin-to-skin." I smiled, somewhere between bitter and nostalgic. "There was a lot of trial and error."

Awkward moments.

Joyful moments.

And I cherished every single one of them.

Tears hung from the tips of her lower lashes. "Can I..." Her hands shook all over. "Can I hold your hand? I've always wanted to."

But she didn't wait for permission. She clasped my palm and laced our fingers together. Dry, cold skin met mine. I remained utterly still as she brought the back of my hand to her icy chapped lips, pressing a kiss to my knuckles.

An unpleasant tremor rolled through me, but I didn't cower, nor did I retreat. Didn't want to hurl myself into the shower and jack up the temperature to that of a boiling kettle. Guess I was cured. Funny, how I'd always imagined all my problems would go away if I just learned how to touch. It never occurred to me that touching came hand-in-hand with feelings. And the only person whose touch I craved was thousands of miles away, on a different continent, probably picking a fight with a crocodile just to show herself that she could.

Mom began full-out bawling.

"She did this?" I could barely make out her hoarse whisper. "She made you touch again?"

"Yes."

You have no idea. She taught me more than I could ever hope to learn.

"But… how?"

The news must've broken a piece of her brain. She'd sunk an entire mega-mansion down payment into psychologists, therapists, doctors, and even hypnotists. Specialists from all over the world. The best in their fields. None of them had ever managed to help me. Not even a little.

"It's simple." I drew my hand from her grip. "She made touching her utterly irresistible. She showed me warmth, and courage, and a passion for life I've never seen before. She made me forget about work. About empty achievements. She made me…" I flashed back to my time with Farrow. A small smile formed on my lips. "She made me eat junk food. And drink shitty beer."

"Oh, Zachary." Mom sounded equal parts appalled and amused. "That is extremely unpalatable." She paused, the makings of a grin starting to spread. "But did it make you happy?"

"It made me thrilled. Before Farrow, I'd forgotten how to be happy. I would give anything to bring her back."

Mom peered down at her blanketed legs. A wrinkle creased the gap between her brows. The woman who tore through thousand-dollar face masks had aged a decade in mere hours. She looked helpless against the world.

"I need to tell you something, Zachary."

I stared at her in silence. I hadn't lied when I'd told Farrow I thought someone in the universe was messing with me. My flight would leave in ninety-seven minutes. The countdown ticked by the second. Meanwhile, I sat in the middle of a deathbed confession, sans the deathbed. Such a cruel trick from fate that, despite endless opportunities to have this discussion at home, we'd chosen to debate weather and stocks over bland lunches.

"What is it?"

"I…" Mom brought her fist to her lips to suppress a cough. Blue-and-purple veins ran on the back of her hand like a familiar map. "I respect Farrow for handling the way I treated her well."

"Beyond the attempted bribe?"

Yes, I'd witnessed that. Through the bay windows on Farrow's first day. The sight of her declining the check had stirred curiosity in me.

"Yes. A few petty tricks to get her off your back." Mom stared at her covered feet. "She fended them off well."

"She's strong like that."

Perhaps I should've been angry. I wasn't. For starters, I expected it. In fact, I'd anticipated worse. Secondly, Farrow Ballantine could hold her own. She thrived on tiny victories. It would be pointless to fight every battle for her when everything that made Octi the woman I loved could be summed up with her heart. Strong, vibrant, steel-coated, and warm.

Mom paused. "She declined the money, by the way."

"I know."

"Her deal with you was probably more lucrative than what I offered."

"I know that, too."

"And you don't find her to be a gold digger?"

"No." I left no room for doubt in my voice. Question answered. Case closed. If she pressed, I'd make good on my threat and leave. Permanently.

"I don't think she's a gold digger either." Mom fingered the cannula in her hand, not meeting my eyes. "But that's not my point."

I checked my watch, unhinged by the prospect of missing my flight and ruining any chances with my feisty little *not*-gold digger. "What *is* your point?"

"That you could do worse." She didn't dare look at me. "I think Eileen is lying to you."

"About?"

"Her personality, her aversion to touching, pieces of her history. Take your pick."

It didn't come as a shock. Mostly because I'd already placed her on the top of my shit list for the crime of refusing to be broken up with when we were never even in a real relationship. Any extra negative trait could only be considered a bonus.

"It doesn't make a difference. The engagement was always a sham. I have no intention of marrying her. The better question is why you would let your son marry a liar."

"Because she molded her life around yours. Someone willing to do that is someone willing to keep you safe."

"I don't need to be safe."

I was finally realizing that. With each touch. Each rainfall. Each god-awful drive in that death-trap Prius. Every time I held myself back, I became smaller as a person. There was as much risk in taking leaps as there was in not leaping at all.

"You do." She shot forward, not quite managing to shout *or* move where she wanted to, but I knew she would if she could. "You are the only thing left in my world. I love no one more than I love you. Don't you realize that?"

"No shit, I do."

She didn't even admonish me for my language, too busy driving her point into me. "You need to be safe. Your dad would want you alive and happy."

"I *will* be happy. So long as I have Farrow. As for alive…" I paused, diving my fingers into my hair. "I can't promise to be perfect in every single moment, but I've certainly learned that life is valuable." *And not through Oliver's so-called lesson.* "I won't take unnecessary risks. But make no mistake—I won't cower in fear, either."

The *tap-tap* of my heel against the tiles startled me. I hadn't realized how upset the prospect of cutting Mom off made me. Truly, before the accident, we shared an incredible bond. Every time I saw Mom behave like a stranger, latent childhood memories pried at my mind, cracking apart my anger. Late night movies. Surprise arcade dates. Make-your-own dumpling nights. Even Romeo wanted to move into our house. Granted, he had other reasons.

I waited with baited breath for Mom's response.

Let me live my life the way I want. Be happy for me.

She lowered her chin into her neck. "What will it take for you not to cut me out?" On cue, the beeps from the heart rate monitor drummed faster, picking up speed.

I answered immediately. "Accept the end of my engagement."

"Done."

"Accept Farrow." This time, I collected her hand in mine, setting it on my palm. "And eventually, love her like your own daughter. She's never had a family, Mom." I looped my fingers with hers. "She's never held a mother's hand. I promise, when you get to know her, *really* get to know her, you'll love her as much as I do."

With her free hand, Mom traced the seam where our palms touched, almost transfixed. "Do you really love her?"

"Yes." No hesitation. Just the easy truth. "I am utterly deranged when she's not here."

Mom squeezed my hand after a moment, dragging her eyes up to mine. "Deal."

"Also…"

She leaned her head back on the pillow, lips forming around a groan. "There's more?"

"Last thing. Promise." *And the thing you might resist most.* "I want you to seek help. For your anxiety."

"I don't have anxiety."

"You do."

"I refuse to take pills."

"There are other methods, but if a doctor recommends them and pills are the best option, I need to know you'll do everything to get better. At the very least, I want you to speak to someone qualified to help you."

The heart rate monitor went wild. She shook her head. "But—"

"I need all or nothing, Mom."

"Fine." She heaved out a breath, staring off to the side for a moment. Finally, she returned her gaze to me. "I see you staring at your watch every ten seconds. Take the jet. Go get your wife, Zachary."

CHAPTER NINETY

Farrow
T-Minus 1 Day.

*T*his will be where I die.

In the sacred, never-before-seen art gallery no one was ever allowed to enter. Splayed across the lifeless epoxy floor. Surrounded by priceless art. Blood splatters camouflaged by the creepy black-and-red Jackson Pollock.

At the very least, I couldn't find a single alternate explanation for why Zachary Sun had sent me down to his creepy subterranean garage. Over the weeks, I'd cataloged every item Romeo and Oliver brought to my studio. Nothing went missing, and I didn't own anything else. No way did he just want me here to show me all the things I'd never own.

I crept out of the elevator, half-expecting something to jump out at me. The electronic key spat back out from a slot on the other side, eliciting a startled yelp from me.

"Welcome, Miss Ballantine."

And another yelp, courtesy of the robotic AI voice at the entrance.

Two glass double doors slid open, inviting me into the main space. If this were the night of his bridal hunt, no way could I ever have broken into this fortress. Projectors lit up white arrows on the floor. They led to the furthest end of the gallery. So deep, I couldn't even make out anything beyond a blur.

"Please, follow the guided path."

I stepped on an arrow, keeping my feet directly on the column, as if it were a wooden plank on a rope bridge. One wrong step and *vamoosh*. The thought of swerving out of line and breaking a five-million-dollar masterpiece pricked the back of my mind as I strolled past statues, paintings, divots, and corridors, too focused on my steps to soak it all in.

Once I reached the last arrow, I dared to glance up. Dozens of boxes, tubes, and racks scattered across the otherwise empty section of the gallery.

"Please, collect your belongings, Miss Ballantine."

I pointed to myself, feeling fifty shades of ridiculous. "Me?"

"Yes."

"Oh."

I hadn't expected an answer. Nor had I planned for this, for that matter. In fact, I'd need a moving truck and a crew to get all of this out. Still, curiosity got the better of me. I fingered a random suede box, tugging off the lid. My knees gave out a little. Something golden swam in a sea of red satin.

No way.

I snatched it in an instant, reeling it closer to admire. "Dad's pinky ring."

A pure gold behemoth. Naturally, Vera had auctioned it off with the first batch of his valuables two years ago. I slid it onto my thumb. Still loose, but I decided to wear it at all costs.

The robotic voice interrupted the moment. "Mr. Sun repatriated Mr. Ballantine's belongings."

That spurred me into action. I raced to the art rack. Dad's replica paintings took up thirty or so rows, sorted alphabetically. Even Da Vinci's *Salvator Mundi*. Slotted in a gallery-grade sorting rack as if the replica deserved as much care as Zach's billion-dollar collection.

Zachary Sun had managed to collect every item Vera ever sold off. The Rolex, the gems, the antique china.

Oh, my God.

Oh, my God.

It must have taken so much time and effort. When did he start planning this? *Why* did he start planning this? I couldn't wipe the goofy grin from my lips even if I tried. I didn't *want* to. To think I'd spent the past thirty days so scared of that damn key.

Such a coward, Fae. You should've known better. The best gifts are wrapped in the way you least expect.

I tipped my head back, scanning the corners of the room until I spotted a camera. A flashing red light blinked at me. I waved back. "Thank you, Zach. Truly."

Then, I ran to another box, popping the lid off with a giddy bounce. A mosaic sculpture of two lovebirds that used to occupy the nightstand beside Dad and Vera's bed. He'd obsessed over this piece during their fourth honeymoon in Venice. This one came with a letter from the reseller. I slid the heavy cardstock out of the envelope.

Mr. Sun,

I do not appreciate being threatened to fork over what amounts to a penny in your wealth of art. In the future, should you wish to pilfer my far more modest collection, I suggest a polite exchange.

Regards,

William St. Eve

P.S. Did you gain such an expansive collection by threatening every collector on the globe? Kamran Izadi recently informed me that you commandeered a Lobster Telephone replica from his home, as well.

I squealed, heels squeaking across the garage as I raced from box to box, trying to find it. When I finally unearthed the lobster, I brought it to my chest, twirling in circles. "I always wanted it for my own room."

"Did you say something, Miss Ballantine?"

I ignored the robot voice, a lone stand catching my eye. A hand-carved box I didn't recognize sat on top of it. Heart in my throat, I popped the lid off, gasping at its contents. The pendant. There, in all its glory. With its lush green tassel and hand-carved lion. I pushed my hair from my face, squinting to make sure I saw it right. It really was here. Down to the crooked trimmed tassel, courtesy of yours truly.

I brought the pendant to my lips, sealing it with a kiss. My eyes caught on a hand-written note, wedged in the roof of the box.

I'm a greedy bastard, Farrow Ballantine. That you're enough for me says it all. — Z

Chapter Ninety-One

Zach

T-Minus 1 Day.

Ever so charitable, the rain added to my misery when I landed in Italy. I descended the stairway without a peacoat, too pressed on time to hunt one down. A driver stood before the open rear door of a Rolls Royce Droptail. I didn't know a lick about him. Didn't deep-dive into a background check. And soon, I'd let this total stranger drive me in the rain. For Farrow, I'd officially broken all my rules.

I waved him away, sliding inside and closing the door myself. "Casa al Mare. 10k if you can get me there in half the time."

Four minutes. The conversation needed to be completed in four minutes. That would give me enough time to fly back to Maryland, change and shower, then track down Farrow. We passed row after row of lush villas. I ignored them all, checking an alert from my security system.

Farrow. In the gallery. Twirling around with random sculptures like a schoolgirl. She finally got the pendant. It only took her thirty fucking days. But it wouldn't be Octi if she didn't push me past my comfort zone.

The Rolls Royce rolled up to a limestone manor, overlooking a private strip of the gulf. I swung the door open and stormed up the cobblestone steps before the car even pulled to a stop. Pachelbel's "Canon in D" blared from somewhere out back. I followed the heavy notes to the oversized terrace, expecting to yank out speakers. Instead, I came face-to-face with a cellist.

He paused, tilting his head at me, lips curled down at the sight of my untamed hair and two-day-old outfit. "Can I help you?"

"If you'd like to continue your music career, I suggest you set down your bow and shut the fuck up."

"Zee Zee." Eileen stretched on a yoga mat, soaring from the staff pose into the mountain pose. "How lovely to see you."

Zee Zee? Of all the worst nicknames I'd ever been called, that topped the list. Above Oliver's Rumpleforeskin and Ayi's Zachy Poo Poo.

I ignored her greeting, strode to the table beside her, and set down my phone, starting the timer.

She paused, pointing at it. "What's that?"

"This conversation needs to be completed in four minutes."

"But—"

"I would say that we're done, Miss Yang, but we never really started." I collected my phone, glancing at the timer. *3 minutes and 56 seconds left.* "That took longer than I expected."

I left behind a gust of wind in my wake as I redirected to the exit. The place was everything I expected from Celeste Ayi's second ex-husband. Gaudy, over-the-top, and dripping with gold. Gold couch. Gold tables. Gold-plated espresso machine.

Eileen chased after me. "Wait. That's *it?*"

I kept walking. "What else is there to say?"

"I don't know?" She waved her hands, jogging now. "Anything."

"Unfortunately, your desperation has rendered me speechless." I slid into the car, sparing her one final thought before I bid her farewell for good. "Keep the fucking ring. Goodbye, Eileen."

CHAPTER NINETY-TWO

Zach
D-Day.
So much for no unnecessary risks.
    A violent storm greeted me near the end of my flight home. I sat at a table, drafting what I planned on saying to Octi. The cabin jostled back and forth, knocking my drink onto my notepad. Iced tea, not scotch. I needed to be sober for this.

The words on the page grew before they blurred together.

Lovely. Not like it mattered. I'd gotten approximately three words written down, stuck on how to convince Farrow to spend the rest of her life with me.

"Mr. Sun?" The flight attendant approached, clinging onto the edge of the table for support. "We're flying through severe turbulence. The captain has advised you to put on your seatbelt."

"Is it safe to fly?"

"I'm sure it is."

"Yes or no answers only."

She fidgeted with her pencil skirt, eyeing the cockpit. "I'll bring back the co-pilot. Just a moment."

As she scurried away, I returned to the bigger problem at hand. I had no experience with people, let alone relationships. Romeo's forced marriage with Dallas could hardly be considered the pinnacle of romance. As for Ollie, his only commitment to date was with his right hand. (And even that could be considered dubious, given the entire wing in his mansion dedicated to sex toys.)

"Mr. Sun?" The co-pilot claimed the seat across from me, propping his tablet up on the stand. "A sudden storm hit our path. We're above Delaware right now." He pointed to a speck on the map. "We may have to travel around the storm and circle in the air until it's safe to land."

404 | *HUNTINGTON & SHEN*

I checked my watch. "Will it add time to the flight?"

"Maybe an hour to travel around the storm. No ETA on how long we'll be circling until visibility thresholds are met and we can land." He zoomed out on the map. "As is, we're a little over thirty minutes until landing. We have enough fuel to hold for ten hours if needed."

I couldn't even afford a minute. According to Romeo, Farrow would be at a fencing competition in a couple hours. I planned on watching the entire thing with her after convincing her to marry me.

I held his gaze, tossing my ruined notepad to the side. "We'll keep on this path."

"We can't. Potomac Airfield contacted us. It's not safe to land there. Or anywhere in the D.C. region, for that matter."

"I need to be in Potomac. *Now.*"

"Our alternative choice is to land now in Delaware. It's about a four-hour drive to Potomac, but there's a storm here as well. The visibility is better but not great."

"Is it safe to land?"

"Safe? Yes." He slanted his head, shaking it a bit. "Comfortable? No."

"Let's do it."

At least driving would guarantee I'd arrive before the event ended. I couldn't take the risk of not making it at all.

The co-pilot still loitered.

"Why are you still here?" I arched a brow. "You have a plane to fly."

Not well, apparently, because minutes later, it plummeted headfirst. I swung forward, grunting as my stomach dug into the desk.

The flight attendant rushed to my side and double-checked my seatbelt, yanking hard on the loop. Another violent shake sent her flying into the chair across from me. She dragged herself into a sitting position, fighting every cruel jolt.

"Keep your seatbelt on, Mr. Sun."

No shit.

I flipped the window up, staring into the abyss. White confetti swept by in a blizzard of alabaster and gray. Midway into our descent, the snow transformed into rain. Heavy drops smashed against the glass.

"Is it always like this?" The stewardess white-knuckled her armrest, dropping her head back. "I'm only three months into this job. This is my first storm."

I ignored her, fighting to keep upright as the plane tossed us round and round like a blender. The co-pilot's tablet tumbled from the table to the carpet, triggering its playlist. "I Want to Hold Your Hand" by The Beatles. A vicious lurch slammed my head into the wall. The song switched. "Bookends" by Simon & Garfunkel. The same song playing when Dad died.

Suddenly, I couldn't hear my own thoughts.

Cars honking. Rain pouring. The sword and octopus on the window.

Another sharp jounce.

The pendant.

I flew up in my seat, landing back down with a thump.

Souls are priceless, Zach. Try to protect yours any way you can.

I tucked my chin into my chest, battling the turbulence. "I'm trying, Dad."

One day, you'll learn to appreciate beautiful things.

"I did, Dad. Her name in Farrow."

More honks. Star-crossed lovers. A horn.

I'd finally learned to appreciate beautiful things, and I would die in the air before I ever got to see her again.

Dad's wide eyes. His torso colliding with mine. Drip, drip, drip.

The plane dropped quick, slicing through rain.

You're okay, Zachary. You're fine.

"I'm not, Dad." I dug my fingers into the handles, almost tearing them off with my nails. "We're dropping too fast."

The rake. The blood. The knife.

I didn't want to remember any of this.

Dad's lips moving. His single tear. His last words.

We slammed into the runway with a huge *thunk*. My hand flew off the rest, smacking into the window. Rain shot from the sky like bullets. The plane slowed to a crawl, but I lowered my head to my knees, brows crushed together.

His last words, his last words, his last words.

"What are you saying, *dammit?*"

The flight attendant unbuckled, sprinting to me. She rested a hand on my back. "Are you okay, Mr. Sun?"

"*No.*"

I finally remembered Dad's last words.

CHAPTER NINETY-THREE

Zach
D-Day.
Nature: 3. Zach Sun: 0.

It took five hours to reach the sporting arena. Five hours in a shitty rental car held together by Gorilla Glue and prayers. I hadn't showered or changed in three days, forgetting my luggage in Chiang Mai. It seemed particularly cruel that, for someone who forbade staff from wearing scented products, I had to suffer through five fucking hours of my own stench.

In the last thirty-minute stretch, the heater died a cruel death. The temperature plummeted to forty degrees within minutes. I still hadn't found a damn coat. I slugged through rain, knuckles the color of milk, hoping to hell I'd make it before the competition ended.

The arena sign glistened in the downpour like a beacon. Thousands of cars filled the lot from end to end. With no chance at finding a spot, I parked in a tow zone right out front, slamming the door behind me.

"She better be here."

It would be just my luck to be misdirected by a horrible game of telephone. I'd gotten Fae's location from Romeo, who had gotten her location from Dallas, who had gotten her location from Hettie, who had gotten her location from Frankie, whom I considered as reliable as the pull-out method.

I shoved my entire wallet into the ticket booth and stormed past the barrier without waiting. The contents of my inner suit pocket smacked my chest with each step. My right loafer fell off as I tore through the halls like a bull. I didn't have time to pick it up. A child darted out of my path. He dropped his cotton candy, crying at the sight of me. I could only assume how I looked. Cheeks flushed pink from being frozen just shy of frostbite. Lips set in a firm line. Hair dancing with the wind. Truly, Farrow had chosen the worst season to cure me. *So fucking cold.*

The corridor bled into the arena, where thousands of people cheered from stadium seats. I would never find her in this crowd.

"Attention: the final match begins in three minutes."

The words echoed from speakers in every corner. It came from a booth at the edge of the bleachers. I marched over, snatched the mic from the horrified announcer, and paraded to the center of the piste, too determined to process any embarrassment.

I tapped the mic. "Farrow Ballantine?"

The buzz of the crowd lulled before picking up again. A row of uniformed fencers halted a few feet away, staring at me through masks. One of them nudged another and pointed at me with the tip of a sword.

"Farrow." I spun one-eighty, trying to spot her in the sea of faces. "Are you there?"

"The fuck are you doing?" It came from a random dude in the stadium.

I worked a thumb over my jaw, speaking into the mic through gritted teeth. "The fuck I'm doing is trying to get my girl back."

The crowd erupted in pandemonium. Most hollered. Some jeered. And I'd officially run out of fucks to give.

"Good Lord, that man is fine." A woman whistled. "Dress me up like an ice cream cone, and let me lick him."

I'd become a laughingstock in the span of a minute, and *fuck it.* I didn't want to extend an olive branch. I wanted to give Farrow Ballantine the whole damn tree.

"Farrow..." I pulled my shoulders back, gazing into the throngs of faceless people. "Our entire relationship has been a secret. Tucked in the dark alleys of our lives. No more. Whether you accept me or reject me, I am done pretending I'm not yours."

"Hey, man." Another damn heckler. "Where is your shoe?"

The entire audience laughed.

I carried on, ignoring them. "I spent my entire adult life living without actually living. You blazed into my life so unexpected. A breath of fresh air. You taught me how to move on, how to overcome my past, and how to *live.* I can *touch* again."

Someone catcalled. More snickers. Maybe I should've cared about revealing my secret to the world, but I didn't. Getting Farrow back mattered more.

"Just now, I drove five hours in the rain in a shitty rental, and I didn't pull over, didn't vomit, didn't stop. That's all you, Octi." I pivoted, facing the other half of the crowd, covering my bases. "I'm sorry I didn't see it sooner. That I didn't make you my priority the minute I met you. You deserve so much more."

I gripped the microphone harder. My vision blurred. I was running on approximately six hours of sleep, spread across four days. "Remember when you told me about the *Lobster Telephone*? You were right. Everyone has a favorite work of art. You're mine."

Silence. Every person in the entire arena had gone utterly silent. Where the hell was Farrow?

Dammit. I'm going to burn all your credit cards, Frankie.

"Excuse me?" An official tapped on my shoulder, shuffling from foot to foot. She toyed with the end of her ponytail. "We have a match right now."

"Postpone it."

"But—"

I glared at her until she scurried away. Alone again, I swung to the other half of the stadium, adjusting my grip on the mic. "Farrow, I tried to fight the spell you put me under. I lied to myself. I lied to *you*. Life is messy. Love is risky. And I was perfectly safe in my sterile bubble."

I didn't care that I had a faceless audience. Didn't care that I was pouring my heart out. For once, I needed to be courageous with my heart.

I sucked in a breath. "I didn't want to admit that I didn't have total control over myself. But it's true. I don't." I gestured down at my unkempt state as proof. "I am so uncontrollably mad for you. Since I met you, there hasn't been a single day that's passed where every second isn't consumed by thoughts of you."

At my words, a single fencer among the row of competitors edged back. *Farrow.* Her shoulders began shaking, rattling her whole frame. She looked so much skinnier in her uniform, so slight, I barely recognized her. It never occurred to me that her month of soul searching would be so hard on her. Dallas had assured me, over and over again, that she was thriving.

My heart sank to the pit of my stomach. The sight of her crying unleashed chaos in me.

I strode to her, snatching up her gloved hand. "I didn't have the chance to grab the engagement ring from home, but I brought this."

When I pulled back, her arms crossed over her stomach, shoulders still shaking.

I reached into my inner suit pocket and produced a beatdown, torn-apart sneaker. The one she'd left behind all those months ago. The crowd began clamoring again, whispers snaking down to us.

"Is that a shoe?"

"Maybe he should find his own shoe first."

"Ew. That thing belongs in hazmat containment."

I ignored the noise, got down on one knee, and collected Fae's hand again, speaking into the microphone to silence the stadium. "I know the world is awful, and ugly, and tiring. I know it hurt you, betrayed you, and shattered your soul. But if there is any ounce of love left in you, would it be selfish of me to ask for it? I promise I'll protect it. I promise I'll protect you." I squeezed her hand through the heavily padded glove. "I love you, Farrow Ballantine. Will you marry me?"

From the seats, a tiny black dog sprinted to us and snatched the shoe out of my hand, running in circles with it clamped between its molars. *Little shit.*

"Did you say love?"

I snapped my head up at the voice, spinning around when I realized it had come from behind me. Farrow Ballantine stood before me in all her glory. Beautiful, and breathtaking, and glowing, and *mine*. She wore flushed cheeks, a sheepish smile, and a coaching uniform draped over with an ID lanyard. For the first time in a month, I felt alive again.

"*Octi.*"

The fencer I'd mistaken for Farrow tore off his mask, revealing a skinny preteen with his face painted in a grimace. "Sorry, bro. One second, I was laughing. And the next, you stormed over here." He shrugged, backing away. "You just grabbed my hand, dude. I didn't know what to do."

In the distance, Oliver's distinct laughter pierced the moment. The crowd remained silent, eager to catch our conversation, now that I had ditched the mic.

Farrow collected my hand, intertwining our fingers. "Did you say love?"

Despite the near frostbite, all I could feel was warmth.

I cupped her cheeks, bringing our foreheads together, breathing her in. "I'm madly in love with you, Farrow. You have completely consumed me. Heart, body, and soul. There's no one else. Never has been. Never will be."

"Zach…" She glanced down at the piste, then peered up at me beneath a curtain of impossibly long lashes. "What is this?"

I rubbed the back of my neck. "A declaration of love. A groveling scheme. And… a marriage proposal?"

For the first time since the accident, I relinquished control. I was soaring into the unknown without a plan, completely at the whims of Fate, and scared shitless. With only Dad's dying words and the woman of my dreams to accompany me. I'd never felt so damn alive.

"You do realize this is so unlike you."

"I do."

"And that everyone in the state will know about this by the end of the hour."

"I don't care."

"Including your mother."

"She approves of our relationship."

Farrow's lips parted. "She does?"

"I swear it."

At my words, she nodded, processing the news. Finally, she squeezed my hand, staring down at where we joined. "Tell me something about the octopus."

I answered without missing a beat. "The octopus ranks highest in the animal kingdom at camouflage. It can change colors in an instant, contort its own body, and rearrange its arms. That's what you did. You slipped into my life pretending to be a problem and turned out to be my solution. My salvation."

On cue, the dog sprinted over to our heels, dropping Fae's shoe on the piste with a bark. I'd kill the little shit's owner if I weren't so eager to propose to Octi right this second. Dropping to my knee, I collect her ankle, slid her sneaker off, and replaced it with her old shoe she'd left behind. A tiny gasp rushed past her lips.

"Perfect fit. Just like you." I peered up at her, thumbing a circle on her ankle. "Say yes, Farrow."

She sank her teeth into her lower lip, feigning hesitation, but I knew she hid a grin beneath that bite. "Are we endgame now?"

"Baby, we're not only endgame. We're in our own goddamn league. Please, put me out of my misery and say yes."

Our friends—correction: our *family*—materialized at the edge of the piste, shooting out their unsolicited opinions in rapid succession.

Romeo flicked something off his suit. "I'm embarrassed for you, Zachary."

Dallas swatted his shoulder. "Why haven't you confessed your love for me in public?"

"I took a *bullet* for you in public." He turned to Fae, nodding in my direction. "The only way he'll be able to show his face in this town again is if you say yes."

Farrow snorted, her ankle waving in my palms with the movement.

Frankie shoved Romeo out of the way, fighting to get closer to us. "We all know your answer, Fae. Can you hurry it up? He's been a miserable asshole since you left."

"Say yes, girl." Dallas jumped up and down, holding her belly still. "Also, did you know octopus brains are shaped like donuts? Epic."

Fae burst into a fit of giggles. She clutched her stomach, struggling to stay upright with a foot in my hands.

You wouldn't have to struggle so much if you'd just say yes, dammit.

"This is too good." Oliver slow-clapped. "I'm the last bachelor standing. Does this mean I won the bet?"

Hettie stood off to the side, carrying a tub of something in front of her. "Good thing I bought popcorn."

Farrow's fingers curled around her throat. An audible *whoosh* soared past her lips. She admired our friends for another moment before returning her gaze to mine. "You gave me a family."

"I had nothing to do with it." I shook my head. "You earned a family all on your own. They love you."

Her fingers dropped. She pulled back her shoulders, all business now. "If we get married, I expect to maintain my independence."

"Done."

"I'll continue to work full-time. As a coach."

412 | *HUNTINGTON & SHEN*

"Of course."

I knew, firsthand, she'd be the best at it.

"And… and… and…" She brought her fingertip to her lips, thinking hard. "I'll still argue with you constantly. You won't be able to burrow your way back into my good graces with designer bags."

"That's fine. I'll burrow my way back into your good graces with your favorite things."

"And what are those?"

"Hard facts and orgasms."

Farrow sucked in a breath. My heartbeats intensified. Euphoria decanted over me like spring water. My stupid heart swelled to an impossible size, a balloon about to pop.

Say yes, baby girl. Come on.

A grin crept up her cheeks. Laughter danced across her lips. She swallowed it down. Finally—*finally*—she gave me her answer. "*Yes.*"

I shot up, scooped her into my arms, and gave her the deepest, hungriest, realest kiss we'd ever shared. Our friends broke out in cheers, sending the crowd into chaos, too. Everyone around us clapped, whistled, and hollered. Even the asshole dog started running in circles around us, barking.

"Oh." Fae giggled into our kiss, snapping her fingers as she remembered something. "I have a dog now."

"*We* have a dog now." I spoke against her lips, refusing to part. And goddammit, we had a dog now.

"Oliver says you hate messes."

"Only when that mess is Oliver himself."

She pulled back a little. Her thumb traveled to my neck, brushing right beneath my ear. "I figured out why I love you."

Our noses touched. I nuzzled mine against hers as we tried to steady our breaths. "And why is that?

"You're my home."

"I figured out why I love you," I countered.

"And why is that?"

"You make my soul breathe fire, my beautiful dark desire."

EPILOGUE

Zach

One Month Later.

I wake up to an elbow to the ribs. Instead of answering, I spoon Farrow from behind, fanning her hair away from my eyes.

"Babe, are you awake?"

With an exhale, I glance at the clock on the nightstand. Five-fifteen in the morning.

Am I awake? Depends. Am I awake to hear Octi tell me Mom begged her—*again*—to consider a New York wedding, though Fae clearly wants to stay in Potomac? No. That can wait until morning. But am I awake for a third round of taking my fiancée against the shower wall? Why, yes. After all, hygiene *is* my passion.

Farrow reaches for the nightstand and snatches her vibrating phone. Her brows furrow at the screen. "Zach." She elbows me harder, eliciting a small grunt. "Tell me you're awake."

I close my eyes, squeezing her closer to my chest. I have a good guess at what she's about to say, and I don't want to get out of bed for it. In fact, I'd be happy to keep doing what we've been doing the past month. Not leaving the house. Every time Dallas comes to drag Farrow to a girls' night, I fight the urge to hook a donut to a fishing rod and shepherd her back onto the road like a sheep.

"Zach." Octi swivels in my arms, tracing a fingertip down my nose. "Wake up."

I keep my eyelids glued shut.

"This isn't funny."

No response.

"Let's have sex."

My eyes shoot open. I pounce on her, covering every inch of her face with kisses.

"You horn dog." She giggles, wriggling away from my embrace. "Dallas is having the baby. We need to get to the hospital now."

"Why? We weren't the ones to get her pregnant."

I kiss my way down her neck, cupping her breast and bringing the nipple to my mouth. We sleep naked for obvious reasons. There hasn't been a single night where we haven't woken up—sweaty and needy—to have sex, just to remind each other that we can. Now that I no longer fear touching, it's my societal duty to make up for lost time.

Fae rolls away and leaps to her feet. "It's an emergency meeting." I prop my head on my fist, watching her from our bed. She plucks her underwear and bra from the floor. "Dallas said she wants everyone to be there, so we can finalize the name."

"I couldn't care less if she wants to name him after her favorite restaurant." Farrow shoots me a warning glare. My smile drops. "No, she doesn't."

"She does." She winces, striding to the walk-in closet, only to return with an oversized gray sweatshirt and a pair of mom jeans that still somehow make her look like a model. "In her defense, the restaurant's name is Antonio's."

I stare at her, grinning. Just watching her exist is enough to get my rocks off.

She buttons her jeans and tilts her head sideways. "Zachary."

"Ma'am?"

"Put your clothes on. We're going to the hospital."

"I don't even like Dallas," I lie. She's fine, I guess. For a human.

Farrow grabs her backpack, flinging it over her shoulder. "You like me, though."

"I *don't* like you, Farrow Ballantine. I'm fucking obsessed with you."

The steady *beep, beep, beep* of the hospital machines echoes down the corridor of the maternity wing. Fae's sneakers squeak against the linoleum floor. She clutches the box of donuts tighter to her chest, racing faster than the situation requires. I punctuate each of her gallops with an obvious sigh, though I've never been happier in my entire damn life.

Farrow has already knocked on Dallas' suite by the time I slip beside her. Per usual, Dallas and Romeo's greeting makes me want to bleach my ears.

Octi barrels past the door before Romeo even manages to get out, "It's open."

"Just like my vagina, apparently." Dallas plucks her blanket up as if we need visual confirmation. "Hey-yo, third-degree tear."

Kill me now.

Why is this couple so obnoxiously TMI? I can't imagine letting anyone near Farrow so soon after giving birth to my child. But I *can* imagine very vividly a situation where she gives birth to our baby.

"Here." My fiancée deposits the box from Gwenie's Pastries into Dallas' eager arms. "Two dozen shakoy donuts, just like you asked. You look amazing."

She does not look amazing. She looks like she just returned from wrestling a bear. And lost. But I appreciate how Farrow always has a kind word to spare when it comes to the people she loves.

I bro-hug Romeo, a recent but not unwelcome development. "Congrats."

"Thanks, man." I shit you not, the tips of his ears turn red.

I peer around the spacious room. "Speaking of, where's the baby?"

"The nurses took him to give me some time off." Dallas shoves a shakoy down her throat. "He'll be right back, so we can all see him and choose a name." She boomerangs upright, tossing the donut into Romeo's chest in order to clap. "I shortlisted it to thirty."

Yay me. This will be a long day.

Romeo goes rigid, his palm stopping mid-brush above his crumby shirt. "*All?*"

With perfect timing, Oliver and Franklin burst through the door without knocking. They wear matching states of dishevelment. Messy hair. Wrinkled clothes. A streak of red lipstick runs down to Frankie's chin. My first assumption, of course, is the horizontal tango. My second is the more unhinged—and therefore, probably correct—option.

And surely enough, a chirp blasts through the air.

No, they did not.

Dallas shovels donuts into her mouth, too busy to notice the state of her two visitors. "Hey, guys. Thanks for coming."

Ollie tucks his shirt into his slacks, clearing his throat. "Pleasure's mine." Nobody other than Dallas misses *that* innuendo.

Farrow sends me a horrified WTF look. For good reason. Oliver and Frankie are a bad idea. Not only is she scandalously younger than him, but they also both have zero morals or principles. These two fiends would set the entire world on fire if they feel like frying a steak.

Luckily, it's as I expected, and Frankie produces a jar filled with holes from behind her back, setting it on a coffee table across the room. "Sorry, we're late. We caught these all by ourselves."

Oliver flicks grass off his shoulder. "Almost died wrestling one of them."

Frankie collapses onto the sofa, hand over her forehead. "Zach told us crickets are a symbol of luck and a good omen for lots and lots of children."

"I didn't say to catch them." I push Ollie away with a single index finger when his mud-crusted ass weasels by a little too close for comfort. See? Passionate about hygiene.

Oliver peeks under the hospital bed. "Where's the little addition to the family?"

Romeo dusts crumbs from his shirt with one hand and strokes Dallas' head with the other. "On his way."

Frankie rushes to the mini fridge in the corner, plucking two water bottles from inside. She waves at her face. "My gosh. Am I the only one who's super hot?"

Ollie pops his head up from beneath the bed like a groundhog. "To a nuclear point, baby."

She hands him a Voss, and they chug them down.

"It's pretty chilly." Dallas screws her nose. "Then again, maybe that's because I tore the skin between my vagina and rectum, so basically, I feel like a Thanksgiving turkey about to be filled with onions, sweet potatoes, and herbs." She frowns. "God, that sounds delicious."

Once Oliver collapses onto the sofa, the entire room descends into chaos. I sit in the corner, scrolling through my phone as everyone fusses and bickers, hovering over Dallas like she just came back from a fourteen-month trip to Mars.

"More painkillers?"

"Have you had water? You need water, Dal."

"Are you craving a Thanksgiving feast? I'm sure February is pumpkin

season, too."

A knock stops the madness. I peer up from my phone in time to spot a nurse wheeling in a see-through hatch. Oliver, Frankie, and Farrow crowd around it, holding their breaths. I trudge over, figuring I'd see what the fuss is all about.

I'm not a fan of babies. They're loud and entirely useless, even by human standards. I do, however, have to admit that the baby Dallas and Romeo produced is a good-looking one. Unlike the majority of newborns, he doesn't resemble a bitter politician berating a lowly staffer. He turns his head just a tad, offering me a better view. Dallas and Romeo's best features war across his face. From Dallas—a button nose and prominent red lips the shape of a strawberry. And from Romeo—a shock of black hair matting his tiny head and enough lashes to warm a herd of llamas.

"My God." Frankie slaps a hand to her chest, sticking her whole body in the hatch. "Sissy, he's gorgeous!"

"I know." Dallas slips off the bed with a grin and wheels the hatch to Romeo's side. "He's going to break a lot of hearts."

The baby is fast asleep, just as I should be at this hour.

"And baseball bats." Oliver mocks a swing. "Those dads won't know how to handle Baby Costa."

Romeo and Dallas grin down at their son. A sudden feral desire to produce an heir with Farrow slams into me. I don't want to wait for tomorrow. I want to do it today.

"Let's go over the thirty names." Dallas clears her throat, unraveling a list that is very obviously longer than thirty.

Farrow shakes her head, eyes clinging to the child. "Luca."

"Huh?" Dallas' head snaps up, her mouth ajar. "No, that's... that's not even on my list." She waves the note roller in her hand, paper flapping in the wind.

"Think about it." Farrow meets her gaze, a small smile on her lips. "Luca."

"Luca." Romeo toys with the name, mouthing it a few times. He caresses a knuckle over his son's cheek. "I like the sound of it. Strong. Italian."

"Means bringer of light." Dallas holds up her Google search. "He did bring a lot of light into my life, even before he was born."

And so, Luca Salvatore Costa was introduced to the world, surrounded by family.

Later, I manage to make it to the parking lot before I can't help myself anymore. "I want one, too."

"What? A Toyota Camry?" Farrow glances at the nearest car, which happens to be a rusty vehicle that has seen better days. In the eighties. "I'm sure we can afford it."

"A baby."

I stop by her Prius. Because, yes, Farrow still drives her stupid Prius, which she loves to no end and also named Priscilla. Another annoying remnant from her pre-engaged life—the apartment. Once she moved back in, she converted the studio into an office for business meetings. *Fine.* I love her fierce independence.

"You want a baby?" She staggers against her car. "Zach, it's illegal to just take one—"

"Not from the maternity ward. *Christ.*" I chuckle, loving that she messes with me. "One of our own."

"We're not even married yet." She furrows her brows. "In fact, we cannot even come up with a date or a *state* for the wedding."

True stuff. A problem courtesy of my overbearingly enthusiastic mother. We managed to patch things up quickly after our showdown in Thailand. Mainly because she showed up on my doorstep her first day back, promised to process her grief with a therapist, and even helped me hunt down my wedding ring. A stunning emerald bracketed by sparkling rubies. It belonged to Mom's family for generations. Rare. Just like Octi.

I snatch the keys from Farrow's hands. "We can have a baby without being married."

She hides a giggle with her fingertips. "Your mother would have another heart attack if we have a baby out of wedlock."

"True." I stroke my chin. I now live life on my own terms, but that doesn't mean I'll piss all over Mom's wishes if they don't interfere with my happiness.

"How about Vegas?"

"Vegas?" Farrow's eyes light up. "Like, elope?"

I nod. "No catering, no arguments over venue, no floral arrangement you need to book three years in advance. You can wear your favorite sneakers and fencing gear, and no one would flinch." Lies. Mom would. But I don't care. A small price to pay. Plus, we'll still hold the traditional tea ceremony.

Farrow bites down on her lower lip. "What about Ari? I was single when she started planning her wedding."

I shrug. "You snooze, you lose."

Also, she'll probably be the first to show up—and with a truckload of champagne.

"You really want to marry this bad, huh?" Farrow scrunches her nose. "Look a little desperate to me."

"Baby." I hook a finger into the collar of her sweatshirt, yanking her to me for a kiss. "I'm past desperate when it comes to you."

Farrow
Three Weeks Later.

"And do you, Farrow Talia Ballantine, take this man to be your lawfully wedded husband?" The Elvis impersonator turns to me, holding a book I'm ninety percent sure is an alien romance I once caught Dallas reading.

Mysterious stains litter the chapel's red carpet. Plastic flowers spurt from dusty Dollar Tree vases. A flamingo-pink ceiling towers above our heads, overseeing the whole ceremony. Elegant? Nope. Perfect? Absolutely.

I grin at Zach. "I do."

He can't see me in my fencing mask. In fact, we're both dressed in head-to-toe fencing gear. Truly, we meant to, at the very least, pick out a proper dress and suit, but we ended up spending the past three weeks in bed, distracted by something much, *much* larger. Neither of us care. I wanted all my dear friends to watch us make complete fools of ourselves, and Zach made that wish come true.

Elvis turns to Zach, peering at him behind oversized sunglasses. "And do you, Zachary Yibo Sun, take this woman to be your lawfully wedded wife?"

"I do."

"You may kiss the bride."

We both take off our masks, sweaty and grinning. He slips a glove off, tosses it behind him, and dives his fingers into my hair, kissing me to the soundtrack of our family's hoots and hollers. Constance throws flowers at us. Celeste twirls in her fancy seventeen-thousand-dollar ballgown. Dallas and Frankie hurl candy at me. Ari and her fiancé grin at each other.

When we finally break off the kiss—mainly not to embarrass our family—I find myself breathless still. My heart beats too fast, too loudly. I feel like jelly, too warm to stand. Zach catches my elbow when my knees wobble. I expect him to swoop me up bridal style. Instead, he loops an arm around my waist and smashes me to his chest, carrying me with my legs wrapped around his torso. Perks of the fencing uniform.

I throw my head back, warm and fuzzy and, I realize, so truly, unabashedly, utterly happy. He presses a kiss to my forehead, striding down the aisle with ease. I relax into my husband's arms. The only true home I've ever known.

"Zach?"

"Yes, Wife?"

"Tell me something about the octopus."

"I'll give you something better."

"Oh? What's that?"

"My father's last words."

I freeze. He presses a kiss to my temple before leaning into my ear, whispering them for only me to hear.

The pendants unite two souls. Fate knows what we don't.

SCAN TO READ

NEED MORE ZACH AND FAE?
WE HAVE AN EXCLUSIVE BONUS EPI.

visit: shor.by/morezach

ABOUT THE AUTHORS

Parker S. Huntington is a stay-at-home dog mom from SoCal, where she discovered her allergy to rain. In spite of her shoddy attendance record and strong aversion to homework, she earned a B.A. in Creative Writing from the University of California, Riverside and an A.L.M. in Literature from Harvard. When she's not writing or exchanging food pics with her friends, she's binge-watching an unhealthy amount of Netflix while curled up with her dogs.

L.J. Shen is a Wall Street Journal, USA Today, Washington Post, and #1 Amazon bestselling author of contemporary, new adult, and young adult romance. Her books have been translated in over twenty different countries, and she hopes to visit all of them. She lives in Florida with her husband, three rowdy sons, and even rowdier pets. She enjoys good wine, bad reality TV shows, and reading to her heart's content.

Check us out on social media here:

VISIT PARKER

VISIT L.J.